"More than just the average fantasy book, Bourne gives increased depth to her own series of books while simultaneously telling an entertaining, well-crafted story in its own right."

The *US Review of Books* RECOMMENDS *Lennox's Story*.

LENNOX'S

STORY

BOOK FIVE

In the
Tales of Avalon Series

BY DAISY BOURNE

To Tess
I hope you are enjoying
the Tales of Avalon Series
Daisy Bourne

For Sophie

CONTENTS

MAP 1

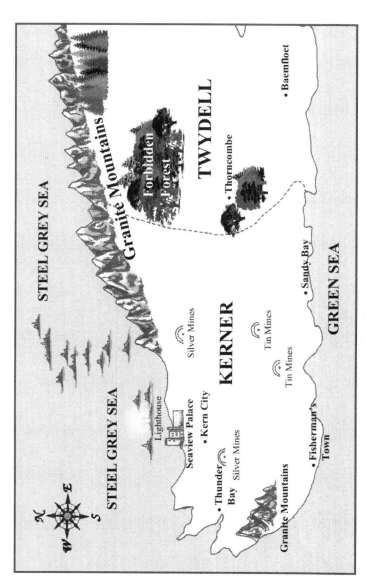

MAP 2

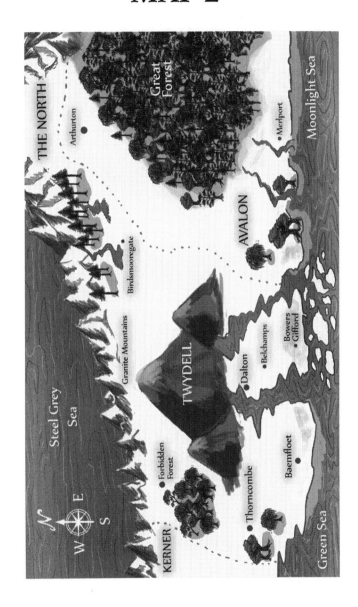

MAP 3

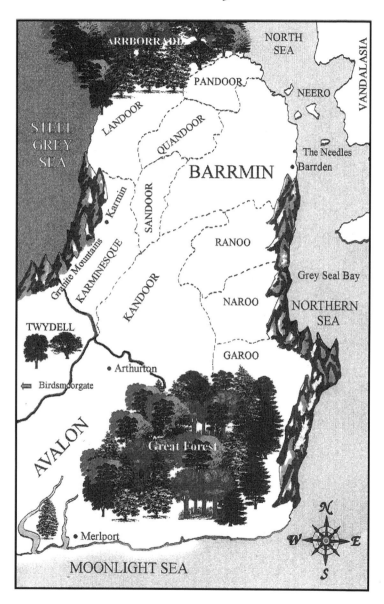

ARRBORRADE

NORTH SEA

VANDALASIA

PANDOOR

NEERO

LANDOOR

STEEL GREY SEA

QUANDOOR

The Needles

• Barrden

BARRMIN

Karmin

SANDOOR

• Karmin

RANOO

Granite Mountains

KARMINESQUE

Grey Seal Bay

KANDOOR

NAROO

NORTHERN SEA

TWYDELL

GAROO

← Birdsmoorgate

• Arthurton

AVALON

Great Forest

• Merlport

N

W   E

S

MOONLIGHT SEA

Prologue

*L*ennox's Story is the fifth book in the Tales of Avalon series.

Merlin, the mighty sorcerer, has established a safe haven in Avalon for those who feared for their lives in Briton.

Magical folk and humans live side by side and have built small towns which they have named Merlport and Arthurton in honour of their founders. The witches and wizards of Avalon amicably refer to non-magical people as plainfolk. The plainfolk refer to witches and wizards as wizzwits. The names do not appear to offend either party, who now live together in harmony.

This story takes us back to Briton and the perils faced by Lennox and the few remaining magical beings.

PART ONE: Briton

CHAPTER 1 – The Fugitives

The sun rose, a golden coin, above the purple horizon spreading the first fingers of daylight across the forest canopy. The dawn chorus brought the forest to life.

Lennox and his family edged cautiously into the clearing where the unbroken melody of birdsong told him that there were no lurking huntsmen. Nevertheless, whilst Tamarie and her foal moved further into the meadow, Lennox remained alert, carefully scanning the surrounding area, searching for movement in the shadows of the trees. He sniffed the air for the scent of those who would send their souls to join the spirits of so many other unicorns.

The first sign of danger was a cacophony of bird cries in the east. Startled crows flew up into the air forming an ominous black cloud. The unicorns pricked up their ears.

Bryant, young as he was, felt his parents' concern. He stood stock-still listening to the sounds of the forest. Tamarie nuzzled him, not too gently, urging him into the protection of the woodland.

Should they hide in a thicket of trees and bushes? Or, should the family flee in the opposite direction from the oncoming danger? Humans prized the silky white coats and silvery horns of unicorns. The hunters would feel no guilt in slaying such beautiful animals for greedy profit.

The unicorns could now hear men shouting and thrashing in the undergrowth. They knew it was huntsmen. *Why are they making so much noise? They cannot be skilled huntsmen to make such a din*, Lennox told himself. However, his instinct said otherwise. Hounds were barking which meant that they already had the scent of their prey.

Tamarie nudged Bryant, urging him towards the west. The colt needed no further bidding and shot forward. The youngster would not be able to keep up with his parents in full gallop so they cantered behind to provide their offspring with protection. There was no whinnying of horses so even at a canter the unicorns could easily outpace the humans – but the pursuers had dogs with them, making escape more difficult.

Lennox heard the chasing dogs draw closer. He stood still whilst Tamarie and Bryant raced ahead. A well aimed backward kick with two hooves lifted the first pursuing cur into the air. It fell back to the ground onto a fallen tree, across which it lay whimpering.

The stallion turned to confront the second beast face to face. The dog faltered, realising that its prey was now the aggressor. Lennox charged head down, grazing the hound with its horn. The dog turned and limped off; it had no desire to do battle with the angry unicorn whose silvery horn now glistened with its blood.

Without the hounds in pursuit Lennox felt more confident of escape, but a sixth sense made his stomach clench with fear for his family's safety.

Tamarie slowed down waiting for her husband to catch up. Bryant was tiring but his parents urged him on. They cantered forward continuing westward. The

4

sound of the huntsmen could still be heard but their pursuers were falling behind.

Suddenly Lennox caught sight of three small, bright figures descending from the trees. He had seen fairies in the forest before and the tiny beings always seemed harmless. Indeed, although their bodies resembled that of the dreaded humans, woodland animals regarded fairies as being no more than large butterflies.

The fairies were pointing north. They swooped down, one at a time, indicating to the family to change course. But the unicorns were confused; north would take them nearer the river where the humans gathered to catch fish. The little winged beings wanted them to take a path which could bring them closer to humans.

Just then, Lennox was surprised to see an old woman hobbling towards them. She wore a long cloak and a tall pointed hat. Lennox recognised her. He had seen her with his old friend Merlin on several occasions. She turned in the same direction as indicated by the fairies and signalled to the unicorns to follow. The old woman looked worried and, as the unicorns hesitated, her gestures became more frantic.

There must be danger in front of us. I am sure Merlin's friend would not see us harmed. And so Lennox whinnied instructions to Tamarie and Bryant to follow the old lady.

They didn't travel far.

The old woman stopped in front of a dense thicket of brambles. And with a wave of the small stick she carried, she opened an entrance into what had appeared to be an impenetrable clump of thorns. She signalled to the unicorns to enter.

Lennox and Tamarie looked around, astonished. They had passed the thicket on many occasions but never before seen the narrow archway. Stepping cautiously inside, they found that the thorny entrance opened out into a small dwelling. There was just enough room for the three unicorns to stand amongst the rickety human furniture.

Once the family was safely inside, the old woman hurried back to the pathway. They watched her walk, as fast as her legs could carry her, whilst spreading handfuls of powder on the forest floor. Then she made her way back to the little house, uttering strange sounds and waving her stick across the ground on which they had just walked. The unicorns were mystified to see their hoof prints disappear and the trampled undergrowth spring back to life.

Then the old woman joined them in the dwelling, carefully sealing the entrance behind her. Brambles fell back into place as if they had never been parted.

The old lady started to push the table into a corner to make more room for her guests. Realising what the frail looking ancient was trying to do, Lennox and Tamarie helped by pushing the table with their rears.

The old lady grinned. A small area, high in the wall of thorns, was partially open, forming a window of sorts. She widened the window with her wand but left a few spindly branches across the aperture so its existence would not be obvious to anyone passing by.

Then she put her crooked finger to her lips. Instinctively the unicorns understood, though they needed no bidding to be quiet. The old lady pointed to the opening. Bryant was too short but his parents joined the witch at the window to see what was happening outside.

Lennox could just about make out one of the fairies, perched in the branches of a leafy tree. He guessed the other two were concealed nearby. It was then that he realised why he and his family had been diverted from their original course. More hunters were coming into view from the direction in which they had sought escape. It had been a trap! The noisy pursuers from the east had been deliberately driving them in the opposite direction towards fellow hunters in the west. The fairies and the witch had saved their lives!

As the huntsmen appeared below the trees in which the fairies hid, gold coloured sparkles dropped like rain. The oncoming huntsmen stopped in their tracks, watching the spectacle with mouths open wide in astonishment.

"There's money falling out of the trees!" yelled one as he fell to his knees to try to find the gold he'd seen.

"It's raining gold coins!" cried another.

"There must be a jackdaw's nest up there!" shouted a third huntsman. "It must have stolen a bag of money."

Soon all of them were on their knees searching for the gold. However, no matter how diligently they searched they could find no shiny coins.

It was obvious to Lennox that the fairies had somehow been responsible for the gleaming shower. And though he could not understand the human words it was evident that they were looking for the golden hailstones.

"What's going on?" bellowed a huntsman to his companions who were grovelling in the undergrowth. He was mystified by their behaviour. "Where are those unicorns? Don't tell me you let them get away. There were at least two of them!"

"Gold was dropping out of the trees," shouted several voices from the group, as they continued to search the ground on hands and knees.

Angry human voices were raised as the two groups of huntsmen started to argue.

"It was just sunlight shining through the branches reflecting on the forest floor, idiots!" one of the new group yelled in exasperation. "You've let our only gold escape in the form of two valuable animals."

One of the injured hounds had followed the pursuing group. Now his master set him to work tracing the unicorn's scent. The dog sniffed the ground but soon started sneezing as it inhaled the pepper the witch had scattered.

A man, more interested in finding the source of the gold, started to climb a tree. He was determined to find the jackdaw's nest from which he thought it had fallen.

Lennox caught a glimpse of one of the fairies slipping through the branches, away from the climber, towards the little dwelling. A few minutes later all three small beings had made their way down a chimney opening and into the room with the unicorns and witch.

The fairies hovered near the roof, giggling like naughty children. One raised her wand to demonstrate to the unicorns how she could produce a shower of yellow glitter. Like golden rain the sparkles disappeared as they hit the floor.

Through the makeshift window the magical beings watched the humans outside. It was a farcical scene: some were still crawling through the undergrowth in search of gold. One was now in the tree trying to find a jackdaw's nest. Others were gesticulating angrily. Eventually the huntsmen moved away, still arguing among themselves as they went.

Everyone in the room breathed a sigh of relief. The old lady looked at Tamarie and, pointing at herself, repeated the same word over again. "Elvira". Then she touched the mare's heart and then her own.

The mare understood the witch's body language as a sign of friendship and she stretched her neck forward to allow Elvira to stroke her face.

Lennox watched his wife. She was a beautiful creature. Her coat, like his, was white but her face was flecked with shades of ebony which matched her dark eyes and long eyelashes. Her black tail swung gently as if in acknowledgement of this new friendship with the witch.

Elvira reached out to Lennox and he too stretched forward to allow her to stroke his face. Then she put her hand on her heart before placing it on his. He felt the warmth and friendship of her touch and acknowledged it by gently nodding his head.

Next, the oldest of the fairies fluttered in front of him. Pointing to herself she uttered the word, "Maud." He allowed her to fly forward and stroke his ears. Soon Elvira, Maud and the two other fairies, Mia and Tia, had all introduced themselves.

There was a bucket half full of water in the corner of the room, which Elvira offered to her guests. Lennox and Tamarie allowed Bryant first drink. The youngster finished off the water without realising that his parents would be left thirsty.

Elvira pointed to the bucket and told them that as soon as it was safe she would go to the stream for more. Neither Lennox nor his family comprehended her words but understood by the old witch's sign language what she was trying to tell them. They also understood, from the signals and indications made by

9

the fairies, that they were flying off to check whether humans still lurked in the woods.

The day passed and evening drew in before Maud returned. She pointed her wand to her throat to raise her voice and spoke to Elvira. The witch nodded and, raising her own wand, opened the entrance to reveal the forest without.

Taking two buckets she signalled to the unicorns to follow her. Lennox and his family followed the witch to a stream, which flowed to the main river, where they drank thirstily. Then, leaving the two buckets beside the stream, Elvira led her guests down to the clearing where grass grew in abundance.

All the time they were in the forest, Lennox was aware that Maud was flying overhead. He spotted other fairies too, darting in and out of the branches, and realised that they were maintaining a vigil so he and his family could feed safely.

Whilst the unicorns sated their hunger, Elvira sat at the edge of the forest humming to herself. When at last the unicorns were satisfied she led them back to the stream where they quenched their thirst again. The old woman filled her buckets before leading the trio back to the safe haven which was her home.

Before sealing the entrance she called to the birds and a pigeon swooped down following her inside. Elvira scribbled on a piece of parchment, which she tied it to the pigeon's leg. "Merlin," she said. The bird flew away and Lennox realised that some sort of message was being sent to his friend.

The following days formed a pattern: the unicorns stayed in the old lady's house. Every now and then they saw hunters searching for them or looking for the gold which they had seen fall from the trees. The fairies would let them know when it was safe to go outside. When they did go out, the fairies kept watch while the unicorn family fed, watered and for short periods of time, enjoyed the freedom of the forest. However, three wild animals could not endure such constraints for long.

Bryant was restless spending day after day in the witch's dwelling. Being cooped up in such a small place was also uncomfortable for his parents. Lennox and Tamarie considered what options there might be. Their thankfulness to the witch and her friends, for their continued safety, was without question. However, they could not stay here indefinately. They talked about travelling further afield to find a place which was free of hunters. The problem was where would they go and how would they get there?

Then one morning the monotony was broken by the sound of whistling. Lennox rose from the place on the floor, to peer out of the window. Walking towards the thicket (which doubled up as a house) was *Merlin*. The wizard was dressed in his grey travelling robes and hat with a long pointed end. Butterflies and small birds circled around him as he walked, the birds singing in tune to his whistling. He was an old man with long, flowing grey hair but he walked tall and straight like someone half his age.

Elvira was delighted. She busied around trying to tidy up before opening the archway. As Merlin walked in she sprang into his arms, and the two embraced warmly.

Lennox waited for the two magicians to finish their greetings before stepping forward. Merlin patted Lennox on the neck, greeting him in the language of the unicorn.

"Lennox, my old friend, it is so good to see you again and to have the opportunity to meet your family. I've seen the beautiful Tamarie before but I don't believe we have ever spoken."

Tamarie, hearing his words, lowered her head to show her appreciation for the compliment.

"And this must be your foal. A fine animal. He looks so much like his father."

"This is Bryant," replied Lennox proudly. "Yes, he does look like me: pure white. Nevertheless, I would have been proud to have him born with the ebony flecks and black tail which I admire so much in his mother."

Bryant was perplexed. He had never heard anyone other than his parents speak Unicornian before.

"I am very proud that our son is pure white like his father," Tamarie spoke shyly.

"Merlin, please tell Elvira and her fairy friends how much we appreciate her kindness towards us. If it were not for them we would have been dead by now. Your friend has been so kind to shelter us." Tamarie lowered her head towards the witch as a mark of respect.

"Elvira sees your gratitude in your eyes," replied Merlin. The old lady gave Tamarie one of her near-toothless smiles.

"I had warned Elvira about the danger you were in and asked her to keep an eye open for you. She sent a message by pigeon telling me that you were hiding in her cottage. It's very cramped in here though," continued the wizard, looking round the little house.

"Yes, we are very grateful to Elvira and the fairies for what they have done for us," Lennox responded, "Nevertheless, the time has come for us to move on.

We cannot continue to let these good people put their lives at risk for us."

"Indeed," Merlin agreed. "But in so doing they have saved what are probably the last unicorns in Briton. We cannot allow your kind to become extinct."

"Extinct!" Lennox was horrified. The very thought made him shiver. "Are we really the only ones left?"

"I know of no others, my friend. Do you?"

"No, I do not." The truth of Merlin's words started to dawn on the unicorn. "Once, I had a fine brood of mares and other sons and daughters. I do not need to tell you that. All my family except Tamarie and Bryant are now gone. But there must be others. There must be families of unicorns elsewhere. There are other forests. Bryant must find a wife and have children of his own."

"Alas, I do not think anywhere in Briton is safe for magical beings and I'm not just talking about unicorns. My own kind and our sister witches are being hunted down and murdered by the humans and it's much the same overseas."

The wizard continued, "Many fairies and elves fled from the fields as they were cultivated by mankind. They moved into the forests, but those woodlands diminish as trees are cut down. Many small magical beings have been killed by a plough or falling timber."

Lennox gave a sigh.

"But all is not lost, my friends. I have travelled far and wide and found a place of safety for us all. Wizards and elves have worked hard to build a fleet of fine ships. Over the years we have taken those who live in fear for their lives to the new land. Indeed, even Arthur who was once king of the Britons is there." Merlin laughed. "Poor old Arthur, we didn't have the fine ships when he went and he had a very bumpy ride in a small boat. But he's all right now."

"So there are humans in this place you have found?" queried Lennox.

"Yes, but only a few. A few who, like Arthur, have helped and respected us in the past."

Merlin had a smug look about him as he added, "The balance is in our favour."

Lennox and Tamarie exchanged glances.

"Listen, my friend, the only safe place for you and your family is Avalon. Our ships leave each full moon in the sunshine months. It's too dangerous in the winter. I can arrange for you to be on the next sailing."

"Do unicorns dwell in this place called Avalon?" Tamarie asked.

"Well, I have not actually seen any," admitted the wizard. "But none of us has ventured into the forest which stands some distance from the village we are building. There may well be unicorns there."

"As my husband says, Bryant will need a wife one day," Tamarie stated. "We know that unicorns have lived here in Briton. We don't know if any dwell in your new land. I believe we should stay here until we are sure that there are no others left."

"Merlin, you and Elvira seem to be able to send messages by bird," Lennox stated. "Can you send messages to your brethren elsewhere to find out whether they know of other unicorns? If there are, then perhaps there is still a safe haven for us somewhere in Briton. Or, if your brethren are aware of others, and believe them to also be in danger, then perhaps we should all leave for Avalon together."

Merlin sighed. "I will do as you ask, Lennox. But if there were other unicorns I am sure I would have heard by now. My brethren and sister witches have been searching Briton to find any lingering magical beings and impress upon them the need to leave as soon as possible. If they had found other unicorns they would be doing what I am doing now; urging them to sail on the next ship!"

"And how safe is the journey to Avalon?" asked Tamarie. "Is it a long way?"

"In my opinion, the most dangerous part of the exodus is the gathering together at the coast before departure. A large number of magical beings in one place is always at risk of being spotted by humans. We cast as many charms as we can to protect ourselves but, yes, you are right, there is always a danger. As for the journey, we sail for several days and nights but there are no humans en route and I am pleased to say all our ships have arrived safely. Our departures are nearly complete for this year. Once winter is over we will start sailing again in the spring, but next year will be the final year of travel."

"Does anyone who has gone to this new land ever return?" asked Lennox.

"Only those of us who have escorted parties to Avalon. Elvira's daughter Esmerelda and her young man are prime examples. They first travelled to Avalon to reunite a young boy with his father some years ago. They came back to Briton to help others escape. You may meet them soon. Esmie will no doubt wish to visit her mother before setting off for Wales. She is going there in search of any remaining magical beings who are not aware of the exodus."

Tamarie looked at her husband. "So there are people who are not yet aware of this new land," she mused. "Of course, Merlin is right; this is no longer a safe place for us. But I think we should wait till next year in case there are other unicorns still here. I cannot bear to think of going to this new land and Bryant living without a wife. It is hard to believe that there are no more of us in Briton but perhaps Elvira's daughter will come across a herd in Wales. If other unicorns are found in a safe haven, then we will join them. I am sure there must still be others like us somewhere. If I am proven to be wrong then we will leave for Avalon next year."

"I met a Welsh unicorn once," Lennox reminisced. "He was a sturdy chap who came looking for a wife. I told him to leave my brood of mares alone! He found a mare from another herd. In those days there were several herds in this forest. Now they are all gone. But I agree with my wife. We should wait before making a journey, several days long, on board a ship. We were not born to travel on water or any way other than on our hooves."

Merlin nodded reluctantly before exchanging words with Elvira. "Elvira urges you to travel sooner rather than later. But she also says you are welcome to the safety of her home until you are ready to go. She will be one of the last to depart. Elvira is Queen of the Witches; she will wait until all her sisters have had the opportunity to go before she herself leaves.

"In the meantime, I have a spell which might create a little more space for you. I will show Elvira how to work the charm, as I must leave tomorrow to escort those living in danger to the coast. I will be glad when the last voyage has taken place and my work here has finished."

True to his word, Merlin taught Elvira how to create a wall which was invisible to people on the outside. The shielding wall was placed around an area encompassing her small dwelling, giving them a little more room and better security. The top was left open, to allow those who could fly to go to and fro without the need to bring the structure down and raise it again. However, it was still a cramped space for three unicorns, who by their nature yearned to roam free.

No one on the outside of the invisible wall could look in, although those on the inside could look out. If an outsider walked into the wall they would merely step out on the opposite side without causing any damage. The problem was that if you walked through the wall from the inside the whole structure disappeared, and Bryant kept getting too close. On the first day he forgot he was confined and walked straight through the wall. On two other occasions, that same day, he just got so close that his horn pierced the framework.

Bryant's clumsiness meant that after having built the wall once, it had to be rebuilt three more times. It was good practice for Elvira but magic is tiring. Even Merlin felt exhausted by the extra workload.

After an early night and confirmation from the fairies that there were no hunters nearby, they all rose early. Merlin strolled down to the stream with Elvira and the unicorns. During the walk he urged the unicorns to re-think their decision to stay in Briton until the following year. "Avalon is a lovely place. The green hills are a haze of lavender and there is a very inviting forest not far away – true, I haven't visited it myself yet but I am sure it is an ideal spot for unicorns."

However, his ministrations were politely rejected. "This new land of yours does indeed sound a tranquil spot, but we will wait till we hear whether our kind still dwell in Wales."

The wizard wished them all a fond goodbye before he left on his mission.

Lennox's cry of agony pierced the peace of the night. The trio, led by Elvira, had left their enclosure to find food and water during the hours of darkness. In only the light of a waning moon the forest can sometimes be a dangerous place. The unicorn's hoof had slipped into a rat hole, and as he fell his shin hit a large stone.

Elvira raced home on her broomstick to fetch potions. She gently bathed the stallion's wounds with cold water and cooling balm. Eventually Lennox was able to stand on three hooves but could hardly bear his weight on the fourth.

Hobbling back to the cottage on an injured leg made matters worse. Next day his leg was even more swollen than it had been the night before. Lennox spent the next few days lying down. He lay in the shade of the branches of an oak tree which fell across the top of the invisible enclosure. Elvira always left the top open so that she could use her broomstick to get in and out. The aperture also allowed a cooling breeze to blow within the enclosed space, bringing a little comfort to Lennox who had a slight fever.

Lennox's injury caused Elvira to become more cautious when taking Tamarie and Bryant to feed. She stayed out for as short a time as possible. However, without his father to keep him in check Bryant had become rather a handful – he kept running away and, in doing so, put everyone else's safety in jeopardy.

Though the pain of his injury had diminished his appetite, the witch picked a sack of grass for Lennox each day, and the fairies each brought a small carrot every morning. Lennox was grateful for the gifts but more often than not left them for his son to eat. Bryant relished the baby carrots, which for a wild unicorn were a delicacy.

Then, one morning the fairies came to say their goodbyes. All except Maud were leaving on boats flying this coming full moon. Of course they did not speak Unicornian but made the family, who were now their friends, understand by body and sign language. Finally they waved their farewells and set off to start their new lives in Avalon.

Lennox and Tamarie were both left wondering whether their decision to stay till the following year was a wise one. However, even if they had changed their minds there was no way that Lennox could limp to the coast.

Elvira was spending more and more time fetching food for the injured stallion. Maud seemed to be darting everywhere keeping watch for hunters. With no one else to share their workload, the strain began to show in their tired faces. Sometimes Maud's husband Selogon joined them, but he too was helping others to ready themselves for departure to Avalon.

Bryant's continued boredom resulted in more bad behaviour. One morning Elvira scattered some breadcrumbs for the pigeons who flew into the enclosure through the roof opening. However, Bryant saw the birds as entertainment. He spent the morning chasing them and greedily ate the crumbs himself.

When Tamarie realised what had happened she didn't hold back on giving him a well deserved scolding. She too felt the frustrations of confinement and the responsibility of trying to keep the headstrong colt in check without her husband's support.

Bryant was upset by the severity of his mother's reprimand. He was fed up with being cooped up in such a small area, especially as there had been no sign of danger for a long time. Without warning, the colt decided to break free. He bolted straight through the invisible wall and galloped away.

Immediately, Tamarie set off after him intent on bringing the disobedient colt back. However, Bryant had grown bigger and stronger and could easily outpace his mother. Now the colt was free, he had a sudden desire to wash away the dust from the enclosure floor on which he had slept for months. He headed towards the river where he and his parents had once bathed in the cool running water.

Elvira wasn't sure what to do. Lennox had managed to get to his feet but was incapable of walking. Replacing the invisible wall took time so instead she helped the ailing stallion inside the house where he would remain hidden once she closed the brambles behind him.

Taking her broomstick, the witch flew towards the stream, thinking that Bryant had decided to quench his thirst. Not finding him there she headed to the grassy clearing, but there was no sign of the colt or his mother.

Now panicking, she made her way to the river.

The sight that greeted her was one of the cruellest of her life: Bryant had been caught in a fisherman's net. His hooves stuck out through damaged netting as though he had been fighting to free himself – but he was no longer moving. The young unicorn had drowned.

Tamarie's body lay on the sloping riverbank as if she had been making her way into the water. She had obviously sought to rescue her son but, in the attempt, been shot in the neck by arrows. Now she lay lifeless in the mud, facing her drowned offspring.

The tears rolled down Elvira's face. There was nothing she could do. She wanted to avenge the friends she had tried so hard to protect but they were already dead. Any form of retaliation would only put herself in danger.

Elvira could not bear to watch as the victorious humans hauled the dead bodies up the bank. She turned homeward with a heavy heart.

CHAPTER 2 – The Revenge

"I am absolutely positive this is where my mother lives!" said the young woman to her tall dark companion. "It's very odd. I know our little house was right here, in the middle of a thicket."

"Are you sure you've got the right place, Esmie?" asked the man. "After all, it's been a long time since you've been home."

Elvira had been sitting with Lennox behind the house but the sound of her daughter's voice brought her round to the front to see what was happening. She gave a little laugh as she watched Esmerelda puzzle over the missing cottage. She could see her daughter stepping into the enclosure's invisible wall on one side only to emerge on the other.

Even Lennox, who had hardly stirred for days, pricked up his ears at the sound of new voices.

Elvira mounted her broom and levitated swiftly towards the branches of the overhanging oak tree. "I'm here," she called.

Esmerelda looked up at her mother, whose head peered out from among the oak leaves. She stepped back to her friend, but although she had only taken a single step she had unknowingly crossed the entire width of the enclosure.

"That's strange," her companion whispered. "Step forward, Esmie."

Esmerelda did as she was bid.

"Esmie, you only moved one step but your mother's head turned from left to right as if you had moved a much greater distance. There is some sort of structure here which you are stepping through; like the enclosure wizards use when they hold a Wizzen."

Esmerelda stepped backwards and forwards watching her mother's head turn obligingly from left to right.

"How do we get in?" she laughed. "Or don't you want to meet Tannus?"

"You'll need your broomsticks," Elvira called back. "There is an opening at the top but be careful not to pierce the wall once you're inside otherwise I'll have to rebuild it – again!"

Esmerelda and her male companion removed their brooms from the carrying cases strapped to their backs. They flew up into the tree and carefully negotiated the opening before dropping down into the enclosure. The young witch gave her mother a warm hug and both shed joyful tears at sharing a long awaited reunion.

"This is Tannus." Esmerelda introduced the warlock to her mother.

"Ah, Tannus, son of Tannitus. You look just like your father when he was young."

"Do I?" the young wizard looked genuinely surprised. "But my father is short, has blue eyes and white hair."

"He may be short now but he was once over six feet tall. After you reach a certain age you start to grow shorter. How old is your father now – he must be what, nearing his two hundredth year?"

"Not quite," laughed Tannus. "Was he once dark haired like me?"

"Yes," responded Elvira. "His hair was as dark as yours but he always had twinkling blue eyes. You, on the other hand, your eyes are as dark as your mother's. But you remind me more of your father."

"I just can't imagine Tannitus being over six foot tall." Esmerelda smiled at the thought. "I met him when I was in Avalon. He is a very kind man – and he still has twinkling blue eyes."

"You would have been better off staying in Avalon when you took that young boy there. You should never have returned to Briton. What were you thinking of? Not of your own safety, that's for sure!"

"We came back to rescue other people." Esmerelda spoke firmly to her mother. The young witch was clearly a woman who was used to having her own way.

"And talking about rescuing others," Tannus broke into the conversation before an argument could ensue, "where are the unicorns?"

Elvira's expression changed from delight at seeing her daughter to one of guilt and sadness. "I've lost the mare and her foal." Water began to fill her rheumy eyes.

"The colt ran off. His mother pursued him to bring him back. Lennox, the stallion, was injured and couldn't move. He had to stay here. Perhaps it was a good thing he did or I might have lost him too. By the time I caught up with the mother and her foal they were both dead; killed by the fishermen at the river."

"*You* didn't lose them!" Esmerelda took her mother by the shoulders and looked into her face. "From what Merlin has told us, *you* did everything you could to save them. Don't blame yourself, mother."

"Where is the stallion, now?" asked Tannus.

"He's behind the cottage," Elvira sighed. "Come and meet him."

Lennox had lain in the same spot for days. He had hardly eaten and the outline of his ribs was beginning to show through his white coat which had lost its lustre. Despite his poor health he was still a magnificent creature. He raised his head as the two witches and the warlock approached.

"Lennox, this is my daughter Esmerelda; we call her Esmie for short." Elvira pointed to her daughter and repeated the word Esmie over again. Then she pointed at Tannus and reiterated his name several times.

Lennox raised his head. *This must be Elvira's daughter and her young man who Merlin told me about – the ones who have been to Wales.* He tried to stand but it was too painful, nevertheless he managed to turn just enough to better see the visitors. *I wish I could speak their language. How will I know whether they have found other unicorns there?* He snorted and made a few strange noises in his effort to communicate with the young woman who knelt down beside him.

Woman and unicorn looked deep into each other's eyes. There was no need for words. Esmerelda's pained expression told Lennox what he needed to know. *There are no unicorns in Wales.*

Esmerelda flung her arms round Lennox's neck and both started to cry. They wept together, face against face. As the witch's tears mingled with those of the unicorn they fell in droplets to the ground.

Tannus and Elvira looked on helplessly.

It was the warlock who was the first to spot the tiny green shoots. "Look, where your tears are falling new plants are growing."

The witches looked down and saw the shoots sprouting out of the earth and increasing in height at a steady pace.

Lennox lowered his eyes to see what they were looking at. He too was mystified by the strange phenomenon.

"That's strange," Elvira commentated. "I've watched Lennox shed a bucket load of tears since Tamarie and Bryant were murdered, but no flowers have grown before."

"I hope you kept the bucket load of tears," commented Tannus. "A unicorn's tears mixed in a potion can make a very powerful charm."

"No of course I didn't collect his tears!" Elvira was irritated. "How could I bother him when all I hoped for was that he wouldn't die of grief?"

Tannus was a very practical man. "Well, if no flowers grew when a unicorn's tears fell to the earth, then why would they grow now? The only reason I can think is that Lennox's tears and Esmie's have mingled and somehow made a spell of their own."

"There are little buds forming now," Elvira remarked. "Yes, you are right Tannus. I should have asked Lennox's permission to collect his tears. We may need some powerful charms to escape Briton safely. The journey from the wood is going to be especially difficult now the huntsmen think unicorns might still be here."

The group watched as more shoots pushed through the soil. When fully grown at just a few inches high the buds opened out into flowers with orange petals and purple centres.

"It's a sign of new life," Elvira spoke wisely. "There may not be any unicorns left in Briton or Wales but perhaps it's a sign that all is not lost."

Lennox sensed her words and tried again to stand. Tannus, who was much stronger than he appeared, helped him. The unicorn leaned heavily against the warlock. The warlock stood his ground. At last the beast managed to stand.

They all stood and stared at the little orange flowers which continued to blossom.

"I've got a spell for orange flowers! Do either of you have anything orange to wear?" But before either of the visitors had chance to answer, Elvira, ancient as she was, ran off into the cottage.

Inside her home she dragged a wooden clothes box out from under the pallet which served as her bed. She pulled out the clothing inside, throwing it carelessly around the room as she searched for the item she wanted. The box held much more than a normal box and clothes ended up being strewn across the table, chair and window ledge as well as on the floor. At last, having delved right to the bottom, she found the orange scarf which she had been looking for and hung it round her neck.

Next, she searched her shelf. This time she was much more careful, making sure she put everything back in its rightful place. Eventually, she found her jar of wild garlic cloves. She took one clove. In another jar she kept a few scraps of parchment which she used to send messages via birds; she removed a piece and did her best to flatten it. Using a feather, and some dye she had made from plants, she scrawled a wish onto the scrap of parchment. Then she wrapped the clove of garlic in the parchment.

Still wearing her orange scarf, she picked up the garlic enclosed parchment and took a spade from the corner of her house; she then returned to the spot where about ten plants now grew. Without offering any explanation she started to unearth one.

"What are you doing?" asked Esmerelda, who was upset at her mother's destructive actions.

"I told you I have a spell. I think the last time I used it was when I was a child. First, you wear something orange."

"Well that explains the gaudy scarf," commented her daughter.

"Next you plant an orange flower, but I need to dig one up before I can plant it – that's what I'm doing now."

After unearthing a plant with root attached, Elvira dug a new hole in which to put it. Putting down her spade, she turned to pick up the little package she had brought with her. However, her daughter snatched the package away.

Esmerelda unwrapped the garlic and read the scrawled note in which it had been wrapped: "I wish that unicorns will not become extinct."

"Look and learn," said her mother, snatching back the parchment. She re-wrapped the garlic clove in the parchment and placed it in the hole she had dug. Finally, the flowering plant was placed above the package and made firm in the ground with soil. As Elvira pressed down the soil around the orange bloom she repeated her wish.

Esmerelda and Tannus copied the older woman's example; they too patted the soil around the plant with their bare hands. Witch and warlock each uttered their own spells in the hope that they would strengthen that of Elvira's.

Lennox watched. The intuitive animal sensed what they were doing. He nuzzled the earth around the plant with his nose before gently treading the surrounding ground with his hoof.

The new flowers had somehow put life back into Lennox. Instead of lying back in the spot where he had lain for days, he hobbled around the enclosure. He followed the witches and warlock listening intently to their speech and understanding as much as he could.

Esmerelda, who often disguised herself as a fruit seller, had brought him some apples. The unicorn still didn't have much of an appetite. Nevertheless, everyone was relieved to see him attempting to eat and just as importantly making an effort to move.

Over the next few days, the young witch and warlock each borrowed Elvira's gaudy orange scarf and repeated the spell she had taught them; eventually every new bloom had been re-planted above a clove of garlic enclosed in a written wish.

Lennox always joined in as best he could. Like his friends he hoped with all his heart to find other unicorns.

But he also made another wish.

He wished to avenge the deaths of his wife and child.

Both Elvira and Lennox were sad to see Esmerelda and Tannus go. Esmerelda, who was a skilled healer, had spent over a week treating the unicorn's injured leg.

The swelling had much subsided and, under the protection of his magical friends, he had even managed to get to the stream to drink and nibble at clumps of grass. However, they stayed away from the clearing as Lennox would never have got home in time if danger lurked nearby.

Lennox gradually grew stronger until he felt sufficiently confident to venture out on his own. He started off by going to the stream at night, and eventually further afield to the clearing where he grazed.

Elvira fretted when the unicorn wandered off. There were no longer any fairies in the forest to forewarn of approaching hunters. However, despite her misgivings she knew that the unicorn, by his very nature, must be free to roam. But although he no longer had his foal to consider if he met danger, the witch never stopped worrying about the stallion when he was out of sight.

"It's no wonder my brow is furrowed," she said to him one day. "What with you wandering off on your own unprotected, and my Esmie travelling here, there and everywhere looking for lost magical beings. Why, it's a wonder my grey hair hasn't turned as white as your coat!"

It was early spring when Lennox ventured towards the river. He wanted to see the place where his wife and foal had died. He spotted two men on the nearside bank where two men were fixing one end of an elver net. Several other humans worked on the other side trying to secure the other end so that the net stretched across the full width of the river. Two horses, hitched to a cart, stood on the near side bank close to a narrow bridge.

Lennox moved stealthily around the shrubbery which grew near the river. He gently pushed his head between some branches to get a better view. What he saw made him sick with horror. Pinned to the back of the cart were two tails – one long black tail and another shorter white one. The long strands of the tails swayed gracefully in the wind.

The horses sensed Lennox's presence and tried to alert him to the danger of which he was already aware.

"Stay away unicorn. These are not good people," said one.

"Be gone, if you value your life," warned the other.

Lennox ignored the warnings and came out in the open.

"I valued my wife and son's lives," he told the cart horses as he trotted past. "It is their 'trophy' tails which are attached to the back of the cart you pull."

The men were so engrossed in fixing their net across the river that they did not see him. The two on the nearside were both bent over. Lennox charged head down. He lunged his horn into the backside of one of the men and lifted him off the ground and into the air before tossing him into the river below. The other tried to straighten up but, before he could do so, Lennox's front hoof hit him on the head and he too fell backwards into the water.

On the far side of the river, men started to run across the bridge. They didn't give their fellow fishermen, who were struggling in the water, a glance. They were more anxious to capture the unicorn than to rescue their comrades. The two cart horses made as if they were bolting with fright. They lurched forward, crashing the vehicle they pulled into the entrance of the bridge. The horses' action not only blocked the way but prevented the men crossing from taking their weapons from the damaged cart.

"Thank you, horses!" Lennox snorted his gratitude as he raced back into the safety of the woodland.

Although the men's route was blocked, two hounds managed to crawl under the broken cart and made chase. It was the same two hounds that had followed Lennox all those months before.

Lennox hoped that Elvira would hear the commotion and open up the entrance to her house for him.

The old witch always kept an ear open for the sounds of danger and heard the dogs barking. She opened the thorny archway to her home and just had time to conceal some of the unicorn's tracks before closing the entrance behind them.

Unicorn and witch watched the humans from the window of their safe haven.

The men soon caught up with the dogs, who were sniffing the ground for unicorn scent. Elvira hadn't had time to spread pepper on the ground.

One of the men scratched his head. "This is the same spot where we lost them before!"

"And this is the same place where gold coins fell out of the trees," said another. "Look, that's the tree I climbed. Some of the branches broke when I stood on them."

"There were no gold coins," snapped one of the other men. "I told you before it was the sunlight playing tricks on you as it shone through the branches!"

"Why do the tracks end here?" queried the first. "This is odd. Can't those hounds of yours pick up the scent?"

Elvira watched the dogs drawing closer and closer. "This needs drastic action," she told Lennox, hoping he would understand.

Taking her broomstick, she levitated through the hole in her roof, and into the branches of the overhanging oak tree. She waved her magic wand and uttered a spell which created a light wind. She emptied some pepper, from a bag she carried in her pocket. The wind took the pepper and blew it in the direction of the hounds. However, the hounds already had the scent and were nosing the ground only a few yards from the cottage.

Lennox watched as a silvery mist arose from the ground. The dogs growled and the fur on their backs started to rise in spiky tufts. In the mist he could see the outline of two creatures emerge. The hounds could see them too.

He could just about make out the glimmering shape of a white unicorn with a black mane and tail; by her side stood a pure white stallion even taller and more powerful than Lennox. *It's my wife Tamarie and my father Fennox!*

Both lowered their heads, horns pointing menacingly at the hounds. The silhouettes of other unicorns started to appear around the dogs, which barked frantically. Lennox recognised other members of his long dead family emerge in the fog.

The dogs started to back away. One of the men walked over to see what was troubling them. He walked right through the silhouette of one of the defensive unicorns.

"What's going on?" he asked. "It's very cold over here and something's upset my dogs." The dogs turned tail and ran through the circle of unicorns as if their lives were at stake.

Lennox looked at Elvira. She smirked as the dogs ran off. However, she seemed oblivious to the mist or glimmering shapes within. The mist started to subside and the outlines of his family dissolved as mysteriously as they had appeared.

"This place gives me the creeps," one man stated.

"It gives me goose pimples," another added. "I'm going back to the fishing. The elver season only lasts a short time and we're wasting valuable time. The unicorn can wait till the season is over then his tail will hang from our wagon with the others."

Soon men, dogs and mist were all gone.

"You've played a dangerous game, my friend," Merlin stated when he heard the story.

Lennox had told the old wizard how he had seen the tails of his wife and son hanging like trophies on the back of the cart.

"I can sympathise with you. However, you have succeeded in putting not only your own life in danger again but also that of the Witch Queen. She tells me that the hunters were within just a few feet of her home. They have never ventured so close. She is worrying herself sick over you."

"We were protected by my family." Lennox told him about the spirits of other unicorns who had come to their aid.

"How I wish I had been here!" the sorcerer admitted. "I wonder if I could have seen them. In all my one hundred and thirty odd years I've never seen a ghost. You say that you don't think Elvira saw them? No, I am sure she didn't otherwise she would have told me."

Merlin eagerly relayed Lennox's tale to the witch. Her eyes opened wide with astonishment. She smiled her wide, near-toothless grin, before stroking the unicorn's silky coat.

"I'm glad you saw your family again," she whispered in his ear and somehow the unicorn understood.

LENNOX'S STORY

CHAPTER 3 - The Final Departure

Elvira and Maud were already in the meadow when Lennox appeared. The unbroken dawn chorus of this spring morning told him that no humans lurked nearby. Nevertheless, he sniffed the air for the scent of man.

Satisfied that he was safe, at least for the time being, Lennox trotted into the open. As his hooves trod the moist grassy soil beneath, his pace gathered to a canter and finally a gallop. It was good to feel the breeze blowing through his mane. These days it was seldom that he was able to enjoy the freedom he once took for granted.

The Queen of the Witches and the Queen of the Fairies were searching for a four-leafed clover. Their task was urgent but, at the sound of hooves, they stopped to watch the breathtaking sight of the beautiful white unicorn pounding across the meadow.

To a naïve onlooker the stunning white stallion might have appeared to have been taking pleasure from the beauty Mother Nature had provided. However, looks can be deceiving. Lennox now knew that he was the only surviving unicorn in Briton. This was his last day in Briton. He would never again run through this green and pleasant place.

Lennox felt his heart pine as he remembered his first canter, near this very spot, under the watchful eyes of his parents. He had tried to protect his own children in the same way. Many a time he had taken pleasure in seeing his herd run and frolic in this same field. They had once been a happy, playful and loving family. But now he was the only one of his kind left.

The unicorn's melancholy was broken by Elvira's shout. He trotted over to where the two magical women waited but he did not stop. He passed them by and again broke into a canter. As he reached the edge of the meadow, he turned, raised himself on his two hind legs, and whinnied before racing back. Again, he passed Elvira and Maud.

The fairy was fluttering above the witch's shoulder. To Lennox, she resembled a giant butterfly. Her opaque wings quivered as they reflected all the colours of the morning hues.

Elvira's bones creaked as she knelt. "Here it is!" She plucked a stem from the selected plant, and smiled a crinkled near-toothless smile at her fairy friend. "I knew there was a patch hereabouts where the four-leafs grow."

A four-leafed clover was a lucky charm in its own right. However, a four-leafed clover picked in the morning dew, after a unicorn had run through the meadow, could be used to create a far more powerful talisman.

Lennox trotted over to his friends. Maud fluttered towards him and lovingly kissed his cheek before settling herself down on his muscular back. First making sure that Maud was securely seated, the unicorn offered his greeting to the witch.

The old woman let him nuzzle her withered face as she patted his neck. The three friends spent a few minutes in the pleasure of each other's company before their idyllic sojourn was broken. A flock of birds flew up in the air, their cries giving warning of approaching humans.

No word needed to be spoken. Full of fear the three made their way back through the trees and hurried along a rugged dirt track. The bridle path that ran across the forest was often used by horsemen so it was imprinted with hoof prints throughout its route. The trio left the track at a point marked by a gnarled elm tree. Lennox hurried along the now familiar bridle track into the middle of the thicket. As soon as the stallion was inside Elvira took a broom, which she had hidden in the bushes, and carefully brushed away Lennox's hoof prints. A wave of her wand and the trampled grass and bluebells sprang back to life. Not even the most skilled tracker would suspect that the owner of one of those hoof prints had deviated from the main route. With Maud's help the witch made sure that the sprawling thorns fell back into their original positions around the front door.

Lennox had continued to find shelter, when needed, in Elvira's home since Tamarie and Bryant had been murdered. The witch was as caring and considerate as ever. She always made sure that there were buckets of water and hay in her house in case the unicorn needed her safe haven. He drank some water and felt refreshed. Then, he stood and watched with interest, as he had done many times before, whilst the two magical beings cast their spells.

They look so different, thought Lennox, *yet inside they are so much alike – kind and gentle.* Maud was no more than eighteen inches high. She was an elegant little lady dressed in fine seamless gossamer. The fairy's skin was soft and clear, the colour of a peach. In contrast, Elvira looked and probably was ancient. The

41

witch was undoubtedly ugly. Elvira's back was hunched. Her face was a map of wrinkles and there was an unsightly wart on the end of her long pointed nose.

No matter what they looked like, the unicorn loved them both and felt a true friendship in their company. He respected their knowledge of nature and he feared for their safety as much as they feared for his. *One thing we all have in common*, he thought, *is the desire to survive – a shared need for each of our kinds to continue.*

The witch chanted her spells in a croaky voice whilst the little fairy almost sang the words she needed for the combined spell. Eventually the four-leafed clover was placed in a jar of clear wax. Lennox further obliged by shedding a tear drop into the setting wax. A unicorn's tear added a powerful ingredient to the charm. It is always hard for a strong creature to cry but in Lennox's case little effort was required. All he needed to do was think about the tails of his last wife and foal, pinned like trophies to the back of the cart owned by their slayers.

Just before the spells and potions were complete a little man appeared through the opening in the roof. Like the fairy, he was less than two feet tall, but he had no wings and his ears were strangely pointed.

"This is Allarond," said Elvira, introducing the King of the Elves to Lennox. The unicorn nodded. He had seen beings like Allarond in the forest before but not for a very long time. *He must be one of the people who helped build the ships. Like Elvira and Maud he must be supervising the last of his kind to leave Briton.*

Now all the companions had to do was to wait for nightfall. Lennox lay on the hay resting his body but not his mind. He considered the foolhardiness of mankind. Mammoths and aurochs had been hunted, like unicorns, until there were none left. Yet, he had heard that man liked eating the flesh of those large animals and made clothing from their skins. The thought of eating another animal's flesh made Lennox feel sick. *Why do they do it?* he asked himself. *If the humans needed to eat animal meat, and use their skins to keep warm, then why did they hunt those same creatures to extinction? Why not leave some to breed?* It just doesn't make sense.

Lennox wished that he had someone to talk to. He looked forward to seeing Merlin again, the only person who understood his language. Hopeful of pleasant dreams he imagined other unicorns, in a forest far far away...

However, full of anticipation, none of the companions slept well. As soon as darkness enveloped the forest they left the little house in the thicket for the last time. Elvira brushed away Lennox's tracks and put the straggly thorns back in place, as she always did. She did this so that her former home remained hidden, and available to any remaining witch or wizard seeking safety.

They crept as quietly as they were able, making their way towards the edge of the forest and the beach beyond. Their destination was several miles away. A brown fox slunk ahead, ready to run back and warn them if it saw any sign of danger.

However, it was outside the forest that the main dangers lurked and the fox would go no further. Although they trod carefully, and tried to stay in the shadows, a full moon cast light over the land.

They passed a courting couple who cuddled together on a hayrick. Despite the travellers' attempt to

43

walk in silence, the man heard a noise. He stood up and squinted, saying something to his girlfriend, and pointing towards the mythical beast. Lennox shivered and prepared to break into a gallop before they could alert anyone else to his presence. But Elvira simply pointed her wand at the young couple. They each stretched, yawned and lay back down, before falling into a deep slumber, enveloped in each other's arms.

The group continued on their way to the beach.

As they passed a farmhouse a dog started barking and ran towards them. Allarond leapt on to the dog's back with surprising agility and strength. The dog tried to shake the little man off but Allarond grabbed its collar and sat firmly on its back. Leaning forward he whispered in the dog's ear. The cur stopped barking and became calm, wagging its tail happily. It even allowed Allarond to remain seated so that the elf rode the cur like a man would ride a horse.

Nevertheless, the occupants of the house had heard the dog barking. One of the windows became lit by a candle. A half dressed man hurried outside. He carried a sword. As soon as he saw the unicorn with what seemed to be a harmless old lady he raced forward, weapon at the ready.

"Don't you know it's unlucky to kill a unicorn?" Elvira asked.

"You're the unlucky one," said the man as he lunged at her with his sword. He chuckled as he saw the old woman raise a small stick to defend herself.

Elvira parried the blade with her wand. As the weapons clashed a red glow appeared in the centre of the sword where the wand struck. The smirk was wiped off the man's face as the sword started to smoulder. The red glow spread upwards from the centre causing the tip to melt; at the same time the heat moved downwards towards the man's hand. He was so astonished he continued to hold onto the burning weapon until the heat seared his palm. A few words from Elvira and the man stood still as a statue and the molten metal slithered to the ground.

Allarond laughed as he gave the dog a gentle kick, urging it forward past its rigid master. Maud decided to rest her wings and flew down to ride in a side-saddle position behind the Elf King.

At last they reached the beach. Lennox looked back at the forest. He could feel the spirits of his ancestors around him and part of him wanted to stay. If he stayed he would be murdered but his spirit would remain here with those of his family. However, his doubt was soon stemmed. Although he could not see them Lennox could feel his ancestors pushing him forward. Their warm bodies touched his and urged him on towards a different life in a new land.

Tears trickled from his eyes. Elvira stroked his neck. If she saw his tears, she pretended not to. When they reached the water's edge, Lennox trotted into the sea. It was good to feel the seawater on his fetlocks. Elvira had no intention of getting wet so she straddled her broom. Allarond hopped from the dog he had been riding and boarded the handle of Elvira's broomstick; the dog was left standing on the beach as if in two minds whether to go home or follow the elf. Maud, and her passenger, flew ahead to meet the others who were making their way to the waiting ships.

Elvira was soon greeted by other witches and wizards on broomsticks. The newcomers welcomed Lennox and urged him forward. The water grew deeper and it was soon nearly up to his neck. The unicorn had never before walked so far into the ocean but he had no fear. When he reached the ship a gang plank was lowered for him. Clambering up this steep piece of timber was not straightforward and he was nervous of falling. Nevertheless, unsteady on his feet at first, he let his hooves press back against the rungs in the plank to force himself up until at last he was on board.

The cheers which greeted the unicorn made Elvira and Allarond fear that humans would be alerted to their presence. But it would have been too late for pursuit. Whilst mortal men slept in their beds, the boats followed the moonlit path which sparkled on the rippling waters below. They sailed as far as the eye could see from the shore and then, at the point where the ocean disappeared into the skyline, the boats lifted into the air.

Hay, water, carrots and apples had been provided for Lennox. Unfortunately though, Lennox was not used to the sensation of sailing or flying and he felt nauseated for a while. He lay quietly on the deck listening to the magical beings around him celebrating their departure from Briton. They seemed certain of a future where they could all live in peace and harmony.

Later, once recovered from his initial sickness, Lennox watched his fellow passengers entertain each other with magic tricks. He liked listening to their amiable chatter but most of all he enjoyed the singing. Often the passengers on one ship would sing one song and the passengers on a ship flying alongside would sing another. There seemed to be some sort of competition going on to see which group could sing the loudest. On a couple of occasions Lennox joined in with whinnies, bringing loud applause from his fellow passengers.

Day after day the boats sailed through the air. Each dawn as the starlight faded, the cool of the night was replaced by a warm sun. One morning, as the sun rose, the travellers could at last see their destination. The unicorn was as excited as his travelling companions. He headed towards the front of the boat and stretched his neck over the side to see the outline of the green land ahead.

As the ships drew nearer, sailing high above the new land, he could see the outline of a vast meadow. Gradually he could make out a forest standing in the distance. He sniffed the air, anxious to locate the scent of any unicorns, but at first there was nothing. It was only as the ships flew down to land that he recognised a familiar scent on the breeze. *Can they sense me as well? Will I be welcome?*

The enchanted vessels descended slowly towards the ocean below. Lennox watched the smiles on the faces of his fellow travellers grow wider. Many impatient witches and wizards took to their broomsticks and fairies to their wings and flew ahead. It was a beautiful sight but all Lennox wanted to do was to get ashore. He pawed the deck anxiously. He needed to seek the unicorns whose scent he recognised.

At last the ships landed on the water and the gang plank was lowered. A boat, slightly larger than those being used to take the travelling humans ashore, had been arranged for Lennox. Lennox stepped down into the waiting vessel. He stood in the boat whilst human oarsmen rowed towards the beach. But as soon as he sensed that the water was sufficiently shallow, he could wait no longer. The unicorn jumped down into the water, white surf drenching his silky body as he cantered towards dry land.

The other disembarking travellers chattered and laughed. They greeted old friends who awaited their arrival. However, silence swept over them as a tall imposing figure standing on the beach raised his staff. The end of the staff was encrusted with a round crystal from which emanated a purple glow. As he raised his staff the purple glow spread across the crowd of newcomers.

Lennox wanted so much to gallop on towards the forest but he knew that it would be impolite to do so. He watched as Allarond, Maud and Elvira joined Merlin. An elderly man, scarred and crippled, stepped up beside them. *That must be Arthur*, thought Lennox, *the man who was once King of the Britons.*

Fortunately, Merlin did not speak for long and the crowd dispersed as they met friends and family who had come to Avalon before them. Lennox trotted up to his old friend as soon as he lowered his staff and stopped speaking. The two exchanged a few words but Merlin sensed the unicorn's urgency.

"Go, my magnificent Lennox," Merlin whispered in his ear. "Go forth and find the companionship you seek. I pray to Mother Earth that you will find it."

The unicorn rose up on his hind legs, whinnied his goodbyes, and galloped towards the forest.

The travellers who had been making their way towards the village stopped and watched the splendid creature race towards the meadows, making his way to the huge distant forest. They waved their fond goodbyes. Elvira and Maud wept openly to see him depart but nonetheless, urged him on. Some Avalonians shouted, "Good luck," but few thought Lennox would need it. They had a good feeling that, like them, the unicorn would find happiness.

PART TWO:
The New Land

CHAPTER 4 – Avalon

"What are you doing out of the forest, unicorn?" The horses grazing on the prairie showed genuine concern. "There are humans living in the new village. They will slay you!"

Lennox didn't stop. Much as he would have liked to have other creatures to talk to, the scent of another unicorn was fading in and out of the breeze. After spending days on a ship the firm ground beneath his hooves was welcome and he had been in full gallop for a while. However, the sun at its zenith brought searing heat rather than comforting warmth. Despite slowing down to a canter, and then a trot, the unicorn's body was bathed in white lather. He had to rest.

A group of horses was gathered under the spreading branches of willow and cherry trees nearby. *"If there are willow trees there will be water."* Lennox sniffed the air. He had been so keen to follow the unicorn scent, and in fear of losing it, that he had not bothered to sense whether there was water nearby. Now he could smell the sweet fragrance of a nearby spring. He trotted over to a spot under the drooping shade of a tall willow.

The horses moved aside to allow him access to the spring. They were naturally curious. "I've never seen you here before," said one of the horses. "Have you escaped from the humans and those other strange creatures who have come to live here?"

Lennox quenched his thirst noisily before answering. "The people in the village below have helped me escape. I come from a land called Briton where my kind has been hunted to extinction. They brought me here so that I may find others like me. I yearn for companionship and it is good to meet you but tell me, I can smell the scent of a unicorn, do they inhabit the forest ahead?"

"Yes," replied the horse. "But we hardly ever see them. They never come out of the forest and chase us away if we trek too deeply inside the woods. We are not forest creatures so we do not bother the unicorns and they do not bother us. It is the new people in the village that concern us. They capture our kind and ride them. Worse still, they tie horses to wagons and make them pull heavy loads."

"There are several beings in the new village," responded Lennox. "Humans, who ride horses and tether animals to carts, and not just horses but donkeys and oxen."

The small group of horses snorted their disapproval.

"The other kind in the village are wizards and witches. They have no need of horses as they fly around on the handles of brushes."

"Hmmm," responded one of the horses. "We've seen them. They brought those little creatures with them, too." He raised his head to indicate a cluster of fairies and elves in the tree above.

The unicorn whinnied his greeting. The little folk raised their hands in response.

"There used to be a lot of them around here but over time they grew fewer. They are too fragile to cope with the number of animals treading these plains. It's nice to see them back. My grandfather told me that they could speak the language of the horse but they do not seem to understand us."

Lennox was puzzled. "I have never known a fairy or elf who spoke Unicornian, or the language of the horse as you call it. But I have found that, if we try, we can understand each other. There is only one of the magical beings who speaks our tongue and his name is Merlin." Lennox went on to tell the horses about his friends, the loss of his family, and how Elvira and the fairies had saved him. However, he hadn't realised how tired he was, and begged the horses' forgiveness if he now lay down and rested for a while.

"Sleep, Lennox," the horses told him. "We will stay here until it cools down. We will watch over you and wake you if any danger approaches."

"Danger?" asked Lennox

"Aurochs or mammoths," responded the horses. "They like the spring to themselves and if they come near we move on before they drive us away."

"Ah, I have never seen either in Briton. They used to exist there but were hunted by men until there were no more left."

The horses snorted their disgust. "Yes, indeed, aurochs and mammoths may drive us from our watering holes, but humans are our greatest enemy."

Evening was approaching when Lennox awoke. He had never intended to sleep for so long. The horses were grazing in the pastureland nearby. The little folk, who had been up in the tree, were now playing hide and seek among some large leafed plants near the spring.

Lennox drank deeply but did not stop to feed. Instead he whinnied his thanks to the horses who had watched over him while he rested. But he did not dally;

the scent of the unicorn had disappeared. He knew he must hasten towards the forest.

I have slept far too long. I have lost the other unicorn's scent. What a fool I have been to slumber so long.

The pastureland grew steeper so that Lennox found it hard to travel at any more than a walk. He sniffed the air frequently until at last it was there again. The scent had moved towards the edge of the forest nearest the sea. He changed direction and gathered pace.

It was nightfall before he saw her. Beneath the light of the waning moon he caught sight of her silvery mane glimmering in the moonlight and the unmistakable glisten of her single horn. The unicorn, whose scent he had followed, stood at the top of the hill.

"Who are you?" she demanded. "Where have you come from? What do you want?"

"I am Lennox, the last unicorn from a place known as Briton, where my kind has been hunted to extinction. I come seeking companionship."

"I have never seen a white unicorn before," she answered, looking the newcomer up and down.

As Lennox got closer he could see the mare had a pale chestnut coat. The only white on her fur was a wide blaze on her face.

"I have only ever seen white unicorns before. That is, except, for my wife Tamarie, she had a black tail and mane and the most endearing ebony flecks on her face."

"If you have only ever seen white unicorns then you have not seen a brown foal on your way here?" The mare's statement was really a question.

"A foal! I wish I had. Our foals are few and far between and I would glory in seeing a brown one."

"Even a colt?"

"Yes, of course." Lennox was puzzled by the mare's response. "Colt or filly, any foal is a glorious gift from Mother Nature."

The mare looked surprised.

"I am tired and thirsty after my steep climb," said Lennox. "Pray, tell me, is there water nearby? I would welcome a drink."

"Yes," replied the chestnut mare. "There is a small waterfall less than half a mile away. Walk with me and tell me more about this land called Briton. I am intrigued by what you have to say."

Lennox, delighted to find a companion, told her his story as they trotted along.

The mare, who introduced herself as Sheba, listened intently. As they neared the falls Lennox gathered pace. It had been a long and tiring day but it was worth it to find another unicorn. Water trickled down the granite cliff into a small tarn.

Sheba watched him as he quenched his thirst. As he raised his head she said, "I am sorry to learn that you have lost your wife and your son. I too have lost my son, Fiery. He is a colt. He was driven out of the forest by his father. I am trying to find him. Will you help me?"

Lennox was stunned by Sheba's revelation. He could not understand how a father could drive a young foal away. He remembered Bryant, his own son, leaving the protection of Elvira's home and Tamarie racing after him.

Sheba explained that Tyzon, the leader of the unicorns in the Great Forest, would not allow any other stallion to live in his territory. It was customary for the leader of the herd to kill any male foal who was not his exact image. Sheba had already lost one son so this time she had run away to give birth. Her worst fear was realised when her newly born foal turned out to be a little brown colt and looked nothing like his father. She fell in love with her newborn child whom she called Fiery, because he was quick and nimble, darting here there and everywhere as soon as the opportunity arose. She vowed that she would not let his father kill him, and so she had dared to leave the safety of the forest. She sought refuge around the edge of the woodland and hoped that Tyzon would not find her or her newborn foal.

However, after searching for several weeks Tyzon found Sheba – but not her son. She had kept her foal well hidden in a hollow tree trunk which was surrounded by wild garlic. The pungent smell of the garlic had concealed her son's scent. She had told Tyzon that the foal had been born dead and she dutifully followed the stallion and his herd back into the forest. She stayed with the herd for a few days, to allay any suspicions that Tyzon might have that the foal still lived, and then she crept away to return to her son again. She planned to run away with him in the hope of finding another forest where his father would not follow. However, when she reached the hiding place Fiery had gone! Now she was searching for her foal.

"So no luck yet," said a small voice. Sheba was in the middle of her story when a small man appeared from between the mossy stones behind the waterfall. He was dressed in a cloak made of leaves which was pinned with an acorn. Oak leaves adorned his hair. On his legs he wore leggings made from the bark of trees but his feet were bare.

"No," she replied with sadness to the little man's question. Then turning to her new unicorn friend, she asked, "Lennox, have you ever met an elf before?"

"I have, but not one who looks like this," he admitted. "Nor ever one who could speak Unicornian! I am most pleased to meet you."

"I'm Tifflin," the elf bowed to the newcomer, "but you can call me Tiff. I'm pleased to meet you, Lennox."

"And I am pleased to meet you!" Lennox bowed his head in acknowledgement.

"Have you had any news from your friends? Has anyone seen Fiery?" Sheba asked anxiously.

"I am afraid not," replied Tifflin. "I would be out there searching for him myself but I must stay at home to look after Dana."

As he spoke a young elf woman stepped out from behind the stones. She too was dressed in leaves but her legs were bare and so too were her feet. Her stomach was swollen

"I am sorry we cannot help you, Sheba, but our own child is due any day now." Dana turned to her husband. "Tiff, why don't you ask the trees if they have any news yet?"

"Good idea," responded Tifflin. He leapt over to the nearest tree and climbed its trunk with ease, as if the bark somehow stuck to his feet. Half way up he pressed his body against the trunk and put his arms as far around it as he could reach. He whispered a few

57

words into a knot in the bark then put his ear next to the small hole as if he were waiting for an answer.

"Were you speaking to the tree?" asked Lennox, who was puzzled by what he had just witnessed.

"Yes," replied Tifflin. "They have an incredible communication network. Their roots intertwine and talk to each other. It may take a long while but they can reach every other tree in the forest and even a few in the copses beyond. They are all looking for Fiery but they have no information yet."

"No news is better than bad news," Dana stated wisely. "If Fiery had come to any harm in the forest we would have heard by now. He must have wandered into the meadows. You both look tired and in need of rest. Why don't you make a fresh start in the morning? You won't see much in the dark."

The unicorns were both weary. Much as they would have liked to continue the search for the missing foal, they agreed that Dana's suggestion was the best option. They settled down for the night, each glad to have found a new friendship.

CHAPTER 5 – In search of Fiery

The unicorns awoke to the sound of the creaks and groans of a nearby willow. They had slept under the trees at the edge of the forest. Woodland was their natural home and Lennox had slept well. Sheba, however, was not only awake but out in the open. She seemed agitated. Her tail was swinging, and she seemed unable to keep her hooves still. She pawed the ground at the edge of the tarn, calling the wood elf.

"What is it?" Lennox asked, concerned about the mare's behaviour.

"Don't you hear them?" asked Sheba, irritated by Lennox's naivety. "Surely a unicorn knows the sound of tree talk!"

Lennox shook his head in bewilderment. "Before last night I had never heard of such a thing," he responded.

"Well, let's hear what they have to say," Tifflin said, emerging from behind the cascading water, stretching and yawning as he did so. The little man's eyes were bleary with sleep, but he walked forward, breaking into a run just before leaping onto the willow tree which was making the most noise.

Lennox noticed that despite the lack of breeze the tree was swinging its long branches, as if a strong wind were blowing. Some of the other trees were swaying too.

Tifflin ducked and dived with skilful agility to avoid being struck by the swinging willow branches, as he made his way up the trunk. Despite the elf's nimbleness the tree struck his legs and he yelled out in pain.

Lennox winced in sympathy.

The little man shouted something and the tree became still. Now he could walk with ease up the trunk, stopping when he reached a large knot. In the same way as he had done the previous evening, Tifflin flattened his body against the trunk with his ear pressed firmly against a knot.

Lennox watched as the wood elf nodded his head, as if understanding whatever the tree was saying. Finally he added a few words himself, before making his way back down and perching on a lower branch.

Sheba moved forward, her eyes full of anxiousness, to hear what Tifflin had to say.

"They say my second cousin Wifflin has news and is on his way here. He and Marje are skirting around the edge of the forest. Why don't you go and meet them? I would come with you but I don't want to leave Dana here alone."

"I understand," said Sheba, bowing her head in acknowledgement. "And I am grateful for your help, Tiff – I am sorry to have awoken you and Dana so early."

"Don't worry about it," Dana's musical voice responded. She was sitting on a boulder beside the tarn. "If I couldn't find my child I would be sick with worry, too. I wish you every bit of luck I have in me to bestow on you. Now go!"

Sheba whinnied her thanks to both elves and trees before setting off at a canter.

"Wait for me!" Lennox called to her. He too whinnied his thanks to the wood elves and copied his new found friend's example in thanking the trees – though he didn't know if the trees had understood.

Sheba was setting a fast pace, and Lennox soon started to build up a sweat. "Slow down," he called. "You will not do yourself any good travelling at this rate."

Realising the wisdom of his words, the mare started to slow. "Let's continue until noon and then find a shady place to rest until the day cools."

"How long will it take to reach the other side of the forest?" Lennox asked.

"About two days if we travel through the forest. About three if we travel around the outskirts, but Wifflin is flying so he will not venture in among the trees."

Flying? I didn't know elves could fly but perhaps this Wifflin and his friend Marje have wings. There is so much I do not know. Until yesterday I had never before seen a chestnut unicorn, nor did I know that trees could talk. I will let Sheba take the lead and simply follow.

At midday they sheltered from the sun, finding refuge under overhanging branches at the edge of the forest, and water in the hollow of a broken tree.

"Hello," said a small voice. "I heard you were travelling this way to meet Wifflin."

Lennox looked down to see a wood elf seated on the back of a large brown hare. The elf had obviously been riding the hare because it had reins made of ivy around its neck. Nevertheless, despite being used as a beast of burden, the hare looked quite content and interested in everything going on around. It sat on his haunches, staring wide-eyed at the white unicorn, as it let its rider dismount. The elf lifted the ivy twines above the hare's long ears, over its head, and left the halter lying on the ground.

"I'm Pifflin," said the elf, introducing himself, "but you can call me Piff. I am on my way to see my cousin Tifflin and his wife Dana, but when I saw you stop I thought I'd come over and say 'hello'. I'm pleased to meet you. I've seen your good lady on several occasions but never a *white* unicorn."

"I'm pleased to meet you too, Piff," said Lennox. "Though I'm afraid Sheba is not my lady. I only met her for the first time yesterday. I am helping her find her foal."

Sheba snorted a greeting to the elf who nodded in return.

Lennox went on to tell Pifflin how he had lost his herd in Briton. Pifflin and Sheba listened intently.

"So you came with those other humans and strange looking creatures in the flying ships? Tiff was out of the forest climbing trees in the coppices below when he first saw them arriving. They have brought other fairies and elves with them but we avoid them. We consider any friend of a human to be our enemy."

"Not all humans are bad," stated Lennox, "but I agree. It is best to keep away from them. You have no need to fear the fairies and elves from Briton though. Like me, they came here to avoid extinction."

All four took an afternoon nap under the shade of the trees on the edge of the forest. The hare curled up beside Pifflin. Lennox took pleasure in lying in the soft undergrowth but Sheba could not relax; she tossed and turned with worry about her missing son.

Nevertheless, it was the wood elf who was first to rise. He had been woken by the sound of a creaking elm tree. Lennox awoke to see him climbing the tree and pressing his ear against a knot in the trunk just as he had seen Tifflin do earlier. The elf muttered his thanks to the elm before hopping down.

"Tyzon has your scent," he warned. "Be careful. Now, I must be on my way to cousin Tiff and Dana. My good wife will have beaten me to it. She has taken the forest route but Moffat here preferred to travel with grass under her feet. They'll wonder where I am and worry that Moffat and I have found my way into a human's stew pot.

"Now be careful, Lennox. Humans do not often travel near the forest because they are afraid they will awake the giants within, but huntsmen sometimes cross the prairie below. But as Sheba has no doubt told you, the biggest threat to your safety is Tyzon. He will not tolerate another stallion in the forest and it does seem as if you have already stolen one of his wives!"

Sheba gave Lennox an embarrassed side glance.

"I will take care, Piff. Thank for your warning." Lennox bowed his head to acknowledge Pifflin's words.

"I hope all goes well for Dana and that her baby arrives safely," added Sheba. "I am thinking of her."

Goodbyes said, the unicorns set off in one direction, the wood elf seated on the bounding hare in the other.

Lennox started to feel sorry for the animals here in Avalon. It seemed they had lived here contentedly for some time. Now Merlin had brought people on flying boats, from another land, who might spoil their lifestyle.

The stallion didn't have time to think too deeply. Sheba was setting a fast pace and he needed to focus his attention on the unfamiliar terrain beneath his hooves. Every now and then he glanced wistfully at the forest as he sped along beside it. He longed to explore its depths and meet Tyzon. He wanted an explanation as to how a father could kill his male foals. Colt or filly, surely every young unicorn was a precious gift from Mother Nature?

It was dusk when a stork swooped down in front of them. The pair came to an abrupt halt. So abrupt that Lennox almost ran into Sheba.

Sitting on the stork's back was another wood elf. "Hi ya!" he called as the stork circled in the air before landing.

The happy little elf slid off the stork's feathery back. The unicorns whinnied in response. The large bird started pecking at the grass in search of worms.

"I'm Wifflin," said the elf, giving Lennox a little salute. "Please call me Wifflin and don't abbreviate my name. This is my friend Marje." He nodded towards the stork who continued to peck at the ground.

"I'm pleased to meet you Wifflin and you too, Marje." Lennox bowed his head in greeting, hoping that Marje would understand but she seemed uninterested.

Sheba was impatient and butted into the conversation. "Wifflin, thank you so much for meeting us. Tiff said you had news of Fiery, my foal."

"I do indeed," said the little man, and beamed a smile which revealed a set of even white teeth. His green eyes twinkled as he told them, "And not just Fiery but other unicorn colts, too!"

"What?" the mare exclaimed.

"Fiery, Flambeau and Feerce!" Wifflin's grin could not be any wider.

"Why, Flambeau was Blaize's young son and Feerce was Luna's."

"Not was – is!" Wifflin laughed, enjoying the surprise that he had brought. "But Flambeau must be nearly a year old now. He ran off before his father could take his life, we assumed he had been killed by wolves as we could not find his body. Luna told Tyzon that she had killed Feerce herself rather than let anyone else do it. Poor mare, she must have done the same as me and allowed him to escape. Are they safe and well?"

"Yes, that is, as safe as they can be outside the forest. Flambeau is, er... different now, you'll know what I mean when you see him. It was Marje here who found them, or rather her family did. There's a lake near the granite mountains where her family lives. We'll take you to the unicorn colts but they remain hidden till nightfall. We won't make it to the lake tonight but if we continue westward around the forest by day, then head across the prairie at dusk, we should reach them tomorrow night before they go back into hiding."

"That will give me time to find Blaize and Luna and tell them that their children are alive and well." Sheba was excited.

"But Sheba, if you go back into the forest Tyzon will not allow you to leave!" exclaimed Wifflin, the smile wiped from his face.

"I will not allow him to keep Sheba," Lennox stated meaningfully. "Fiery will need his mother to guide him."

"You cannot enter the Great Forest, Lennox. I will find a way of contacting Blaize and Luna which will not involve you." Sheba was concerned. "No other stallion is permitted in the forest. Tyzon is a powerful beast and will slay you."

"Or I will slay *him*," answered Lennox. "I cannot understand how a stallion can kill his own sons. It sounds almost human-like. No, I will come with you and protect you. If I am to die by another unicorn's hoof or horn so shall it be. I am old now and may not sire another son but you, the other mares, and your sons must live on and breed other herds. I am prepared to meet this Tyzon."

Sheba bowed her head in acceptance.

"Then let us rest awhile," said Wifflin, who had been listening wide-eyed. "If you are to meet Tyzon then you will need every ounce of strength you can muster."

To a human, the shadow of trees on the forest floor would have woven an eerie pattern. However, to a unicorn they were familiar and welcoming. The smell of the nearby herd should have been welcoming too, but the unique, musty scent of the forest stallion was formidable.

The moon was waning but nevertheless it spread light through the trees. Lennox and Sheba came to an abrupt halt when they saw the moonlight glimmer on the horn of a tall and muscular unicorn. Tyzon stood on a mound in a forest glade, making him seem even taller and more formidable than he already was. His wives stood in a semi-circle on the lower ground behind him.

Tyzon had been awaiting Lennox's arrival.

"So, here you are!" he stated in a meaningful tone. "You are a newcomer and unaware of the laws of the

Great Forest so I will give you this one chance to leave, but you will go without my wife."

Lennox looked in amazement at his rival. He was the biggest unicorn he had ever seen, probably twice his own weight. His body was jet black, but even in the waning moonlight he could see the shine of his ebony coat and the ripple of his powerful muscles. However, Tyzon's most striking feature was his horn, which glistened pure gold.

"I have never seen a black unicorn before," Lennox stated, as much in bewilderment as in an effort to make conversation and ease the tension. "Let alone one with a golden horn. Let us speak for a while, my friend, I have no wish to offend you or to fight with you. Unicorns are rare – as are our children whom we should cherish. I do not understand how you could wish to kill your sons, or not allow another herd to thrive in this vast forest. If you are not careful our kind will become extinct here, as they have done in my former homeland known as Briton."

"Ha! White unicorn. You have answered the question yourself! It is to stop the forest herd becoming extinct that I must slay my sons, much as it grieves me to do so. It pains me almost beyond endurance to see them die but I must stay strong and obey the laws of the forest. It is those same laws which have enabled this herd to survive whilst others have perished."

"I do not understand," replied Lennox. "Pray explain the law that states you must kill your children in order for the herd to survive. It makes no sense to me."

"Very well," Tyzon answered. "It is rare that I have the opportunity to speak to anyone other than my herd so I will tell you. And it will do no harm to remind my wives as to the reasoning behind our laws, and why they must allow their male offspring to die at the tender age of 49 days."

He looked at Sheba. "Are you listening, Sheba?"

"I am listening," the mare replied. "But Tyzon, I beg you to reconsider these laws which are old and may yet turn out to be our downfall."

Tyzon pointed his golden horn towards Sheba and pawed the ground as if he were about to attack. Lennox tensed himself ready to protect the mare, but Tyzon raised his head and spoke.

"Our herd has thrived for hundreds, perhaps thousands, of years. It has always been led by a stallion with a golden horn. A golden horned stallion will only be born once in a generation. If other males are allowed to survive they will breed other herds in the forest – eventually there will not be enough food for all of us.

"Furthermore, there are creatures known as 'humans' who would take our lives. If there are so many of us here that our existence is known, then it will attract these humans who would slaughter us all. There was a time when my forefathers sent their sons, born without the golden horn, out of the forest to find new homes. We heard through our friends the elves that they had perished at the hands of these humans. Many had suffered cruel deaths. Some tried to capture our sons and tame them, but to a unicorn captivity is worse than death. Others were slaughtered for their meat, horns, coats and blood. So, it was decided that the leader of the herd, or the foal's mother, would kill any male born without the golden horn with one strike through its gentle heart. A quick death, as painless as possible."

"But what if anything happens to you?" asked Lennox. "How would the herd survive without any other stallion?"

"A foal has always been born whose horn turns to gold within 49 days of its birth," replied Tyzon. "Such a child will be born again soon."

"But Tyzon, my love," said a black mare, with a white blaze down her face, "I remember when your father, grandfather and even your great grandfather lived with the herd. Now it is just you. This newcomer speaks sense. If you were taken ill or if we were attacked by humans and you fell, who would protect the herd then? How would we survive without you?"

"As long as we obey the laws of the forest," the black stallion bellowed, "laws which have kept us safe for centuries, we will survive. Now, I have had enough of this nonsense. Leave, white unicorn, or die!"

Tyzon leapt down from the mound on which he stood, lowered his horn and walked solidly towards Lennox. In response, Lennox lowered his horn. Tyzon lurched forward but the newcomer, less powerful but more agile, leapt to one side, and as he did so turned in mid-air, scratching Tyzon on the shoulder.

The black stallion let out a terrible sound as he felt the sting of the cut. No one had ever struck him before. He lashed out with front and back hooves, catching his white rival on the nose.

Blood leaked from Tyzon's shoulder but poured from Lennox's nose, smearing his white coat with splatters of red. Horns clashed and hooves struck for what seemed like hours. The watching mares whinnied and snorted nervously.

Sheba cried out in anguish, "Stop! Please stop! Listen to me! Fiery, my colt, is still alive. He has travelled out of the forest to a place across the prairie. I have heard that he is safe and well and has found shelter with Flambeau and Feerce."

The two stallions came to a standstill. Blaize moved out of the semi-circle of mares behind Tyzon. She was followed by another black mare with a mark like a half moon on her forehead.

"What did you say?" asked Blaize.

Sheba repeated her story that Fiery, Flambeau and Feerce were well and living on the other side of the prairie. She added, "If we leave tonight we could be with them by this time tomorrow. I will go, and if you wish me to care for your colts as well as my own I will do so."

"But Tyzon will not allow you to leave," exclaimed the black mare with the crescent moon on her forehead and whose name was Luna.

"Leave now!" Lennox shouted. "I will not allow Tyzon to keep you here even if I die stopping him. Go. Quickly. I am old. The lives of your colts are more important than mine."

The three mares sped off. Sheba turned momentarily and gave the white stallion, who was covered in blood, a wistful glance. But she knew if she did not leave him at that very moment, the chance would be lost forever.

And so the fighting resumed: Tyzon lunged at Lennox again. Lennox managed to avoid the larger animal's thrust which would have easily killed him if it had struck.

Lennox raced around the larger beast to avoid its deadly horn and heavy hooves.

Will this black beast never tire? Lennox asked himself. *I cannot continue much longer. I just hope that*

I have given the mares sufficient time to get away and that my end will be swift.

Eventually the two stallions stood opposite each other. Lennox was so tired he almost felt it was time to let his opponent do his worst. Tyzon lowered his horn and pawed the ground readying for his final assault. Then a movement in the trees caught Lennox's eye; a small round object shot from the tree above hitting Tyzon on the neck. It happened again and again. Tyzon's concentration was broken as he turned to see where the pellets were coming from.

Lennox took the opportunity to turn and run. His tired limbs acquired a new found energy and he broke into a gallop. He could hear hoof beats behind him but his heavier assailant was slower. At last he reached the edge of the woods where he could see Wifflin flying on Marje above him. The little elf signalled him forward, down the hill, and across the plain.

Tyzon reached the edge of the forest. He came out in the open but would go no further. He had no intention of leaving the forest border. He stood watching his opponent flee. His remaining wives emerged either side of him. Tyzon had chased his opponent away but in so doing he had lost Sheba, Blaize and Luna who had fled ahead of the white stallion.

Later Lennox wondered whether it was really the forest laws which had prevented Tyzon leaving his woodland home, and chasing after him; or whether the golden horned stallion secretly hoped that his three male offspring might survive elsewhere.

Lennox staggered down the hill. He was tired and his old injury had started to flare up again. His leg grew more painful with each step. Wifflin and Marje flew ahead, guiding him until they reached the shelter of one of the small coppices that dotted the vast prairie. The mares were waiting there. Lennox's nose had stopped bleeding but his body had many superficial wounds which the mares licked clean.

"I'd hoped we would have been on our way to the lake by now," Wifflin commented. "But perhaps we need to rest for a day or two."

"Not one day!" protested Lennox. "Give me a few hours' respite and I will be fit to travel again."

"Fit to travel?" quipped the wood elf. "I thought you were a goner in the forest."

"I nearly was," agreed the unicorn. "If something hadn't fallen from the tree and hit Tyzon on the neck he would have slain me."

Wifflin gave one of his mischievous grins, and his green eyes twinkled with amusement. With one hand he withdrew a catapult from the inside of his cloak; with the other he produced a handful of acorns from his pocket. "Acorns can sting when fired from tree tops," he laughed.

"So it was you who saved me, Wifflin! I thank you. I ran like a coward but because of you I am still alive. Thank you!"

"Coward?" the mares uttered in astonishment.

"Only the bravest of unicorns would challenge Tyzon," Blaize stated.

"He gave you the opportunity to leave without a fight," Sheba added. "Instead you decided to stay and gave us the chance to escape. You are the bravest unicorn I have ever met."

The other two mares snorted their agreement at Sheba's words.

"Now, rest, Lennox," ordered Blaize, who was the oldest and wisest of the mares. "If it takes more than a day to recover then I will stay here with you while Sheba and Luna go ahead. My child Flambeau is almost a year old now. He has managed without me for all this time so another couple of days won't do any harm."

Despite Lennox's protests he and the mares rested until a herd of aurochs walked menacingly into the coppice. They wanted to drink from the spring, and so the unicorns had no choice but to move out into the pastures.

"Be careful!" horses from a nearby herd snorted. "Humans sometimes pass by here. If they see you then their huntsmen will certainly follow."

"What are you doing out of the forest?" others asked. "Your white stallion won't outpace the hunters with that injured leg."

"We are looking for our foals," Sheba replied, adding simply, "They were lost but this wood elf and his stork are leading us to them."

"Ah, yes," replied the horses. "We have seen them playing with the cefflars at the lake."

"Let us help you," offered a piebald stallion. "We will walk with you; it will be nice to bathe in the cool waters. We will surround you so that if any humans pass by you will not be so easily seen."

The unicorns thanked the horses for their kindness. They also asked them what the cefflars were but, mystified by the replies, decided to wait till they could see for themselves. They took their time walking down the hill to the lake chatting among themselves as they went. It was good to be among friends. The slow pace eased the pain in Lennox's shin. Meanwhile, Wifflin and Marje took the opportunity to fly around and scout for signs of danger.

The afternoon heat was such that the equine friends sought shade under a small grove of wild fruit trees. As they rested the peace was broken by the sound of hoof beats – someone was travelling fast from the direction from which they had come.

Lennox's stomach clenched. *Surely not Tyzon. Not now. He had his chance to follow but did not take it. Have we been spotted by hunters?*

All the unicorns were alarmed by the sound of approaching hooves but their fears were soon allayed when they saw Wifflin and Marje flying above. The pair were weaving circles in the air and showed no signs of panic. As they drew nearer Marje swooped down and Wifflin called out triumphantly, "Look what I've found!"

Cantering into sight, above the undulations of the meadows came three unicorn mares. They slowed to a trot when they saw their counterparts mingling in the herd of horses.

"We have come to join you!" they shouted. "We do not want to risk losing any sons we may have!"

The horses were mystified by the comment, so whilst Sheba and her sister mares welcomed the newcomers, Blaize explained the laws of the forest to them.

"Then you cannot return to the forest," one horse commented. "You must hide with your sons. They disappear during the day and we do not know where they go."

"They cannot live with the cefflars," Wifflin stated. "Their home is under water."

As dusk fell the unicorns continued their journey, surrounded by the horses, with Wifflin and Marje flying overhead ever conscious of impending danger. It was near midnight before they reached the lake.

Lennox was glad to bathe his aching leg. Some other equines followed him into the inviting cool water. Marje joined her family who all seemed to be standing on one leg asleep or fishing in the shallow borders of the lake.

It was a peaceful scene but the unicorn mares soon started to fret. "Where are they? Where are Fiery, Flambeau and Feerce?" they asked.

"They will be here soon," answered the horses as they frolicked in the lake. "They come out from wherever they are hiding in the dead of night. Be patient, ladies."

Lennox was more concerned about where he would lead the mares once they had found their lost sons. He did not know this new land. He asked the advice of the horses who told him that they had heard of forests further afield but to get there the unicorns would have to travel through human-occupied country.

Wifflin heard the conversation and came down from his tree top vantage point. "Wherever the foals hide during the day is a mystery. Even the storks don't know. I suggest you share their hiding place for a while. Give yourselves time to think and that leg of yours time to heal."

Lennox did not have chance to respond. Everyone's attention was drawn by a sudden loud plop from the lake as a small winged horse jumped out of the water. It was followed by more plops and black winged horses

which flew out of the lake on to dry land. Half a dozen of the delicate creatures frolicked for a while. They were no more than three feet tall, all were black with large protruding black eyes and wings which were so fine that the bony structure on which they were hung was visible. All were slender and agile.

So these are the cefflars! A horse with wings which lives in water. Lennox and the other unicorns looked on full of wonder.

The cefflars appeared to be dancing as they pranced on the pasture land surrounding the lake. Everyone was so absorbed by the site of the winged horses that no one actually saw the arrival of the three unicorn foals until they joined with the cefflars; prancing and dancing.

The equine audience stared at the spectacle before them until Fiery shouted, "Mother!" and ran to Sheba. Flambeau and Feerce looked around to see their own mothers pacing towards them, trying not to alarm the cefflars as they did so.

Mothers and sons nuzzled each other, each weeping with the joy of their reunion. Lennox's eyes filled with tears too, as did those of his new equine friends – there was hardly a dry eye among them.

Although Blaize greeted her son tenderly, she now stood back. "Flambeau, what has happened to you?"

Flambeau no longer had a horn. It had been broken off. Only a furry lump remained where his precious horn had once been. Blaize looked at her son with eyes full of tenderness but the colt simply bent his head as if he were ashamed.

"It's a long story," stated the colt, who was jet black just like his father. Flambeau's strong physique looked as if he might one day be as big and as powerful as Tyzon. He added quietly, "And not a tale for other ears."

Although Flambeau had spoken softly he had his father's clear voice and his words were overheard by some of the horses.

"Ah, you have secrets yet to unfold," said one horse to Lennox whom he assumed to be the leader of the herd.

"We will stay a while," the horses told the unicorns, "then we will leave you. No doubt your sons will share their hiding place with you and you will no longer need our protection."

The unicorns thanked the horses who had escorted them to the lake. True to their word, the horses moved back to their more familiar territory but before they went each and every one of them came forward to wish the unicorns good luck.

The adults watched the youngsters feed and frolic with the cefflars for several hours. The colts would not disclose their hiding place but told their mothers that all would be revealed soon. "We hide by day. At night we feed and play," they explained. "The cefflars are our friends." Despite having been parted from their mothers they appeared happy and, with the exception of Flambeau's missing horn, all seemed in good health and high spirits.

Lennox tried to speak to one of the cefflars but as soon as he approached the small winged horse, it shied away. Almost as suddenly as they had appeared the cefflars 'plopped' back into the lake, allowing themselves to be swallowed into the depths of the waters.

"I've never heard of cefflars before," Lennox confided in Wifflin, who had lain beside a bush using Marje as a feather pillow.

"They are rarer than unicorns," the little fellow responded. "Now, I must wish you good fortune and return to my forest home. I am a woodland elf and although I like watching the lakeside life style, I never stay away from my homeland for long."

Lennox had grown very fond of Wifflin and was sorry to see him leave. He would never forget how the wood elf had saved his life. He and the mares thanked Wifflin and Marje warmly for all the help they had given them. It was twilight as they watched the pair fly away and gradually disappear from sight.

With the departure of the horses, cefflars and wood elf, only the unicorns and birds remained at the lake. The colts were looking tired. Except for the sound of early morning bird song the world seemed at peace until a loud crash broke the tranquillity.

Storks flew up in the air, crying out in alarm. Not one of the big birds remained at the lake. Lennox swirled around to see what he thought was a small avalanche tumbling down from nearby mountains. He instinctively stepped back, as did the mares. Until now, it had been too dark to take in the entirety of his surroundings. Now he could see that the lake was close to tall granite mountains. It was not unlike the spot where he had met Tifflin and Dana but the lake was much bigger and trees separated the mountains from the lake and pasturelands. He had seen the trees earlier and thought that they might be a good hiding place but the sight of the falling stones now gave him the impression it was a far too dangerous location.

The colts, however, stayed where they were and showed no alarm. Despite their mother's warnings they ran towards the falling rocks rather than away.

Lennox, having seen so many strange things over the last few days, thought that he was beyond surprise, but that was not the case. He watched in astonishment as the tumbling stones rolled together, bumping into each other and nudging as they found the correct place to fit. Finally the stones assembled into what looked like two men made of rock. Arms began to move as the rock men shook off the dust and slowly rose to their feet.

"These are Mason and Flint," Flambeau told the mares. "They are guardians of nature over mother earth and are called gnomes for short. They guard us too when we come out to play."

"Come out from where?" asked Blaize who, having spent all of her life in the Great Forest, was naturally bewildered.

The rock men beckoned the unicorns forward, with their stone arms and hands, but Lennox, like the mares, stepped back rather than forward. They had never seen such odd looking beings before. They bade the colts stay where they were.

However, although the adults tried to stand firm, Flambeau, Feerce and Fiery walked towards the gnomes. Feerce even nuzzled one of the stone creatures. Realising the adults' concerns, the colts tried to encourage them to follow.

"Mason and Flint and the other gnomes protect us," they tried again to explain. "You must follow us. It is dangerous out here. Not just humans but mountain lions. We have heard tales of dragons and other large creatures seeking animal flesh, too. Don't be afraid. Follow us to Zanadoo."

It was a stalemate; the colts wanting to follow the gnomes and the mares begging them stay where they were, until a white mule appeared. The newcomer seemed to have come from what looked like a dark opening in the mountain.

"Hello," the mule greeted them happily. "I'm Muffle."

Muffle appeared to be white and pink and from its wide legged stance Lennox could see that the mule was very old. The colts were pleased to see the old timer and ran to him, lovingly nuzzling him.

Lennox stepped forward to speak to the mule, and as he did so he saw that the strange pink colour was actually the mule's skin showing through his sparse white coat. The mares drew closer to the mule but remained behind Lennox.

It was Muffle who spoke first. He looked directly at Lennox, accepting the stallion to be the leader of what was now a small herd. "My master, who has cared for your young ones, bids you welcome. He has been expecting you and will give you refuge and a safe haven for most of your journey to the Forbidden Forest."

"Expecting us?" queried Lennox. "The Forbidden Forest?"

"Yes," replied the mule. "Although Zan lives within the mountains, he has a gift which allows him to know what is going on in other lands."

"Really?" This time it was Blaize who asked the question.

"Yes, come and meet him," the mule responded. "I'm going to take you inside the mountain. It will be unusual surroundings for unicorns, and you will no doubt be nervous at first, but I beg you to follow. You will be safer inside the mountains than out and it is not just humans that you need to fear. We had another foal here but he was attacked by a pair of mountain lions. I used to bring the foals out here to play and graze. Alas, it is a long way for me to walk and I could not defend the young colt. Fairfax, he was called."

Lennox could hear the mares behind him repeating the name. It was obvious that they had once known Fairfax.

"There was nothing I could do. I am old and slow. The gnomes threw their spears at the lions, and rolled their stone bodies towards them, but the big cats were too quick. Fortunately a giant was passing by, we don't see too many here; he drew a sword and killed the male lion. The lioness ran off and we have not seen her since. If it were not for the giant we may have lost Flambeau as well, or the lions may have taken me!"

"A giant?" Lennox had heard of giants but never seen one.

"They live in the Great Forest," Muffle explained. "Your mares will have seen them. They do not harm unicorns."

The mares snorted their agreement.

"As well as the Great Forest there is a family of giants who live on the far side of Twydell. The giant must have been on his way to visit relatives. It was sad to see such a magnificent beast killed, but if it had not been slain then the lions could have easily had your other foals for dinner."

84

"I was here at the time," Flambeau confirmed. "I was lucky not to have been killed, too. I was so very sad to see what happened to Fairfax. He was my friend."

Blaize moved forward and comforted her son.

The mule spoke again. "The path, upon which I am about to lead you, is inside the granite mountain. It is a far, far cry from your forest home. Nevertheless, it is the only safe route especially for your precious youngsters. It will be worth spending a week inside the mountains in order to spend the rest of your lives in your new home – the Forbidden Forest."

It was with some reluctance that the unicorns finally agreed to follow Muffle towards the hole in the granite mountain wall. Lennox and the mares still hesitated as they left the sunlight to enter the darkness. But it was clear that the colts would continue with or without them; they showed no fear whatsoever as they followed Muffle and Mason into the cave. The mares whinnied anxiously, but not wanting to let the youngsters out of their sight again, continued along the gloomy tunnel. Lennox brought up the rear. He heard a strange movement behind him and a crash of stones. Somehow Flint had sealed the entrance to the cave. Like it or not the unicorns were now inside the mountain and would not be able to retreat.

The unicorns were used to the darkness of the forest at night but this was different. The mares whinnied and snorted uneasily. The echo of their hooves and the heavy footsteps of the gnomes added to the eeriness of the place in which they now found themselves.

Muffle called the group to a halt whilst the gnomes lit torches on the walls. "There are torches already burning further down," he told them. "But we do not

85

light the ones near the entrance when the foals are out, in case they attract any humans passing nearby.

"We don't get many humans near here but we are careful, not just for the foals' sake but for the safety of Zanadoo."

"Who is this Zanadoo?" asked Lennox.

"Not who!" Muffle stated. "Zanadoo is the country you entered when you stepped inside this cave!"

The stallion and the slow walking mule had now taken up the rear whilst the colts trotted ahead deeper and deeper inside the mountain. The youngsters appeared to be very confident in their unusual surroundings and the mares followed. All the unicorn horns glistened in the light of the flaming torches; that is, all except Flambeau's.

I wonder what happened to Flambeau's horn, Lennox mused. But he had little time to puzzle about it. He was concerned for the safety of the mares and kept looking ahead watching for any signs of danger. He could see Sheba's silvery mane bobbing up and down in the torch light as she pushed ahead, keeping Fiery within her sight. He felt glad she had found her missing foal but knew their present whereabouts must be causing her more concern. Lennox realised his feelings towards Sheba were growing tender.

Every now and again the colts would come to a standstill and wait for Muffle to catch up but it seemed impossible for them to keep still for long.

It was about a mile or so further along the winding track that it gradually became brighter. The passage opened up into a large cavern. The top was high, with openings carved into the ceiling through which sunlight trickled but not enough to light the cavern sufficiently. Flames from torches flickered on the walls which sparkled with shades of mauve and plum. Whilst one wall appeared to be a sheet of purple glass, others were streaked with gold and silver.

Lennox remembered the golden coins falling out of the trees in Briton – an event which seemed so long ago. *This is like the gold that the humans prized so highly.* The reflection of the slim rays of light and flames glinting on the sheet of shining purple stone made Lennox squint for a few seconds. Like the mares he stamped his hooves and snorted in wonderment at his new surroundings.

Hearing what he thought were human voices, Lennox turned to see small men bringing buckets and placing them on the floor of the cave. There seemed to be two types of newcomers. Some resembled small wiry men, bigger than a wood elf but smaller than any human Lennox had ever seen. The others were what looked like very squat humans with short arms and legs compared to their body size. The one feature that the two groups had in common was that their faces were lined with hard work.

The mares were nervous of the newcomers but neither Muffle nor Lennox showed any fear. Lennox had become accustomed to the humans on the flying boats and knew that not all were bad. Meanwhile, the colts trotted towards the small men with no concerns whatsoever and dipped their heads eagerly into the buckets.

"Come," called Muffle. "Our friends the goblins and dwarves have brought oats and carrots for us. Not as much as we would have liked. Our supplies are somewhat rationed these days but very tasty nonetheless. Fresh water falls from the mountain above into a pool in the corner over there." The mule indicated a place where they could quench their thirst.

As Lennox looked around he saw not only the goblins and dwarves but also a very old man lying on a couch. A man so pale that if it were not for his clothes, he might have been transparent.

Lennox stared at the old man. He knew it was rude but he couldn't help it – the man reminded him of his friend Merlin, although clearly this person was much older. The man smiled at him kindly and said something.

"Zan bids you to enjoy some oats before those greedy foals eat the lot!" Muffle told Lennox. "He will speak with you later."

"He speaks Unicornian?"

"No, he does not speak the equine language or Unicornian as you call it, but Zan and I have been together for so long now that we understand each other. When he speaks in the human tongue it somehow translates in my head. When I speak he understands me too."

"Ah, much the same as I grew to know what Elvira was saying to me," said Lennox.

Zan was right. The mares and their offspring had almost finished their share of the oats but Blaize had made sure some had been left for the stallion. Lennox enjoyed the nutty flavour of the small seeds which he had never tasted before. The mares ensured that a few carrots were also left for him.

In spite of their misgivings, the unicorns were fascinated by this splendid cavern in which they found themselves. Nevertheless, they were anxious to learn more about their future home.

Muffle, realising their apprehensions, spoke to Lennox. "Zan saw you coming some time ago and has been making arrangements. He believes he has found a place for you in the Forbidden Forest, a woodland on the other side of Twydell. The Forbidden Forest is not as big as the Great Forest in which your mares have roamed, but nonetheless it is a woodland where Zan believes you can all live peacefully.

"When you are ready, get your mares together and I will tell you as much as I can."

Lennox whinnied for all the unicorns to gather around Muffle. His whinny echoed in the cavern and Lennox was embarrassed to realise his friendly call sounded more like a command. Nevertheless, the mares did not seem offended and did as they were bid. And Lennox realised that they had accepted him as the leader of what was now a new herd.

Muffle trotted over to the corner of the cavern where Zan lay back on his bed. The pallet was covered in soft blankets. Thick cushions pushed his back upwards into a sitting position.

Mule and man had lived together for so long that there appeared to be a resemblance between the two. Muffle's pink skin could be seen through his sparse white coat. Zan had thin strands of long white hair and, although his face was pale, the skin on his head was as pink as that of the mule's. Both had long thin faces and kind grey eyes. Both had a strange serene air about them.

Lennox looked around. His mares and the colts had gathered in a quarter circle around him as he faced Zan and Muffle; stone gnomes seemed to appear from nowhere to ensure the torches kept alight; flickering flames and slender streaks of light from the windows reflected on the amethyst wall giving the cavern a purple glow. Lennox remembered the purple glow of Merlin's staff and felt strangely comforted.

This is a splendid sight which I may never see again, Lennox mused.

Muffle sat on his haunches, amid a pile of straw, beside the very old man. Zan spoke to the mule who stared at the purple wall as if he were in some sort of trance. He hee-hawed and wiggled his ears several times as if in response to Zan before speaking in the equine language.

"Zan welcomes you to Zanadoo. This is a secret place and you must never speak of the location to anyone – neither equine nor human. We are only aware of one human who speaks our language, a fellow called Merlin, who came to this land with Lennox."

Lennox was surprised to hear the wizard's name mentioned.

"Lennox, you must swear now in front of your mares and these young unicorns that you will not reveal the secret of Zanadoo to Merlin, until given a sign to do so."

"I do so swear," said Lennox solemnly.

"And you, the mares of this new herd, you must swear never to reveal the secret of Zanadoo to anyone. Your sons have already made their vows."

The mares whinnied their oath of secrecy.

Zan said something in his human voice. Muffle's ears twitched and he hee-hawed again. It must have been a minute or two before he continued.

"One day, Lennox, you will tell Merlin about Zanadoo. I don't understand all that Zan says but it is clear that he has been following you. Zan looks into that glass ball on the table and seems to know what is going on elsewhere. The glass ball is like a window to the outside world. Sometimes I look in it with him. I saw you, Lennox, in a ship which flew through the air. The fact that I saw you meant that you must have been on your way to Zanadoo."

"But I had never heard of Zanadoo before today!" protested the unicorn stallion. "I was not on my way here. I was on my way to Avalon."

"You may not have thought so at the time, but look, here you are! And, as I said, one day you will tell Merlin about Zanadoo but not until the time is right. Merlin will have his hands full for the time being. Now, let me tell you about our home.

"Zanadoo stretches from Karminesque in the North to the far side of Twydell in the south. Zan and his four white mules used to travel the length of Zanadoo regularly but we grew old. I am the only one of the four mules left. We decided to spend our last days in the Zanite cavern near Karminesque. The people of the land known as Karminesque were our friends till they were annexed by a bigger country in the North. We still have friends there; in fact, it is the only country where we have human friends. They used to sell us supplies but Karminesque has been taken over by a strange poisonous vine and they can no longer spare food. That is why we have moved here to the amethyst cavern in Twydell."

"It is a very beautiful place," commented Lennox.

"Beautiful indeed," agreed Muffle. "We share our home with dwarves and goblins... or perhaps it is the other way around; the dwarves and goblins share Zanadoo with us. Our friends the dwarves go out to the towns and villages in Twydell and pretend to be jugglers which earns them a few coins. Whilst in the towns they sell a piece of jewellery or two – not enough to raise suspicions or soon the people who live there would be searching for our mines. The little money they earn keeps us in food. Of course they could sell much more jewellery, but as I said, if the humans found out about this place it would soon be destroyed.

"Our home was nearly taken away from us recently. The dwarves like mining; it seems to be their natural skill. The goblins are skilled craftsmen who make things from the minerals the dwarves mine. We are all happy enough, but the dwarves dug so far into the ground over the centuries that one of the holes reached middle earth. Middle earth is full of horrible creatures known as gudgers. The gudgers climbed the tunnel and attacked us. Now rather than digging tunnels, dwarves and goblins are busy filling them in!"

Zan said something and Muffle turned his head towards his master. The mule's ears twitched and he hee-hawed for a few moments before continuing.

"Enough about Zanadoo. Let us tell you more about the journey to your new home in the Forbidden Forest. As I said, it will take longer on this route through the granite mountains but believe me, you will be much safer. We will give you a guide and make sure you are fed on your journey. The gnomes will let you out into the open when it is safe to do so and guard you while you graze."

"Thank you," stated Lennox as he bowed his head in gratitude. The mares echoed his word and actions.

Zan said something and Muffle repeated his hee-hawing and ear twitching actions before speaking again.

"As you make your way through Zanadoo, you will meet more of the dwarves and goblins who live here.

At times the paths are narrow but do not be afraid. They are well built and will serve you till you reach your final exit from the mountains. The most dangerous part of your journey, on this occasion, will be after you leave the mountains. Then you will have to cross the prairies. It is an area roamed by large beasts and hunters. Nevertheless, Zan sees your safe arrival at the Forbidden Forest. No other unicorns live there. You will be greeted by a group of women including one lady in a colourful dress. That is the lady you must follow. All the women will care for you but the one in the bright clothing is the one to whom you must remain close."

"Thank you," said Lennox, bowing his head once more. "Your words are comforting but I have a question. You used the term 'on this occasion' when you spoke about travelling from the mountains to the Forbidden Forest. Will there be another occasion?"

Muffle again hee-hawed and wiggled his ears. Zan said something and Muffle repeated his mouth and ear actions again.

"Zan says you will return, Lennox."

Zan fumbled about in the pocket of the robe he wore and drew out a pendant. It consisted of an opaque yellowish gem enclosed in intricate gold casing and hanging on an equally ornate chain. As the stone in the pendant caught the light of flickering torch flames its colour changed to shades of pink, mauve and green. He showed it to Lennox.

"When you see this pendant again you will know that you can tell your friend Merlin about Zan and our home in Zanadoo. Until that time you must tell him nothing. Merlin has a great number of tasks to perform and he does not need Zanadoo's problems to distract him."

"One thing I would like to know," Blaize asked Muffle. "What happened to Flambeau's horn? Each time I ask my son what happened to it, he avoids answering. Please tell me."

Flambeau made an impatient snort and kicked his back legs in the air. Blaize gave him a look half of annoyance and half of hurtfulness.

"On your journey you will see the spot where it happened and Flambeau will tell you the story. I understand how concerned you must be, Blaize, but please be patient for just a few days longer. For now, please just be happy and rejoice at seeing your son after almost a year."

Blaize gave a sigh of reluctant acquiescence.

"I will add," the mule looked at Blaize with compassion, "that Flambeau is one of the bravest equines I have ever met.

"Now, if you do not mind, it is time for me and my master to take our mid-morning nap." Muffle looked at Zan, who appeared to have already fallen asleep. "When we wake up, please let us know whether you are ready to start your journey now or whether you wish to rest here in the amethyst cavern for a day or two."

With nothing else to add the mule lay down on his bed of straw beside his master's couch. Within seconds, like his master, he was snoring

After some discussion, Lennox and his mares decided to start their journey that day. The unicorns did not realise that anyone was listening to their conversation.

"Hi there!" said a new voice.

The unicorns turned to see a small dun-coloured pony with black tail and flecked face. Her ebony tail and flecked face reminded Lennox of Tamarie and for a moment he felt his heart strings tug at the memory.

"I'm Bunty, your guide," announced the newcomer. "I heard you make your decision so I will go and arrange for a couple of cart loads of food to follow us through the mountains. We won't see grass until late tonight and only then if the gnomes think it is safe for us to go outside. Once the two ancients have had their slumber we'll make a start on our journey. Just relax here a while. They never sleep more than a few hours."

Before departing to make the necessary arrangements the pony gave a wink. An action the unicorns had never seen before.

With time to spare, the newly formed herd of unicorns took Bunty's advice and the opportunity to rest.

CHAPTER 6 – Journey Through Zanadoo

After saying their goodbyes to Zan and Muffle, the unicorns followed Bunty along one of the tunnels out of the cavern. The rear was brought up by two donkeys each drawing a slender cart full of carrots and oats.

"I feel guilty that we have made you beasts of burden." Lennox lingered behind to speak to the jack and a jenny who pulled the carts.

"Not at all," replied the jenny. "We are proud to serve you. We are treated with kindness here. If we roamed the plains we might have been captured by the humans who would make us work much harder. Besides, we like to keep busy."

"And don't wait for us," added the jack, "Bunty will stop more than enough times to tell you about this special place we call home. Indeed, she enjoys talking so much we will probably not only catch up with you but overtake you."

Lennox heard Bunty's voice ring out ahead, "Right folks, the paths are fairly even but just watch yourselves in case any small stones have fallen. I've asked the dwarves to light the torches for us and then put them out when we've passed – we don't want to waste the pine resin, do we? We don't like harming trees for the sake of burning torches unnecessarily."

Sure enough a dozen dwarves, both ladies and men, ran, cartwheeled or tumble-tailed ahead. They stood on each other's shoulders to ignite lamps when the light trickling through the openings in the high ceiling was insufficient. After the herd had passed, the small people would perform other balancing tricks to put the torches out. Lennox and his mares were fascinated by their antics.

Lennox soon understood what the jack donkey had meant about Bunty enjoying talking. Every now and again she would stop to show the group of unicorns the various minerals which had been formed in the rocks they passed.

"Gather round, folks. Now do you see this seam of bright blue? It's a stone called lapis lazuli. Some of our Zanadoonian dwarves and goblins actually have eyes this colour."

She neighed and stomped her hooves to draw the attention of the dwarves. They turned and looked at her. One of the dwarves cartwheeled over to where she was standing. He stood in front of the unicorns pointing to his eyes. The equines could see that they were a similar colour to the lapis lazuli.

The mares snorted with interest.

"Told you so," Bunty stated in a 'know it all' manner.

"I know a wizard with blue eyes," Lennox commented, remembering Merlin.

"What's a wizard?" asked Bunty and the mares.

"Well, they are like humans but they dress a little differently and can perform magic." Lennox went on to describe his friend and how he had brought humans and magical beings, who feared for their lives in Briton, to Avalon.

"Isn't that the man Zan was talking about?" Blaize raised the question. "The one you will meet up with again in the future?"

"Yes," confirmed Lennox. He went on to describe his witch friend Elvira who had eyes the colour of grass.

"Why, yes," agreed Bunty. "Some of our dwarves and goblins have eyes of that colour, too. Now, let's continue our journey and later on we can see stones in several shades of green."

On the group went until, true to her word, Bunty showed them dull green stones.

"This is jade," stated Bunty. She stamped her feet and whinnied; this time a female dwarf performed a series of tumble tails across the floor towards the unicorns, who took it in turns to look at her green eyes.

Lennox heard the sound of metal cart wheels and looked around to see that the donkeys and their carts had caught up with the group and were indeed overtaking them. The donkeys looked at him, and hee-hawed in a knowing manner.

"Now remember the shade of these jade stones because, at some stage, we will come across a much brighter green stone called emerald," Bunty told them as she gave her audience one of her winks.

Each day was much the same as the last, with dwarves or gnomes lighting torches to illuminate dark passageways and extinguishing them once the party had passed. Bunty led the way and made the route more interesting by her descriptions of the minerals and stones they passed. They learnt all about stalagmites and stalactites and bathed in underground pools. Sometimes the cefflars came out of the pool to play but the shy little creatures were reluctant to join in any conversation. Lunch consisted of oats and carrots but at night the gnomes opened up hidden exits and let the equines out into the pasturelands to graze. The gnomes would watch over them until dawn, when they would be called back. As soon as everyone was safely inside, the gnomes re-sealed the opening.

New cartloads of oats, hay, carrots or apples appeared each day. They seemed to have been brought from somewhere in the outside world by the dwarves, via other carts, to refill the ones pulled by the jack and jenny.

It soon became apparent why the carts were long and slender. Sometimes the tunnels became tight passages, but more often it was to allow the carts to cross narrow bridges built over deep caverns where dwarves and goblins worked together.

The unicorns found the bridges very frightening. The echo of picks and shovels and the people singing or shouting in the quarries below made the bridges even more terrifying. Eventually, the workers understood that the echoing sounds of their work alarmed the unicorns and they learnt to stay silent whilst the travellers crossed above them.

Sometimes the people below would climb ladders or stone staircases to get a closer look at the unicorns. The mares found this unnerving at first, especially if anyone tried to touch them. The three colts made it their business to shield the mares from the small people who only wanted to pet the exotic creatures.

The donkeys often set an example. With sure hooves they trundled their slender carts across the narrow bridges. On the first occasion Lennox, copying the donkeys' example, acted as the pioneer showing that the crossing could be completed safely and with ease; although secretly he shivered with dread. Despite being the role model in the first instance, Lennox subsequently took up the rear. Bunty was the first to cross, encouraging the mares to follow, whilst Lennox stayed on the other side gently nudging them onwards. Such delays made the journey slow. Even the younger colts seem to have some trepidation on the most elevated overpasses but Flambeau, the eldest and the bravest, trotted across each link they encountered without hesitation.

The little dun pony called her group together and gave them one of her now customary winks. "Now, folks gather round, please!"

The unicorns expected another geology lesson but today this was not the case.

"Today I'm going to take you a little off the direct route to your exit in order to show you a few things which will be of interest."

"But Bunty, although we love your lessons about stones and the history of Zanadoo, we are anxious to get to the Forbidden Forest," Sheba put in.

"Quite so," replied Bunty. "However, Zan has told me that he wishes you to take this route, particularly Lennox. It will give him the knowledge he needs for when he returns."

"Will it mean more bridges to cross?" asked Blaize

"Well, maybe an extra one or two," the guide admitted. "But you have done so incredibly well so far, I'm sure another couple won't hurt."

"Those bridges really scare us!" Blaize responded.

"Mother," said young Flambeau. "I know where Bunty is taking us. You have asked what happened to my horn and it would be a lot easier to show you than try to tell you. I think it is a lesson everyone here needs to learn. I wouldn't want what happened to me and Sprike to happen to anyone else."

"What did happen to you? Who is Sprike?" Blaize asked, looking directly at her son and what was left of his horn. His head drooped towards the ground as if he were ashamed.

"I agree with Flambeau," said Bunty. "I think that it will be easier to show you what happened rather than try to explain."

Realising their guide's dilema, Lennox stamped one hoof and spoke with authority. "I am sure Zan would not have instructed Bunty to lead us elsewhere unless it was vital. The Zanadoonians have led us safely thus far and provided us with food and water for our journey.

"Ladies, you have followed me this far. Please indulge me a little longer and join me on this detour which we are told will not be overly long."

Copying Lennox's authoritative stance and tapping his hoof, Flambeau added, "I do think this is important, ladies. Please follow Lennox and me."

Blaize's eyes opened wide as she watched and listened to her son. "Very well," she relented.

The other mares conceded too. There were several comments from them:

"So be it."

"What's another day in the scale of things?"

"Although Lennox may pay another visit to Zanadoo, it is unlikely that we will, so these are memories to cherish forever. Well, maybe not the bridges."

"I want to know what happened to Flambeau's horn and more about this Sprike."

"Who is Sprike?"

✿ ✚ ✿ ✚ ✿ ✚ ✿ ✚ ✿ ✚ ✿ ✚ ✿

The party made its way along the winding tunnels which were now well lit from openings in the mountain above. Torches were no longer needed.

So we are quite high up, Lennox mused.

Whilst Bunty took the lead, Lennox usually took up the rear to look after stragglers. However today, in the brighter and wider passage ways, he sought the company of Blaize. "Your young son shows all the characteristics of a leader," he told her, "I am old. Flambeau would be a good replacement for me. I would like the opportunity to train him."

"A leader of a unicorn herd who has no horn?" Blaize responded.

"Ah, it is a pity he has lost such a unique feature. It must have been soul destroying for him to be rejected by his father but to lose his horn as well is so very sad. Other than his horn he is such a magnificent creature and so much like his father. I would be proud to have a son like that."

"Oh, Tyzon was very proud of him. As you say, he is the image of his father. Tyzon was deeply disappointed when Flambeau's horn did not turn to gold within the 49 days allowed. Everyone in the herd thought that the new leader had been born. Tyzon even decided to give him an extra couple of days, to see if any specks of gold appeared. That was when I encouraged Flambeau to run."

"Interesting," mused Lennox. "I wonder whether Tyzon knew young Flambeau would run?"

"I've often wondered that myself," Blaize agreed. "It's the only time that I have known Tyzon defy the laws of the forest.

"Where did this 49 day rule come from?"

"I don't know. Someone said once that humans think seven is a lucky number. They have seven days to their week and seven times seven is forty nine."

"But unicorns are not governed by human laws or symbols."

"No, but there is a Lord of the Forest whose name is Heres and he is in human form, except much bigger apparently. Perhaps it is something to do with him if he really exists. I've never seen him and neither has anyone else I know. I once heard a wood elf say that Heres looks like them but much bigger."

"So, this Heres is Lord of the Great Forest." Lennox considered the information which Blaize had given. "Is he Lord of the Forbidden Forest, too?"

"I don't know," she replied honestly. "I just hope that our sons will not suffer the same fate in the Forbidden Forest as in the home we have just left."

"They most certainly will not!" Lennox stated firmly. He meant what he said.

Lennox pondered over his conversation with Blaize, and feeling his place at the rear of the herd was no longer required, he moved to the front next to Flambeau. He realised that whilst he had taken a place at the back of the group to encourage stragglers, who feared this new environment, Flambeau had trotted ahead. The hornless black stallion had, without thinking, taken the position as head of the herd; even Bunty now trotted behind him. *Ah, this boy is already a natural born leader without realising it.*

"Flambeau, can you tell me how you came to Zanadoo? Did you follow Wifflin and Marje, as I and the mares did?"

"I knew my father was going to kill me," the black colt replied frankly, "so I ran away." He remained silent for a while before adding. "I saw one of the giants leaving the forest. I had seen the giants before and they had never harmed us so I traced his footsteps. The giant knew I was following because he kept looking over his shoulder.

"I made my way behind him, at what I considered a safe distance, for a whole day. I became alarmed when a bull buffalo saw me; I had probably wandered too close to a calf. I let out a fearful shriek when the bull lowered his head and made as if he was going to charge. The giant heard me and raced back just in time to chase it away. Even the buffalo are afraid of giants. After that I just kept following him."

"Until you reached the lake, I suppose?" Lennox hoped Flambeau would tell him the whole story.

"Far beyond the lake," the colt replied. "The giant took a path between the granite mountains and the trees. I kept him in sight. Each time he stopped to drink at a watering hole, he moved away and waited for me to quench my thirst at the same place he had just left. Once I had drunk my fill, he walked on and I followed."

"So he knew you were following him but he never approached you?"

"No, he never once attempted to touch me or speak to me – not that we would have understood each other."

"Ah, but you understood his actions. He sounds like a good person to me."

"Yes, he must have been. I followed him all the way to a large wooden house where other giants live. I grazed on the land near their house for a couple of days. It is not far from here.

"One day a cart, driven by dwarves and pulled by donkeys, passed by. They went to the house and left again with the cart filled with cauliflowers, cabbages and potatoes. I thought I had hidden myself behind some rocks but the donkeys must have sensed I was there. One of the donkeys shouted something out to me. Something like, 'What are you doing standing there? Don't you know how dangerous it is here for a unicorn?'

"The next day the dwarves returned with the same donkeys pulling the cart, but this time Muffle was seated in the back. He looked very funny. The dwarves had to lay a plank from the cart to the ground, otherwise he wouldn't have been able to step down. He came straight over to what I thought was my hiding place and spoke to me. He persuaded me to follow the cart back to Zanadoo. The entrance I used when I arrived is the exit you will leave by."

"Don't you mean 'the exit *we* will leave by'?" queried Lennox.

Flambeau remained silent for a while. "Perhaps," he eventually answered, "but I have unfinished business here. Please do not ask me any more questions until I am ready to answer them."

"Very well. I will not ask you any further questions but I will make a statement. You are a fine young unicorn, Flambeau. I have fallen into the leadership of this herd which I will take to the Forbidden Forest but I am old. A new leader will be needed one day. It seems to me you would fit that role perfectly. I would deem it an honour to train you for that role."

"I thank you for your words, but a unicorn without a horn leading a herd?" Flambeau replied scornfully. "I think not."

Lennox trotted along beside Flambeau, in silence considering all he had said, until he could no longer hold back his curiosity. "I know I agreed not to ask you any further questions but there are still some things puzzling me. Pray tell me what are cauliflowers, cabbages and did you say *pots of atoes?*"

Flambeau laughed. "Cauliflowers and cabbages are a delicious form of food. The other colts and I enjoy them raw but the dwarves and goblins boil them in hot water until they are ruined and eat them that way. Potatoes are tubers which come out of the ground. Potatoes don't taste very nice to me but the small people cook them until they become soft and then they find them edible."

"I see," said Lennox, "I have so much to learn."

"And another difficult task to perform coming up," replied the black colt. "The next bridge is very high, narrow and above a quarry. You will need to use all your skills of persuasion to get my mother and the other mares across this one."

Having spoken, Flambeau trotted straight across the bridge with no qualms whatsoever. Feerce and Fiery followed. Lennox and Bunty were left to coax the mares over the pass.

"Right folks, gather round," said Bunty as the party neared the end of the day's travels, "now take a look at this!"

Ahead of the group was a balcony overlooking an expansive grey sea. Two goblins sat on stools staring out at the ocean. They appeared to be on guard duty, but stood up to welcome the unicorns as they approached. Flambeau walked over to greet them both.

Bunty started her commentary. "This is where the goblins and dwarves come to rest. We have a large project going on not too far away and they need time off to recuperate." Lennox and Sheba moved forward and stretched their necks over the balcony railings to see a small sandy cove below where goblins and dwarves were enjoying the sunshine. Some paddled in the sea; others lay on blankets on the sand; quite a few were perched on the rocks with fishing rods. Women were building fires on which to cook the day's catch, whilst young children played nearby.

"This is the only place where the workers can get out without intervention from humans," Bunty continued. "Apart from ships which pass we see nothing else. The sea is quite hazardous in this area, so smaller boats don't venture in these waters. We just have to watch out for bigger ships on the horizon. If a vessel does happen to pass then we do this... please step aside, Lennox and Sheba."

Lennox and Sheba dutifully moved back. Bunty turned her head to one of the goblins who, as if on cue, took action.

A canvas, painted the same colour as the granite mountains, was rolled upon a bar which hung from the ceiling. One of the goblins used a pole to unhook the canvas which quickly rolled free at one end. The goblins hastily covered the balcony with the loose end.

"You see, if a ship passed by then our balcony would be hidden from view; from the sea it would look just like part of the cliff. The people outside would have to hurry in of course. But from up here the look outs would see a large ship on the horizon long before anyone on board could see us. From that sort of distance we would be mere specks on the beach."

"Very impressive," Lennox remarked as the two goblins started to hoist the canvas up into a rolled position again.

"Just think, Lennox." Bunty sounded envious. "You are one of the few beings who has travelled all the way from the Moonlight Sea to the Steel Grey Sea!"

"From where to where?" asked Lennox puzzled.

"Oh," Bunty replied. "I was told that the sea where your vessel landed was the Moonlight Sea, the sea which humans fear because of the ghost ships."

"I didn't know it was called the Moonlight Sea," Lennox mused, "I just thought that I had arrived on the coast of Avalon. I saw the Great Forest in the distance and went straight there in the hope of meeting other unicorns."

"And so you did! But you are in Zanadoo now and the ocean before you is the Steel Grey Sea. Tomorrow, or the day after you will be in the Forbidden Forest which is in Twydell on the border of another country called Kerner. What an incredible journey you have undertaken."

Lennox felt confused with all the different locations which rolled off Bunty's tongue with ease. *It is indeed a strange journey I have taken, and not just from sea to sea but from Briton to Zanadoo. No matter all these different places. I am here now with six mares and three colts. Soon we will be in our new home in the Forbidden Forest, in the land of Twydell, where our kind will live on.*

Whilst the unicorns admired the view, the dwarves released the donkeys from their harnesses. They were keen to get outside and urged the unicorns to join them.

The herd followed Bunty and the donkeys down stone steps, carved in the mountains centuries ago, on to the beach. The people on the beach, some seeing unicorns for the first time, stopped whatever they were doing to come together to welcome the new arrivals. The unicorns, however, were nervous of so many individuals approaching at once and shied away. The donkeys, understanding their friends' nervousness, pushed their way in between them and the admiring goblins and dwarves. The small people understood and moved back, much to the disappointment of their children. Both boys and girls held out their arms longingly, hoping to touch one of the beautiful creatures they saw before them.

Flambeau, however, was not at all nervous. Instead he moved towards the watching crowd, trotting around and even brushing his tail up against them in greeting. The crowd rewarded the black colt with a clapping of hands. The children were delighted.

Lennox wondered whether he should copy Flambeau's example. *I have a lot to learn. I will not copy him now but I will make sure that I acknowledge these people appropriately before I leave this place.*

Flambeau trotted back towards the herd. "Follow me, there is a path here which takes us up to the top of the granite mountains. There are patches of grass up there which have quite a unique salty flavour – you won't taste anything like it anywhere else. Careful though, make a single file and watch your footing; the path is crumbling away in places."

Having spoken, Flambeau made his way up the steep slope with an agility which surprised Lennox. Feerce and Fiery followed without hesitation.

"Well, let's go folks." Bunty gave her now customary wink. The mares followed their guide up the path which at times yielded beneath their hooves. Lennox took up his usual place at the rear to ensure no stragglers were left in difficulty.

The view from the top of the mountains was breathtaking but most of all Lennox enjoyed the gentle wind blowing on his face and mane. He looked around and knew instinctively that his new herd felt the same. The craggy mountains held a beauty of their own; the rugged rocks formed ridges in between which grew the grass which Flambeau had described to them.

In the distance Lennox could see the mountain goats dancing and balancing on slopes which he would not even consider trying to scale. *I wonder if Flambeau has learnt his agility from the goats.*

The grass was coarse but very tasty. The herd grazed for several hours, wandering from one isolated patch to another, before Bunty called them together. "We have to go, folks, the tide is coming in."

The sure-footed donkeys were already making their way down the cliff. Flambeau and the other colts followed. Bunty led the procession of mares with Lennox bringing up the rear. The sea had already

111

covered the sand as the unicorns reached the cove. The mares, who had never experienced the sea before, swiftly made their way back inside the granite mountains.

However, Lennox decided to stay where he was. He pranced and splashed in the salt water, enjoying the opportunity to bathe in the sea. He was aware that people had gathered on the balcony to watch, and turning to face them, rose on his hind legs to acknowledge them in his own way. It was a surprise though when Sheba cantered up beside him and copied his actions. Not long afterwards they were joined by Flambeau and Feerce, who frolicked and jumped the oncoming waves.

"This is great fun," Flambeau snorted. "I've never thought of exercising in the sea before."

Fiery started to make his way down to the beach, too. However, he was not as tall as the others and became nervous of the rising tide; he stood on the stone steps afraid to go any further. As soon as his mother saw him she left the beach and ushered him back to the open area behind the balcony. Lennox, Flambeau and Feerce remained in the sea until the water rose to a level where it was perilous to stay longer.

Before the stallion and his male companions reached the top of the stairs they were met by the smell of roasting fish. The Zanadoonians were cooking their evening meals.

Cauliflowers, cabbage and carrots had been provided for the unicorns.

"Delicious!" commented Lennox. He had eaten carrots before but never previously experienced cauliflower or cabbage.

"Look over there, Lennox." Flambeau indicated the fires where vegetables were boiling in water, in pots, on the fire. "That's what they do to good food. They put it in water and cook it till it's soggy."

"Ugh," Lennox was disgusted. "What a waste!"

"And those odd shaped things on the fire, placed on beds of clay, are potatoes."

"Oh," replied Lennox. "Even at my age I still have so much to learn."

"With more to come." Flambeau nuzzled Lennox's neck. It was the first time the colt had shown any affection towards the older stallion.

The unicorns spent the night on the hard floor. Some straw had been spread for them but not enough to be comfortable. Interesting as the day at the seaside had been, they were glad to set off the next day. Some of the dwarves and goblins waved their goodbyes, others it seemed intended to leave with them. They organised themselves into a marching formation with picks and shovels thrown over their shoulders. Even Bunty looked surprised.

"They are going back to work," explained Flambeau. "They have had their little holiday and now it is time to return to their unenviable task."

"Well, that makes sense," Bunty stated with a nod of her head.

It may make sense to Bunty but I'm not sure it makes sense to anyone else, Lennox mused.

It was a few hours' march, with the army of workers making steady progress behind the trotting equines, before the crash of falling rocks could be heard. The noise grew louder as the travellers neared a quarry where black holes could be seen in the quarry floor. The surrounding walls had seams of a rose coloured mineral which might have given the place a peaceful ambience, were it not for the sound of plummeting rocks.

The unicorns looked down to see male and female, dwarves and goblins alike, pushing boulders or emptying rubble into the dark tunnels beneath them. Sometimes they could hear the rumble of the boulders, bumping along the sides of the tunnels, growing fainter as they tumbled further than the sound could reach.

The unicorns waited for Bunty to call them into a group as she usually did. On this occasion, however, it was Flambeau who called everyone together. The mares snorted as if to say 'what's going on?' but as the ebony colt stamped his hoof they obeyed.

"You've all been wondering what happened to my horn." Flambeau spoke in a loud clear voice. "The loss of my horn is nothing compared to the troubles that are happening here. Those troubles could one day spread outside of Zanadoo to other parts of the lands in which we, other creatures and the humans live. They may eventually spread as far as the Forbidden Forest or even the Great Forest."

"They could indeed," Bunty put in. She didn't give her customary wink on this occasion.

"Let me tell you how I arrived here," said Flambeau, who proceeded to repeat the story he had told Lennox the day before. He finished up by telling them how Muffle had offered him refuge and ended his story with the words, "And so I became a Zanadoonian."

Lennox considered the colt's words. *He became a Zanadoonian. What was it he said yesterday, 'the exit you will leave by'? That colt is not intending to come with us to the Forbidden Forest – what is going on?*

"I was so glad to have other equines to talk to but I also became a close friend of Sprike, the King of the Goblins. He didn't speak equine but he took care of me, grooming my coat and tending the little cuts I had suffered from thorns when hiding from larger creatures.

"Sprike was a spritely man, always laughing and he was very clever. In Zanadoo, the dwarves mine and the goblins turn just a small proportion of the minerals they find into jewellery or ornaments. They sell some of it, that is true, but most they keep for themselves. Sprike was a very skilled craftsman; he made some beautiful and intricate things."

"He did indeed," Bunty joined in. "The jewellery Sprike created was quite fantastic. I wish the goblins would make some equine jewellery, too. We could easily wear emerald necklaces and ruby bracelets without hindrance to the tasks we perform."

Flambeau ignored Bunty's interruption. "Look at the quarry below, this is the place where the dwarves dug so deep that the gudgers were able to enter our world. Apparently there was some sort of legend which nobody really believed; nobody could remember where it came from. Legend said there was a middle land below this one where it is hot and humid and where horrible animals lived. The gudgers are indeed horrible animals. They are like lizards except they can walk on two legs as well as crawl. They are muscular, very strong and smell atrocious."

"You've seen one of these creatures?" asked Lennox.

"I have, more than one. On the first day the gudgers came out of the ground there were only a couple of them. The dwarves threw stones at them and they ran back. But they reappeared, bringing others with them. Dwarves and goblins alike fought them back."

"We ponies and donkeys got involved in the fighting, too," stated Bunty.

The donkeys hee-hawed their agreement to her words.

"I kicked one with my back legs," Bunty added. "He fell right back down the hole he'd just climbed up."

"I used my back legs to kick a load of rubble at one of them before he could reach the top," the jack donkey put in. "I heard him coughing and spluttering as he tumbled back down to where he came from."

"I stamped my front hoof on a gudger's head as he rose out of the ground. That was another one who went straight back down; and he took a few others with him as he went," the jenny donkey stated. She tried to wink, like Bunty, but instead gave the appearance that she had something in her eye.

"Sprike always wore his gold crown," Flambeau continued. "It wasn't just gold; it sparkled with diamonds large and small. He was very proud of the crown, which had been handed down by his family over generations. It seemed as if the gudgers like pretty things, too. They came out of the tunnels one day and made a beeline for Sprike. Sprike held on to his crown and the gudgers dragged him to the tunnel. I ran over and pierced one of them with my horn and killed it. Sprike was still struggling; the gudgers were all over him trying to either pull off his crown or take him with them. I used my hooves to try and beat them off. Then it was as if they wanted to take me too. Perhaps they thought a unicorn might be as great a prize as a gold and diamond crown.

"Other dwarves and goblins came to our rescue but the gudgers were determined to take me and Sprike. I saw Sprike being pulled inside a hole. I shook off my attackers and did my best to free him. I stabbed several of his assailants but others were rising out of the depths to take him. My own attackers had started to climb on top of me. Next thing I know, a gudger is hanging on to my horn and another gudger was holding on to the first's tail. My head was hanging over the tunnel and I could see them carrying Sprike below. He was looking up for help but there was nothing I could do. Then another gudger held on to the one which was hanging on to the one holding my horn – that was three of them all trying to pull me below with Sprike. Part of me wanted to go after Sprike to try to rescue him; but the other part told me to place my hooves firmly on the floor and stand firm. I stood my ground alright, but my horn tore away from my head. The three gudgers who were hanging on to it fell into the depths below, taking my horn with them."

"He was the bravest young unicorn you could imagine," put in the jenny. "When he shook off his own attackers he could have run away, but instead he stayed to try to fight off the gudgers who were stealing Sprike. Flambeau put up a real battle as did the rest of us but in the end there was nothing we could do. The King of the Goblins disappeared into the ground with the gudgers."

"I can imagine Flambeau going into battle," commented Lennox. "I have seen his father fight. Like father, like son."

"So that is how you lost your horn." Blaize spoke now in a comforting voice. "It is no shame, my son; the shame is mine that I did not run with you and was not here to protect you."

"This is not a time for self blame, mother." Flambeau looked at her. "What is important now is that the gudgers are stopped from entering our world. I have prayed that Sprike would escape and find his way back, however unlikely that may be. Even if he did escape his captors, the tunnels are being blocked forever."

"So now you know about the gudgers and the middle lands," Bunty stated in a more serious tone and without her customary wink. "If we leave now we will be at the exit by nightfall."

The herd felt a cold gush of wind as they reached the ultimate leg of their journey. A large opening in the walls revealed a storm-streaked sky. Much of the view beyond the entrance was obliterated by rain and fog.

"We are here," said Bunty but, instead of her usual wink, tears filled her eyes. "I shall miss you all."

"Are you not taking us all the way to the Forbidden Forest?" asked Sheba.

"No. I have never roamed far from the confines of Zanadoo. I'm too afraid of being captured by humans."

"Or dragons," commented a new voice. The voice belonged to a grey donkey whom they had not previously met. His coat was wet as was the load of fresh greens and carrots he had just brought from outside.

The dwarves emptied the contents of the cart on the ground for the equines.

"Have something to eat before you go," Bunty stated tearfully.

Lennox was more interested in what the donkey had to say than the food he had brought. "What do you mean, dragons?" he asked.

"They are monsters flying around Twydell. They breathe fire which burns land and crops," stated the donkey. "They are so big they can even carry off goats and sheep, perhaps even a small pony or donkey. My name's Ned by the way."

Ned looked at Fiery. "I wouldn't let that one out in the open when they are around. That little fellah wouldn't stand a chance. The dwarves carried bows and arrows and swords when we went out today but if we had seen a dragon, or more to the point if a dragon had seen us, then I'm not at all sure they could have fought it off."

"Is it too dangerous to travel to the Forbidden Forest tonight?" Lennox asked.

"No. Tonight is probably a good night. There will be no hunters about in this storm and most of the predator animals will be in their lairs. I still wouldn't risk taking that little foal though."

"Then Fiery will stay here with us," announced Flambeau.

"What do you mean," cried Blaize, "stay here with *us?*"

"I mean I am not going to the Forbidden Forest with you, mother. I left you when I was fifty days old but I have been in Zanadoo for the best part of a year. I miss Sprike and if he manages to escape then I want to be here for him. If I have the chance to help in any rescue attempt then I will take it."

"Then I will stay, too," stated Blaize firmly.

119

"If it is too dangerous to take Fiery the last six miles of the journey then I will also stay," added Sheba.

"I am sorry," said Ned. "But that is not possible: supplies are growing scarce in Twydell at the moment what with these attacks by dragons and this bad weather. You will have to leave. It is not far to the Forbidden Forest and I can't imagine large beasts like you, in a group, being attacked by other animals. Flambeau and Feerce are part of our family now so they can stay if they wish to do so. As for the little one, the trip would be too dangerous so we will care for him."

"Ned is right," responded Bunty. "We have had food shortages in the North for some time. If we are now facing shortages in Twydell too then we cannot cater for you all. Zan has seen your safe arrival at the Forbidden Forest. He did not see, or if he did he did not tell me, whether the colts were with you. Tonight is a good night to travel without the fear of hunters or mammoths." The little pony shuddered at the thought of the dangers in the open.

"You won't stay, will you?" Luna asked Feerce. The expression on her son's face told her that he would. She lowered her head before going over to nuzzle his neck and say goodbye.

Blaize continued to protest but gave up in the end. Flambeau was adamant that he would remain in Zanadoo.

Sheba did not protest. Instead she turned to Lennox. "I will not put Fiery at risk by taking him with us if he is safer here. Zan told you that you will return one day. When you come back, and if it is safe, will you return my son to me, please?"

"Yes, of course," responded the white stallion. His heart went out to Sheba. He remembered how worried she had been when she could not find her foal. Now, she had to leave him again but Lennox knew it was the sensible option.

Now Lennox turned to Bunty. "We have reached the exit and we know that the forest is about six miles from here. If you are not coming with us can you at least give us directions?"

"I can do that." It was Ned who answered. "I do the trip to the giant's house regularly. One day when I was off the reins I wandered up to the top of the hill and I could see the forest in the distance. I can take you to that spot, but that's as far as I will go. If you have your final destination in sight then I can't think it would be take very long to get there. Now you will need to hurry. If the weather improves you don't know what creatures might come out of their lairs!"

"Then we had best leave straight away," stated Lennox.

There were cheerless goodbyes. The excitement of the anticipated journey to the herd's new woodland home had lost its thrill. Saying goodbye to the colts was painful for both the mothers and the other mares. Even saying goodbye to Bunty, and the jack and jenny who had accompanied them on their journey, was heartrending. The equines who were departing nuzzled and licked those who were staying.

As the mares shed their tears in droplets on the floor, Lennox's thoughts reverted back to Elvira collecting his tears for her spells. He missed the old witch.

121

True to his word, Ned led the herd along a stony path down the mountainside and on to the plains. From there they trotted as quickly as they were able across open land and past a large wooden house.

That must be the house where the giants live, thought Lennox, remembering Flambeau's description.

The party travelled up an incline for a while. By the time they reached the top the donkey was tired and breathing heavily. He indicated the route ahead.

"Well, you may not be able to see it now because of the fog but the Forbidden Forest is directly in front of you. Keep straight on and you will eventually see it. I am tired, cold and wet. Now it is time for me to return to my home in Zanadoo."

The unicorns continued down the hillside and straight ahead at a fast canter. Just as Ned had told them, the forest eventually loomed up out of the mist.

Lennox and his mares came to a halt. They had thought that they could simply walk into the forest but the woodland was surrounded by a vine which was thick as rope. The vine twisted and turned to form different patterns which bound trees and bushes together. There was no way through.

"There must be an entrance somewhere." Lennox was puzzled.

"Some of us could go in one direction to try to find it and the rest in the other," suggested Blaize.

"No, let us stay together." Lennox was firm. "If there are dangers around the outskirts of this forest then we are safer in numbers."

They walked around the border looking for an entrance. Lennox pricked his ears. He thought he heard human voices from within the forest. Next came a rustling of branches and bushes as the vines which bound them unravelled before their very eyes. As the vines fell back, an opening was revealed. In the gap stood a group of seven witches, whose ages ranged from young to very old. Beside them, just as Zan had predicted, stood a handsome woman dressed in colourful clothes.

CHAPTER 7 – The Forbidden Forest

"You were right! You were right!" one of the witches cackled. "However barmy your dreams seem to be, you were right yet again!"

The women moved aside to allow the unicorns access to the forest.

"Helen-Joy's always right," the very oldest witch stated firmly, as she clapped her hands with glee. "It wasn't just a dream neither; she saw it in that crystal ball of hers."

"One, two, three…" the witches started to count out loud as Lennox cantered through the gap with his mares following, "four, five, six, seven."

Two of the witches ran to the entrance and scanned the plains to see if any more unicorns were on their way. Their heads turned one hundred and eighty degrees, from left to right, as they looked around the hedge but they barely stepped beyond the opening as if afraid of what lay beyond. Satisfied that all were now inside, they waved their wands and watched the vines, that had unravelled to allow the unicorns access, rewind. The rope-like vines soon twisted and turned around the shrubbery and trees to again seal the forest from the outside world.

Helen-Joy, the handsome woman dressed in floral clothing, beamed. Even she had doubted her own prediction. *Who would have thought that a herd of unicorns would seek refuge in **our** forest home?*

125

Soothsayer and witches watched the unicorns frolic in and out of the trees. The animals' happiness to be in their new home was apparent. The witches started to dance around in a circle, humming and singing to show their pleasure.

Helen-Joy just stared, eyes wide with wonder, at the spectacle going on around her. She saw the white stallion watching her, then he stood on his hind legs as if in acknowledgement. The soothsayer heard her witch friends applaud the stallion's trick but he seemed to be looking only at her. *Is he watching me? What a magnificent creature!* She felt her heart miss a beat as he trotted towards her. He lowered his head to allow her to pat his neck. The witches started to rush forward to touch the beautiful creature too but he shied away.

Although there were sighs of disappointment at not being permitted to touch the new arrivals, smiles of pride soon appeared on the faces of the witches. After all, this was their forest and certainly not everyone had unicorns come to dwell with them.

"This woodland home of ours is turning into a magical place," stated the very oldest as a wide near-toothless grin appeared on her wrinkled face.

"You mean *even more* of a magical place," stated one of the younger witches.

"What I mean is that this enchanted home of ours has become even more blessed."

"What are we going to do with them, though?" another asked no one in particular. "Where are we going to keep them?"

"Don't be a fool, Maura," replied a witch, who looked remarkably like the one who had just asked the question. Her tone of voice was sarcastic. "They will be free to live in the forest; it won't be up to us to keep them."

"Yes, Nora," replied the other. "We all know that they must be free to roam as they please. What I mean is that the vines which run above the treetops form such a powerful canopy that it doesn't let in enough light for sufficient grass to grow. I don't think they eat tree leaves."

"Oh, I see what you mean, Maura my dear," Nora responded in a more gentle tone.

"Well, I suggest we take them home to the cottage and they can share the orchard with the goats for the time being," stated one of the other witches. "In future we can open the canopy in spaces to enable grass to grow. It'll be nice to have a bit of sunshine."

"I don't mind opening the entrance from time to time," stated the youngest of the witches, a girl of about sixteen. "I would watch over them while they grazed and then let them back in. I mean at night when there is no one around."

"I'm sure you would, Heather!" snapped Sally, who was Heather's mother. "I've seen you striving to look through the bindweed; trying to see what's going on outside. There's nothing good happening out there in the land of Twydell, my girl! Nothing at all! You stay here where it's safe! We don't want what happened to your father to happen to you!"

Heather looked forlorn but Sally, sorry for her sharp reaction, gave her daughter a hug.

"Well, we may have to consider opening up the entrance for them from time to time," stated the very old witch, who was obviously the head of the family. "Providing we issue protective spells and keep a careful watch we can soon re-seal the entrance again before any unwanted human trespasses on our property. Now, in the meantime I suggest that we try to persuade these lovely creatures to follow us home to the orchard."

The oldest lady, who was also fat, marched with surprising nimbleness towards a narrow path. Her family followed. She beckoned, in fact they all beckoned, to the unicorns to follow.

"Come along," she called to the white stallion who watched but stood firmly where he was, as did the mares.

However, when Helen-Joy joined the line of witches walking towards their home, the white stallion followed and behind him trailed his six mares. The long line of walkers made their way through the trees to a topsy-turvy wooden house in a clearing. Beside the house was an orchard where a couple of goats grazed. The very old witch swung her arm towards the orchard as if to offer it to the unicorns. She smiled as they reacted by trotting on to enjoy a field rich in clover and fallen apples.

"I think we could all do with something to eat and drink," Maura stated matter-of-factly.

"I'll help you make a brew," Nora offered. "We still have some blackberry crumble and fruit cake."

"Good idea," stated the very old witch. "It's been an early morning and a long walk but I wouldn't have missed seeing the arrival of our new residents for all the full moons in a year!" Then she added, "You'll stay and have something to eat won't you, Helen?"

"How could I refuse a portion of the Bramble family's delicious blackberry crumble?" the soothsayer laughed. "Oh, Great Grandmother Bramble, what a morning it has been!"

The family arranged themselves on the rickety verandah of their home, and on stools situated in the garden. It was a warm morning. It had rained earlier and their shoes and socks were wet from the walk to the entrance and back. Now they took the opportunity to hang their socks out on the fence to dry while they lined their shoes up along the porch.

Helen-Joy wore open toed sandals which she too took off to dry. She sat on a stool outside the house and put her cold feet up on a stone ornament to warm in the sunshine. It was a lonely life in the Forbidden Forest with just the seven members of the Bramble Family of Witches for company but she felt today was special and perhaps the beginning of something new. She had seen lots of strange things in her crystal ball of late. The white stallion had appeared on several occasions in the past but he was always on his own. It was only yesterday she had seen him arriving at the forest entrance with others.

"I'm so glad you believed me when I told you about the unicorns seeking refuge here, Bertha." She spoke to Great Grandmother Bramble.

"And why should I have doubted you?"

"Well, it all seemed so incredible. Don't you think?"

"Incredible, it might have seemed, but here they are. Never doubt yourself, Helen, you are a skilled soothsayer. What fools the Twydellers were to oust you from your home. If they had an ounce of sense they could have made good use of your skills."

"There seems to be so much happening at the moment. I keep seeing dragons in both my crystal ball and my dreams. There is a lot going on outside the forest, Bertha."

"Then I'm thankful we are locked inside. As long as what is going on in Twydell doesn't affect us then I'm not worried," the very old witch stated as she took a mug and plate from Nora.

"A nice bit of fruit cake for you, mum, and a cup of acorn tea." Nora smiled affectionately. She knew her mother always enjoyed a piece of her cake.

"And blackberry crumble, laced with honey, with just a tad of cream. I think that's how you like it," said Maura as she handed Helen-Joy refreshments.

When everyone was settled with breakfast, Helen-Joy revealed the content of more of her visions and strange dreams. "I can see a wizard flying through the air on a broomstick and keep hearing the name *Merlin*."

"Very interesting," agreed the witches.

"I also see dragons – and they are frightening. Sometimes when I dream about them I wake up with a start and my heart is racing with fear."

"Oh, Helen, you know you are always welcome to stay here," Sally offered.

"Thank you, so much, but my home is my home. I'm not sure if I could see the future anywhere else."

"I could stay with you and keep you company," offered young Heather.

"That would be nice. I certainly will take up your offer if it all gets too much." Then the soothsayer added, "If that's alright with you, of course, Sally."

Sally laughed. "I think my daughter is trying to get away from her family. What with offering to open the entrance for the unicorns and now offering to stay with Helen."

"Oh, mother," Heather sighed.

Sensing antagonism between mother and daughter, Helen-Joy finished breaking her fast and got up to leave. "Well, I'd best be on my way now. All these dreams have had me waking up tired and, what with such an early start this morning, I'm hoping to go home and get a bit of dreamless sleep."

She gave the unicorns what she thought was one last look before giving each of her witch friends a brief hug and setting off along the track. To her surprise she heard the sound of hooves behind her; turning, she saw the white stallion following with his mares behind him.

Helen-Joy stood where she was, trying to take in what was happening. The white unicorn, staring straight at her, halted too, as did the mares. She looked over to Great Grandmother Bramble. "He wants to follow me Bertha, what shall I do?"

"Well, they are free animals, my dear. It seems they want to go with you so let them do so. If they wish to come back here they are more than welcome."

With a little sigh and a girlish giggle, the soothsayer shrugged her shoulders and walked on with the seven unicorns trailing behind. It was a good hour's walk to her home. She kept looking over her shoulder. Not once did the unicorns wander off track or attempt to overtake her.

Her feet were aching by the time she reached the waterfall which hid her home. Helen-Joy was weary but decided to watch the unicorns for a little longer before going inside to take a nap. She sat down on a boulder and took off her sandals, which were still slightly damp. She expected the unicorns to graze on the green area surrounding the pool which was fed by the falls, however, the white stallion decided to jump

131

in. Water splashed all over her. Her clothes were drenched.

"Well, the bottom of my skirt was spattered with mud anyway," she spoke aloud to the animal who understood nothing of what she said. Laughing at her foolishness, she removed her colourful skirt and blouse, and washed them in the pool, leaving them on the rocks to dry. Then she retired to the cave behind the waterfall, which she called her home. *Oh, please no dreams… not unless they are sweet ones.*

"So you are still dreaming?" Heather asked

Helen-Joy had awoken to find the young witch sitting outside watching the unicorns. Some were grazing, a couple splashing in the pool and others simply lying in the warmth of the late afternoon sun.

Over a cup of hot mint tea the soothsayer confided the content of her recurring dreams. "I see the same man flying through the air on a broomstick. Then there are fires and people screaming. I even see the old house where I used to live in Dalton burnt to the ground. Sometimes I see dragons and at others great big birds causing havoc."

"That's awful," the young witch sympathised.

"I saw that beautiful white stallion and that was a good dream which came true. I kept hearing the name Merlin when I saw the unicorn, now I hear it over and over again when I dream about the dragons and the burning – I hope that doesn't come true, too."

The white stallion who had been rolling in the grass pricked his ears, stood up and looked directly at the two women.

"Perhaps it's his name," Heather gasped. "Look, he stood up when you said that name and now he's watching us!"

"Are you called Merlin?" Helen-Joy asked, beckoning the animal to come to her. The unicorn just stood and stared. "No, I don't think so. But I think it is a name you recognise, don't you, fellah?"

Now she did exactly what Elvira had done back in Briton. She pointed to herself. "Helen-Joy," she said. Then she pointed at the young witch. "Heather." Next she pointed to the unicorn. "Merlin?" she asked.

The white stallion paced backwards. The two women spoke in unison. "No, he is not called Merlin."

"I'm glad," said Heather. "I want to call him Prince Magnificent or King Wonderful."

Her friend pulled a face. "King Freddy was a prince when I lived in Dalton and it was his father, the king, who had all the magical beings and soothsayers expelled. The last thing I want is to be reminded of royalty and their commands."

"Oh." Heather was disappointed. "Well, what about Snowy, then?"

"Come here, Snowy," she called. The unicorn stood where he was.

"No, I think he already has a name," Helen-Joy was thoughtful, "His reaction to the name Merlin though might mean that he knows this person. I wonder if Merlin is the old wizard flying through the air. I saw him earlier fighting his way through thick smoke. Whoever he is, that wizard is a brave man."

"Do you know *Merlin*?" she asked in a very precise manner. "Is he the wizard flying through the air? Did he send you here?"

The unicorn moved forward again and allowed the soothsayer to pat his neck. This time he even allowed the young witch to touch him too.

"Well, he certainly knows the name *Merlin*," Heather agreed. "Look, did you see his ears twitch when I said *Merlin*?"

"I think that when you go home you should tell the rest of the Bramble family to expect a wizard by that name. Ask them if they can charm the bindweed to open when he arrives, in case I cannot predict the day or the time. It is such a long way to walk if he is not there."

"I don't mind the walk. I don't mind taking the unicorn herd to the entrance occasionally, and letting them out to graze either."

"I know you don't but your family worries about you. And, as I said, it is a long way to walk."

"Great Grandmother has an old broomstick. I could use that."

Helen-Joy felt sorry for the young girl who had only ever known the forest, and was naturally inquisitive to learn more about what went on outside. "I'll talk to your mother. Using the broomstick seems a good idea and the unicorns will need to go outside occasionally. Now, I'm going to read my tarot cards to see if they can help put together the pieces I spy in my crystal ball and see in my dreams. You will talk to your family about making arrangements for this Merlin to access the forest when he arrives, won't you?"

"I will, of course I will." Heather planted a kiss on the soothsayer's cheek before she made her way home. "It will be the most exciting thing that has ever happened here; except for the arrival of the unicorns, that is, *nothing* could beat that!"

✿ ✛ ✿ ✛ ✿ ✛ ✿ ✛ ✿ ✛ ✿ ✛ ✿

Days passed. It had been another stormy night and dawn had barely broken when Helen-Joy came running out of from her home behind the waterfall. She found the white stallion sheltering between the underhang of the mountain and some leafy trees.

"Here, boy," she called, beckoning him to come to her. She carried a glass ball.

The unicorn stayed where he was until he heard her say the name *Merlin* very clearly, followed by the word *entrance* which she also pronounced in a precise manner.

Helen-Joy pointed towards the path which led to the edge of the forest. The unicorn understood. He bid his wives to stay where they were and he set off alone to greet his friend. For the last week or so the young witch, who called herself Heather, had led the herd to the place where the vines released to provide an opening to the prairie beyond. She had been accompanied by the woman who wore the colourful clothing, who called herself Helen-Joy. Both had repeated the words 'Merlin' and 'entrance' over and over again to the white stallion.

As Lennox cantered towards the entrance he could see Merlin flying above the forest canopy on a broom. *Ah, he is trying to find a way in.* He saw Merlin turn mid air and make his way back to the boundary; he had expected to see Heather there, but there was no one else. He was surprised to see the vines disentangled as he approached.

The wizard stood on the other side. At first he stayed where he was, obviously afraid to venture forward in case it was a trap, but when he saw Lennox cantering towards him he stepped through the aperture. He put his arms around the unicorn and told him, in the equine language, how good it was to see him again. Lennox nuzzled the old man's neck and both felt the warmth of their genuine friendship.

"I am happy to see you, old friend." But despite his words, Lennox was worried by the old man's haggard appearance. He had never seen the wizard look so pale or tired. He made a quick decision. "I am not a beast of burden but on this occasion, if you climb on my back, I will take you to the lady you seek."

Merlin hesitated. "What lady?"

"The lady who is expecting you." The unicorn lowered his front legs to make it easier for the old man to clamber on to his back. "I have never carried a human before. If you do not wish to take up my offer then I will walk ahead and you can follow."

The wizard gratefully accepted the offer. As man and beast moved forward they heard a rustle behind them. They turned and saw that the vines were rewinding, to seal the woodland from the outside world once more.

"How did you do that?" Merlin asked.

"I did nothing. The lady you seek made it clear through her sign language that you were arriving today. I did not know how you would get in or out. I just did what I understood she wanted me to do."

"How did you come to this place?" asked Merlin.

Lennox recounted the tale of how he met the other unicorns and his fight with Tyzon, and some of his adventures. But, as he had promised, he did not mention Zanadoo.

Eventually, they reached the clearing where the mares grazed in what was now bright sunshine.

"This is my new herd," Lennox stated with pride.

"Why, I don't believe I have ever seen such a fine brood of mares before!"

Merlin made towards Sheba but Lennox, concerned that the mares may have forgotten their oath to Zan, drew the wizard's attention.

"The lady you seek lives behind the waterfall. She is expecting you. It is best not to keep her waiting. She seems to spend a lot of time sleeping, so it is best to catch her while she is still awake."

"Thank you, I will go straight away."

"Will you do me a favour when you speak to her, please, old friend?"

"Of course."

"Please tell her my name is Lennox. She has a friend, a sweet girl but she keeps trying to invent names for me like Prince Magnificent and Snowy."

Merlin chuckled. "Prince Magnificent, how very grand!"

"My name is Lennox. The same name as my grandfather was known by and if I am fortunate enough to have another son it will be the name by which he will be known."

Lennox hoped that his old friend would have more time to spend with him, but Merlin seemed extremely busy. However, next morning it was good to see that the old man had bathed and combed his hair. It was also a relief that he no longer smelt of bonfire as he had done the day before. He looked well groomed and Lennox guessed Helen-Joy had washed and cut his hair and beard for him.

The next morning the Bramble family of witches, who had also visited the evening before, came again. They sat in a circle on the ground in discussion with Merlin and Helen-Joy. This time there seemed to have been some sort of altercation which resulted in Heather being slapped across the face by her mother. Heather wept, her shoulders shuddering with each sob.

Merlin came to say goodbye to Lennox and his mares. The wizard told him that he must leave immediately because of his growing concerns about the land of Twydell and a missing dragon egg. He was looking for some large birds who might know the whereabouts of the egg. He said Heather would walk to the entrance with him and would point him in the direction of where she suspected the large birds lived.

Sheba overheard the conversation and whispered to Lennox that she would be willing to carry the young witch. "I feel sorry for her. She is a young woman. When she takes us to the entrance to graze I see her looking longingly at the open land beyond. The Forbidden Forest is a beautiful place but she is lonely and seeks love. This is a happy place for me because I have found my true love." She nuzzled her husband fondly. "But that poor girl has yet to find hers."

And so it was that witch and wizard rode to the edge of the forest on two unicorns, Heather on Sheba and Merlin on Lennox. The antagonism between mother and daughter had subsided. The earlier anger even turned to pride as the witches applauded their youngest member having the privilege to ride a unicorn.

At the edge of the forest Lennox told Merlin how sad he was to see him depart again. "I hope whatever problems there are in Twydell and with this dragon egg will be resolved. I look forward to your return to the Forbidden Forest... and give my regards to Elvira and Maud."

"You sound very certain that I will come back and you are right to do so. Take care, Lennox, my old friend. Elvira and Maud will be delighted to learn that I have seen you."

Several weeks passed.

The herd was grazing by the pool when Helen-Joy hurried down the stone steps from her home and started running down the path. Lennox sought to follow but she turned and shooed him away.

That's odd, thought Lennox. He couldn't read the expression on her face. She wasn't smiling but she did not look afraid either. She simply looked wide-eyed and distracted.

Lennox told the mares to stay where they were and not to follow. He waited for Helen-Joy to run ahead and then crept behind her, carefully concealing himself in the shadow of the trees and tall shrubs.

She ran almost all the way to the house where the Bramble family lived. Lennox knew she must have been exhausted by the time she got there. *Humans do not travel well without support.* Whatever she said to the Brambles caused a lot of excitement. Lennox could hear their voices all talking over each other. Shortly afterwards all seven of them marched purposefully out of the house with confident strides. Helen-Joy, who still appeared out of breath, lagged behind the line of witches but she too headed towards the entrance.

The unicorn trotted along behind careful not to be seen. However, Lennox soon caught the scent of one of the mares and turned to see Blaize not far behind him. "What are you doing here?" he asked. "Are you alone? I told you all to stay behind. There may be danger ahead and I don't want any of my mares harmed."

"I am on my own," replied Blaize. "We know you do not wish to put your wives in danger but we do not wish you to be harmed either. You are a brave stallion, Lennox, and we cannot afford to lose you. If someone needs to put themselves at risk then better an old nag like me than the only stallion in the forest."

Lennox was annoyed with Blaize but she made it clear that she would not leave him so the two followed the seven witches and the soothsayer to the edge of the woodland.

They were surprised to see the witches form a horizontal line, in front of what would be the entrance, holding their wands in front of them. Helen-Joy stood to one side.

"They are in defence formation!" Lennox was startled. He had not seen the witches act like this before.

Blaize sniffed the air. "I smell horse."

"Yes, and I can hear hoof beats in the distance. The Brambles are expecting visitors but are in fear of whoever it might be. Look at the expressions on their faces; Helen-Joy has turned almost as white as my coat. Why on earth would they open the entrance if they were frightened of what was on the other side?"

The unicorns looked at each other as they heard horses approaching and human voices. Lennox came out of hiding and took up a position behind the witches with horn lowered in attack mode. Blaize copied his example.

"No, no," whispered Helen-Joy who tried to shoo the unicorns away.

"She wants us out of sight," Lennox told Blaize.

"Okay, then let's stand out of sight of the entrance but close enough to give them help if they need it. I must admit though those witches look a pretty formidable sight to me. I've seen some of the tricks they can perform with those little sticks of theirs."

Lennox stood one side of the entrance; Blaize stood on the other. The witches were now releasing the vines just an inch or two at a time.

"We are soldiers from King Frederrick of Twydell's army," stated a man with a loud voice. "We have been to Kerner, on the bidding of our king and a wizard named Lord Merlin, to receive three men released from prison there. We were instructed to bring them to the Forbidden Forest."

Lennox pricked his ears at the sound of his friend's name. *So Merlin has had something to do with this! I should have known.*

The women had become very excited but would not leave the forest till the soldiers had departed. The witches watched the men retreat before unwinding the hedge sufficiently to let themselves through.

Lennox and Blaize stuck their heads through the loose vines to see what was going on. There on the other side were three men sitting in a cart. The younger witches were fast in stepping up into the cart. They were all trying to talk to the men at once and, at the same time, lift them down to the ground.

141

The unicorns were horrified to see the vehicle had been drawn by a small pony whose bones stuck out through a coat mottled with sores from a whip.

"That little chap needs help!" Blaize stated. "You stay here, Lennox. Your white coat is too noticeable. If the soldiers look back and see me, at this distance they will think I am just a horse." With that statement she trotted around the women who were busily getting the men off the cart. She could see that all three looked sickly but so too did the little pony. Nobody else was paying the animal any attention.

Blaize started licking the sores borne by the poor little creature. Lennox, throwing caution to the wind, joined her, stamping his feet and snorting sounds of annoyance. Helen-Joy, recognising the unicorn's concerns over a fellow equine, ran to help. She unharnessed the pony who looked barely able to stand. Blaize and Lennox escorted the animal into the woodland.

"What is your name?" asked Blaize.

"Pit pony fifty nine," it replied.

"Do you mean there are there fifty eight other ponies like you?" asked Lennox.

"More than fifty eight," replied the pony. "I am one of the older ones."

Blaize tut tutted. "Well, in future you will be known as Lucky. You are Lucky because you now have a new home in the Forbidden Forest, with the unicorns, and we will look after you."

Lucky looked up at the tall black mare with the white blaze; his eyes were full of tearful gratitude.

I wonder if Elvira would collect those tears, Lennox pondered. *What an absurd thought! I should be thinking about how to care for him and help the Brambles with these men. Concentrate!*

The Brambles had got the men out of the cart but were struggling to get them to stand for more than a few seconds before their legs gave way. Only one seemed capable of walking. There seemed to be a lot of discussion and shaking of heads until they all drew their wands again and pointed them at one of the men. The man rose to his feet or rather his feet rose off the ground; as he started to float in the direction of the path leading to the Brambles' house. There was a little cheer and some clapping before the same spell was cast and the second man started floating behind the first. The third man walked with the aid of Sally and her daughter Heather.

"I've not seen men in the forest before," commented Lennox.

"No, we wondered what had happened to them," Blaize responded. "If young Heather is Sally's daughter then Sally must have had a husband once. Perhaps it is the man to whom mother and daughter are giving assistance."

"They have come from the mines in Kerner," Lucky told them. "There are many men and children who are forced to work there. None of them are cared for. If they are magicians, like the three in the cart, they are given drugs to prevent them using magic and running away."

Lennox was disgusted at the revelation. "The men outside mentioned the name Merlin earlier. He said he would return and when he does I will make sure he knows what this pit pony has told us."

"Lucky," Blaize reminded him. "His name is Lucky."

❀ ✦ ❀ ✦ ❀ ✦ ❀ ✦ ❀ ✦ ❀ ✦ ❀

At the Brambles' house, the unicorns let the little pony rest and take sustenance. They watched as the witches busied around their men folk whilst Helen-Joy sat in a rocking chair on the verandah and fell asleep.

"That woman falls asleep anywhere at any time," Lennox commented.

He and Blaize were just about to leave when the soothsayer stood abruptly and, looking directly at Lennox, said the word, "Merlin." She walked towards the white unicorn, repeating the wizard's name and pointing back, in the direction from which they had just come.

Then she hesitated and called to Great Grandmother Bramble, "The entrance is still charmed to open if Lennox is on one side and Merlin on the other, isn't it?"

"It is indeed," responded the old lady. "Oh, I do hope he is here. His powerful magic could help mend our boys."

Lennox didn't understand the exchange between Helen-Joy and the witch but knew what he must do. "Blaize, please take Lucky to the rest of the herd. I must return to the entrance to let the wizard in."

Blaize gently nudged the pony who struggled to his feet and walked beside her in one direction whilst Lennox hurried off in the other.

At the entrance Lennox not only met Merlin but also his old friend Maud and other magical beings from Avalon. He was delighted to see the Queen of the Fairies but sorrowful to hear that Elvira, the witch who had saved his life back in Briton, was dead. "She died fighting at the Battle of Merlport," Merlin told him. "Esmerelda, who I believe you know, is now Queen of the Witches."

The unicorn acknowledged Esmerelda, and her warlock companion Tannus, but greetings were brief. He needed to take the wizard and the other visitors to the Brambles' house. As they made their way along the path, Lennox told his friend that an old pit pony was also in need of care and attention. He said the pony had been taken to the pool, next to Helen-Joy's abode to be looked after by the mares. Merlin promised to go along to see the pony and do whatever he could for it.

Lennox left the Avalonians at the witches' cottage and headed back to his herd. He was concerned for the pony. *I have done what I can for the three sick wizards. I am so glad that the Avalonians are here. They will help the Brambles care for their men, now I must make the pit pony my priority.*

Over the next few days there was much toing and froing from the soothsayer's abode to the topsy-turvy cottage. With so much going on, the unicorns were grateful that Helen-Joy and Merlin had found time to help tend Lucky. No one had expected him to live long but he was growing stronger and happier day by day.

Over the following months more prisoners were released from Kernan gaols. All were young witches and wizards who arrived at the Forbidden Forest along with more poorly pit ponies. Merlin and other magical beings from Avalon came back and forth to care for the new invalids. The equines looked after their own. Lennox did not altogether understand what was going on; he was aware that Merlin and other wizards were working elsewhere clearing faraway lands of a poisonous weed. Even Great Grandmother Bramble and Heather had left to help, much to the consternation of the rest of the Bramble family.

The unicorns waited, some impatiently, to see if Merlin would show their stallion Zan's pendant on one of his visits. However, no sign of the pendant was forthcoming.

Lennox wanted to ask Merlin about the pendant. He thought that with so many other things going on, the wizard might have forgotten about it. Nevertheless, he knew he must keep the oath he had made to Zan. He also remembered what Zan had said about Merlin being very busy and should not be distracted from the tasks in hand. The unicorn did not give way to temptation and, true to his promise, did not mention the pendant or Zanadoo to his friend.

It was obvious to everyone; magician and equine alike, that Helen-Joy and Merlin had become very close. Nevertheless when the old man proposed to the soothsayer it was a surprise to everyone. The equines were delighted to be invited to the exchange of rings ceremony which they watched with interest.

"Helen is expecting twins," Merlin told Lennox one day, in earshot of the herd. His face radiated with pride.

"I have an announcement, too," Lennox told him. "Sheba is with foal."

The other mares whinnied. All welcomed a foal into their herd.

"Then double congratulations are in order. I'll see if Helen has some red apples in the back garden."

"Mmmm… I love red apples." Sheba brushed against her stallion.

"So do I," replied Lennox. "But I would prefer to see that pendant again."

"Even if it takes you away from me?"

Lennox looked uncertain. Whatever the outcome he knew that one day he would go back to Zanadoo. *But will I return? Perhaps the longer the pendant stays where it is, the better.*

PART THREE: Gudgers

CHAPTER 8 – The Pendant

Merlin was still in Avalon. He wasn't supposed to be. He should have returned to Helen-Joy, his wife who was expecting twins.

Of course it was only right that he should attend the Wizzen, the meeting of wizards, where his successor was chosen. It didn't really bother Merlin that he had to step down from his role as leader. After all, everyone knew that he was the most powerful and knowledgeable sorcerer who had ever lived and it would free him from some of the more menial tasks involved in the role. Wormald the Wise would have been far better at risk analysis, attending boring meetings and the like. However, it had come as a surprise, and somewhat of a worry, when young Tannus had been elected to replace him.

Instead of going home after the Wizzen, Merlin stayed on. All the wizards had been intrigued by Tannus's revelations about the King of Barrmin and his long term intentions. They were worried about what was going on in the North.

Initially, he had declined the request to officiate at Prince Edward and Daisy's wedding. However, with the exchange of rings ceremony only the day after the Wizzen, it was a good excuse to linger on and try to gain more information from Tannus. The new wizard leader had been very secretive about his escapade which had brought him to a place called Zanadoo.

Whilst Merlin's human friends were happy to have him stay on in Merlport, his magical peers were not. The leaders of the magical folk in Avalon had met Helen-Joy and felt sorry for the woman, who was giving birth so late in life and was at home on her own. Queen Esmerelda never ceased to chastise the old man for what she deemed as his selfishness. Merlin knew his magical friends were suspicious that he lingered in Avalon with the intention of joining them on the planned trip to Barrden, the capital of Barrmin.

It was clear when he saw Tannus and Esmerelda approaching that he was in for another scolding but he didn't care. Tannus had been exhausted when he had arrived at the Wizzen the previous night and, what with urgent Wizzen business, Merlin had had no chance to question him further about his trip to Zanadoo.

The Witch Queen's lips were drawn tight and her eyes glinted with annoyance. "You should be on your way home."

"I'll only be away an extra couple of days and, if you remember, Edward had specifically asked me to officiate at his wedding. Wormald says he does not mind me taking over at the last minute." Merlin was standing at the buffet table and stuffed a large portion of apple pie into his mouth.

"But Helen needs you at home. Promise you will return first thing in the morning," Esmerelda pleaded.

"Well, I must admit that I am considering staying a little longer and sailing up to Barrden with you all. It would be nice to call in and see Azgoose again. I would also like to meet Queen Issyluna, her father King Xargon and…"

Tannus interrupted. "I can understand you staying an extra day or so for the wedding and you must be disappointed not to be travelling to Barrden, as we all know you enjoy your trips. However, I have a message for you and you must take it seriously, I ask you to tell no one."

He turned to Esmerelda. "I must bid you to say nothing of what I have to tell Merlin."

Merlin and Esmerelda looked at the serious expression on the young wizard's face. Both realised he had something significant to reveal. They uttered their promises to keep the secret he was about to unfold.

From out of a concealed pocket in his green velvet gown, Tannus withdrew a pendant and handed it to Merlin. The pendant consisted of what appeared to be a clear stone set in an ornate gold surround and hung on a matching chain.

"I was asked to give this to you. It is a gift for Helen-Joy, but first you must show it to Lennox."

As Merlin took the jewel, the stone within glimmered a pale yellow and then a light green. As it caught the light at different angles the colour changed to shades of pink and mauve. "What is it?" he asked. "Where did it come from?"

"It is a stone called zanite. As you know I am sworn to secrecy. I am sorry. I am allowed to say only two things: first, that we must take a more careful look at the Kernan mines. Second, that you must show the pendant to Lennox. When he sees this gift, he will know that he can tell you about his journey to the Forbidden Forest."

The old man shook his head. "I have had so many adventures of my own since coming to Avalon, I had not thought to ask Lennox about his. I just assumed that when he left the ship and headed towards the Great Forest he had taken some of the mares which lived there, and moved across country to a new home. What a fool I was not to ask about his own journey."

Esmerelda was more concerned about the instructions to look more carefully at the Kernan mines. "Are you telling me that there are more of our kind and children being forced to work in those horrendous mines?"

Tannus put his arm around the woman he loved. "If that is what I thought, I would be in Kerner ready to do battle with King Jeffrey. No, I believe it is something else.

"Let Lennox tell you his story, Merlin. He knows more than I do. We all know that there are mysteries around those Kernan mines and what goes on there. Don't forget what that man said, the one who brought the children to us, about the children not being needed any more because they had stronger creatures working in the mines."

"I'm intrigued…" Merlin was about to say more but a horn sounded in the distance. "Ah, Daisy is on her way. I must officiate. Thank you, Tannus." He slipped the pendant into an inner pocket of his colourful ceremonial gown. "We'll talk again later."

"I have no more to say," said Tannus. "I told you all I intended saying about Zanadoo at the Wizzen last night. I repeat, I am sworn to secrecy. You must speak to Lennox – and you should waste no time in doing so."

Merlin nodded and hurried off to the dais where the exchange of rings would take place. Guests hurried to their allocated seating. The exchange of rings ceremony, for which they had all been patiently waiting, was about to begin.

✿ + ✿ + ✿ + ✿ + ✿ + ✿ + ✿

It was a restless night's sleep. Merlin couldn't decide whether to stay on in Avalon and join the travellers to Barrden or to go home and find out what Lennox had to say about the pendant. He was torn. Tannus had had so much tantalising information about the King of Barrden and his family but surely the pendant must be important too. Tannus was right; there was a lot to learn about the Kernan mines. The significance of what the man who brought the children from Kerner had said had not been lost on him. He wanted to find out more about the strong and willing creatures which were being employed in Kernan mines.

He decided to visit Tannus to try to glean more information about how he came by the pendant. He rose early and made his way to Esmerelda's house and knocked on the door. The loud knock echoed in the otherwise quiet street.

Esmerelda opened half of an upstairs window and leaned out. Her long black hair, which was a mass of tangles, tumbled over her shoulders as she bent forward. It was clear that he had woken her. "What do you want?" she snapped, green sparks shooting from her eyes.

"I'd like to speak to Tannus, please." Merlin was very polite. It had not occurred to him that the Witch Queen would still be in bed.

Tannus opened the other half of the upstairs window. Like his lover his hair was tousled and his eyes half shut. "What do you want, Merlin?" The new leader of the wizard's tone was abrupt. His face showed that he was not at all happy to be roused from his slumber. He had had weeks of hard travel and long days. He needed rest.

"I'm sorry to have woken you but I'm considering going home today and I wanted to find out if there was anything more that I needed to know about the present you have given me for Helen." Merlin was aware that neighbours were opening their bedroom windows to see what was going on. It was the day after the wedding and they had all had a late night with plenty of ale and good wine. Everyone had looked forward to a relaxing morning to recover.

"As I told you last night." Tannus spoke in a loud measured tone. "You must show the pendant to Lennox and he will tell you his story. I have nothing more to add except that I am glad you are going home to your wife and no longer considering joining us on our visit to Barrden." He slammed his half of the window shut.

Esmerelda put on a sweet voice. "Oh, I am so glad you are returning to Helen. Please give her my love and tell her we will be thinking of her and casting spells for the safe delivery of her twins. We wish you a safe journey, Merlin, and will visit you when we return from Barrden." Then she too slammed her half of the window.

The old wizard was left standing in the street, in front of a house with closed windows and door. Meanwhile, neighbours had started to lean out of their windows and were asking what the noise was about. Embarrassed, he made his way back to Arthur's house, where he was staying. The choice as to whether to go home or stay and join the trip to Barrden was no longer a difficult one. He would return home without further delay and still have time to visit Kerner before Helen-Joy gave birth to her twins. King Jeffrey couldn't object to the visit because, after all, Merlin had spent a lot of time in Kerner clearing the land of the poisonous weed which had killed their crops.

Arthur and his family were still in bed when he took his leave so he left a note on the kitchen table: '*I would very much have liked to have gone to Barrden with you but I have decided that my place is with my wife. Wishing you and your companions a safe trip. Your friend, Merlin.*' His magical counterparts may not have wanted him to join them but he knew Arthur would be more than a little disappointed not to have the wizard at his side when dealing with the Barrmin king. Leaving before the old king awoke would save an explanation for his change of heart.

Plenty of food had been left over from the wedding feast and deposited in Arthur's kitchen. Merlin wrapped a few chicken legs in a cloth. He packed scones and strawberry cake in another and tucked his packages away in the deep pockets of his travelling cloak.

Comet, his white horse, was in the king's stable. Merlin never used a saddle. He put a thick blanket, with pockets on either side, over Comet's back and filled the pockets with leather canteens of ale and wine plus a round of cheese. He felt a pang of guilt at the load his white steed had to bear but the food and ale would soon be gone.

With his broom strapped into a carrying case on his back Merlin set off. Sometimes he rode and other times he took to his broom to give Comet a break. He enjoyed flying although sitting for too long on such a narrow stick was uncomfortable and made his ancient bones ache. Nevertheless, he liked to feel the wind in his face and breathe the air, well above fires and chimney stacks, where it was still fresh. The views across Avalon and Twydell from so high above were always pleasant to behold and the old man was always interested in what was going on. Sometimes when he flew low people waved to him because he was now a well-known figure in Twydell as well as Avalon. The journey passed without incident and the old man's head was full of so many thoughts that he was home before he had time to get bored.

Since her pregnancy Helen-Joy had lost her powers of foresight so no one was there to meet him when he arrived at the edge of the woodland. Great Grandmother Bramble, knowing his need to go back and forth, had taught him the charm to open and close the protective vines which sealed their home from the outside world. As soon as the periphery opened and he stepped inside he felt he was at home again. He took the blanket off Comet's back and put it across his broom. He swept ahead, leaving Comet to meander through the trees. The horse knew his way to Helen-Joy's home and would get there in his own time.

When he reached the waterfall, which hid the entrance to Helen-Joy's cave, he was disappointed to find that Lennox and his mares were not in their usual spot. They often spent time at the small patch of grass beside the pool which was filled by the falling water. On entering, he found the dwelling which he shared with Helen-Joy was empty. He hurried through the length of the cave, to the red velvet curtains which served as a back door, and into the sheltered garden beyond. The garden was a green haven on the edge of the forest with the granite mountains behind. His wife was sitting on the bank of a shallow stream with her feet in the water.

"Helen, my sweet, you look so lovely there under the apple tree. I can see the twins are growing; your belly has swelled since I last saw you."

"Not just my belly! My ankles are swollen too. I thought the cool water might ease them. But enough about me. Tell me, my love, what have you been up to?" Helen-Joy welcomed her husband with a warm smile but did not stand to greet him. She looked tired but nonetheless had her usual smile on her face and a myriad of questions on her lips.

"How did the Wizzen go? Was it a success? Are the other wizards happy with Wormald the Wise as their new leader or did they think they would miss you? What about the wedding…"

"Let me answer one question at a time, dear. Wormald was not elected as leader and it was young Iwan's vote that made the difference. You know, the lad who was rescued from the mines who the Brambles took in. The one we had to move to Avalon because of his lack of control in creating fire."

"How could I forget Iwan? We were afraid he was going to send the Brambles' house up in flames or worse still, set the whole woodland alight."

"Yes, true, but when he came to the Wizzen I couldn't deny him the right to vote. We need to control him and if he were to go off on his own and become a hedge wizard, goodness knows what damage he might do."

"So, who did Iwan vote for? I'm surprised he knew anyone in Avalon – Hold on! I thought you told me that Wormald had no rivals."

"I didn't think he had but Tannus was nominated at the last minute, and won by just one vote. Iwan's vote."

"Well, you can't blame Iwan. He knows Tannus, whereas he had never met the other chap. Anyway, I'm pleased for Tannus. He's a nice young man who has done a lot to help the magical folk released from Kernan mines. Why don't you look happy about it? You're face is nearly as long as Lennox's."

"Tannus and Esmerelda are both highly skilled magicians but they are both very young. I miss Elvira, Esmerelda's mother, she was a sensible old witch. Tannus and our new Witch Queen are impulsive, to put it mildly. Tannus has just made an unauthorised visit to the North."

"Who should have authorised his visit?"

"Well, I don't exactly mean authorise. Nonetheless he should have told me and Wormald what he was up to."

"Did he do any mischief or cause anyone any harm?"

"Er… no. He didn't cause any harm, but he might have done."

"But he didn't. Did his visit have a useful purpose?"

"Oh, I suppose it did but it might have turned out otherwise." Merlin realised that he was not making sense. He could not divulge more without revealing some matters considered confidential by the Wizzen. Any wizard who betrayed the Wizzen would be self cursed. He swiftly changed the subject.

"Do you know where Lennox is?"

"Oh, the unicorns have found another clearing where they can graze. One of the Brambles opens up the canopy by day and closes it in the evening. They still come back here at night though. I don't think they like me to be here on my own."

Merlin felt a pang of guilt. "I am sorry, my dear, I should have asked you whether you had been alright here alone."

"I've been fine. I've been on my own here for what, eighty years? One of the Brambles comes round every day. It's too far for me to walk to them nowadays. Sometimes young Heather stays over but she's been away again – clearing more poisonous weed in the North apparently. I'm really pleased you are home. Let's go and have a cuppa. I fancy a nice mint tea and a plate of peas."

The sorcerer thought of the delicacies he had enjoyed at the wedding feast and the titbits he had savoured on his way home. A cup of mint tea was one thing but a plate of raw peas was quite another.

They decided to drink their tea beside the waterfall at the front of the cave. It was always a cool spot and they both delighted in the way sunlight formed flickering rainbows on the cascading water. Whilst Merlin found a red apple to eat, his wife dined on a plate of peas. Helen-Joy was eager to hear about the wedding. As Merlin described the ceremony he also relayed the many messages from the guests, wishing her good health and a safe confinement. He was in the midst of 'setting the scene' for her when they heard the sound of hooves.

Lennox appeared with Comet beside him. He was followed by his mares and the rescued pit ponies who seemed to have joined the herd of unicorns. Sally Bramble flew above them on her broom.

"Ah, Comet, I wondered where you were. You must have sensed the unicorns and gone to find them."

Sally landed in front of the wizard. "Hello, Merlin. I knew you must be back when I saw Comet and came straight away. The herd decided to follow. Are Heather and Isaiah back, too? I wasn't expecting them for another day or so." The witch was anxious to know whether her husband had returned safely from the Wizzen and had hoped that her daughter was with him. She was always worried when either of them left the forest. Her husband Isaiah had been captured by the Kernans, held prisoner, and forced to work in the mines there for seventeen long years.

"Er... no. I saw them at the wedding and they were enjoying themselves. I left in rather a hurry the next morning as I was keen to get home to my dear wife. I'm afraid I didn't ask them when they would be leaving."

Sally looked downcast.

"Would you like a cuppa, Sally? I'll go and get you one. I could do with another myself. Would you like another, Merlin?" Helen-Joy didn't bother waiting for replies. She simply started making her way back up the steps.

"I'll come and help you," Sally offered, as she traced the other woman's footsteps.

Lennox came forward and greeted his old friend. "I'm pleased to see you home. We have done our best to keep an eye on your wife. We return each night to make sure she is alright. One of us is always ready to gallop to the Brambles if the need should arise."

"That's very good of you. Please thank your herd for their compassion." Merlin felt another pang of guilt but nevertheless was eager to solve the mystery of the pendant. "Now," he said, "I have something to show you."

He took the pendant from his pocket and, holding it by the chain, swung it to and fro. The unicorn pricked his ears and his mares whinnied at the sight of the necklace which they had last seen, held by Zan, in the amethyst cavern. Even though they had left Zanadoo some time ago, their memories were still fresh.

"Where did you get that?" he asked. "I knew you would show it to me one day, and that when you did that I would be able to tell you my story."

"I got it from Tannus," responded the wizard, "and before you tell me your tale I must apologise that I was so absorbed in my own adventures that I never asked you about yours. I simply assumed you had gone to the Great Forest, stolen some mares, and made your way here. I am all ears and anxious to hear what you have to say."

Suddenly behind him Merlin heard a crash. He turned to see that Helen-Joy had dropped the two clay cups she was carrying. Mint tea was spilling down the steps.

"Where did you get that necklace?" she gasped. She hurried down the stone steps, almost slipping on the last one. Merlin sprang to his feet, and grasped her to stop her falling.

Helen-Joy, seemingly unbothered by her near fall, clutched the hand in which he held the chain. Then she gently brushed the pendant with her fingers.

"Have you seen it before?" asked Merlin.

"It was my mother's. I lost touch with her when I came here. I've seen it in my crystal ball many a time, but not my mother. Where did you get it?"

"I got it from Tannus."

"Tannus?"

"Yes, he brought it back from his expedition to the North. He said it is a present for you. However, I was instructed to show it to Lennox first, who had been sworn to secrecy about certain aspects of his journey to get here, until he saw the pendant again."

"Then let Lennox tell you his story," Helen-Joy stated firmly. "Then you can translate to me." She took the necklace and held it next to her heart as she spoke.

Sally looked puzzled. "I'll make another brew," she said, picking up the pieces of the crockery that had smashed on the stone steps, before returning to the stove.

Lennox told Merlin how relieved he was to at last be able to tell his story.

He started by describing how, after leaving the ship, he met Sheba and his subsequent clash of horns with Tyzon. Merlin was horrified to learn that male unicorns were slain at just 49 days old if they did not grow a golden horn. He tut tutted when he heard about the forest laws. The mares joined in with sounds of disapproval.

Then the wizard gave the unicorn a break, and a chance to sup at the pool, while he told his wife and her witch friend what he had heard. They too looked aghast when they heard about the slaughter of the baby unicorns. However, their frowns soon turned upside down when Merlin relayed the story of the wood elves and little Wifflin who rode upon the back of a stork called Marje.

As Lennox continued his story, Merlin was intrigued and excited to learn about the cefflars. He interrupted the unicorn to translate. "I've heard about those small flying horses in Ireland but never seen one though I travelled there on several occasions."

Helen-Joy and Sally were captivated by the story and bombarded Merlin with questions which he then had to translate.

"Translating to the ladies is time consuming and I have not yet reached the most important part as far as you are concerned." The unicorn and his herd were growing impatient. "Remember we were all sworn to secrecy," he said. "I saw your good wife's reaction to the necklace, so she may already know the secret that I have to tell – but I cannot reveal any more to the witch."

Merlin apologised to Sally. Although the witch was disappointed not to be invited to stay longer, she was nevertheless keen to get home and tell the rest of her family about the story to which she had been privy. She said her goodbyes and hurried off.

Lennox continued.

He told Merlin about his meeting with Zan, and his journey through Zanadoo. He ended his tale with Flambeau's revelation about the gudgers and how they had carried off Sprike the goblin king.

"So that's it!" Merlin slapped his thigh and shook his fists in the air in triumph.

"They must be the creatures that work in the Kernan mines," he said to his wife – who had no idea what he was talking about.

"What has this to do with my mother's necklace?" she asked.

In explanation he added eagerly, "You remember the man who brought the children who had been held prisoner to work in the mines? He told us that they were no longer needed because the Kernans had strong creatures who were willing to work and would replace the children."

His wife just looked at him, waiting for a more detailed explanation.

"Tell me, my dear. Have you ever heard the name Zan?"

"I had an uncle called Zan, or he may have even been a great or great great uncle. I never met him. He left Twydell when he was a young man. My mother told me he was a very skilled soothsayer. A farmer once asked him if he could tell him what had happened to his missing cattle. He told the farmer that the cattle had been stolen by a wealthy nobleman. The nobleman denied the accusation and was furious. He demanded my uncle Zan's head. He was an important man and he offered a reward to anyone bringing the soothsayer to him – alive or dead. So Uncle Zan ran away before he could be caught."

"Do you know where he went?"

"Yes, and I suspect you do too. He went to a place called Zanadoo. A place hidden in the mountains."

"Well, he is still there – and this is his gift to you."

"And my mother?"

Merlin asked Lennox if Zan had told him anything about Helen-Joy's mother.

"No. He did not mention her at all," was the reply.

"After he went into hiding, mum used to go and meet him somewhere at a secret place. She always went at night when no one was likely to see her leave. On one occasion she came back with this necklace. She said that Zan had discovered a stone which he had called zanite. His friends in Zanadoo had cut some of the stone out of the rocks and made this necklace. She was very proud of it."

"And so she should be. It is an intricate piece of jewellery. The stone is most unusual. Look, it changes colour in the light," Merlin observed as his wife held it up to look at it once again before continuing.

"When all magical beings, soothsayers or anyone who was a bit different were expelled from Twydell, mum said she was going to Zanadoo. But I didn't want to spend the rest of my life living in a cave. At least," she said turning to look at her current home, "not one where I could never have a garden or see the light of day. I chose to go with Bertha Bramble's family. They knew the wizard who lived here. I've been here ever since. Mum had hoped that Zanadoo extended to the granite hills behind the Forbidden Forest. That's why I chose to live in this spot with the mountains just behind. I always hoped mum would pop out through a concealed entrance one day, but I never saw her again."

Merlin felt alarmed. *If the gudgers have tunnelled their way into Zanadoo and Kerner they could tunnel their way here, too. I will not frighten Helen by telling her my concerns. It would be very unwise to alarm her at this stage of her pregnancy.*

"Is there anything else you can tell me about Zanadoo?" Merlin asked, trying to sound casual.

"No, nothing," said Helen-Joy. "Mum was always reticent to talk about Zan or Zanadoo. I was never allowed to go with her when she met him. But she always told me that he was watching out for us. Sometimes, when I see this pendant in my crystal ball, I think I see a grey eye watching me."

"Does Zan have grey eyes?" the wizard asked the unicorn.

"He does," responded Lennox.

Merlin translated for his wife.

167

Helen-Joy clapped her hands, "Then it is my uncle's grey eye which I see in my glass. But he must be ancient now – even older than you!"

"If he is your great great uncle then he must be!" A smile appeared on the old wizard's face.

"Oh, I'm sorry," said his wife. "I didn't mean to be rude. But we are both of an age, aren't we?"

"We are indeed, my love. Tell me, do the Brambles know about Zanadoo?"

"Well, Bertha will know. She will remember my mother. There were always rumours about a magical country hidden away somewhere but very few people knew where. The whereabouts of Zanadoo was a well guarded secret. I'm not sure if it is a magical place though. Would you call living in the middle of a mountain magical?"

"Lennox seems very taken with it, as do his wives." Then, knowing that his wife was aware of Zan and the place in which he lived, he related the rest of Lennox's story to her including the way the gudgers had kidnapped Sprike. He tried not to sound as if he were worried by the story.

"My goodness, I hope they never dig their way through to the Forbidden Forest. It sounds as if they have managed to get in to Kerner, too."

She has worked it out for herself and I must warn the Brambles of our fears, but I do not wish to cause too much alarm.

"From what we have been told, the gudgers have been welcomed by the Kernans." Merlin stopped to think, then he turned to Lennox and asked him a question. The unicorn relayed the question to the former pit ponies who had joined his herd.

168

"Yes, the ponies have seen the gudgers. They described them in much the same way as Flambeau did. They are large lizard-like creatures who walk on two legs. They have a very unpleasant odour about them. Their tongues are very long and they catch flies in mid-air. Lucky says they have started to wear human clothes and can now speak to the humans in their own language."

"They must be very clever creatures!" said Helen-Joy.

Merlin nodded. "And hard working creatures too. I need to find out more about these gudgers," he continued. "It is strange that they are despised in Zanadoo but welcomed in Kerner. Perhaps, like humans, they are a race made up of the good and bad. But as always, you are right my sweet, we do not want them suddenly climbing out of the granite mountains where we live. Our home is surrounded around the edge of the woodland by the bindweed and from the sky by the forest canopy. I had thought we were protected on the far side by the mountains but perhaps I am wrong. But there is no need to worry, I am sure that Bertha and I can come up with a solution."

He stopped to think for a while.

"I must take a trip to Kerner. King Jeffrey cannot deny me a visit to his palace. After all the work I have done in destroying the poisonous weed which nearly destroyed his arable land, I should be made welcome. I will go to Kerner without delay and find out what I can."

"Oh..." Helen-Joy's face showed her disappointment.

"Obviously, I do not want to leave you here on your own, my sweet, but this could be urgent business. If what we have heard of the gudgers in Zanadoo is correct then people in Kerner are in danger. I feel that I should visit your uncle Zan and find out more about this place called Zanadoo, too. As you say there is a risk, albeit a slender one, of gudgers burrowing into the Forbidden Forest.

"I know I should not leave you on your own. Would it be possible for you to stay with the Brambles for a few days? Or perhaps one of the Brambles could come and stay with you?"

"There is no way I could ask one of the Brambles to stay here. They are so busy at the moment with the children to look after, especially with Heather being away again. I must admit, I would have liked to stay with them. But it just isn't possible. My feet and legs are so swollen at the moment I'm not getting around very easily; there is no way that I could walk to the Brambles' house."

"I will ask if Lennox or one of the mares would be willing to take you." Without waiting for an answer, Merlin called out to the unicorns.

Helen-Joy stopped him mid question. "I don't think I could or should ride in my present condition. Being bobbed up and down on a unicorn's back wouldn't do the twins any good either."

"Ah… yes," said Merlin. "I understand." The wizard told the unicorns that he had changed his mind as his wife riding in her current condition would not be sensible.

The equines, however, after discussion among themselves, came up with a solution. Lucky, the former pit pony, approached. "I am a lot stronger now than when I arrived as are the other ponies. The cart I pulled here was heavy and far too wide for these narrow paths.

My friends the unicorns have told me that when they were in the place they called Zanadoo they saw slender carts which donkeys pulled along the narrow tunnels. I believe the old carts, which brought the Bramble men and the children here, are still outside. The men from the mines were too afraid of the magicians to collect them. If you could make a slender vehicle from one of those old carts we would be pleased to take the lady as our passenger. She has tended our wounds and found so many fine vegetables for us to eat. We would be delighted to have this chance to repay her."

Merlin thanked the ponies profusely and when he told his wife she clapped her hands, stood up and walking to each pony in turn, looked into their eyes and told them how grateful she was. Although she did not speak their language there was no doubt her actions told them the message she wished to convey.

"Well. I am sure we can halve one of those carts. Isaiah, and hopefully Jonathan, may be back later today or tomorrow; they will help. I shall rest with you for the remainder of the day and start work on the cart tomorrow. Now, my dear, I think I have half a round of cheese left in my pocket, shall we have that for tea, with some of the apples from your garden?"

It was a question which required no answer. Helen-Joy relaxed, with her feet in the pool, while her husband waited on her.

CHAPTER 9 –
Preparations for the
Journey to Kerner

Merlin started the day with an abundance of energy. Helen-Joy thought he would sleep in but he left her, in her comfy bed, on the broad stone ledge in her cave. The ledge was padded with a goose down quilt on top of a layer of straw. He looked back at her; she lay in a deep slumber, wrapped in the patchwork silk bedspreads which she had made. She was no longer disturbed by the dreams which informed her of what was happening elsewhere or foretold the future – good or bad.

Will she ever regain her skills as a soothsayer? I hope so. I would like to think that our children inherit my magical talents and their mother's abilities as a seer. What marvellous children they might be. Marvello, now that's a good name for a wizard. I'll have to suggest it to her.

Taking his broom, he found the unicorns, ponies and Comet waiting outside, ready to leave. As the broom whizzed along the track they kept pace at a slow canter, zigzagging in and out of the trees.

Merlin took a detour to the Brambles' cottage. He was afraid he would find them all in bed but he was very wrong. The magical children, who had been rescued from the Kernan mines, and were now being cared for by the Brambles, were outside. They had made ropes of plaited bindweed. Some were using the 'ropes' for skipping and others tied them between chairs to see how far they could raise the rope and still jump over it. He noticed one girl use a quick flick of the wrist before springing even higher than the chairs and landing a good six feet beyond. A smile appeared on his face. *Very clever, levitation with no wand required.* He memorised the girl's face.

"Hello, Merlin. How lovely to see you." Dilly and Dally spoke almost in unison. They broke off from their task to each plant a kiss on his wrinkled cheeks.

"What are you doing?" asked the wizard. He was puzzled as to why the witches were hollowing out small loaves of bread.

"We're making trenchers," explained Dilly. "We will use the scooped out loaves like bowls."

"But what about the bread you scoop out?" Merlin looked worried. "You won't waste it will you?"

"No," laughed Dally. "Surely, you know us better than that, Merlin? Nothing gets wasted here! We'll use it to make a bread and cheese pudding for tonight's tea."

Sally Bramble was the next to embrace the visitor and plant yet another kiss on his cheek. "Hello, Merlin. I see you have brought the herd with you. I was just going to find them and open up the canopy above one of the clearings."

"No need. I am taking them outside of the forest today," and he went on to explain his plan to halve the width of one of the carts so the ponies could transport Helen-Joy without the need for her to walk on her swollen ankles. Before he could ask whether his wife could stay at the witches' abode for a few days, Great Grandmother Bertha Bramble appeared at the door.

"Merlin," she shouted, "you are just in time for breakfast! We are serving mushrooms in a rich butter sauce this morning."

"Mmm... I can't think of a more enticing invitation than breakfasting with the Brambles. My mouth is watering at the very thought."

The witches called the children to help lay the outside tables. Chequered cloths were spread across long tables with benches on either side.

These tables and benches are new; one of the visiting wizards must have made them. Place settings consisted of wooden plates and spoons. Merlin took a seat at the end of one of the tables. The children scuffled and pushed as they all tried to sit next to the wizard, who they had been told was probably the most powerful magician in the world.

A cauldron full of steaming mushrooms in butter sauce floated across the lawn, directed by Dilly and Dally Bramble's wands.

"Settle down!" Nora shouted at the children who were still jostling for a place next to the wizard. "You're going to knock the cauldron over if you are not careful. Take a seat *now* or you might end up going without! Merlin won't be happy if you spill his breakfast."

"No. I will not." Merlin spoke in a measured tone and tried to look stern.

Two men followed the cauldron, carrying bread trenchers piled on top of one another. Their faces were pale and bore vacant expressions. One dropped the top trencher and as he bent to pick it up others fell to the floor. A young boy, who had been given a wand, left his place to help the man who was fumbling to pick up the fallen bread. He raised each trencher individually

175

and made sure that each fell in front of one of the diners. The first trencher landed in front of Merlin. The boy smiled as the wizard praised his mastery of the wand.

"I am sorry." Dilly Bramble smiled wryly at her wizard friend. "You don't mind a bit of dirt do you, Merlin? We try to encourage Jerry to help with mundane tasks but sometimes I wonder whether he will ever recover from his ordeal in Kerner."

"A bit of dirt never hurt anyone," replied Merlin. "Actually, Jerry and Garod both look much better than when I was here previously. They have come a long way since the day they came home."

Great Grandmother Bramble, taking her ladle, filled his trencher. Taking his spoon he sipped the sauce before it seeped too deeply into the trencher. He finished off by tearing the now moist bread and chewing it, for as long as he could, to relish its rich buttery flavour.

As he ate he watched one of the younger children tear off a piece of her bread. She turned around on the bench and, placing the crust in the palm of her hand, she held it out. A blue tit flew down from the tree, perched on her hand and pecked at the bread.

"Young Maisie has a way with birds," Nora commented. "Sometimes she sits out here, for hours, surrounded by them. They each have a knack of their own. Little Gawin over there, next to Maisie, has a way with plants. He's going to be like our Jonathan and his father."

Our Jonathan. Merlin smiled. Jonathan was a warlock from Avalon. He and his father were herbologists. Jonathan now spent much of his time with Heather, the daughter of Sally and Isaiah. *I can see there will be another exchange of rings soon. I wonder how long it will be before Jonathan proposes.*

"You have done an outstanding job with the children," said Merlin. "You should all be very proud of yourselves and what you have achieved."

The Bramble witches beamed with pride. Their wide smiles revealed many missing teeth.

The two men sat at the table spooning their food. They seemed to hear nothing of what was being said and took no notice of what was going on around them.

"I don't know what we are going to do in the winter though," sighed the great grandmother. "This time of year it's still warm enough to sleep under the stars and when you are away and Heather is home, she stays with Helen-Joy. Now you are back Heather will want to sleep in her old bed again; Maisie is in it at the moment. We will need a new wing added to the cottage if the children are going to remain here."

"Ah, yes," said Merlin. "I can see there will be a problem. Perhaps it might be best to move some of the children to Merlport? Wormald the Wise is giving training lessons to all the young warlocks in case there is another attack by the Trajaens. They would benefit from some defence training."

"What if an attack takes place while they are there?" Sally snapped, as her cheeks started to turn red. "It's safer to keep them here out of harm's way. Speaking of which, do you have any idea when Heather will be home? Both she and her father are away and I've hardly slept a wink since they left." Sally always fretted when her daughter was away. Heather had been helping Jonathan clear the poison weed which destroyed crops in the North. Her husband had recovered more quickly than the other wizards from the

Forbidden Forest and had attended the Wizzen near Merlport with all the other wizards and warlocks. She knew that Heather would have gone to Merlport with Jonathan rather than attempt the journey home on her own.

"As I said, I saw them at Daisy and Edward's wedding and they seemed to be enjoying themselves. I am hoping that they will be back today. I have a job I would have liked Jonathan to help me with, but I think I will have to do it on my own." Merlin explained his plan to make a slender cart so that the ponies could transport his wife from one place to another.

"What a good idea. Why don't you ask young Dexter to help?" Maura stated, indicating a tall boy with a mop of unruly red hair. "He is very good with human tools. He helped Jonathan and Tannus make these tables and benches. We have some hammers, wrenches and a box of nails and screws."

I should have guessed Tannus had a hand in making the new furniture. Merlin felt annoyed.

Young Dexter had been listening and looked directly at Merlin when he first heard his name mentioned.

"Would you like to help me?" asked Merlin.

"I would regard it as a privilege to help the greatest sorcerer in the land." The boy smiled confidently.

However, it seemed like all the children had been listening. A number of other voices joined in. "Can I help, too?"

"Can I go with you, please?"

"Can I watch? I want to learn how to do human jobs as well as magic spells."

"Well, I am rather hoping that I can find a spell to do the manual work, or at least most of it for us."

Merlin smiled. He liked children, and was very proud of the progress they had all made since he had organised their rescue.

He looked at the Bramble family. "Is there any reason why they can't come? I can't look after all of them but if perhaps one or two of you would join us, then it would be a nice little outing."

"You mean to take them out of the forest to where those carts are left?" Sally was aghast.

Maura Bramble spoke. "But if your mother and I went with them, Sally, then they would be well protected. Two witches and a wizard should be able to manage a group of magical children, especially as those children are learning spells themselves. We are only going just outside the entrance so we could easily dart back inside if any danger approached."

"I could jump back in less than a second," stated the girl who Merlin had seen jumping the rope earlier. She flicked her wrist again, sprang up in the air and landed ten feet in front of where she was originally standing with no effort whatsoever.

"Yes, very good, Gemima," said Sally in a gentle tone – although the cracks in her voice revealed to everyone just how upset she was.

"I don't want to go." Little Maisie's voice was so soft it was difficult to hear her. Her face was full of apprehension. "I remember being chained in those carts. I never want to see them again. I want to stay here with Aunty Sally."

"Then of course you will stay!" Great Grandmother Bramble stated firmly. "No one will be forced to go." When Bertha Bramble spoke everyone else stayed silent. She was the head of the family, a position which earned their respect. "Nevertheless, it is my opinion that if any of the children wish to go and Merlin promises to take care of them, then I don't see why they shouldn't take the opportunity. However, even the most powerful of sorcerers cannot take responsibility for too many children. If Maura and Nora are willing to accompany him then any who wish to join the expedition should be able to go."

Maura and Nora looked at each other then nodded their heads in agreement.

Sally and her sisters looked worried; all three of their husbands had been captured by bounty hunters working for the Kernans. They had been sentenced to a lifetime of hard labour simply for being wizards, and forced to take drugs which robbed them of their magical powers. Although Sally's husband was well on the road to recovery, the other two wizards were not; they both remained seated at the breakfast table with lifeless eyes staring out of pale faces.

"Don't forget, since Merlin made peace with the humans, I've been brave enough to venture further afield," Great Grandmother Bertha told the three sisters in a gentle tone of voice. "It was an experience and I enjoyed it. Nevertheless, I have to say that the best thing about going on my adventure was the pleasure of coming home to my family again."

"We missed you and we worried about you all the time you were away," said Nora, wrapping her arms around her mother.

"I came back though."

"But you had Merlin, Jonathan and Yzor with you," argued Sally.

"And the children who wish to come with us will have Merlin, myself and your mother," Maura stated. "Much as I love having the children here, I think

Merlin is right. Some of them should, if they wish, go to Avalon. This expedition will help them adjust to the outside world. It would be good for them to learn some of these defensive spells which Wormald the Wise is teaching. He must be a very powerful wizard to follow in Merlin's footsteps as the new wizard leader."

"Er... Wormald was not elected as leader," Merlin admitted.

"Who was?" asked the six members of the Bramble family in unison.

"Tannus."

"Hooray!" shouted the children, who all knew the handsome warlock who had visited them and helped them regain the magical talent with which they were born.

The Brambles clapped their hands. All, except for the two men, got to their feet and started to dance around in a circle. The children joined in.

Merlin sighed. *So Tannus is revered as the new wizard leader here as well. How I wish they were aware of the perils into which his impetuous nature could lead us.*

"I will certainly be very grateful for all the help I can get with the cart," said Merlin, changing the subject before he got irritable. "I need to leave for Kerner as soon as possible. Dexter, I would be delighted to receive your assistance. I never cease to be surprised by how clever all..."

Great Grandmother Bramble stopped still in the middle of the dance, as did her daughters and granddaughters. The children dancing in the circle, unaware that the adults were going to come to a sudden halt, each bumped into the person in front of them. A couple fell on the ground.

181

"Going to Kerner? Your wife is expecting twins and you are off on another one of your escapades?" Bertha Bramble's happy face had grown stern.

The smiles were wiped from the other witches faces as they each fixed the wizard with harsh stares.

"Yes." Merlin tried to sound casual. "You remember the man from the mines who brought the children; he said they were no longer needed because they had found strong creatures to replace them. I believe they are lizard-like beings who have tunnelled through from middle earth. They may be appreciated in Kerner but they have dug their way through in other mines, where they are not so welcome. I am rather worried by them."

"What place with other mines?" asked Bertha.

"Well, it is difficult to say too much. It is a confidential matter and the people concerned wish to keep their problem private for the time being."

"Children, go to the orchard to play for a while," Great Grandmother Bramble commanded. The children obeyed the matriarch's order without question, although several turned their heads as they went. No doubt they wondered what the grown-ups had to talk about that they were not allowed to hear.

"You're not talking about Zanadoo, are you?" asked Bertha, looking straight at Merlin. He knew her watery eyes were concentrating on his face, ready to detect any avoidance of the truth.

"When Sally came home yesterday and told me you had given Helen a necklace, which she said had once belonged to her mother, I guessed where you had been. Don't forget I came here with Helen while her mother and other members of her family hid in the granite mountains."

Merlin was shocked. "So you know about Zanadoo. Why didn't you tell me?"

"Many magical people knew about Zanadoo but we were all sworn to secrecy. If the Twydellers found out about it they would soon be there robbing the mines of their precious stones and minerals. There would be nothing left for future generations and they wouldn't have thought twice, in those days, about murdering our kind. I told my family about Zanadoo in case anything happened here and they needed to leave the forest and find a new place of refuge. Having said that, I don't know where the entrance is. Helen always hoped she would find a way in from her garden. Is that how you found Zanadoo?"

"No. I have never been to Zanadoo," Merlin told them truthfully. Realising that the family was already aware of the mysterious country, he decided to tell them the rest of Lennox's story. He did not, however, mention Tannus's adventures in the North. *That's a story never to be told.*

The witches were horrified to learn that the gudgers had found their way into Zanadoo and had kidnapped Sprike, the Goblin King.

"That's why I must hurry to fix a cart in which my dear wife can ride in comfort," the wizard ended his tale. "Her feet are too swollen for her to walk at the moment."

"We understand now why it is so important for you to go to Kerner." Bertha spoke solemnly. Then a wry smile appeared on her grizzled face. "But you haven't explained why Helen needs a cart to be carried across the forest trails."

"Ah, yes," said Merlin, who realised that he had not yet asked if his wife could stay with the Brambles.

183

"Well, I should have asked earlier. I must ask you a great favour…"

Bertha saved the wizard further embarrassment. "You want us to look after her while you're away. Yes, of course we will. Helen is like one of our own. I just worry about the space, especially when Heather and Jonathan get back." She looked back at their topsy-turvy cottage before speaking again.

"You will return as soon as you can, won't you Merlin?" asked Sally. "You should be here to weave your own magic when the twins arrive. The spells you weave when they are born will help protect them throughout their lives and give them a sound magical base on which they can build."

"Of course, of course," replied Merlin. "I will make haste to settle my business and return before you know I am gone! The twins are not due for a couple of months yet so there is plenty of time."

"Unless they arrive early," Sally stated firmly. She remained tight-lipped and fixed the wizard with a severe look.

The other witches nodded in agreement.

"Well, the sooner we get this cart sorted out the sooner Merlin can leave and the sooner he'll be back." Maura stood up. "Come on Nora, let's fetch the tools and get the children who wish to come with us together. As mum says, the sooner we get started the sooner we'll finish."

When they reached the edge of the woodland two of the children, who had volunteered to help, changed their mind. They preferred the safety of the forest.

"That's all right." Nora spoke in a kindly tone. "You sit there at the entrance and be our lookouts. Watch carefully and if you see any men and no matter how far away they might be call us straight away. Watch out for aurochs and mammoths as well; we don't want them too close. If you see anything unusual, shout."

"Have they been taught stunning spells?" asked Merlin, as he perused the old carts.

"Not yet," replied Maura. "It will be their first lesson when Heather and Jonathan return."

Dexter spread the tools, which had been in the saddle bags on Lucky's back, on the ground. He inspected each one carefully.

"I think before we do anything manually," said Merlin, "I'll try a halving spell. The doubling spell is one of my specialities so if I modify the wording I might just get what I want with one stroke of the wand."

Merlin drew his wand and muttered some words. The cart shrank to half its original size but not only was its width reduced, but so was its length, height and even its wheels.

"Well, it's a nice little cart," Nora commented.

"If you could 'halve it' again it would come in useful in the garden," Maura observed. "We could use it as a hand cart."

The disappointed wizard obliged the two elderly sisters, who looked very pleased with the result.

Dexter was looking over one of the other carts. "It wouldn't take too long to reduce the width of this one by half," he said. "Look, the base of the cart is six lengthwise planks wide. If we take off the wheels, remove one of the side panels and three planks from the base all we have to do is cut the two ends and the axle in half and put it all back together again."

"That sounds like a lot of hard work," responded Merlin, as he examined the cart to check if what the lad was telling him made sense. It did.

"Not hard work at all," said Dexter. "Before they found out that I was a warlock I used to maintain the carts in the mines. I was a sort of a handyman; my job was mending anything that was broken which could be repaired."

"Really?" Merlin raised his eyebrows. The two witch sisters looked surprised, too.

"You never told us that before!" Maura looked at the lad.

"I was so dopey with drugs when I arrived, I didn't think to mention it. It was some time later that I started remembering my past."

"How old are you?" asked Merlin. "You look older than the other children."

"I am. Few of the children in the mines live to be teenagers," Dexter replied in a matter of fact tone. The other children who had come to help turned white with horror.

"I'm sorry, I shouldn't have said that. I am thirteen, I think, maybe fourteen. I sort of lost track of time once the guards started forcing me to drink a potion that robbed me of my magical powers."

"So, you were practising as a young warlock before you went to the mines?" Merlin was curious.

The two witches listened intently to the conversation. They had not yet asked the children about their previous lives in case it caused them upset. They had simply nursed them back to health and taught them a few charms and spells as they grew stronger.

"No. My parents were magicians," continued Dexter. "But they kept their powers well hidden and I was always told not to work spells where people might catch a glimpse of what I was up to. One day we were in the market. We didn't know soldiers were looking for us until they surrounded us. Mum and dad were arrested. They tried to escape by blowing up a dust cloud; I managed to get away. I hid in a crate under a trader's table. I peeked through a knot hole and saw mum on the ground and then a soldier knocked my dad senseless with a wooden club. While they were unconscious they were forced to swallow a potion; then they were put in a wagon and taken away. The soldiers looked for me. I stayed where I was and pretended to be invisible. Perhaps I was, because one of them looked under the table and I was sure he would see me but he walked away."

"The fright you had may well have caused you to disguise yourself in some way," said Merlin as he gave the subject some thought. "Sometimes magical beings do not realise their powers until their emotions take over. An invisibility charm would usually require the skills of a most powerful magician. But if you were frightened of being discovered, then you could have worked an invisibility spell without realising it. Or, one of your parents may have had time to cast a spell, to obscure you, before being captured. What happened to you after that?"

"I started stealing bits of bread and things to eat," replied Dexter. "People used to chase me away and I knew the soldiers were looking for me. One day a man offered me a job. Well, it wasn't really a job. I became a thief. He took me to another town where he looked after other children, who like me had no parents. In exchange for giving us food and lodging, he set us to work climbing into houses through small windows and taking a few bits and pieces which he could sell; or stealing money from people in the markets. I was very good at it because sometimes I could charm purses to come to me, but I was very careful not to be seen using magic. No one guessed I was a warlock."

"I'm sure you must have been a very skilled thief," Merlin observed.

"I didn't like stealing, though!" Dexter looked aghast. "My mum and dad always taught me to be honest but I had to survive."

"I'm sure your parents were very nice people," Nora said kindly.

"And you were only doing what you had to in order to survive," Maura added. "I assume you got caught though."

"Caught red-handed!" exclaimed Dexter. "The other children were friendly and the man fed us well. We were a team. Each time we stole something, we passed it to someone else who passed it to someone else. That way if the actual thief got caught there was never any proof he had stolen anything. I was a successful thief for several years until one day I stole a small purse from a lady in the market. I turned round to give it to my friend but she wasn't there. Someone saw the purse in my hand and called a soldier. I suppose I could have used my magic to escape but I saw what had happened to my parents – knocked unconscious and forced to drink the potion which turned them into zombies. I decided to take my punishment like a human."

"What did they do to you?" asked Merlin. "I know you ended up in the mines with the other children of magic, how did they find out about your powers?"

"They didn't for a long time." Dexter worked on the cart while he spoke. Hammers and wrenches leapt to his hands when needed, and returned to the bag when he had finished with them. "We need to saw the axle to make it shorter. Can you help me, please?" he asked Merlin.

Together they reduced the length of the axle and put it back on the now slender cart. The other children watched with interest.

Whilst they were putting the wheels back, Dexter continued with his story. "I started off in the mines. It was hard work and very hot. We had chains around our feet and I could barely walk more than a few steps. At night when no one was looking I would remove the chains and put them back before we started work again in the morning. No one ever noticed."

"How clever," the older wizard observed.

"One day the wheel cracked on a cart full of rocks, which a pony was trying to heave out of the mine. They whipped the pony, trying to make it pull a heavy cart on just three wheels with one corner dragging the ground. I offered to mend it. The men laughed at me but I knelt down beside the wheel. The mines are not well lit and most of the people who work there have poor eyesight."

The two witch sisters looked at each other and sighed.

"They couldn't see what I was doing and I used a bit of magic to make the cracked wheel stick together enough for the pit pony to be able to pull the cart outside. I pretended to hammer the wheel together with my fists. They thought I was very skilled and after that I worked outside in the yard. There was a carpenter there who was also a prisoner but it was his job to fix this and that and he started to teach me his trade."

Dexter looked at the cart. It was now half the width; exactly how the wizard had described what he wanted it to look like. "I think I'll use one of these planks we removed to make a seat for your wife." He measured the correct width by placing the plank on the cart and making a notch at the point which required cutting.

Will you hold it firm for me, please?" he asked the older wizard, who obliged.

"How did they find out you were a warlock?" Merlin asked, holding the plank whilst Dexter sawed. He was keen to find out more.

"Not in front of the younger children," said Dexter, his voice so soft that only Merlin could hear. "We will talk again later."

Lucky came over to look at the cart. "Do you want me to try it out?" he asked.

"I think the reins will need some adjusting but I'm sure I can manage that task." Merlin drew his wand and started tapping the leather straps. The reins moved into their required size without the need for manual adjustment. He and Dexter strapped Lucky into the cart and soon the little pony was trotting around the grassland with the empty cart in tow.

The witches and the children clapped their hands.

"I don't like him being a beast of burden again," Maura commented, "but he does seem to be enjoying himself."

"As long as we don't expect too much of the little chap," Nora added.

Her sister nodded.

Dexter looked pleased with his handiwork.

"Well done," said Merlin, clapping the boy on the back. "It would not have been done so quickly if you were not here."

Dexter smiled.

He is a quiet, modest boy, thought Merlin. *I am looking forward to speaking to him again. I can learn a lot from him about those dreadful mines.*

Maura rode Comet whilst Nora flew on Merlin's broom. Merlin himself walked beside the children. Dexter trundled the handcart as far as the split in the path where he left it to collect later. One track led back to the Brambles cottage and the other to the soothsayer's home. They all made their way along the path which led to Helen-Joy's home.

Lucky took up the rear with the slender carriage in tow. The children had decorated it with daisy chains and other wild flowers they had collected en route.

When they reached the clearing in front of her home they found Helen-Joy sitting beside the pool with her feet in the water, but she stood up when she saw them coming.

"Well, what a very pleasant and unexpected surprise! I didn't expect to see Maura and Nora today let alone the children." Her smile showed her pleasure until Lucky arrived pulling the cart and then her face dropped and her mouth fell open.

Everyone, except Dexter, had expected her to be over the moon with her new vehicle. They looked at her shocked expression in bewilderment.

191

"It looks like a coffin, doesn't it?" remarked Dexter. "That's why I put the seat in it, so you could sit up and look around."

"Oh, I see. That's very kind of you." Helen-Joy got up and walked over to the cart and started to inspect it. She saw the flowers and realised that she was disappointing the children who had come along to present the gift. Her face lit up again.

"It's wonderful. I am so pleased with my new chariot. It looks very comfortable." She clapped her hands and the party joined in. The equines whinnied and Lucky stamped his hooves and shook his mane.

"May I try it out?" She tried to clamber inside but it was too high for her. Lucky pulled the cart around to the steps so she could get some extra height and Merlin assisted her to climb aboard.

Lucky dutifully trotted around the clearing while Helen-Joy smiled and waved to the onlookers, who clapped their hands to show approval.

Nora sidled up beside Merlin. "What's a coffin?" she asked.

"Some people don't just bury their dead under the trees like we do. They put them in a box called a coffin. I'm afraid the slender cart does rather look like one. Having said that, I've never seen anyone sitting up in a coffin before. She does look pleased, doesn't she?"

"Yes, she does now," Nora replied.

After Lucky had finished his display, Helen-Joy and her witch friends went inside to find some fruit for the children and fresh vegetables for the equines.

Merlin took the opportunity to talk to Dexter.

"You've done a good job with the cart," he said.
"Thank you."

"I'm glad your wife liked it. She looked horrified at first."

"Well, she looked very happy with it in the end. The carpenter you spoke about in the Kernan prison taught you well."

"Until he found out I was a wizard. You asked me how they found out what I was." Dexter looked sad. "Many people die in the Kernan prisons. Few live as long as the three Bramble men you rescued. They must have had very strong minds. People died every week. They would bring them out from their cells or the places where they worked. We would pile them into wagons which took them away. If they came from a family with money, sometimes the family would pay for a coffin – which is how I learnt to make coffins."

The wizard nodded. *No wonder he was able to adapt the cart so easily.*

"It was a part of my work; I hated it but I got on with it. The rest of my work wasn't too bad and the skilled workers were fed quite well in comparison to other prisoners. I no longer had to wear foot chains because sometimes I needed to climb ladders. I was only sentenced to fifteen years' labour for theft so I kept quiet and waited for the day I would be free."

"A sensible thing to do in the circumstances," Merlin commented.

"I must have been five years or so into my sentence when I was sent to the workhouse where women did the washing. I was repairing a gate in the yard when they brought out a body. I looked and looked at it again before kneeling down beside it. It was my mother. Her brown hair had turned grey and she was as thin as a

193

rake but I still recognised her. Her hands were red and sore and I held them. It was then I realised she was still alive. I took hold of her face and tried to rouse her. A guard came over and asked what I was doing and I told him the woman was still alive and needed help. He laughed and told me she was no use any more and to help him load her into the body wagon. I felt my anger rising. I just went like this." The boy demonstrated how he stretched his arm and pointed towards the guard.

"As I pointed at him I felt my fury release. I didn't know what I was doing but the guard stumbled backwards and fell. I felt something strike me across the head and the next thing I knew I was back in chains, working in the mines. My senses were dulled. I tried to remove my chains at night, like I did before, but I could no longer work the spell. It was the man who taught me my trade who had wielded a hammer to strike me. While I was unconscious they must have forced me to swallow the potion which rendered my magical skills useless."

"I am sorry to learn that your mother was treated so cruelly," said Merlin. "It must have been a terrible ordeal for you finding her as you did."

"It was a terrible ordeal for everyone in those prisons, especially for witches and wizards."

"Tell me," said Merlin. "While you were there, did you see any creatures like large lizards working in the mines or elsewhere?"

"Yes, the gudgers. They took on a lot of the mine work which was a relief for the prisoners. We hoped more and more gudgers would come to ease our burden. Mines are the worst places to work which is why our kind was sent there. The mine managers use children to get into the crevices that adults are too big to access. The gudgers are big creatures but they seem to be able to squeeze their bodies to get into the slimmest of crevices; they can even do the children's work."

"Were the gudgers aggressive?"

"No, they seemed eager to work and please."

"I've heard that they speak and wear clothes."

"Yes, they were learning to speak while I was still working in the yard," continued Dexter. "They're not easy to understand though. They sort of mutter. As regards their clothes, sometimes they worked on the lands of noblemen, whose wives regarded their nakedness as distasteful, so they were given trousers to wear. For some odd reason they also started wearing waistcoats but I think that was just because the gudgers liked the style and thought they looked smart."

"So you liked these gudgers."

"Liked them? Well, they saved our kind some hard labour, so yes I liked them in that sense. I always had a strange feeling about them though, I can't explain it but the worse thing was their smell. They smelt horrible, like bad eggs. I avoided them whenever I could because of the stink. It wasn't so bad in the yard but in the mines, where there is no fresh air, it was disgusting."

Just then Helen-Joy brought them both mugs of mint tea and a plate of fresh fruit.

"Thank you so much for my chariot, Dexter. You are a very talented wizard."

"Actually," explained Merlin, "Dexter used his human skills, not his magical ones, my dear."

"Then you have double skills and should be proud of them. I am guessing my husband will want to leave for Kerner tomorrow and I will look forward to travelling to the Bramble Cottage in my new chariot."

"If you like, I could make you a pair of cribs for the babies," offered Dexter enthusiastically.

The wizard and his wife were equally as enthusiastic in accepting the boy's offer.

The next morning Helen-Joy spread one of her patchwork quilts and some cushions in her 'chariot'.

"Perhaps you need to make some more of these," Merlin commented, as he admired the pretty patchwork quilt. "They would look nice on the cribs Dexter is going to make for us."

"I wish. The patchwork is made out of old curtains and dresses, but I have run out of material. I am using what's left of the patches from worn out quilts to make cushion covers!"

"Oh," said Merlin. "I didn't realise."

Lucky waited to be hitched to the cart. Only Comet and one of the other former pit ponies remained. The others were making their way to a larger clearing they had found.

Merlin led the way on Comet, followed by Lucky drawing the cart with Helen-Joy sitting up inside. The other pony brought up the rear.

The Brambles and the children were delighted to see her arrive. The witches promised to take care of her but urged her wizard husband to return as soon as he was able. He promised to do so.

Goodbyes said, Merlin set off on yet another one of his adventures.

CHAPTER 10 – Sea View Palace

It was an interesting but sombre ride through Kerner. The local people who saw him raised their hands in greeting; even if they had never seen him before, they had certainly heard of the wizard with long grey hair, dressed in strange clothing who rode a magnificent white horse.

Merlin contemplated the story Dexter had told him, about how the man Dexter had thought was his friend turned on him when he realised Dexter was different. *It's difficult to think that these are the same folk who despised people of magic and treated them with such cruelty. How did we strike such fear in them? Was there once a wicked clan of magicians or were they simply afraid of our powers? People often fear those who are different.*

He looked at the ground beneath his horse's hooves. The weed which had poisoned the land was dead now but the soil remained dry and powdery. No crops grew and some of the farmhouses had been abandoned. *We need more rain, and a lot of it, to wash the poison deep into the ground.*

The weather had been humid. Grey clouds blotted out the sun but had not darkened enough to bring the much needed rain. *Tannus should be here. He is so good at creating rain. Damn the man, he is good at everything he turns his hand to. I should be travelling to Barrmin and he should be here creating storms. It's too late to change things now, though, and I am intrigued by these gudger creatures. I must find out more about them and make sure I block any burrowings into the Forbidden Forest.*

Merlin recognised a farmer he had met before. *I remember clearing the weed from that man's fields. This could be an opportunity. The ordinary people seemed reluctant to speak to us before; probably because there were always Kernan soldiers around.*

He waved to the man, who waved back. Nevertheless the man looked somewhat taken aback when the eminent magician steered the white horse in his direction.

"Hello," said Merlin. "How are you?"

"I am not so bad, Lord Merlin, thank you for asking." The man gave a little bow.

"I notice that several of your neighbours have abandoned their farms."

"Aye, no crops mean no food or income," said the man. "They've moved to Twydell where that damned weed never spread. We'll be leaving soon, too. My boys have been ill; mumps followed by measles, but as soon as they are fit enough we will be making our way to Twydell, too."

"Have you any fresh water at your house? My horse is thirsty and so am I."

"Aye, clear fresh water from a spring which is still good to drink. We were afraid our water would become toxic when it started to rain and the poison from the weed started to sink deep into the ground."

"Yes, I must admit it is a risk," said Merlin. "Unfortunately, other than gradually washing the poison away I can think of no other way to make the soil safe again."

Merlin followed the man back to the house. It was a well kept place with a tidy yard. The horse trough was already full and Comet drank noisily. The man lowered the bucket into the well and drew fresh water for his visitor.

The only other animal in sight was a carthorse. The man explained that most of his livestock had died when the soil became poisoned. He had sold what remained except for the carthorse, which they would need to pull their belongings to neighbouring Twydell.

"I'd invite you in," he said, "but as I said, the boys are just recovering from their illnesses. I can bring you out a bowl of stew though. It's not much, just some barley we had stored from last year and few beans we had preserved in salt, but you are more than welcome."

"Oh, how very kind," said Merlin. "I'm sure I had mumps and measles when I was a child, so please don't worry about inviting me in. I would love to sit down for a while and meet your family."

Merlin couldn't really remember what childhood illnesses he had had. He simply decided that at the age of one hundred and thirty one, even if he hadn't had mumps or measles, he would be immune by now. Besides, somewhere in the back of his mind he remembered being told that magical beings didn't catch human diseases.

The kitchen was clean and tidy. A row of shiny pans hung above the stove where the pot of stew bubbled. The farmer's wife was not expecting visitors, let alone a revered figure like Merlin. Turning this way and that, she appeared flustered as to how she should greet him. Finally, putting her wooden spoon to one side, she curtsied low.

201

"Oh, please stand up my good woman. Don't bend your knee for me. My kindred bend the knee for no one, and expect no one to do so for us."

"Yes, my lord." The woman stood up before curtseying again. Her cheeks were flushed. She looked down at the floor, too bashful to glance at the wizard who was now standing in her kitchen.

"And I'm not a lord. I am simply Merlin, a wizard from Avalon. Actually now from the Forbidden Forest in Twydell." *I am now a Twydeller; I must remember that.*

He turned and nodded his head in greeting to the two boys. One lay on a couch, his neck so swollen that it stretched beyond his ears. The other sat on the end of the couch, his face a mass of red blotches. Both stared wide-eyed at the man in the strange garb to whom their father was now offering a seat at the kitchen table.

The woman placed the pot, half full of barley and bean stew on the table. "There's not a lot, Lord Merlin," she apologised.

"Ah, I can soon rectify that." In a swift movement the wizard drew his wand from his sleeve.

The husband and wife stepped back with looks of concern on their faces; the wife dropped the ladle she held on the floor. However, the wizard simply tapped the stew pot and muttered a few words. The contents of the pot swelled till the pot was filled.

"How did you do that?" the woman asked; her mouth fell open and her eyes almost popped out of her head.

The two boys stood up. They leaned over the table to see the product of the magician's spell. They were too astonished to utter a word.

The man, on seeing Merlin take something from his sleeve, had grabbed a rolling pin from the shelf. Now, realising that there had been no intention of inflicting any harm on his family, he put the rolling pin back in its original place. However, his actions had not gone unnoticed by the wizard.

Even after all I have done to free this country of the weed which could have killed them all, he is still afraid of me. Merlin felt quite sad.

"Thank you," said the man, a look of relief spreading across his weathered weary face. He shook his head, not knowing what to do. "Your trick is a blessing to us. We only have a little food. We put some cereal by each year in case of a bad harvest the next and try to preserve a few vegetables but it goes so quickly. We sold what livestock we had left to pay the rent and almost all that money has gone now."

"You still pay rent, even though the land is no longer arable?" Merlin enquired as the farmer's wife ladled stew into the bowl in front of him.

"Aye, we still live in the house, and Lord Jecquin's rent collector comes each week to demand what's due. The sooner we leave and find employment in Twydell the better. There is little work here in Kerner for a farmer."

"Perhaps I should have charged this Lord Jecquin for my labour. That weed would have engulfed the whole of Kerner if I had not cast my spells upon it. His land would not have earned much rent then."

The farmer and his wife said nothing. *They dare not criticize their overlord.*

"Do you ever see King Jeffrey?" Merlin enquired.

"He travels through occasionally," the husband replied. "King Jeffrey is more of a sea lord. He prefers to travel by ship than by road. He is a famous sailor."

Well, that's something I didn't know.

"If Lord Jecquin's men tell us the king is coming we go out and line the roads to greet him," the wife added. "We wave to him, and drop to our knees as he passes, as is expected of us. He waves back but never talks to us peasants. He even stopped here once so he and his men could water their horses. We offered bread and cheese which his men took to him and he sent back his thanks. He remained in his tent. He never spoke to us himself."

"Do you see much of Queen Shirley-Poppy?" asked Merlin.

"No, we have never seen her." The man spoke casually, as he supped his stew. "She is very shy. Her carriage travelled through on the way to the wedding of her son Steven to Princess Jeanette of Twydell. Her curtains were drawn shut."

"We hoped to get a glimpse of the queen with the new princess on their way back," the wife commented. "The princess pulled her curtain to one side; she seemed nice enough, she smiled and waved. We never saw the queen; she kept the curtains on her side of the carriage closed."

"We saw Prince Steven, though," the eldest boy joined in. "He smiled and called out a greeting as he rode by."

"Yes, I met him briefly at the wedding," said Merlin. "He seemed a nice young man."

"You went to the wedding!" The farmer's wife was in awe. "Oh, please tell us about it, Lord Merlin. What did the princess wear? Who else was there?"

"Just plain Merlin, please. I am not a Lord. My kind do not believe in all these titles." He paused to think. "I will make a bargain with you. Allow me to rest here the night and I will tell you all about the wedding. I have a little silver to pay for my bed and board. It is only a thin sliver of a Trajaen warrior's arm band. The Avalonians took the Trajaen's gold and silver when they defeated them at the Battle of Merlport."

"The Battle of Merlport!" the boys cried in unison. "Were you there?" asked the eldest lad. "Were you in the fighting?"

"Hmm... sort of," said Merlin. "If your parents are kind enough to allow me to stay I am sure there will be enough time to tell you about the battle as well."

"Of course, you are most welcome to stay with us!" The farmer was completely taken aback. "I never thought we would receive such an honoured guest in our home. We could not possibly accept payment from the person who freed our land of the poisonous weed."

"Thank you," said Merlin. "You are very generous. If you will not allow me to pay for my board, then please may I ask a great favour. If your boys are well enough, would they groom my horse? I am an old man and my bones ache when I make a long journey. If you will not take the silver for my board I will gladly give it to them for tending my horse."

The eldest boy looked eager.

"I'm not sure if my youngest is well enough," replied the man, "My eldest might like to help me feed and groom that fine stallion of yours though. We have a few oats..."

"Which I can double," said Merlin, "and double again, with my special spell."

Smiles spread across the faces of the farmer and his wife.

"Do you think you might be able to do something with our barley, too?" asked the wife timidly.

"Yes, but then I must rest. Magic looks easy but it is very tiring. When we have all finished our tasks for the day I will tell you about the Battle of Merlport to keep the boys happy and then I'll entertain their charming mother by telling her about the wedding."

It was not often anyone paid the farmer's wife a compliment. She beamed. "But before you get to work, I have a jar of cherries preserved in honey. We shall have it for our dessert. I've been saving it for a special occasion and today is very special. I never dreamt when I got up this morning that I would meet a wizard, let alone have one dine in my house!"

Merlin set off following the directions the farmer had given him. Comet's coat shone and his tail and mane flowed free of tangles.

The farmer and his family stood outside to wave their guest a fond farewell.

They are good people, he thought. *The silver will pay their rent and I have doubled sufficient quantities of the supplies they stored to keep them fed for a while.*

Although no one was apparent, he had a feeling he was being watched. It was a further two days' travel to reach the Sea View Palace. The second and third nights were spent at inns where the locals were polite but not as friendly as the farmer and his family had been. On the third night, whilst eating a meal, he saw two other travellers settle in the corner of the tavern. *I'm sure I've seen those two before. They stayed at the same tavern as I did last night.*

As he made his way to his room he smiled at the two burly men, took off his hat, bowed his head, and said, "How nice to see you again. I trust you are having a good trip, too. I am journeying to the Sea View Palace to see King Jeffrey, where are you heading?"

The two men looked at one another before one answered, "Our journey ends here. We have business in the village. We wish you a safe journey."

As was his usual practice when staying at a strange inn, Merlin put a charm on the door so that it would cry out if anyone opened it. He had a good night's sleep and the door remained silent. On enquiry with the landlord the next morning, he discovered that the two men had not stayed overnight. The landlord said he did not know who they were but Merlin sensed that the man had not been truthful.

The palace stood on a hill overlooking the sea. Merlin had imagined it to be like King Jeffrey himself, cold and dreary. He was not wrong. The exterior was austere in appearance – tall and built of grey stones. Merlin moved away from the road for a while and steered Comet to the cliff top. He stopped to take in the view. There was a shingle beach with a small expanse of sand but as he looked across the beach he saw jagged pieces of rock rising out of the steely waters. *A dangerous place for ships*, thought Merlin. *A sailor would have to know what he was doing to navigate these waters without damaging his vessel.* As he gazed across the horizon he saw what he thought was a tower sticking out of the water with no land surrounding it. *I wonder what that strange building is, a lighthouse perhaps?*

All the time that he sat on Comet, staring across the coast, he was aware of soldiers watching him. Some stood on guard duty on the road leading up to the palace; others practised sword craft on the surrounding green. None of the grim-looking soldiers outside the castle acknowledged him but he was allowed to pass unchallenged until he reached the closed drawbridge. A guard on the wall asked him who he was and what business had brought him to Sea View Palace.

"I am Merlin, a wizard from Avalon, now living in Twydell. I have come to visit King Jeffrey and Queen Shirley-Poppy. I have no doubt they will wish to see me."

Whilst the drawbridge guard disappeared others appeared on the wall to see the castle's odd looking visitor. Some might have seen him before whilst he worked to free their land of its poisonous weeds; others were probably curious to see the strange person they had heard so much about.

Merlin heard the drawbridge being lowered. He walked Comet slowly over the bridge and across the courtyard so that his eyes could drink in his surroundings. *What a barren looking place*, thought Merlin. *Not an ornament or flower in sight. Very different from King Frederrick's palace with its decorated walls and blooming rose bushes.*

A man in simple clothing greeted the wizard at a stone arch in front of a heavy wooden door.

"Lord Merlin, I bid you welcome. I am King Jeffrey's secretary. Let one of our grooms take care of your horse. I will take you to our king who is pleased to receive you." The man's smile was not mirrored in his eyes.

A young boy dressed in a rough brown jerkin and trousers bowed his head to the dismounting rider as he took Comet's reins. The boy averted his eyes to avoid any sign of greeting.

The wizard slung his broom's carrying case across his shoulder and dutifully followed the secretary up a long flight of stairs. *I'd have used my broom if I'd realised there were this many steps.*

At the top of the stairs was a long corridor, devoid of any pictures, at the end of which was the king's parlour.

The door was already open. Merlin could see the king sitting at a table laden with bread, slices of meat and a bowl of fruit. Two places were set.

"You were expecting me?" Merlin tried to sound surprised.

"Lord Jecquin's men saw you travelling through his land and sent word," replied the king. "Welcome, Lord Merlin, to what do we owe the pleasure of your visit?" King Jeffrey's face did not reflect the greetings in his words. "Please take a seat and you can tell me over our repast."

The secretary filled two goblets with a rich red wine. Merlin watched the king sip from his cup first before tasting his own. It was a very good vintage. He helped himself to food but waited for the king to start eating first before following his lead. *I've chosen my cuts, now let me watch Jeffrey swallow. I don't think he would try to poison me or drug me but I must be careful.*

"I thought it was time to take another look at the land to make sure that there were no new shoots of the poisonous weed," explained Merlin.

"My men check the land regularly for signs of new growth," replied the king. "If any new plants were noticed we would have called on you immediately. Nevertheless, I thank you for your concern."

"It is a pity that there has been no rain," continued Merlin. "It is so humid; each day I think the weather will break and bring a much needed shower – but no such luck."

"No, it is a pity that young man who created the rain clouds for us before has not returned. Is there any chance you could bring him back?" asked the king. "As you say. Kerner needs rain."

"Ah, you mean Tannus," said Merlin. "No, I am afraid not. You will not have heard our news. I am retiring to the Forbidden Forest with my wife. We are expecting twins, you know?"

"Yes, so I have heard. Congratulations." Jeffrey uttered the words with no warmth in his voice.

"Tannus, the young warlock who is skilled in creating rain, has been elected as the new leader of the wizards of Avalon."

Merlin detected a flicker of interest in King Jeffrey's normally expressionless face.

"Then I must send him my best wishes for success in his new role. I hope the friendship between your people and those of Kerner will continue under Lord Tannus's leadership."

Friendship? Is that what he calls this stalemate? He knows we would take action if any more of our kind or children are found in his prisons. No doubt he remembers the display of angry spells my people cast when we saw how badly the Kernans had treated their prisoners.

210

Just then Merlin became aware of the sound of laughter, and looked towards an open window. Jeffrey paid no attention to the noise coming from outside.

Merlin continued, trying to ignore the distraction. "I'm sure the friendship between your kind and mine will flourish now all magical beings have been released from cells and cages."

"How are the magicians and the children we released into your care? You know, of course, that I had no idea they were being held."

"Yes, you have told me before that you did not know of their existence. I am sad to say that we lost some of the fairies and elves; they were too sick for even the most skilled healers to restore to health."

Merlin expected the king to squirm at the revelation. However, Jeffrey showed no sign of guilt as he continued his meal.

"The children, on the other hand, have all recovered. They are fit and well and being trained to use their magical talents."

"Good, I am glad to hear they are better." Jeffrey's voice was toneless.

"One of the wizards is recovering, but the other two are making slower progress."

"I hope their progress continues."

The sound of women's voices outside rose into shrieks of merriment. "What is that noise?" asked Merlin. "I can hear people laughing." Too curious to remain seated any longer, and without being invited to do so, he rose from his place and crossed to the open window. Leaning out, he was surprised to see a most beautiful garden full of colourful flowers below; it was a marked contrast to the palace courtyard. In the middle of the garden was Queen Shirley-Poppy along with a woman who looked remarkably like her. They held sticks with what appeared to be small clubs at the end. The queen used her stick to strike a small round object which shot through an arch built in a miniature wall. The other lady placed a ball in the same spot as that in which the queen's had been placed. She was about to strike the ball when Merlin called out to them.

"Good afternoon, ladies," he yelled.

The two women looked up. The queen stood with her mouth wide open staring at the wizard waving to her from the window above. Her companion dropped her stick and ran off, pushing herself between a cluster of large plants which hid her from sight.

"Oh, dear, you have alarmed Hyacinth." Jeffrey looked out of the adjoining window. Merlin glanced sideways and could not fail to see the annoyance on the king's usually expressionless face.

"Good afternoon to you, Lord Merlin," called out a friendly voice. He hadn't noticed Princess Jeanette, who had been sitting on a bench beneath an overhanging tree. Jeanette was the daughter of the King of Twydell who had recently married Prince Steven of Kerner. She was now on her feet and waving as she made her way to stand at the queen's side. The queen looked at her daughter-in-law and copied the young woman's example by waving too. She even managed a smile.

"Don't worry about Aunt Hyacinth, I'll explain it is only a friend paying a visit," Jeanette reassured her father-in-law.

"Poppy and her sister are very shy." The king made his way back to the table and indicated to his guest to do the same. "My wife has come out of her shell to some extent over the years but Hyacinth is still as timid as ever."

"I am sorry for frightening her," said Merlin. His apology was genuine. "They seemed to be having such a good time and I spoilt it for them. What were they doing?"

"Oh, it's a game their father devised for them called Strike the Ball. Now come, let us finish our meal. It is a pleasure to have company. We have few visitors. Tell me more about your successor. What are his plans for the future?"

He's showing an interest. He wants to know what Tannus is up to.

"He wishes our young warlocks to continue with defensive training—"

"Defensive – not attack?" King Jeffrey interrupted.

"We are not an aggressive people. We would not attack anyone unless they threatened us first!"

"Then we have much in common."

"Yes, indeed," said Merlin, but he was no longer interested in his conversation with King Jeffrey. "I am intrigued by your good wife's game. I take it they have to strike a ball and get it under the arch?"

"Yes, under the arch and past many other obstacles, too. What else does Lord Tannus have planned?"

"Tannus, just Tannus, and I am simply Merlin. Our kind do not have titles. Now, let me see. Tannus and Esmerelda are travelling to Barrden to the wedding of Princess Delphine of Barrmin to Duke William of Vanddalasia. Sadly I will not be able to attend…"

Jeffrey stopped eating and looked straight at the wizard. "They have accepted an invitation from the King of Barrmin to his daughter's wedding?" He put down his fork. "I am most surprised. You know it was *that* man who sold us the bags of so-called fertiliser which turned out to be the seeds of poisonous weed!"

"Yes, but do you think he knew what was really in those bags?" asked Merlin. "The Barrmen also used it thinking it was fertiliser. Their land endured a far greater devastation than that suffered by Kerner."

"I suspect that when the King of Barrmin realised what the bags really contained he sold what he had left to us!" continued the outraged king. "He intended ruining my country! His fleet could never match mine in battle. But he probably thought that, by weakening my land, his chances of a potential invasion would increase. He has invaded all the small countries in the North. You know he is a descendent of the Trajaens, don't you? The same race which attacked Avalon. The King of Barrmin is not a man I would trust!"

For once I am in agreement with Jeffrey, thought Merlin. *But I will remain diplomatic.* "Barrmin is our neighbour," said Merlin. "That is to say, Avalon's neighbour. Tannus and King Arthur must try to maintain a good relationship with its leader. Avalon and Barrmin are doing quite a lot of trade now."

"Hah, I thought it would be good to trade with the Barrmen. We offered fair bargains and what did we get in return? The seeds of a malicious plant disguised as fertiliser!"

Peals of laughter could be heard again from the garden below.

"Ah, Hyacinth has got over her fright. That's a relief," sighed Jeffrey as he poured more wine for his visitor, and water for himself.

Merlin had a strong desire to take another look through the window but did not dare to do so. Instead he gave the king a genuine smile and said, "It would be such a pleasure to renew your charming wife's acquaintance and meet the lovely Princess Jeanette again. I would also like the opportunity to apologise to the lady who I frightened." Jeffrey gave the wizard a quizzical look. "I would deem it an honour to watch them play that very curious game," continued Merlin. "Do you think they would teach me? If you were kind enough to invite me to stay overnight we could talk politics later but it's been a long journey and I would be grateful for a little respite."

"You are genuinely interested, aren't you? How odd." Jeffrey knitted his brows. "I am expecting other visitors so I will take you down to meet them but be careful not to upset Hyacinth again. She is not used to strangers."

The king called his secretary. "Have the maids make up a room for Lord Merlin. He will be spending the night here. We will be out in Her Majesty's Pleasure Garden for a while. Do not disturb us unless the matter is of importance."

Instructions given, King Jeffrey led his visitor to the garden below.

The back stairs were even longer than the front ones, because the garden was at a lower level. As they reached the bottom King Jeffrey spoke to Merlin. A serious expression spread across his humourless features. "Not a word about politics in front of the girls. They get upset and worry unnecessarily."

"Not a word," promised the wizard.

CHAPTER 11 – Strike The Ball

"Poppy, Hyacinth, look who is here to see you." King Jeffrey crossed the lawn towards the two women. Both stopped what they were doing and stared at the wizard, who was now standing in the garden. "Lord Merlin is interested in your game. He has asked if he can join you."

The queen managed a forced smile. Hyacinth hurried to her sister's side and stood, still as a statue, beside her.

Jeanette rose once again from her seat in the shade of a tree, the like of which Merlin had never seen before. Its drooping branches were covered in large triangular leaves which were so deep a shade of blue that they appeared almost black. The Princess, a natural hostess, held her hand out to receive the visitor's kiss. "Welcome, Lord Merlin. What a pleasant surprise. We are so pleased to see you."

"And I am most pleased to see you, too." The wizard bowed slightly before stepping forward and taking the princess's hand and kissing her fingertips.

The guest then turned towards the queen. Again, he bowed slightly and stepped forward to kiss the hand she offered. As he brushed his lips against her fingers he could feel her trembling. *I didn't realise that she was such a nervous woman.*

"It is such a pleasure to renew our acquaintance. There was so little opportunity to speak at your son's wedding." Merlin spoke in his most gentle voice.

The queen muttered something inaudible, so Merlin simply nodded.

"May I introduce you to my sister-in-law, Lady Hyacinth." Jeffrey looked anxious.

He is worried she will run off again. Merlin understood how worried the king must have been.

This time Merlin took a slight bow but stood back. Hyacinth looked so frightened she had turned white and remained motionless.

"I am so sorry to have alarmed you earlier. It was such a foolish thing to do. I don't know what I was thinking of, shouting out of the window in the way I did. Please forgive me." He stepped forward and took Lady Hyacinth's hand, which continued to lay at her side. He gently lifted her fingers to his lips. *The woman is frozen with fear. She is like a doll with no movement of her own; if I release her hand it will simply fall back to her side.* Merlin carefully returned the lady's hand to its original position.

"Poppy, dear, would you be so kind as to show Merlin how you play Strike the Ball?" The king spoke to his wife in a kindly tone of voice. "He is fascinated by the game. In fact, I could hold him back no longer."

The queen lowered her head and seemed unable to raise it again to look at the wizard or her husband. "Oh, Jeffrey, I would make such a fool of myself. You are such a good player, you should show him." As she spoke her face gradually turned scarlet.

"Isn't she adorable?" said King Jeffrey, smiling at the plain looking woman in front of him. It was the first time Merlin had seen him smile. Poppy, as he called her, was short and plump with a round face and mousey hair. She averted her pale blue eyes as her husband spoke.

So this is the chink in his armour.

"Oh, very well. It is such a long time since I played. This will be a chance to get some much needed practice." The king turned. "Roger, my striking stick, please, and one for Lord Merlin, too."

Merlin turned to see who Roger was. At first he could see no one. A few seconds later a servant, with bare feet and rolled up trousers, came out from behind some bushes. He carried two sticks with club-like ends, very similar to those used by the queen and her sister. However, the sticks were longer than those used by the shorter women and Jeffrey's personal stick was made of silver. The one handed to Merlin was, like those used by the women, made of wood.

"Thank you, Roger," said Merlin as he took the stick from the servant. *I wonder why he has bare feet and rolled up trousers. How very peculiar.*

"Now the object of the game," Jeffrey explained, "is to get the ball around the course, hitting it as few times as possible. Roger will keep a record of the number of strikes you make but, if you wish, you may also mark them down on your personal scoreslate. Experienced as he is, it is not impossible for Roger to make a mistake."

Roger reappeared with two small pieces of slate; each had two silver chains attached. One chain linked to a chunk of white chalk, the other to a hook.

"You attach the hook to your belt, like so," Jeffrey demonstrated how the hook attached to his belt buckle. "As you don't wear a belt around that gown of yours, I'm not sure how you would carry yours."

"I'll keep it in my pocket. Wizards always have deep pockets. We need to carry so many things."

"Wizzzzard..." Hyacinth spoke for the first time. She looked aghast at their visitor.

"Yes, but a good wizard." Jeffrey spoke firmly but kindly. "Lord Merlin has helped us rid our land of a particularly nasty weed. He has returned to make sure it has not re-grown. There is no need to be afraid of him."

The king turned back to his guest so as to draw his attention away from his timid sister-in-law.

"Now this mark is the starting point." He indicated a cross on the ground in front of some brightly coloured flowers. "The course represents my voyage from sunny lands to get home to my dear Poppy. I tell you what, let's put the scoreslates to one side and have a trial run." He removed the scoreslate from his belt and threw it to the ground. "These flowers are lobelia," continued the king. "I brought plants back from one of the islands where my ship docked."

"They really are exquisite," remarked Merlin. "I have never seen such brilliant purple and red blooms before."

"See, there is a little gravel path through the lobelia. You have to gently strike the ball so that it falls into the path and down its slope."

Roger had brought out a selection of small balls, no more than an inch and a half in diameter. They were made of leather but painted different colours.

"Pick a colour," instructed the king. "I will take... grey." The king placed the ball in the allocated spot and expertly struck it with his silver stick. It landed on the path, which was about four inches wide, and rolled down the slope until it came to a halt on a level surface. "Now you try."

Merlin threw his hat and the carrying case, he had strapped to his back, to the ground. He selected a red ball, placed his ball on the marked spot and struck it with the wooden club. The ball landed in amongst the flowers.

The king picked it up and handed it back. "If you miss you have to start again." Merlin tried again. Once more his ball landed in the lobelias from where he retrieved it. "Third time lucky," he grinned, and sure enough this time the red ball landed on the path and rolled down to take its place beside the king's grey one.

"That is three strokes to my one," Jeffrey stated. "In a scored game I would be two points in front of you."

"Well done," said Jeanette. "It took me a lot longer to get started the first time I played. It must have taken me at least five strokes for my ball to find the path."

Jeffery took a wider grass path, to the spot where the ball had ended up, so that he would not have to tread on the flowers. He moved Merlin's red ball to one side with his stick and proceeded to strike his grey one again. This time it rose slightly into the air and landed the other side of a square hole.

"There are animal traps in many of the islands where my ship has been docked. Sometimes I fear they are there to ensnare men, too. You have to hit your ball so that it avoids the trap and lands on the far side."

Merlin took his place and tried several times to hit his ball across the square hole. He got tired of leaning over to pick it up and without thinking held out his hand and called the ball to him. The red ball rose out of the hole and back to the hand he held out to catch it. He heard gasps from the women behind him.

"It's cheating to use magic," Jeffrey said sternly.

"I used it only to retrieve my ball," Merlin protested. "My back is old and aches if I bend too often. I would not use it to give myself any unfair advantage in the actual game."

"Oh, very well," Jeffrey conceded. "But be careful not to alarm the girls if you do it again."

"Alright, I'll shout out 'magic trick' before doing it again."

"Speak, do not shout," Jeffrey stated.

"Agreed. I'll say 'magic trick' next time." Merlin turned towards the women to apologise for his behaviour. He was surprised to see Poppy, as well as Jeanette, smiling at him.

"Oh, please, do use magic." The queen spoke shyly, averting her eyes. "I do so like magic tricks. I remember the falling stars at Steven and Jeannette's wedding. I told Hyacinth all about it, didn't I Hy?"

Although her eyes looked at the ground, Hyacinth nodded her head enthusiastically.

I'm making progress!

Having at last got his ball across the 'animal trap', the red and grey balls advanced through various obstructions within a miniature forest.

"How exquisite. I assume you brought these tiny trees back from one of the places you visited across the sea?" asked Merlin. He was genuinely fascinated.

Jeffrey told him that a race of foreigners he had met had developed the art of cutting tree roots. The trimmed roots allowed tiny forms of the larger varieties to grow and flourish. He had indeed brought some of the miniatures back to create the forest which grew around their feet.

Merlin's ball followed the king's over bridges and through tunnels till it met a rod on which a line of toy monkeys swung. Merlin noticed Roger winding a handle which rotated the row of clay monkeys, which didn't necessarily all turn at the same time. The game required the players to get the balls past the moving animals. The king managed the obstacle in two strikes of the ball. The wizard however found that if his ball was not knocked back by a monkey's head then it would be hit by a swinging tail or a body. It took eight strokes to catch up with the king. After his first failure, he said, "Magic trick," and the ball flew back to his hand ready for another try; on each such occasion the women clapped and laughed. *I don't feel such a failure at this game when I keep them amused.*

Jeffrey, however, maintained a serious expression on his face.

"Now this is an interesting obstacle." The king pointed to a small wooden ship floating on a pond. "You have to hit the ball onto the deck, like so…" He swiped the grey ball but it simply plopped into the water.

Roger appeared from behind some water reeds, stepped into the water which was knee deep and retrieved the ball. He wiped the ball dry with a cloth before bowing and handing it back to the king.

So that is why he has bare feet and rolled up trousers.

Roger gently moved back a pace, ready to act again if necessary. Jeffrey waited for the ripples on the water to calm before making a second strike; he missed and it took several other unsuccessful attempts. Roger dutifully retrieved the ball, dried it and returned it to the king after each failed strike. Eventually it landed on the deck of the model ship.

"At last. That's always a tricky one and I'm out of practice. Now, you must not touch the boat with your stick but gently stir the water around it until it arrives in port over there." Jeffrey walked along beside the ship encouraging it to move forward by gently creating waves behind the stern. "When it reaches port you are allowed to pick up the ball and place it in front of the market."

Merlin copied the king. He found it very hard to hit the ball into the boat. Roger stood by ready to recover the ball but he was not needed. "Magic trick," stated the wizard and the ball splashed back out of the stream to his waiting hand. However, he found this obstacle most difficult and eventually decided to cheat. As he rubbed the ball dry on his sleeve he muttered a few words under his breath and with the next stroke landed the ball perfectly on the ship. The ladies applauded his achievement but the king looked at him suspiciously.

Winding the ball through the impediments among market stands was not too hard to achieve but hitting it up the slope of a volcano and striking it across the top was not at all easy. The top of the volcano was almost horizontal to his arms. He had to hit the ball across to the other side without letting it fall within the gaping hole at the summit. If it fell into the hole it rolled through the volcano and landed back at the wizard's feet, ready for him to start the journey to the top again.

The secretary appeared at one point and told the king that visitors awaited him. The king seemed to know who had come to call because he simply told the secretary to tell them to wait.

The game continued through flowers and over bridges until the balls arrived back at the stream again.

Oh, not another ship, thought Merlin. *I don't want to have to cheat again.* But this time the player was required to hit the ball from dry land, across the water and into the top of a solitary tower which poked out of the water.

Now where have I seen a tower like that one before?

The king took just one stroke to hit the target. The ball could be heard tumbling down the inside of the tower. It then became silent for a while and Merlin was surprised to see the grey ball fall out of a tube onto an area covered by sand on the other side of the stream.

The king apologised that he had to leave as he had people waiting to see him. However, before he left he finished the course in order to show Merlin what he needed to do. He easily negotiated his grey ball through a zigzag path of stone obstacles until it arrived at what Merlin recognised as a model of the Sea View Palace.

Ah, that solitary tower is the one I saw from the cliffs when I arrived.

Jeffrey skilfully struck the ball across the drawbridge and finally into the archway at the front of the palace.

"Home at last," he declared. "Now, please do excuse me, I must speak to my visitors. Lord Merlin, you will no doubt wish to freshen up before dinner? Someone will show you to your room when you are ready. You will be called when dinner is served. I am afraid I will have no time for you tomorrow as I have already arranged a meeting with the lords who oversee my lands."

"Oh, I was hoping to have just a little more time with you before I leave," said Merlin. He had been so anxious to play the game of Strike the Ball that he had not yet broached the real subject of his visit.

Jeffrey levelled his gaze at the wizard. His softened features hardened once more.

He warned me not to talk politics in front of the ladies. "It is just a small matter," explained Merlin. "I wished to seek your advice before making my way home."

"Oh, if you want advice Jeffrey is your man," said Poppy, smiling happily. "He is very wise. He has journeyed far and has gained much knowledge."

"Yes, he has," agreed Hyacinth, who now felt sufficiently confident to speak. "He is a very knowledgeable man."

The king continued to look at Merlin. He did not flinch. "Very well, we will meet before dinner. I will have someone call for you when I am ready."

"Thank you, King Jeffrey." Merlin bowed his head to give the appearance of being humble.

The king gave him a sideways glance as he left.

Then Merlin completed the obstacle course whilst Queen Shirley-Poppy organised refreshments to be brought to them in the garden.

Flowers in a variety of colours climbed over a gazebo providing shade over an ornate iron table. The wizard allowed the ladies to choose their seats before taking his own. Hyacinth selected a seat between her sister and Jeanette.

"Lord Merlin, what would you like?" asked one of the servants who brought the afternoon refreshments. "We have ale, cider, wine or lemon water."

"Lemon water, what is that?" asked Merlin. "I've never heard of it before."

It was Jeanette who answered. "Lemons are yellow fruits from over the seas. They are very sharp and you could not eat them on their own. Cook squeezes out the juice, blends it with honey, or a sweet granulated product called sugar, and then dissolves the mixture in hot water. When it cools it is quite delicious and refreshing."

"I'll try the lemon water, please," said Merlin, full of enthusiasm to have the opportunity to try something new.

"Do try one of cook's cakes, too." Jeanette encouraged the wizard to try one of the delicacies which were placed on a plate in the middle of the table. "Cook travelled with my father-in-law on his ship. He learnt the foreigners' recipes for using the strange fruits and spices they brought home."

Merlin chose one of the small cakes on offer. It was sweet with flakes of a white nut sprinkled over the top.

"Mmm… very flavoursome, I have not experienced anything quite like it before. Well, I have to say, when I set off on my journey three days ago I never expected to be sitting in such a delightful garden, enjoying lemon water and cake with three charming ladies."

Poppy and Hyacinth cooed in harmony, fluttering their eyelashes and averting their eyes. Their cheeks turned pink.

Jeanette smiled. "It is so nice to have a visitor."

"Very nice," Poppy agreed.

"I had a letter from my mother. She tells me you have married a Twydeller and you are now living in the Forbidden Forest." Jeanette had a mischievous look on her face. "My mother tells me your wife is expecting little visitors herself."

"Yes, that it true." Merlin smiled broadly. "I am very proud to admit that I am going to be the father of twins."

"Twins," Poppy and Hyacinth echoed in unison.

"What a wonderful gift, Merlin." Poppy looked at him with a sincerity he had not recognised in her before.

"A double gift," sighed Hyacinth. "We haven't had a baby in our house since Steven was born."

"The only baby in the house that we have ever had." Poppy looked wistful.

"Where is Steven?" asked the wizard. "Will I see him at dinner?"

"Steven is away," answered Princess Jeanette, the smile wiped from face. "He has been appointed Admiral of the Fleet. I am not expecting him home for several months."

"I know how you must feel, my dear." Poppy spoke soothingly to her daughter-in-law. "When I came to live here, and Jeffrey was at sea, I used to climb to the top of the castle every day to see if I could see his ship on the horizon."

"There was no need," commented Hyacinth. "The guards would have raised the alarm as soon as a lamp was lit in the lighthouse. But you were always the same, staring out to sea, hoping his ship would suddenly appear."

"The lighthouse, is that the tall tower sticking up out of the sea?" Merlin asked, looking at the obstacle course, tracking King Jeffrey's journeys home, and focused on the tall piece of stonework in the middle of the water. "Have you ever visited it?"

"Visited?" Poppy looked surprised. "We used to live there!"

"Our grandfather used to be the lighthouse keeper," Hyacinth explained. "We went to live with our grandfather when mummy died."

228

"We were very young. We don't remember our mother," Poppy added. "Our father was Admiral of the Fleet and spent his time sailing the seas. When he was home he was always busy doing reports and things so we didn't see a lot of him." The queen described how difficult it was for the sailors to get home. "The coast around Kerner is full of jagged rocks and the fleet has to dock far out at sea. If the tide is in, the sailors use tender boats to get to the lighthouse. They tie the tenders up at the lighthouse and then they take smaller boats to get to the coast. When the tide is out, all the sailors need to do is use the small boats to come ashore."

"When the tide is out," continued Hyacinth, "there is a small sandy beach around the lighthouse. Grandfather made some wooden hoops and a ball out of seaweed." She stared up at the sky as she spoke, as if visualising the scene. "We took it in turn to use an old broom handle to hit the balls through the hoops. When father was at home he used to play too."

"One day when father came home he brought a handsome young sea captain with him." Poppy giggled as her cheeks turned pink. "We were told he was a prince and we had to curtsey to him. We were petrified in case we did something wrong but he was really very nice. Can you guess who he was?" she asked Merlin.

"Mmm… let me think, was his name Jeffrey by any chance?"

"Yes, of course it was!" the sisters answered in unison, clapping their hands.

"It was love at first sight," the queen sighed, as her face now turned completely scarlet. "After that he came whenever he could – which wasn't often because he spent so long at sea and then when he did come home he was always busy with the affairs of state."

"But he's home now almost all the time," Hyacinth added.

The queen turned to her daughter-in-law and spoke with a tender voice. "Now don't you fret Jeanette, my dear, Steven will be home soon. He will serve his years as Admiral of the Fleet and meet all the foreign leaders then he will come home to stay. Hyacinth and I will help to keep you amused until he returns."

"I know," said Hyacinth. "Let's play another game of Strike the Ball. That will bring a smile back to your face, Jeanette, my dear."

Poppy nodded, "Who wants to play next? I know, why don't we play in teams? We could draw lots to see who plays with who."

"Well, we haven't played in teams for a long time!" her sister commented.

"We haven't had four people willing to play at the same time for a long time, that's why," Poppy replied. "We are so lucky to have Merlin here."

The sisters giggled. They were obviously very happy to have such an informal visitor. Jeanette ordered Roger to bring her stick.

The servant dutifully returned with the princess's personal stick. He also brought four reeds, the ends of which were hidden in his hands. The players chose their reed, two of which were short and two long. Merlin and Jeanette drew short straws and formed a team to play against Poppy and Hyacinth. The sisters had obviously become very skilled at the game over the years and, despite some unnoticed cheating by the magician, they were the outright winners.

"Congratulations." The wizard raised a glass of lemon water to honour the triumphant sisters. "You are very good. I hope we have time for another game tomorrow before I leave."

"I hope so, too," Poppy responded shyly. "Merlin, may I ask you a favour?"

"Please do, my lady."

"I see you have your broomstick in that bag. Would you demonstrate it to Hyacinth, please? I saw you and your friends flying off when you left Dalton Palace. I told Hyacinth about it and she couldn't believe what I was telling her. Would you show her how it works, please?"

"Oh, yes, please let us see you fly!" This time it was Princess Jeanette who echoed the queen.

Merlin didn't hesitate to remove the broom and sit side saddle across its handle. The broom took off vertically. As he rose Merlin could look above the high wall which surrounded the garden and into the courtyard below. He saw horses being brought for two men whom he recognised as being the same pair as he had seen at the inns in which he had spent the last couple of nights."

Ah, spies with very little to tell their king. How I have wasted their time. I'd best make a swift landing in case Jeffrey thinks I am now spying on him!

Returning to the ground, with a round of applause from both the ladies and their servants, he took his leave and asked to be shown to his room.

It was a plain room with basic furnishings but it had a good view of the sea and the solitary tower poking out of its depth. *What a lonely life it must have been living out there with just their grandfather. It is no wonder the sisters are so reserved.*

He lay on his bed considering how best to broach the subject of gudgers with the king. Despite the plain ambience of the room, the bed was very comfortable. The wizard nodded off to sleep.

He was awoken by a sharp knock at the door. *Goodness I haven't brushed my beard nor combed my hair, let alone washed my face.*

"Just one moment," he called out. He splashed water, which had been left for him in a bowl, across his face and wiped it with a towel. He was annoyed to see that the towel was left with streaks of dirt. Next, he delved into his pockets for a comb and tried hastily to remove the worst tangles from his beard.

That will have to do. I must not keep the king waiting when he has agreed to see me for a second time today. It would be very rude and I do not wish to upset him any more than I may have done already.

King Jeffrey sat at his table, his secretary stood at his side. Both eyed the visitor with a cold stare.

"What would you like to drink?" asked the King. "We have ale or wine. I will not partake. I prefer water when I need my wits about me."

"I will take a mug of ale, please." Merlin sat opposite his host. A servant brought a silver tankard and filled it with dark ale.

"Now, I trust, you will tell me the real purpose of your visit." Jeffrey's voice was cold.

"It is a confidential matter, sire." Merlin lowered his head. He decided to be polite and act meekly.

Jeffrey nodded to his secretary and servant. Both bowed respectfully before leaving.

"When your man brought the children to us he mentioned that their places had been taken in the mines by strong creatures. He suggested they were willing workers."

"Do you have any objection to the employment of strong, willing workers in our mines?"

"None whatsoever, sire. I just wondered whether you would you be so kind as to describe these creatures to me?"

"Hah! So that's it! You want some of my gudgers! Well, you can't have them. I want *more*, not less. You go and find your own workers!"

"No, no, sire. That is not the reason for my enquiry. I simply wish to know if they are aggressive and whether they would attack a person. Might they even kill someone?"

"We have had no problem with them." Jeffrey narrowed his eyes. "No more beating about the bush, out with it man, what do you want?"

"It is a confidential matter, sire." Merlin shifted uneasily in his seat.

"I have ordered my secretary and my servant out. No one else is listening to this conversation. Either you have something to say or you don't. If what you have to say has nothing to do with me, or my country, I will have no reason to divulge anything you have to say. If it affects Kerner in any way, that is another matter and I cannot promise to keep your secrets."

He makes a fair point. Well, let's go with it. Merlin had made up a story which he hoped would extract the information he needed, but he didn't like telling lies because there was always a risk he would be found out. If the conversation went as he hoped, he could provide misinformation but, at the same time, not be untruthful.

233

He would make no mention of Zanadoo or the goblins that lived there.

"When we came to Avalon," continued Merlin, "we brought with us what we believed was the last unicorn in Briton."

"Really?" King Jeffrey raised his eyebrows slightly. "I have travelled far and wide and heard of such creatures but never seen one. A horse-like creature with a single horn, I believe."

"Yes, exactly, and reputed to have magical qualities which is why they were hunted to near extinction in Briton. If it were known that such animals dwelt with us, we would be afraid of stepping in and out of the Forbidden Forest in case hunters lay in wait."

"You said you had brought one unicorn with you, now you speak as if there were more."

"Yes, there is a small herd in the forest. Its existence has been a secret. Now I confide that secret in you."

"So there were unicorns in the forest all the time and I never knew! Well then, I give you my oath that I will tell no one. However, I do not see what business it is of mine; the Forbidden Forest borders Kerner but is on Twydell soil."

"I will come to the point and waste no more of your time," continued Merlin. "The vine which seals our forest spreads across the tree tops and lets in little light. We need to take the unicorns outside the forest sometimes to graze..."

"And our hunters sometimes wander on to Twydell land in search of prey; particularly as wild beasts have left our poisoned soil. If you wish me to pass a law banning the killing of unicorns then so be it, but if I do the existence of your herd will no longer remain a secret."

"Er, no, that is not the favour I wish to ask you. A little man used to look after the foals. He was with one of the foals one day when lizard-like creatures suddenly rose out of a hole in the ground. They grabbed the little man and carried him off. They tried to take the unicorn foal too but he fought back. In the fight the gudgers, as I believe they were, grabbed its horn and tore it from his head."

"Now you have my attention." Jeffrey looked Merlin in the eye. "Why didn't you tell me before? This is serious business. I cannot have violent creatures working in my mines. They could harm my guards and if they ventured elsewhere could wreak havoc. However, I have to admit what you say surprises me. When the gudgers first burrowed their way into our mines we were, as you can imagine, concerned. Even the strongest of my men would be no match for those powerful beasts in combat. The guards were on full alert. I posted archers around the mines in case of trouble."

"Very wise," Merlin observed. "Your men may not be able to beat them in arm to arm combat but a skilled archer can easily find his target."

"I went to see the gudgers myself. Despite their formidable appearance they seemed humble animals, or perhaps I should say reptiles. We have had twenty or more working for us for over half a year now. They expect little reward, a few pennies in exchange for hard labour, which strangely enough they like spending on clothing. They have never caused any trouble. Their only downside is their smell; their stench is atrocious. Your story of an aggressive band of gudgers surprises me but I am glad you have told me. I must take precautions."

"But you will say nothing of our unicorns?" asked Merlin.

"I said I would not."

"Thank you, King Jeffrey. I trust your word." Merlin hesitated as if considering his words – although in reality they were already planned. "May I speak to one of your gudgers? We would very much like to rescue the man they kidnapped."

"Kidnapped? You think he is still alive?"

"I hope so," replied Merlin.

"This man," asked the king, "why is he so important to you?"

"Is not every man and woman important?"

"Don't turn this conversation round in circles, Merlin. Be honest with me. Who is he?"

"He is a little man who cared for some unicorn foals which had been abandoned. On that subject I wish to say no more but the foals are very upset. Perhaps if the man had not tried to protect them he might not have been carried away. He was still alive when young Flambeau saw him being carried down the tunnel they had dug; they made no attempt to kill him at the time, so there is a chance he is still alive."

"Who is Flambeau? This is the first mention of him."

"Flambeau is the oldest of the unicorn foals which the man cared for," explained Merlin.

"So how do you know what this unicorn foal saw?"

"He told me what he had seen. He was very precise. The gudgers carried the little man off. They did not attempt to kill him."

"A talking unicorn?" Jeffrey leaned back in his chair. "It is a good thing I decided not to have a glass of wine otherwise I would be sure it had gone to my head."

The wizard remained very calm. "I speak the language of the unicorn." *I won't say horse otherwise he will be afraid to let me near his stables.*

Jeffrey stared at his guest. He said nothing.

He is wondering if I am sane. Merlin surpressed a smile. "Is it so surprising that I can speak to unicorns when your gudgers have learnt to speak the human language?"

Jeffrey considered this for a while. "No, perhaps it is not. A year ago I never thought I would see a man fly through the air on the handle of a brush. Your talents never cease to amaze me. How did you know the gudgers had learnt to speak?"

"One of the boys who you released into our care heard them."

Jeffrey nodded. "I see. Let me think on this for a while."

The servant had left a pitcher of ale on the table. The king indicated to Merlin to help himself and so Merlin refilled his tankard and drank. Meanwhile, the king paced over to his window and looked out across the garden; he was deep in thought. He paced back and forth for a while before returning to the table. He did not sit but stood behind his chair looking down at his guest.

"Merlin, how would you like to spend another night at the Sea View Palace? I have a busy day tomorrow. I believe I told you the lords who oversee my lands will attend to make their regular reports. The following day I will travel with you to one of the mines where the gudgers work. Your request to interview a gudger is granted. I will attend the interview with you."

I did not foresee Jeffrey coming with me but I have no choice other than to accept. I can only hope that, if these gudgers know about the kidnap, they do not refer to the Goblin King or the mines in Zanadoo.

"If you can spare the time," said Merlin, "that would be good – but I do not wish to take up more of your busy schedule than necessary."

"Do you take me for a fool?" asked the king. "I have no doubt there is more to this story than you are telling me. As long as what you fail to reveal does not affect Kerner then I could not care a bean. You can keep your talking unicorns and sealed forest; I'm not interested. What does worry me – and there has been a nagging doubt in my mind since the gudgers first arrived – is whether these creatures have an ulterior motive for being here. At first we treated them as beasts of burden but as you say, they have learnt to talk; they are an intelligent animal."

Merlin looked his host straight in the eye. "We understand each other well, King Jeffrey. I accept your offer. I would be delighted to stay for another night and enjoy the company of your charming ladies. We will speak to the gudgers together."

"Alas," said the king, "there is one flaw in your carefully thought out plan."

Merlin had been feeling smug. Now he did not feel so confident.

"The mines where the gudgers work are situated on lands belonging to Lord Jecquin. The mines belong to the crown but he manages them on our behalf. I cannot simply ride in and demand to speak to the gudgers without him wondering why. I believe you will have to bring Lord Jecquin into your confidence. If you don't, he will simply question the gudgers after we leave and find out for himself. It would only be natural for him to want to know the reason that one of his workers is being interviewed by his king and a renowned magician."

Lord Jecquin, thought Merlin, *the landowner who charges his tenants rent even if they have no income to pay.*

"This Jecquin," asked Merlin, "is he a trustworthy man?

"He is loyal to his king," replied Jeffrey. "If I command him not to speak of unicorns and put down any rumours of their existence he will do as I bid. That should be enough."

Merlin had no choice other than to agree.

The ladies were awaiting the arrival of the king and his guest in the dining room. As was customary they waited for the king to arrive before taking their seats.

"I am sorry we are late for dinner, my dears. Merlin and I have had some interesting business to discuss. Come let us all take our places."

Jeffrey and Poppy sat at either end of the oblong table. Hyacinth and Jeanette sat opposite the wizard.

"Merlin is going to stay another night, my dear. As you know I have a long meeting tomorrow and I hope you will keep our guest entertained while I am busy. The following day he and I will set off for the mines. He is interested in meeting the new workers we have employed."

Poppy and Hyacinth's faces lit up. "That will be lovely," responded Poppy. "We can have another game of Strike the Ball."

"I shall look forward to it." Merlin smiled. "I enjoyed today immensely. I'm considering trying to build something like your fascinating obstacle course in my wife's garden."

"Is your wife keeping well during her pregnancy?" It was Jeanette who made the polite enquiry. "She must be missing you while you travel on business so often. Does she have someone to look after her while you are away?"

"Oh, yes, there is a family of witches who live in the forest…"

"Witches!" Hyacinth's voice was a high pitched shriek.

"They are good witches," Jeanette assured her. "You remember I told you that some came to my wedding."

"Oh yes, I do remember." However, Hyacinth gave Merlin an enquiring look. "You are sure she is safe with them, aren't you?"

"She is very safe," the wizard assured her. "Unfortunately, her feet are swollen and she cannot walk too far at the moment. The Bramble family of witches has very kindly offered to take care of her for a few days until I return."

"I expect she is busy making things for the baby," Poppy smiled. "Hyacinth and I have been chatting. We are going to knit some baby clothes and Jeanette is going to crochet a pair of shawls."

"How very kind of you. I am overwhelmed." Merlin raised his goblet in a gesture of thanks to the ladies around the table.

"Is your wife busy knitting, too?" Jeanette enquired.

"I don't think so." Merlin had to stop to think for a while. He hadn't been at home very much at all but he could not remember seeing any knitting needles. "Helen enjoys making patchwork quilts and cushions but she has run out of materials."

"What is a patchwork quilt?" the princess enquired.

"Well, she gets hold of old pieces of silk; worn out clothing or curtains which are of no further use. Then she cuts the undamaged pieces into small squares." He indicated the size by drawing an invisible square on the table with his finger. He had to think carefully because he had never actually seen his wife working on her hobby. "She sews the squares together on three sides and fills the little packet she has made with down or hay before she stitches the fourth side. She does the same thing over again and finally sews all the little squares together to make a soft blanket."

"What a good idea. We could do that." Poppy looked at her sister enthusiastically.

Hyacinth nodded with equal enthusiasm.

"Did you say your wife had run out of materials?" Jeanette asked.

"Yes, patchwork is a way of using up odd ends of material. I said silk but I think any sort of material can be used. It is just a hobby which my wife enjoys but we have no access to materials in the woodland where we live."

"There must be old oddments of material here, is there not, dear mother?" Jeanette asked the queen.

"I am sure there must be. We could have a look in the attic. That would be fun, wouldn't it?" Poppy's question was aimed at her sister and daughter-in-law.

"Oh, yes, we haven't looked in there for years." Hyacinth smiled at the thought. She turned to Jeanette. "You would enjoy rummaging around all the old bits and pieces the palace has stored over the years. It would help keep your mind off Steven."

"We will find some things and send them on to you, along with the baby clothes we will make." The queen smiled with pride. The king, who rarely showed his feelings, smiled fondly at his wife.

Jeanette took the opportunity to change the subject. "Father, dear, when you and Merlin travel to the mines, may I come with you? I would very much like to see more of my new homeland and I have never been to a mine."

Poppy and Hyacinth looked shocked. They sat upright in their chairs.

The king looked directly at his daughter-in-law but his voice was not unkind when he answered her question.

"No, my dear daughter, I do not think that would be wise. The mines are not a fit place for a young lady. I think it best if you stay at home and help your mother-in-law and aunt with their tasks. I shall look forward to seeing these shawls you intend to crochet when I get back."

Jeanette looked downcast but did not argue.

"When we finish the baby clothes we could make some new shirts for Steven. That would be a lovely surprise for him when he gets home." Poppy tried to raise her daughter-in-law's spirits.

"Yes, what a good idea." Jeanette smiled dutifully at the older woman.

Poor girl, thought Merlin. *She must be so bored. It is so different here from her father's palace where she had so many friends. I hope her husband returns soon.*

❀ ✦ ❀ ✦ ❀ ✦ ❀ ✦ ❀ ✦ ❀ ✦ ❀

Merlin didn't see the king at breakfast. Instead he broke his fast with the ladies in the queen's parlour. They dined on sweet cakes and lemon water. Unlike the rest of the palace the queen's rooms were brightly furnished and boasted an abundance of ornaments and pictures. She and Hyacinth proudly showed the wizard some of their embroideries and paintings.

After breakfast they played Strike the Ball and picnicked in the garden for their midday meal.

Mid afternoon, the king's secretary came down to invite Merlin to meet the Kernan lords. He said they would like the opportunity to speak with him before they left. The wizard was disappointed to leave the ladies, whose company he was enjoying immensely, but nevertheless grasped the opportunity to meet the noblemen of the country which once despised people of magic.

The lords greeted him politely. They spoke of the poisonous weed which had gripped their arable land and thanked the wizard and his people for destroying it before it could spread further afield. However, they also expressed their concerns at the growing friendship between Avalon and the Barrmen of the North.

"I sincerely hope you do not sell any of the timber from your Great Forest to the Barrmen," stated one lord. "They would only sell it to the Trajaens to build ships which would eventually attack your coastline and ours."

"One of the conditions we made with the Barrmen, before agreeing to clear their lands of the weed, is that they would not sell any more timber to the Trajaens," Merlin parried.

"Do you really think they will keep their promise?" Another lord was sceptical. "I heard that after you had fought off those marauding Trajaens, and taken prisoners, your King Arthur let them go again. I don't understand how you could be so lenient. We would have had their heads and hung them on poles." The noblemen nodded their own heads in agreement with the one who spoke.

"It was not altogether Arthur's decision," replied Merlin. "We are a peaceful people. We sent the prisoners back home with a permanent mark on each of their faces and a stern message. We told them that if they, or any of their race, threatened Avalon again we would not show mercy a second time."

Merlin went on to tell them that he was retiring so that he could spend time with his wife and children. He explained that Tannus had been elected as new leader of the wizards. He added that if the Kernans were to send an envoy to Avalon he was sure that they could enter into some mutually beneficial trading.

King Jeffrey told his noblemen that he and Merlin would visit one of the mines the next day. He said Merlin was intrigued to hear about the gudgers, from one of the children who had once worked in the mines, and was interested in meeting one.

The lords, except for Jecquin, departed. They left with words of friendship.

Lord Jecquin had been asked to stay behind to make arrangements for the visit to the mines. It also gave the king the opportunity to briefly explain what he believed to be the real purpose for Merlin's trip and the need for secrecy.

Jecquin was a small wiry man. He had dark hair, a short pointed beard and mocking eyes. His appearance was immaculate and his words polite. Merlin took an instant dislike to him. The wizard's sixth sense told him not to trust this man. He wondered how loyal the lord would be to his king if put to the test.

The nobleman expressed his concerns to learn that the gudgers had captured what he thought to be a friend of the wizard's. He said he had no reason, so far, to suspect that the humble nature they conveyed was not genuine. Nevertheless, he stated that his men never ceased to be aware of the potential danger of working alongside creatures of which little was known. After some consideration he said he thought it best for his king and Merlin to meet Glubber, the gudger team leader in one of the silver mines. The mine was situated close to the route which Merlin would be taking on his way home. Glubber had mastered the ability to speak better than other gudgers.

However, he warned Merlin, "I suggest you bring a nosegay full of petals and herbs. The gudgers stink but have no idea that they smell so badly or why we carry posy bags to cover our noses when close to them."

CHAPTER 12 – Glubber

The ladies had been busy. After Jeffrey mentioned that the mine they were to visit did not smell very nice, Poppy and Hyacinth had set about making each of the men a silk drawstring bag which Jeanette had filled with sweet smelling flower petals and lemon peel.

Merlin said his goodbyes. After a somewhat delicate start to his visit he had enjoyed the company of the ladies and felt sure the feeling was mutual. He told them he would very much like to see them again sometime in the future. *Although I am not sure if Jeffrey would send me an invitation*, he smiled to himself, *unless he had an objective of his own.*

King and wizard set out on their expedition. A group of burly soldiers rode well in front to tackle any danger in advance of the royal party's approach. The king led the main party on a fine bay steed. Merlin followed just behind on Comet. Armed guards rode on either side and also took up the rear. Jeffrey kept his distance and did not speak to the wizard during the journey.

A page rode a few hours ahead of the entourage to let people know that the king would be passing through. People stood by the roadside, as was expected of them, to watch the royal party pass. They bowed and curtsied and the king raised his hand in greeting. Merlin gave the watching Kernans a wave too along with a broad smile.

At night the guards set up tents. The king dined with Merlin as his guest. Merlin asked the king about his many travels abroad and the king told him about some of the places he had visited. The wizard was enthralled but Jeffrey warned him that a sailor's life might not be as glamorous as envisaged. It transpired that his father-in-law, his predecessor as Admiral of the Fleet, had been lost at sea.

"My father sent me and a fleet to look for him. I spent months looking for the ship and its crew or at least trying to find out what had happened to it. We discovered that it had delivered its cargo of tin as planned; from there it sailed on to another port from which it left laden with goods. We found no sign of a shipwreck along the course he sailed. We offered rewards to anyone having information as to what might have occurred. There were other ports at which the Admiral might have docked and other vessels which might have seen his ship at sea but we heard nothing."

"Queen Shirley-Poppy must have been devastated," Merlin observed as he sipped his wine.

"She was, as was poor Hyacinth. Their grandfather had passed away and they had no other family except me. My only living relative was my father. A king's life is always demanding and he was a very busy man. Whilst I was at sea he spent much of his time patrolling the coast. As you know our country is shaped like a triangle and Trajaen raids had always been a threat – as they still are. My father had little time to spend with Poppy and Hyacinth. They had only servants for company."

And so the sisters have learnt to live in their own little world with their ball game and embroidery.

Jeffrey advised that he had despatches to deal with; Merlin took this as a polite way of asking him to leave. He bid the king good night and retired to the small tent which the soldiers had erected for him.

248

❀ ✛ ❀ ✛ ❀ ✛ ❀ ✛ ❀ ✛ ❀ ✛ ❀

The next morning the humid weather broke at last and rain trickled from the sky. It was not pleasant weather for travelling and they made haste arriving at the mine around midday.

Lord Jecquin was there to meet them. He was dressed impeccably in a neatly fitted green jacket braided in gold thread. His finery was a notable comparison to the dull grey riding outfits worn by the king and the wizard.

A tent, where they could enjoy refreshments before the gudger's arrival, had been set up.

"I have wished for rain for many a day now but I hope it will stop before Glubber arrives," said Lord Jecquin. "If we have to meet him in here his stench will turn the cream sour."

Jecquin's wish was granted. The rain stopped and the tables were moved outside. Jugs of ale, wine and water were laid on the table plus a bowl of fruit and a dish of nuts. An ornately carved chair with red velvet cushions was placed one side of the table for King Jeffrey. A lesser chair, without cushions, was placed beside the king for Merlin.

Glubber could be smelt before he was seen. Jecquin raised a small bag made of gold silk to his nose.

The king and Merlin each held their bags of sweet smelling petals, provided by the royal ladies, to their noses; a blue one for Jeffrey and a purple one for the wizard.

Stories about the strange appearance of gudgers had not been understated. The scaly skinned creature walked, or rather marched, on two legs, with a side to side motion, swinging his arms with each step. His long greenish-grey head drooped down on his chest and swung with each walking movement. He was dressed in a black waistcoat with shiny buttons and matching black trousers but his feet were bare, exposing long pointed toe nails. He wore a black triangular shaped hat with more of the shiny buttons sewn on as decorations.

Glubber had obviously been taught how to bow to the king. He removed his hat with one hand which he held in front of himself; he placed his other hand behind his back as he bent forward.

"Good day, Glubber," Jecquin greeted the newcomer as he continued to pat his nose with the gold silk bag. "Please take a seat here." He indicated a bench a distance in front of where he stood behind the seated visitors.

"Thank you for coming to talk to us, Glubber." King Jeffrey wasted no time in idle conversation. "Lord Merlin of Avalon has come to Kerner with some questions about gudgers. I hope you will be able to answer them."

"I am very pleased to meet you, Glubber," said Merlin. "Although I am afraid I am *not* a lord, so please call me just plain Merlin."

"Ello, Just Plain Merling, glub glub."

Merlin was conscious of Jecquin smirking behind him. Jeffrey's face remained expressionless.

"Glubber," continued Merlin, "I am told that you and your fellow gudgers work very hard in the mines here in Kerner. I have heard nothing but praise for you."

"Glubber works hard glub glub. Gudgers work hard glub glub. We like it here."

"Oh good," said Merlin with a nod. "I am envious of the Kernan people having such strong and willing workers."

Just then a fly landed on the plate of fruit. Although Glubber's eyes appeared to be concentrating on the people in front of him, his tongue suddenly struck out sideways. It seemed to stretch over two feet in length. It snatched up the fly and smartly whipped it back into its mouth. The entire action only took a split second.

Merlin hesitated, at a loss for words. Glubber sat motionless on the bench in front of him. He was gathering his thoughts when Glubber's tongue shot out a second time. This time the long pink muscle leapt up in the air catching another fly mid-air, before it could get anywhere near the table.

"Glubber likes flies and other flying insects," said Jecquin, filling the silence and allowing Merlin time to overcome his surprise.

"Glubber likes flies, glub glub, but not very filling." The gudger's tongue struck again but this time it reached out for the nuts, bringing back several, which he crunched between his long rows of razor-sharp teeth.

"Please do help yourself to the nuts." The king pushed the dish nearer the gudger as he covered his nose with his sweet smelling bag. "We have just eaten lunch so these are all for you."

Who would want to eat those nuts after that reptile's tongue has been all over them? Merlin, who was not usually at a loss for words, collected his thoughts. *Now, where was I?*

Merlin continued: "Whilst I appreciate your efforts and all your hard work in Kerner I have heard a story that other gudgers made their way to a place close to my home. They kidnapped a friend of a friend of mine. I am told they carried him off through a burrow which led deep into the middle of the earth. Have you heard of this man who was kidnapped? Do you know if he is still alive?"

"Glubber don't know this word kidnapped," said Glubber.

"It means taken against a person's will," explained Merlin. "Stealing might be another description, but stealing a person not an object. It was a little man who was looking after a young horse, but an unusual horse, one with a horn in the middle of its forehead."

"Did they glub glub kidnap the horse, too?" asked Glubber.

"No just the little man. But they ripped the horn from the horse's head before they made their way back down the tunnel."

"Glubber don't know nothin' about Just Plain Merling's friend's friend."

"Oh, my dear Glubber, I am not suggesting you do," Merlin stated. "But if you could find out whether he is still alive I would be most grateful. I would be even more grateful for his safe return."

The gudger continued to catch flies and devour the nuts.

"Glubber might be able to find out about Just Plain Merling's friend's friend, glub glub. Glubber goes home soon to see his family. Glubber will ask around."

"I am sure Lord Merlin will be able to offer a reward for information about his friend's friend," suggested Lord Jecquin, "or, better still, the safe return of the little man?"

Merlin nodded his agreement. "Oh, yes, there will be a reward."

"Glubber will try to find out."

"Thank you, Glubber. That is all we can ask of you." Jecquin brought the interview to a close. "I will be here to meet you on your return. If you have any information regarding the little man I will pass it on to my Lord King and Lord Merlin."

Glubber sat where he was. He had finished the nuts and was now making his way through the fruit. A passing butterfly was also devoured.

"You may go now," said Jecquin. "Please take all the fruit with you. You can even keep the bowl."

Glubber stood. He didn't need to take the bowl with them. Every plum, cherry and apple was soon consumed.

As he finished his food the gudger let out a loud belch. All three of his hosts immediately dabbed their noses with the posy bags.

"Them pretty bags. Where you buy them, glub glub? Glubber wants to buy one too?"

"Glubber, if you bring me back news of the Lord Merlin's friend I will give you a box full of posy bags," Jecquin offered.

"Glubber find out and come back,"

"Yes, thank you, Glubber." This time it was the king who spoke, standing to indicate the interview was over.

"Thank you, Glubber," echoed the wizard. "You are indeed most kind. I look forward to seeing you again."

The gudger replaced his hat, bowed and walked off, swinging his heavy arms and long head from side to side. Merlin noticed that his trousers had been specially cut to allow for his long muscular tail.

I bet that tail could render a powerful blow, thought Merlin, his mind sweeping back to a meeting he once had with a pair of dragons. He remembered the sharp sound of the male dragon's tail smacking the ground when he was annoyed. As if to reflect the wizard's thoughts he heard a cracking sound as Glubber's tail smacked against a post. *I wonder if tail smacking is an indication of annoyance in gudgers, too.*

❋ ✛ ❋ ✛ ❋ ✛ ❋ ✛ ❋ ✛ ❋

Lord Jecquin fanned the air with his gold posy bag. "Even the yard here stinks from their comings and goings. Look, not one in sight, but the place reeks!"

King Jeffrey had asked to look around the mine before he left. "After coming all this way I should inspect the crown's property," he had said. Now, he appeared to be having second thoughts. There was indeed a pungent smell drifting across the yard.

A dead man was being brought out of the mine, towards a waiting wagon, by men who looked almost as pale as the body they carried.

"What did he do?" asked Merlin.

"Without looking at his name or his records, I have no idea," replied Jecquin blandly. "I oversee the mines. I do not manage them."

"Can you assure our visitor that there are no more children or people of magic working here?" The king's tone was bored, and the question was clearly more for Merlin's benefit than his own.

"There are no children," replied the nobleman. "I was not aware there were any here in the mines. My managers have been instructed not to employ any person under the age of twelve."

"What about people of magic?" the king prompted.

"Not as far as I know," replied Jecquin, "but sometimes they hide their magic skills when they're brought here."

"Why would they do that?" asked Jeffrey, puzzled.

"So that we do not use the drugs on them."

Merlin took a sharp, audible intake of breath.

Jecquin frowned. "If the people of magic had not been drugged then they could have harmed my guards, innocent workers and other prisoners. There was one incident when a boy tried to escape; it was not till he felled one of my men, in his attempt, that we realised what he was."

Merlin, who had been listening, shook his head. He was growing angry. He guessed the boy Jecquin was so casually referring to was Dexter.

"I am sorry if what I say upsets you, Lord Merlin," said Jecquin, who did not look at all apologetic, "but I am being honest. The facts are that no one has been imprisoned here unless sentenced by the magistrates. All wrongdoers, whether they have magical skills or not, have to be punished."

Merlin's face was betraying his growing ire. He wanted to ask what the three Bramble men had done wrong to suffer seventeen long years in gaol. However, he had promised himself to be diplomatic and such enquiries at the present would not be helpful to his mission. *On this occasion I will bite my tongue*, he thought, *but when the opportunity arises...*

"I suggest," Jeffrey continued, before the wizard had a chance to respond, "that Lord Merlin now returns to Twydell. You, Lord Jecquin, will give Glubber paid leave to go home and make enquiries. When he returns you will send Lord Merlin a message letting him know whether there is any news or not. A message will also be sent to me."

The king turned to Merlin. "Now, how will Lord Jecquin get a message to you? I believe your people seem to know when someone approaches the Forbidden Forest?"

"That has been true in the past," said Merlin. "Unfortunately, our, er... mechanism for telling us when people are approaching is temporarily out of action. Nevertheless, I will make sure that someone is posted, from noon each day until the sun goes down, to receive messages."

"Then we can do no more at present than to wish you a safe journey home," said the king. "Please do not forget to tell your good wife that the House of Kerner sends its regards and wishes her a safe confinement."

Jecquin bowed low, in what Merlin considered a mockingly gracious manner.

The wizard was thus dismissed. He remained polite and gave his thanks and goodbyes before preparing for his journey.

"It is not wise to goad such a powerful sorcerer," King Jeffrey advised his nobleman. "Merlin is no fool. Do not underestimate him."

"I failed to tell him that it was you who brought back the magic-suppressing drugs from one of your many voyages." Jecquin's smile was sly.

"Indeed," agreed the king. "Some things are better left unsaid." Jeffrey adopted his usual expressionless face. "Now let us inspect this mine."

CHAPTER 13 –
Homeward Bound

Merlin spent the first night of his travels at one of the inns he had stayed at previously. He was wet, and weary. Comet was tired too. The horse had borne his master's weight all day as the magician had been reluctant to sit on the uncomfortable broom handle on such a miserable day. The wizard ached from head to toe and wondered if he was now suffering from the effects of so many games of Strike the Ball.

Supper came as ordered, cod and sea kale; since the devastation of the previous year's crops there was a heavy reliance on sea food. The plate looked tempting but Merlin found that he wasn't as hungry as he thought, and ate very little.

"Is everything alright, Lord Merlin?" enquired the innkeeper. "Is there anything wrong with the fish? It was freshly caught this morning."

"Oh nothing, nothing at all, thank you, landlord. I'm just rather tired after a long journey in the rain. I'm ready for my bed so I'll bid you good night and see you for an early start in the morning."

The climb upstairs seemed steeper than it had on the last occasion; he felt quite out of breath as he reached the top. He looked out of the window to see the same two men who had followed him on his way to the Sea View Palace. They were standing just inside the stable. *I suppose once the landlord has told them I've gone to bed, they'll come in and sit in a darkened corner.*

The wizard charmed the door as he always did when he stayed at an inn. If anyone opened the door while he was asleep it would start to scream. However, he had never actually awoken to the sound of a shrieking door before.

His eyes opened as soon as the alarm went off. He had slept with his wand in his hand, now he leapt out of bed. Nobody had entered, though the screaming door stood ajar. He tiptoed to the door, wand held high, a defensive spell on his lips. He quickly swung the door open, pointing his wand ready to curse whoever the culprit was who had tried to steal into his room whilst he slept. The landlord stood outside, motionless as if frozen by shock, his mouth and eyes open wide. Other people, hearing the noise, had started to climb the stairs to see what was going on; they now stood with hands pressed over their ears trying to blot out the terrible sound of the shrieking door.

Merlin hastily rescinded the spell and the door stood silent.

"What do you want?" The wizard's words were quick and, like his face, angry. He was not at all amused by someone upsetting the good night's sleep he had yearned for. He stood in his vest and pants revealing his skinny body.

"I was only coming to ask if you were all right," replied the landlord meekly. "You said you were going to make an early start, and it's mid morning now."

"Oh," said Merlin feeling foolish. "I do apologise. I had not realised it was so late. I must have overslept."

"The door," mumbled the innkeeper, "Why did it make that 'orrible racket?"

"A simple spell to let me know if anyone tries to get in while I'm asleep," replied Merlin, with a forced smile, and what he thought to be an acceptable explanation.

"A simple spell?" The landlord was still dumbfounded and remained standing where he was. However, after a long pause he responded in a much louder and aggressive voice, "I was only making sure you were all right because you looked so ill last night. What happens? I get the fright of me life." He turned and stormed down the stairs.

The other people who had been standing and staring made way for his furious steps. As he went he called back, "And don't use any more of your magic on my doors again!"

Merlin stepped back inside and got dressed. He was embarrassed and wanted to leave as quickly as he could. It was too late for breakfast but he was not hungry anyway. *Now, the sooner I leave here and get home the better*, he thought, *I am so looking forward to being back in my own bed and spending a good night's sleep in Helen's arms.*

Before leaving he downed a large mug of ale then ordered another. He had quite a thirst. *It will make up for not eating*, he told himself.

The landlord was terse when he served the ale but brightened up again when a piece of silver was added to the payment for the wizard's bed and board. He had his stable boy bring Comet around to the front of the inn and made sure Merlin's canteens were full of fresh water.

The landlord helped the wizard mount but before releasing the reins he sought reassurance. "That door won't make that noise again will it, Lord Merlin? I don't want any of my guests being scared away"

"Just Merlin, I'm not a lord. No, my good man, be assured I have removed the charm."

The landlord and his family stood outside to wave their visitor off.

"I hope he doesn't stay here again," the daughter muttered. "I don't want any more screaming doors. That commotion this morning fair gave me a headache."

"He can stay as many times as he likes if he leaves an extra piece of silver each time," the landlord grinned.

"He won't be here again." The innkeeper's wife spoke with the matter-of-fact confidence of an older woman. "The silly sod's on death's door."

Merlin couldn't remember much of his journey to the little farmhouse where he had spent his first night in Kerner. He was relieved to see the dwelling in the distance. *I shall offer another piece of silver if they allow me to stay the night. I am sure they will. They were such nice people. I will tell them all about my visit to the palace and Strike the Ball. They will be enthralled by my stories about gudgers burrowing into the royal mine and taking up employment there.*

He looked forward to supping barley and bean stew. The wizard still wasn't hungry but the watery stew would quench his thirst. He had drunk all the water in his canteens. Comet needed a rest so he decided he would ask the family if he could stay an additional night. It would give his aching limbs time to revive.

He had no doubt the family would see him approaching and come out to greet him, but no one came. It was disappointing not to see a welcome party and even more disheartening to find the house empty. *The boys must have recovered sufficiently from their illnesses for them to depart for Twydell. What a pity. Well, not a pity that the boys are better, what was it again, mumps and measles? How fortunate that magical beings don't suffer with those annoying human ailments.* Thankfully, the farmer had left the bucket attached to the pulley above the well. He hauled bucket after bucket; both horse and rider drank greedily. Despite the rain it was still humid and Merlin felt uncomfortably hot and sweaty. He did something he rarely did; he took off his clothes and washed in cold water. He had no towel so he remained naked for a while to allow himself to dry.

No beds were left and the floor in the house was too hard to sleep on, so Merlin chose to spend the night in the stable instead. Although it still smelt of carthorse he considered the straw strewn in the stable to be a more comfortable option. He closed his eyes. When he opened them again he was surprised to see the sun, or what he could see of it from behind dark clouds, at its zenith.

It's noon. I've overslept for the second time! I ache so much I could easily stay here but I must get home. Bertha Bramble will have some soothing cream I can rub into my joints. I must have turned awkwardly in the night and cricked my neck. I can hardly move it from side to side. I must get home. Helen will make me some of her mint tea and the Brambles will send over some blackberry crumble. After that my wife and I will enjoy

263

a tipple of passion fruit wine before nestling under our patchwork quilts.

Merlin's mouth was watering at the thought of home cooking and he longed to lie in a soft bed beside the woman he loved.

He had to ask Comet to stand next to the fence while he mounted. He promised the magnificent white steed that he would groom his mane, which had been tangled by the continued rain, as soon as he got home.

I'm going to build our own Strike the Ball in the back garden when I get back. The children will love it. Will it be two girls, or two boys, or one of each? In between lessons in wizardry they can play in the garden and Helen and I will play with them. We will invite the Brambles and the children to try their skill at hitting a ball around our obstacle course. We will have competitions and the winner will receive a pretty pendant...

Merlin started to dream. He dreamt of flying ships into which players had to strike balls made of seaweed; a forest with a black unicorn whose horn was made of pure gold – the unicorn would jump in the air stabbing any balls which tried to get past him. The appearance of gudgers burrowing into his obstacle course made him wake with a start and he felt himself falling, landing on the ground with a sharp jolt. The pain was such that he lay where he was.

The wizard slipped into unconsciousness. He regained his senses when he felt someone pressing against his already sore neck.

"It's all right," a voice called out, "He's still alive."

Merlin opened his eyes and looked up to see one of the men who had been following him bending over, examining his sore neck. His companion was dismounting. The wizard's first instinct was to draw his wand but the man was kneeling on his sleeve where he kept it concealed.

"You gave us a fright there, old timer," the man said. "Lord Jecquin would have us hung if you came to any harm on Kerner soil."

"You're not going to murder me?"

Both men laughed.

"Murder you?" they said. "As soon as you were spotted roaming round in Kerner, we were sent to find out what you were up to and report to the king himself. When it was time for you to leave we were sent to make sure no harm came to you on your way home."

"What shall we do with him now?" one man asked the other. "He ain't in no fit state for travelling."

"He's got mumps," replied the other, "Look at his neck. It's almost as round as a plum pudding. Good job I had mumps as a kid or I'd be half a mile away already. It's painful when a fully grown man gets it."

"Magical beings don't get mumps," Merlin replied. *I'm sure we don't.*

The other man leaned forward to look at him. "Well, you've got it now. I thank my mother for taking me to stay with my cousin when he had mumps. 'Much less painful to have it as a child than a man,' she said."

"Sorry, old timer, but I don't think you're going to last the night and we don't want you dying on Kerner soil." The man leaning over Merlin turned to his companion. "I reckon we should take him to the border, leave him on Twydell land and let him die there."

He turned back to Merlin, who still lay on the ground listening to what was being said. "Don't worry, old man. We'll make sure you're comfortable before we leave you. We'll tuck you up in this old cloak of yours and you'll just fall asleep and pass away peacefully – much better way to go than crossing swords in a fight."

"I don't have a sword," muttered Merlin. "I use a wand."

"Well, better than crossing wands then. I've heard those wand things of yours can cause some damage."

The wizard decided not to respond. Each time he tried to speak his throbbing neck hurt more than ever.

The two men lifted him, none too gently, back on to Comet. He slumped across the horse's neck.

"Nice horse," he heard one of the men say. "Pity it's not better cared for. What shall we do with it?"

"It'd be worth a fair penny or two when it's groomed."

I'll make sure Comet is groomed till his coat shines when I get home. I will ask young Dexter to take care of him and repay him by teaching him some lesser known spells which he won't learn elsewhere.

"Don't be daft. If we take the horse it will look like we've robbed the old sod and next thing we know we'll be attacked by weirdoes flying on brushes!"

Good. They are not going to steal Comet. If I don't get home then at least he will find his way back and tell everyone in the forest about Strike the Ball. Wait a minute! Comet was in the stable; he didn't see Queen Poppy's pleasure garden so he won't be able to describe the game to them. I must get back. I have a wife and two children waiting for me.

Merlin drifted back into delirium again. His mind did not return to the real world until he felt himself being lifted from his horse and laid on the ground.

"Here you are, old man." One of the men tucked his cloak around him. "We're going to miss you. Don't think we've ever had such an entertaining journey before."

"No," replied the other, "You have a vivid imagination – all those stories about flying ships and unicorns catching balls with their horns."

The wizard's delirious mind jerked back to reality. *Surely I didn't mention Zanadoo or any of the Wizzen secrets? No, if I had I'd be cursed by now. Or, am I cursed? Is that why I have mumps? No, I'm not cursed because the mumps came before my delirium.*

"Don't leave me here," he pleaded. "Please don't leave me here. Take me to the Forbidden Forest. The entrance is just a few more miles away and I have a piece of silver with which I can pay you for your trouble."

"I'm not going to try to get into that place!" stated one of the men.

"People have died trying to get through that vine which surrounds your forest home," the other man added. "I've heard that people who try to get in there disappear off the face of the earth!"

"I don't want you to go into the forest," croaked Merlin. "Just leave me at the entrance. That is enough."

"And you have silver to pay?" asked the other man.

"Yes, I do."

"So what's to stop us taking the silver now?" asked the first man.

"Hah! Do you think I would be foolish enough to travel without charming my pockets? If you try to rob me you will get a nasty shock." The wizard's neck throbbed with every word he uttered, and his voice had turned into a whine.

267

The men looked at him for a while. Then one asked, "Will your pockets start to scream like the door at the inn?"

They both laughed.

"That story will be told for many a year," the other man agreed.

"No, nothing as painless as a scream," Merlin said, trying to sound menacing, but his ears told him that he sounded even more pitiful.

"What if you die on the way?" asked the first man. "How will you pay us then? If we can't take this silver, which you say you have, out of your pockets then we'll have taken you part of the way for nothing?"

Merlin was trying to think of an answer when the other man spoke.

"I been thinking. Lord Jecquin might not be happy with us leaving him here so close to the border. It's only a few more miles to the forest. Let's take him there. If he lives we'll get the silver he says he has, though I'm not so sure he's telling the truth, and if he dies outside the forest then everyone will agree we did what we could for the mad magician."

"I swear I have silver," muttered the wizard before slipping back into his dream world. He felt himself being lifted on to Comet once more and gliding along as his horse flew towards home.

Suddenly the wizard sat bolt upright. "What happens if the gudgers burrow through into the garden? If the balls slip into the gudger's tunnel they could fall into middle earth."

Merlin heard the men's laughter. He decided to go back to sleep. He felt himself falling to the ground once more and his broomstick, which the men had pushed into his saddle bags, falling with him. He fell on top of his broom and automatically grabbed the handle, ordering it to rise. However, he wasn't seated on it properly and as the broom rose he slid off and fell back on to the ground.

The men, who had already dismounted, tried to grab the broom by jumping up in the air to catch it. They missed and the broom glided on. One got back on his horse and gave chase but the broom rose higher and flew on ahead.

"Well, you've lost that flying contraption of yours," stated one of the men. "But I guess you won't be needing it again."

"Pity," said the other. "I would have liked to have had a go on that."

"Won't work for humans," the wizard managed to whine.

"I would still have liked to have had a try though. If we could have caught it we might have been able to sell it. We could auction it." The man mimicked the auctioneer's voice. "'A magic brush once owned by none other than Merlin, the famous weirdo, who killed the poisonous weed which could have destroyed Kerner.' The bidders would go mad."

"Yeah, he did a good job getting rid of that weed. I'm going to miss him."

"Strangely enough, so will I. If we get him home, perhaps one of those magical folk who live in the forest will find a cure for him. You never know; they've surprised us in the past with their clever tricks."

"That would be nice but I think he's too old to be cured. He's past it."

Merlin listened to the men as he slipped in and out of consciousness. It warmed his heart to think they didn't really want him to die.

He felt one of the men shaking him out of his reveries. "So where is this entrance where you want us to leave you?"

"Follow the hedge around till you see some old carts. The entrance is nearby." Then he added, "But the entrance could be anywhere it chooses to open."

He heard the men curse but nevertheless they followed the hedgerow around till they saw the old carts.

"No entrance here," one of them stated.

"Just leave me here," said Merlin, before he slid off Comet's back and landed with a thud on the ground. He saw stars and then nothing at all.

At first he thought he must still be delirious when he heard Great Grandmother Bramble's voice. "Stay where you are! What have you done to him?"

Is it Bertha Bramble? It can't be. I've never heard her sound so vicious before. I wish I could open my eyes but they are too sore.

"Nothing," protested one of the men who had brought him back to the forest. "We haven't done nothing to Lord Merlin! The only thing we've done is bring him home!"

"That's right. He asked us to bring him home because he was so ill he kept falling off his horse," stated the other man, whose voice trembled slightly. "He's got mumps."

"Magical beings don't get human ailments," snapped Great Grandmother

That's what I thought!

Merlin forced his eyelids apart to see Bertha Bramble with Jonathan beside her. They were flanked by Maura and Nora. All had their wands drawn, pointing threateningly at the two men who held their hands high above their heads in surrender. Maura, who was nearest to him was now walking sideways towards him; wand still pointing at the two men.

"Stay away, Maura," Merlin croaked. "I've got mumps."

Maura stood still. She glanced sideways at him. "His face is flushed and his neck is swollen," she observed.

"That's mumps," said Jonathan, turning slightly to get a better look. "I had it when I was a child. It was horrible."

"I thought you just said magical beings don't get human ailments," one of the men stated.

"I'm half human," Jonathan told them. "My mum was a plainfolk. She married a wizard." Jonathan made his way towards the magician who he had revered all his life. His face was full of anxiety.

"What's a plainfolk?" asked one of the men.

"Someone like you, with no magical powers."

The men looked at each other. "We didn't know humans could interbreed with magicians," one muttered.

"My wife is human," Merlin stated, still in a world of half delirium. "We are expecting twins, you know, and when they are born we are going to play a special ball game in the garden."

"If your wife really is human, and she really is expecting twins, then the last thing you want is for her to get mumps," one of the men stated. "Mumps could kill a newborn child."

Even in his dream state, Merlin suddenly felt panic. He hadn't considered the risk to Helen-Joy and the twins.

The witches glanced at one another with eyes full of alarm.

One of the witches made as if to assist Jonathan, who was now holding his hand across Merlin's forehead, checking his temperature.

"Stay where you are, Maura," said Jonathan with a firmness to his voice. "You don't want mumps at your age. I'll see to Merlin. You can only get the disease once so I'm safe to touch him but you are not."

"All we want is to go home," said the men. "We thought we was doing you a favour bringing the old man home. We was only supposed to take him to the border but he promised us a piece of silver if we got him back to the forest."

"Oh, thank you," replied Great Grandmother. The vicious tone had gone from her voice and she sounded more like her usual self. Nevertheless, she still kept her wand pointing at the humans.

Merlin heard a thump and shifted his eyes to see Heather landing beside him on her broomstick and carrying another one.

"Get back, Heather," ordered Jonathan. "Merlin has mumps and believe you me, you don't want to catch it. It is a very painful illness."

"Oh," said Heather as she drew her wand and copied the older members of her family by pointing it at the two men.

"Not another one," sighed one of the men. "We try to do Lord Merlin a favour by bringing him home to die and all we get is threatened by a load of witches."

"I'm a warlock," Jonathan corrected.

"Give them a piece of silver and let them go," croaked Merlin. "There's a piece in my left sleeve pocket. Look right down in the bottom and you'll find a bit of Trajaen armband in there somewhere."

Jonathan did as he was bid. He pulled back the folds of the wizard's cloak and reached inside the pocket. A flash of lightning struck out of the pocket knocking the warlock backwards. His wand fell out of his hand and on to the grass; he was disarmed.

"Arrrgh... That hurt! Have you charmed your pocket or something?"

"I'm so sorry. I forgot." Merlin muttered some words. "There, that's done the trick. You can take a look now."

Jonathan tried again only to be knocked back a second time.

"That's it! I'm not getting struck by lightning a third time. They'll have to come back for their silver another time."

"Merlin is too weak for magic," Maura stated, still watching the ailing wizard from the corner of her eye. "He must be very sick."

"I've got some gold if that's any good," offered Heather.

"Where did you get that from?" asked her Great Grandmother, looking out of the corner of her eye. Like her daughters, she still stood with her wand pointing at the humans.

"Tannus gave it to us when we were working up in the North in case we needed to stay overnight at an inn. I've still got it."

She stepped forward showing the men a piece of gold. "Will this do?" she asked the men as she held the

273

gold in front of them. "We don't use money in the Forbidden Forest, it's no use to me."

"You people…" One of the Kernans stared, wide-eyed, at the chunk of gold as he searched for words.

Heather thought the man's reaction meant that the payment she offered was not sufficient. "I'm sorry. I'm afraid it is all I've got."

"It's enough," the other Kernan stated. "Let us take our reward and go. We have wives and children at home who are missing us. Please let us go."

"Oh, we know what it's like to be parted from our families," Bertha Bramble said, but not unkindly. "Now take that bit of gold, take your horses and walk away backwards. No offence but the humans we have dealt with in the past have not always been good ones."

One of the Kernans quickly grabbed the gold that Heather offered. Then, stepping backwards, both he and his comrade picked up the reins of their horses and still facing the Brambles continued to pace in the opposite direction. When they thought they were safely out of the range of dangerous wands, they mounted and galloped off as fast as they could urge their horses to go.

As soon as the men were far enough away not to be of any concern, the wands were lowered and the women turned their attention to Merlin.

"Stay away," Jonathan warned again. "Mumps are contagious and the last thing we want is for anyone to carry the disease back inside the forest."

Great Grandmother's face was full of worry as she looked at her elderly friend lying on the grass. She turned to the young warlock. "If we can't go near him for fear of bringing this terrible thing into the forest, and you are the only one who can't catch it, then you will have to stay here and look after him, Jon."

Jonathan looked helplessly at Heather, whose face dropped.

"Now, now, dear," Nora Bramble comforted her granddaughter. "It won't be for long."

"I'm sorry, Heather. I don't want to stay here and look after Merlin but I have no choice." He looked back down at the old wizard lying on the grass and smiled. "You know what I mean, don't you, Merlin? I'd much rather be with my girl but you are my priority at the moment."

"Of course you are!" Heather tried to smile at the sick wizard. "You are everyone's priority. We owe you so much. If it were not for you I would not have my father back. We can always get married another time."

"What?" Merlin struggled to speak. His swollen throat felt like it was choking him.

"We were waiting for you to get back and for father to arrive and we were going to 'tie the knot'." Jonathan smiled. "Helen said that she was sure you wouldn't mind staying with her at the Brambles for a while, so Heather and I could spend a few days at your cave for our honeymoon."

"Of course you can. Helen and I will be happy to stay at the Brambles." He remembered his manners. "Congratulations, I am sure you will both be very happy. You are so well..." He wanted to say 'suited' but he broke into a coughing fit.

"Here, Jon, put these on his forehead." Great Grandmother held out some dock leaves which she had moistened with water that had collected in an indented stone. "We need to get him some fresh water and you must get him to drink as much as you can."

275

"Come on, girls, let's go home and get some water and blankets for Merlin and our Jon. It may not be the best of places to spend the night but at least we can make them comfortable."

"If you can move yourself to under one of those old wagons at least you'll keep dry if it rains again," Jonathan suggested to Merlin.

The old man rolled over on his front and crawled under the nearest cart.

"Now you try to get some shut eye," called out Great Grandmother as she left with her 'girls'. "When I come back I'll have some nice chicken soup. You'll need to keep your strength up, Merlin. Those twins of yours will need you. Just keep thinking of your lovely wife and the babies she is expecting. That'll pull you round."

The next morning Merlin felt much better. His eyes were not so painful to open. He lifted his hand to his forehead.

"Don't touch them," said Jonathan, who sat at his side watching a candle burn. "They are dock leaves soaked in cold water. Great Grandmother said they would bring down your temperature."

"Why are you burning a candle in daylight?"

"I've drawn a picture of you on it." Jonathan continued to stare at the candle. "Surely you know how a simple healing spell works. Draw or write the name of the person you wish to heal on the candle and then as it burns wish hard that the person will be healed. Now, stay quiet while I try to concentrate on my wish or it won't work."

"Thank you." Merlin felt blessed by the young warlock's kindness.

"Maura and Nora had a stock of candles. The witches and the children have been casting spells, all night, for your recovery. Now, I must concentrate."

Merlin did not say another word. Tears welled in his eyes. He had not appreciated how much he was loved. He watched as Jonathan waved a piece of wild mint over the candle's flame. He breathed in the herb's essence.

As the warlock chanted a prayer to Mother Earth, beseeching her to heal his friend, a bird added its sweet song. Merlin looked up to see a little goldfinch in the branches of a tree which overlapped the forest boundary.

What a delicate tune! It is as if that pretty little bird is copying Jonathan's chant. I wish I could paint a picture which told this story.

When the candle had flickered its last, Jonathan ceased his chant. He changed the dock leaves on Merlin's forehead for others which had been soaking in cold water laced with mint and rosemary.

"Well, thanks be to Mother Earth; your temperature has dropped. It felt like there was a fire raging inside of you yesterday."

"I feel so much better." Merlin managed to smile. "Thank you. I will never forget your kindness."

"Does that mean you will forgive me for voting for Tannus instead of Wormald the Wise?"

Merlin chuckled, but it hurt his throat. Nevertheless he managed to croak, "Tannus is a brave wizard who has much to offer." He changed the subject despite the discomfort of speech there was a lot he needed to know. "How did you know I was here? How is my dear wife?"

"We knew you were here because Maisie was flying above the canopy and saw a riderless broomstick. Heather set off to retrieve it while Maisie and I flew up to take a look around. We could see you approaching with those two men. We knew it was you because no one else has a pure white horse. You were slumped across Comet. I kept an eye on what was going on while Maisie got the Brambles. We didn't know what had happened or who the men were.

"As for Helen, she was doing very well until she heard you had been taken ill. The Brambles tried to play it down and told her you had caught a cold and thought it best to keep your distance for a while. The play acting didn't work, she might have lost her soothsayer skills but she still has a sixth sense. She demanded to know what was going on so Great Grandmother had to tell her about your mumps. Maisie has just flown off so she will be on her way to tell everyone that you've pulled through the night and look a lot better now."

"Who is Maisie?" Merlin was bewildered. He was wracking his brain trying to remember where he had heard the name before. He had not seen anyone else nearby.

"One of the rescued children. She was the goldfinch up in the tree just now."

Merlin recollected the little girl, with red hair and freckles, who fed a blue tit from the palm of her hand. "She can transform?"

"Yes, she has only just discovered her ability. Apparently she wanted to see outside the forest but was afraid to go with the others when they took the unicorns and ponies to graze. Suddenly she transformed but she still doesn't fly further than the forest edge. Sally is worried sick about the child. She's afraid she will fly off and get lost."

"Sally is right to worry," said Merlin. "Men capture pretty birds and put them in cages. It is still a remarkable achievement for the little lass. Now, tell me, is Helen getting around? Are her ankles still swollen? How are the twins?"

"Too many questions at the same time! I told you Helen is well. I haven't looked at her ankles myself but she seems to be getting around okay. I have no reason to believe that her twins aren't in good health. Your wife is blooming. Her only worry is you, and Maisie will soon be able to put her mind at rest on that score. I can't tell you a lot. Heather and I only got home yesterday."

"Of course, of course. I am sorry and most grateful to you. I wish there was someone else who could share the burden of looking after me with you."

"My mother will be here soon. If she nursed me while I was ill she has either had the disease or is immune. I don't think father caught it while I was ill either. Apparently magical beings don't normally suffer with human ailments."

"Not in my case. Why is your mother coming?" It was unusual for the Brambles to permit humans into what they deemed as their forest.

"She's coming to the wedding. Do you remember I told you Heather and I were going to 'tie the knot'? We have asked Great Grandmother to officiate the exchange of rings ceremony for us, here in the forest. Heather didn't want a wedding in Avalon because her family wouldn't be willing to travel. Can you imagine

Sally leaving the forest even to go to her daughter's wedding?"

Merlin tried to shake his head but it was too painful.

Jonathan continued: "We are looking forward to spending some time at your cave. It is such a peaceful spot."

"Stay as long as you like." Merlin had talked too much and his voice was husky but he managed to add, in an effort not to disappoint his warlock carer, "I will have to be off again soon so it is best for Helen to stay with the Brambles."

Jonathan just stared at the old man. "What! Leaving your wife again when she is due to give birth in just a few weeks? I think you have said enough, Merlin. I hope it is just the mumps which is affecting your brain because if not, you and I are going to fall out."

Merlin decided it was time to close his eyes and return to his dreams.

Dexter and Jonathan, with a little help from Maura, had used some of the timber from the old carts to build a shack just inside the forest. Merlin had moved from beneath the remains of one cart outside the entrance to the shack, made with pieces of another, inside.

Merlin had been left on his own for a few hours one evening whilst Heather and Jonathan got married.

Whilst Ethel spooned chicken broth into her patient's mouth, she told him yet again about the exchange of rings which had taken place. "It was a quaint little ceremony. Jonathan and Heather were made for each other. She is such a shy little witch, I'm looking forward to getting to know her better."

It must be very disappointing for Jonathan's mother. She is one of the few human beings ever invited to the Forbidden Forest and she ends up sitting here nursing me.

Far from being disappointed, Ethel, as she was called, seemed to relish being a nurse. Merlin would have been able to spoon the soup into his mouth himself but Ethel insisted the task would be best performed by her.

Merlin didn't dare object. If he objected and Ethel got upset, there was no one else who could spend time with him. Jonathan was on honeymoon and the only other candidate was Yzor, Jonathan's father. However, Yzor was busy helping Dexter build a wooden extension on to the cottage before winter set in. Besides, Ethel seemed happy talking to him without feeling the need for a response.

Lennox and his herd had stopped by a couple of times. Merlin did not want the pain of talking more than he had to but he appreciated the company. He spotted Maisie, in her goldfinch form, sitting in the trees above him on several occasions, singing in her dulcet bird voice. Each time he saw her he waved and she fluttered her wings in acknowledgement.

His mind was most often on Helen-Joy. He longed to see her again but knew he must go back to Kerner to speak to Glubber as arranged. *Surely a messenger will arrive any day now? How I dread meeting that stinking creature again, but I must find out what happened to Sprike. Lennox will need to go to Zanadoo to fetch Fiery soon. If Sprike is dead, as I suspect he is, Flambeau and Feerce will join us in the Forbidden*

Forest – they will have no reason to stay in Zanadoo. After that I can spend the rest of my life in the Forbidden Forest. I will never wish to leave again.

A few days later, Merlin's neck was back to its normal width and he was feeling fairly fit and well. His eyes were still sore but he felt ready to move on. The only thing stopping him going to the Brambles' house and his wife's loving arms was Ethel.

Ethel stated that humans were still contagious for fourteen days after infection. She insisted Merlin stay where he was for the time being. Merlin had argued at first, stating that he had contracted the illness in less than the fourteen days so he was unlikely to remain infectious for such a long period. But after giving the matter some consideration, he decided to err on the side of caution; besides, everyone else considered prudence to be the best policy.

Now that Merlin was active again, Ethel spent more time with her family and he was left on his own. Of course he had the companionship of Lennox and the herd. He had been allocated the task of guarding the herd whilst they grazed. Sometimes Jonathan would accompany him and on other occasions it would be one of the Bramble witches, but the latter kept their distance.

Today he was on his own when Ethel arrived with a late brunch. He was just sitting down to enjoy mushrooms, in a gravy soaked trencher of bread, when he heard Maisie's startled cry. He looked up to see the goldfinch flapping her wings. He put his food to one side and made an opening in the hedge just big enough to poke his head through.

The goldfinch flew off and Merlin knew that Maisie had gone to the Brambles' cottage to alert others of potential danger.

At first he could see nothing, then he saw a cloud of dust. As the cloud drew nearer he could see a small group of soldiers and a wagon heading in the direction of the forest. *Ah, perhaps my friend King Frederrick of Twydell has heard I have been sick and is sending me a few casks of good ale and wine in that wagon. Maybe even a roast chicken or two.*

However, as the party grew nearer he could see the flag of Kerner, a silver sword on a plain green background, not the three mountains and two valleys of Twydell. Merlin was equally excited to receive a message from Kerner as he would have been to receive gifts from Twydell.

They must be coming to tell me that Glubber is back and to ask me to return with them to meet him. I can do that. I'm not allowed to see my wife yet so this is an ideal chance to return to Kerner. I wonder why they are bringing a wagon and what can be in those chests it carries?

Merlin wasn't sure if he was glad or not that the person leading the party was not a soldier but one of the men who had brought him back to the forest. *Better the devil you know*, he thought to himself. He drew his wand. After his failure to dispel the charm on his pockets he had practised a few simple spells. He felt well enough to cast stronger spells if the need arose.

"Hello, old man, it's me, Jed. It was me who brought you home when you was ill. Do you remember?"

Merlin didn't think he had ever known the man's name before. "Hello, Jed."

"Glad to see you've got over the mumps," said Jed. "Lord Jecquin said a guard would be on duty from midday till sunset. I didn't expect to see you on guard duty though. I thought you were too important for that sort of thing."

"Er... we all take turns. Everyone has equal responsibility in our society." Merlin felt Ethel's eyes on him.

"I've got a letter from Lord Jecquin and three boxes to deliver," stated the man. He and the soldiers were dismounting. They showed no aggression but Merlin was cautious and stayed where he was.

"Can you read, or do you want me to read it for you?" The man offered a rolled up parchment.

"Of course I can read," said Merlin, snatching the parchment through the hole in the hedge. "If Lord Jecquin wanted you to read it to me, he would not have put a seal on it."

"All right, all right. Keep yer pointy hat on."

The wizard sealed the vines.

"What are you doing?" asked Jed from the other side of the foliage. "Don't you want these boxes we've brought? They were sent from the Sea View Palace itself."

"I need a little time to read this letter," replied Merlin. "Just be patient. I'll be right back to you."

Merlin ripped open the seal. The parchment unrolled. It was so long it almost reached the ground. He read the contents:

Dear Merlin

Glubber has returned to work and states that your friend's friend is still alive but held prisoner by a group of rogue gudgers. Glubber says there are good and bad in all races. He states he is a good gudger and wishes to help you rescue your friend's friend. If you wish to free the man you must meet Glubber at the gudger end of the tunnel on the night of the full moon. He thinks that will give you time to clear the tunnel, which is now filled in. As days and nights are different in his land he suggests you keep a careful track of time. Glubber does not ask for any payment other than for you to bring a unicorn with you. He has never seen one before. He states that the sight of such a mythical creature is reward enough.

This matter has been discussed with His Majesty, King Jeffrey, who states that there is no more we Kernans can do to help you. We can only wish you luck in bringing your mission to a successful conclusion.

p.s. His Majesty has asked me to say that he is very disappointed that you did not confide the true identity of the little man concerned. When Glubber mentioned that the victim wore a golden crown, he was easily identifiable by King Jeffrey. Our king saw Selogon, consort of the Fairy Queen, at the wedding of his son to Princess Jeanette – a little man with a golden crown.

Merlin breathed a sigh of relief; not only did he not have to travel to Kerner again but the Goblin King's identity remained secret. His continuous reference to a little man had, as he had planned, led to King Jeffrey believing the kidnap victim was someone completely

285

different. Goblins were known to be expert miners. If it were suspected that there were miners working near the forest, it might have led to people searching for the mines where they worked. Ultimately, the whereabouts of the legendary land of Zanadoo would no longer be a secret.

A broom landed nearby, then another and another.

"What's going on?" asked Jonathan, who was now looking over Merlin's shoulder in an attempt to read the parchment.

Yzor and Heather had also landed.

"There are Kernan soldiers outside," Ethel explained to her husband and new daughter-in-law. "They've brought a letter and a wagon with boxes on."

Merlin gave Jonathan the parchment. "Everyone on guard," he said. "I'm going to open the entrance, but I don't think there will be any trouble. They seem harmless enough. Stand back, please," Merlin ordered the Kernan soldiers, as the vines unravelled.

The soldiers did as they were bid.

"Thank you for bringing this private correspondence from your lord. Please send him my best wishes and tell him that I will meet our mutual friend on the date he has suggested. Now do you think you can repeat that for me, Jed? We don't want any mistakes."

The man dutifully repeated the message word for word.

"What about these boxes?" asked Jed. "Come on lads, let's get them off the cart and then we can all go home."

"No need," said Merlin in a haughty manner. He wanted to show off. The last time Jed had seen him in action he had failed to dispel the lightning charm on his pocket. He couldn't have anyone reporting to Jecquin that he had lost his powers.

A flick of his wand and the smallest box lifted itself off the wagon and on to the ground. *That was easy.* A second flick saw the middle sized box slowly edge its way to the side of the wagon before falling clumsily with a thud. *Oh dear, that wasn't very good. I'm going to make a fool of myself when I can't shift that large wooden chest.* However, the chest started to move on its own. He looked out of the corner of his eye and saw Jonathan and his father, Yzor, manipulating the large box for him. He joined his strength with theirs and the chest moved gracefully on to the ground. The Kernans, whose gaze was fixed on the display of magic in front of them, did not notice the assistance being given by the two other wizards.

Jed shook his head, "Well, you certainly got your strength back, Lord Merlin. The last time I saw you I didn't think you would last the night. I thought those mumps would be the death of you. But now, even though you've got the measles, you're back to doing magic tricks."

"Thank you, I…" Merlin was about to extol his own virtues, when he realised what Jed had said. "What do you mean measles?"

"You've got red blotches on your face."

"What? Have I?"

"Yes, you have," said Ethel. "I saw them this morning but didn't say anything at the time because I didn't want to spoil your brunch."

Merlin touched his face and felt the spots which had appeared. He felt both annoyed and foolish. *How could I have contracted yet another human illness and not realised it?*

"We'll be off now," said Jed. "Oh, I'd best give you the keys otherwise you won't be able to open the boxes."

Merlin did not accept the offered keys. He was indignant and felt the need show off again. He aimed his wand at the large box. Sparks flew, the lock turned on its own, and the lid flew open.

The Kernans stood back. They had not seen fire fly from a wand before. Everyone stared at the contents of the box which appeared to be folded cloth.

Ethel stepped nearer and lifted a layer of the cloth at the top. She stepped back, allowing the material to unfold, revealing a moth-eaten velvet curtain. She pushed it to one side and found the other matching one. One of the soldiers helped her lift the heavy pair of curtains out of the box. Underneath were the silk hangings from a four poster bed which had been faded on one side by the sun. Other torn lengths of worn material were piled one on top of another.

"Who would want all those old curtains and oddments of material?" asked the sergeant in charge of the soldiers. "When we were asked to bring these boxes from the Sea View Palace itself we thought there was something valuable inside. We've been guarding those boxes every night. What a waste of time!"

"There's a letter in the bottom." Ethel picked up the parchment and read it aloud.

Dear Merlin

We all had great fun looking through the attic and finding these old items for your wife to use making patchwork quilts. They are not all silk but thought you might be able to use other types of material too. We are

going to try to make a patchwork quilt ourselves.
Jeffrey will be so surprised when he sees it.
Kind Regards
Poppy

"How kind," Merlin said, his heart filling with emotion. The Kernans looked mystified. "Would you like to do the honours with the next box?" Merlin asked Yzor. He wasn't sure whether he had exhausted his powers for the day. Yzor unlocked the box and opened it with ease. He did not need keys either. Ethel picked up the items in the box while her wizarding family and Merlin still held their wands aloft. "It's full of baby clothes. There's two of everything – two pink, two blue, two white, two yellow, two purple – cardigans, bootees, leggings, bonnets, mittens... and look, right here at the bottom, two crochet shawls. I've found another letter." Again she read the contents aloud:

Dear Merlin
We enjoyed making clothes for your twins as much as we enjoyed playing Strike the Ball with you. There is two of everything so if you have two boys you can give the pink clothes away and vice versa. Hope to see you again soon.
Love
Hyacinth x

"Hyacinth? That's not Queen Shirley-Poppy's mad sister, is it?" asked the sergeant.
Merlin gave the sergeant a very stern look. "How dare you refer to the Lady Hyacinth as being mad!

Your good queen's sister is one of the nicest people I have ever met. I am sure His Majesty, King Jeffrey, would not wish to hear his sister-in-law being so described."

The soldier reddened. "I am sorry. I will always refer to the Lady Hyacinth with the greatest respect in future. It is just that we never see her so assumed there was something wrong."

"She is simply shy," the wizard responded.

"I suppose you want me to do the honours with the little box?" Jonathan enquired with a slight grin.

"Please do," responded Merlin graciously.

The small chest flew open to reveal a pair of child-sized matching silver mugs, the lips of which were decorated with alternating stars and half moons.

Ethel gasped as she took the mugs from the box. "They are beautiful. They must be extremely valuable." She read the letter enclosed with the gift so everyone could hear:

My Dear Lord Merlin

It was a pleasure to have your company at the palace.

We commissioned the royal silversmith to make these mugs for your twins, using the finest silver from our Kernan mines. We wish your wife a safe and healthy confinement. Please do let us know when the twins arrive.

Yours sincerely

Princess Jeanette of Twydell and Kerner.

"Please convey our most sincere thanks to the royal ladies. Tell them I will write to them as soon as my children are born," was all he could say as his tears continued to fall.

"Well, we had better be on our way then," Jed stated. "I hope you get over the measles as easily as you did the mumps, Lord Merlin."

The wagon driver got back in his vehicle and picked up the reins. The soldiers mounted and gave a salute before turning and heading back to their own country.

Jonathan picked up the parchment from Lord Jecquin which had been thrown to the ground. He handed it to Yzor. "Look at this, dad." His tone was even. "I think, now Merlin is better able to speak, he had better tell us what is going on."

Ethel and Heather, realising their menfolk wanted a meaningful word with Merlin, exchanged glances.

"Shall we walk back to the cottage together?" Ethel asked her daughter-in-law. "It would be nice to get to know each other better. I've hardly had chance to see you since I arrived."

The two women walked away arm in arm.

The three wizards sat cross legged on the grass. Two waited for an explanation from the other.

Chapter 14 – On The Road Again

"So, you have been to see one of these creatures that works in the Kernan mines, and have agreed to meet him again?" Yzor shook his head with annoyance as he asked the question.

"The Brambles told us you were off to find out more about gudgers," said Jonathan, disappointment on his long face. "All the time I was here, listening to your delirious babble about striking a ball into a boat and hitting it across a forest; you never once mentioned meeting one – or the risk of them burrowing into the cliffs near your home. The same home in which I've been spending my honeymoon!"

Merlin sat in guilty silence.

"Now we are part of the family, the Brambles decided we should also know about Zanadoo," Yzor added. "There were surprises all round because they didn't know Jonathan and I had been already been there with Tannus. They didn't realise that Zanadoo spread across the Twydell Granite Mountains to the North and we didn't know it spread, in the opposite direction, almost to Kerner."

"Heather and I didn't actually go into Zanadoo," Jonathan corrected his father. Then he added, "Only Heather and Great Grandmother have ever left the forest, so the other Brambles won't have a clue as to how far that chain of mountains actually spreads."

Merlin spoke at last. "I am sorry I didn't tell you about my meeting with Glubber, Jon. I was so hot and feverish when you were caring for me I wasn't sure what was fact and what was fantasy. I certainly didn't want to worry you before your wedding. As far as gudgers burrowing into the Forbidden Forest, I suppose they could tunnel their way through anywhere; you are just as safe staying in my home as anywhere else. If they really live in some sort of underground world in middle earth, what's restricting them to tunnelling in the mountains? They might turn up anywhere in Avalon or Twydell."

Jon continued to look down at the ground. His face remained sullen.

"So, it seems you are off to meet this creature again in less than three weeks?" asked Yzor.

"Yes, but I will have to leave long before then. If the passage through which the gudgers took Sprike has been filled in; I will have to find an alternative way through."

"I hardly think that the goblins will want to re-open a way to gudger land." Yzor pulled at his beard as he thought about it. "It would put them all at risk again."

"It won't be necessary to re-open the passage," said Merlin. "That would be a very silly thing to do, even if it gave them the opportunity to free their king."

"If he is still alive!" Yzor was sceptical. "How do you know this Glubber creature is telling the truth?"

"I don't," admitted Merlin. "The only way I will find out is by meeting Glubber as arranged."

"How will you do that without opening the passage? Sad as it is to think that Sprike is held prisoner, it would only put more lives at risk to try to free him – yours included!" Yzor levelled his gaze at the former leader of his wizard clan and spoke in no uncertain terms. "You are a very brave wizard, Merlin, but you have a wife and soon you will also have two children to think of. You should be putting your adventuring days behind you and concentrating on your family. My advice is to call another Wizzen, and let Tannus deal with this problem."

Merlin felt a mixture of rage and jealousy rise within himself. *Tannus is little more than a warlock*, he thought. *How dare Yzor suggest such a thing? I thought he was older and more sensible.* He tried to calm himself.

"Are you all right?" Jonathan asked. "You've started to go red again. Here, mum left some dock leaves soaking for you. Let me put them on your forehead."

"Thank you," said Merlin, holding onto his temper and reluctantly allowing the warlock to tend to him again.

"Take off your hat and lay back."

"No, no. I'll just sit here and hold them on my forehead. We still have much to talk about."

"Do we?" asked Jonathan. "Surely all we need to do now is call a Wizzen. I don't think there is much else to do except think of ways to prevent these gudgers digging through anywhere and everywhere." Exasperated with the situation, the young warlock could no longer hold back his feelings. "You amaze me, you really do! You and your cronies didn't like the idea of Tannus going off to the North doing his own thing but that's exactly what you have done. You should practise what you preach!"

"Careful, Jonathan," Yzor intervened. "Respect your seniors. Merlin is the most revered wizard to have ever lived." He turned to the former wizard leader. "However, my Jon has a point. Tannus was criticized

295

by the elders for taking action without telling anyone else what he was doing. Now you have done the same."

"Tannus and the Queen of the Witches received an invitation to the Princess of Barrmin's wedding," Merlin reminded his two counterparts. "He will be setting off soon if he has not done so already. A Wizzen could not be arranged until after his return and in the meantime I would have missed my opportunity to meet Glubber."

"But haven't we agreed that it would be too dangerous to re-open the tunnel leading to gudger land?" Yzor looked puzzled. "I don't understand how your mind is working."

Merlin threw his hat aside. He decided it would be better to lie back after all, that way he would not have to face his two fellow magicians. He pressed the dock leaves to his forehead and let the cool water soak his heated brow. In the branches above the spot where he lay, he could see Maisie in her goldfinch form. He watched her for several minutes, flitting backwards and forwards, chirping prettily.

"I often think it is foolish to share the form of your familiar with others." Merlin spoke as if his thoughts were elsewhere. "It is something private that every witch and wizard should keep to themselves."

"Is he delirious again?" Yzor asked his son.

"If he is, we will soon start to hear about this ball game again."

"Strike the Ball," Merlin stated, sitting up abruptly. "It is a game I learnt at the Sea View Palace. When I have time I will make such a game in my back garden, but I have other things to do first. No, I am not delirious again. I agree we need to hold another Wizzen but first I need to find out more about this middle earth and the gudgers who live there. I have a plan which will enable me to meet Glubber without putting the Zanadoonians at risk. If Sprike is still alive we may even be able to rescue him."

"We?" Yzor queried.

"Yes. I will need your help."

Yzor and Jonathan looked at each other as if they had no choice.

A few days later the party set out for Zanadoo. Merlin was much better thanks to his counterparts. His face was still blotchy but he was in good spirits. Fortunately, a new supply of candles had arrived to enable new healing spells to be performed.

Seth, the father of Isaiah and grandfather of Heather, had attended the wedding with his wife. When he left he was asked to come back with a new supply of candles. Merlin had retrieved the silver he had in his pockets. He had given one piece to Seth which was enough to pay for the candles plus all the other items on Bertha Bramble's list. The Brambles had always had to fend for themselves so, when Merlin suggested it, they found the idea of a shopping list to be a luxurious experience.

Seth was a wizard but had always hidden his skills and was untrained. When his three sons had exhibited magical talents, he had brought them to the forest for the Bramble family to bring up. His wife was a plainfolk and they had other non-magical children they wished to protect. Since witches and wizards had been accepted in Twydell he no longer had to hide what skills he had. He had been surprised to be invited to the

Wizzen and accepted as a wizard. He had joined what was now Tannus's clan.

It seemed that Seth had no sooner arrived with the shopping than he was asked to leave again. This time he was to take the long journey to Avalon and, in Tannus's absence, seek out Wormald the Wise and tell him about the gudgers.

Thanks to the rain dance that had been performed at the cottage the previous evening, the night had been speckled with light showers. However, as the party set out at first light a strong wind blew up, bringing with it an assembly of dark clouds. Merlin, alone at his shack, had performed his own version of the spell. He had chanted, paced and scattered burnt sage to purify the air; he even put his supper, of home-made spinach pie, into the fire as a sacrifice. He was satisfied that he had regained his power which had diminished so much whilst he was ill. *They would never have got such dark clouds if I had not done my bit*, he reasoned.

The party set off. Although it would have been more pleasant travelling in fair conditions, they were pleased to see the rain. Human huntsmen were not usually so active in bad weather and it was not a long journey. Jonathan flew overhead acting as a scout on the lookout for danger. Yzor hovered above the driverless slender cart, drawn by Lucky, which was half full with cabbages and cauliflowers that Seth had bought. The gardens in the forest were fast running out of supplies with so many more mouths to feed than in previous years. Both Yzor and Jonathan were skilled garden wizards but both had been away so long that they had not had the opportunity to re-stock the gardens. Even now when they were back in the forest there were other things which needed doing like nursing Merlin or building an extension to the Brambles' cottage – or joining Merlin on one of his adventures.

Merlin rode Comet. Lennox kept between Comet and the cart so that his single horn would not be so easily spotted by any lurking humans.

Sheba had wanted to go with them. She longed to bring back Fiery, but had been dissuaded by Lennox. "You are with foal. It would be foolish to put our child at risk. I promised that I would bring Fiery back to you one day. If he is willing to leave then I will keep my promise. The dangers which prevented us bringing him here before no longer exist."

Blaize and Luna had also demanded the right to join the party. Lennox had argued with them. He was relieved when Merlin told them, in no uncertain terms, that they could not go.

"Whilst we can shield Lennox to some extent, it is not possible to hide three fully grown unicorns. Lennox will keep his head down to hide his horn. Like my Comet, he is as white as snow. If we were seen, people would think that I now owned two fine steeds; they would probably think they were brothers."

Blaize and Luna had reluctantly yielded but not before Lennox had promised both that he would do his best to persuade their offspring to come back with him.

Although Lennox had only done the journey once, in the opposite direction, he recognised the spot where Ned the donkey had left him and his herd. They passed the giants' house. The giants watched from their garden and waved as they went by, but did not attempt to approach. Merlin and Yzor waved back. Lennox kept his head down as he maintained his place between

Comet and the cart, hoping his horn would not be visible.

Lennox was worried that he might not recognise the part of the mountain from which Zanadoo was accessible.

Merlin told him not to worry. "If Zan is anywhere as proficient as his niece with a crystal ball he will know we are on our way."

Sure enough, Ned found them before they went too far off track. Lennox was so pleased to see the grey donkey he cantered forward, breaking his cover to greet him.

At the entrance two stone gnomes stood guard. They stamped their spears on the ground in welcome. Unfortunately, the gesture made Lucky and Comet shy away. Ned apologised to them but horse and pony still refused to enter the cave. Lucky said it reminded him too much of the mines he had worked in and Comet said he would simply prefer to stay outside with his friend.

Hooves could be heard beating along the stone passageway. Bunty emerged from out of the gloom and raced towards Lennox. They rubbed noses and brushed against each other. "I've missed you so much," she said.

"My mares and I missed you, too. It is a delight to see you again."

"Now, let's hurry along," Ned advised. "Zan and Muffle will want their mid morning nap soon and once they are asleep it is difficult to rouse them. What is more, they are very grumpy if their sleep is disturbed."

Bunty said she would stay with Lucky and Comet. There were patches of grass outside the cave. "It will be nice to have another pony for company," she stated, giving the visitors a wink. "Not that I don't enjoy the company of donkeys and mules of course," she added, glancing at Ned.

Before leaving the equines, Merlin uttered his doubling spell over the cart half filled with vegetables. "There you go, that should be enough to keep you going and some to share if required." The quantity of cabbages and cauliflowers increased to such an extent that they spilled over the sides of the cart, on to the ground.

Ned and Lennox led the way, trotting alongside each other, followed by the three wizards on brooms. After a few hundred yards the passage was lit by pine resin torches; the adventurers continued onwards. The sound of tumbling rocks could be heard before they reached the rose cavern. Zan was waiting for them on a platform overlooking the quarry. He sat propped up by cushions on his couch. On one side was a small table on which was placed his glass ball. Muffle sat on his haunches on the other side of his ancient master; beneath him was a bed of straw.

"So, this is the wizard who stole my niece's heart," said Zan as he looked Merlin up and down.

"I am Merlin, your niece's husband, so I suppose that would make me your nephew-in-law. It is a pleasure to meet you. Please let me introduce you to Yzor and his son Jonathan."

Zan moved his pale face towards the other wizards. "Ah, yes, I have met Yzor before – the magician who speaks to those large birds. How is your friend young Tannus? A very resourceful person."

301

Yzor bowed his head in acknowledgement. "I am honoured that you remember me. It was actually Merlin who taught me to speak the thunderbird tongue – he is an expert in languages. Tannus is probably on his way to the North by now; he is attending the wedding of the Princess of Barrmin to a count from another country."

"Yes, you are right; I have seen Tannus on a ship with the Witch Queen. She is a beautiful lady. Such a well-matched couple, they will achieve much together."

Zan slowly turned his head to Jonathan. It was as if his head was too stiff to move easily. "I recognise this young man, too. You helped your father and Tannus seal Zanadoo's entrance in the North. Pity, but it had to be done to protect us. Congratulations on your exchange of rings with that nice little witch. You are well suited and will be very happy together. It was brave of her to accompany you to the North."

"Heather and I have never met you. How did you know we had wed?" asked Jonathan, but he knew the answer.

"I saw you in my crystal ball, of course! Just as I watched you both rid the North of that poisonous weed. I actually saw your matrimony before you did. It was such a touching little ceremony. It was a pity Merlin could not be there."

"Alas, I was suffering with mumps and could not go near the Brambles' cottage for fear that Helen would catch it."

"And now you have measles," said Zan. "Your wife has hardly seen you!" There was a sudden change of tone in Zan's voice, a certain harshness was detectable. "Even though young Tannus has replaced you as leader of the wizards you still find it hard to stay at home, don't you?"

"Zan," Merlin defended himself, "I felt I had no choice but to find out more about these gudgers. They have burrowed into both Zanadoo and Kerner. I wish to protect the Forbidden Forest; even if there are colonies of these reptiles which are non-aggressive, we cannot allow them to enter our forest. A unique enchantment protects our home which would peter out if too many creatures found their way in."

"That is for sure," agreed Zan. "The Forbidden Forest's enchantment has evolved with nature because it has been barely inhabited for many years. You must not allow too many people to enter the forest or its charm will ebb away."

Zan turned to Yzor and Jonathan. "I am not referring to you when I utter my concerns about the growing number of people in the forest. You are skilled gardeners and I see you doing much to help the evolving wilderness. You will also help Merlin with the silly game he wants to make in Helen's back garden."

"Will we?" Jonathan looked confused.

"For sure." Zan even gave a little laugh and Muffle joined in with his hee-hawing and ear wiggling.

"Now, it will soon be time for our mid morning nap, so let us talk business. I gather you have some sort of scheme which will put a stop to these gudgers and their burrowing."

"I do indeed have a plan but it will mean that the goblins and dwarves I see working in the quarry below will have to stop filling in the tunnel leading to the gudgers' world."

"Well, they are not going to like that!" Zan stated. "You had better tell Sprikeson and Dorf what your plan is and persuade them that we will all benefit from it."

"Rose-Grace," called the ancient man and a tall graceful woman seemed to emerge from nowhere. Like Zan she was nearly transparent; it was only her rose coloured skin and clothing and burgundy hair which made her visible. "If you please, my dear, would you be so kind as to fetch Sprikeson and Dorf?"

The woman floated rather than walked away.

"Sit," suggested Zan. "Partake in water and oat biscuits – they are very tasty."

Other women similar to Rose-Grace brought chairs and refreshments for the visitors. One had skin the colour of pale lilac and hair of deep purple; another was bathed in yellow and yet a third in shimmering white; all resembled the different colours of the mineral stones within Zanadoo.

The wizards took their seats. Lennox found the spot where water drizzled down the walls into a stone basin, next to a bucket of oats which had been placed there for him. Ned snuggled down beside Muffle as if he too were ready to enjoy a well-earned rest.

"Who are those women?" Merlin asked.

"They are the stone graces," responded Zan. "They are very lovely, are they not?"

"They are exquisite," replied Merlin. "I have never seen a race quite like them before."

"I first saw one when I visited you in the North," Yzor said. "She was a yellow colour but as she was touched by the light she changed to shades of pink and green."

"That was the zanite grace." A smile flickered across Zan's ancient face. "Each stone has its own grace who cares for it, not just keeping it polished and clean, but making sure our hard working dwarves do not mine it to extinction. The graces have been here since long before the dwarves and goblins arrived and far longer than me. I fell in love, or was infatuated, when I first saw them. I was a young man then. If the gudgers take over Zanadoo the graces will not survive. This is why I wish your mission to be successful. I am not a magician, merely a soothsayer, but I know there is something magical about the graces. You have chosen to undertake an arduous and perilous venture. Somehow I feel their will alone will give you the strength you need when you need it most."

The rose woman returned with a burly dwarf and a younger, sinewy goblin; their face and clothes were covered with dust from the quarry below. They were accompanied by the three young unicorns who had remained in Zanadoo.

Like the other women, Rose-Grace glided from view as effortlessly as she had emerged.

After introductions, Zan told the newcomers that Merlin wanted them to stop blocking the tunnel.

"Are you mad?" Dorf the dwarf stood with hands on hips looking at Merlin as if he were insane.

"If we stop blocking the passageway which links Zanadoo to middle earth we would soon be overrun with gudgers!"

Sprikeson was aghast. "The gudgers are removing the rocks we use to fill the passage, almost as fast as we can put them in. It is a job that will never end. We will spend the rest of our lives filling that tunnel; any delay just gives the gudgers a better chance of getting through."

"But I need to travel to middle earth," Merlin persisted. "I am meeting a gudger there, called Glubber. He says Sprike is still alive and, in exchange for sight of a unicorn, he will help us free King Sprike…"

"Ludicrous," bellowed Dorf. "No one in their right mind would expect us to open up the passageway to middle earth."

"Even if my father is still alive," stated Sprikeson, "which I doubt, he would not want everyone in Zanadoo to be put at risk for the sake of a failed rescue. I say failed because that is what it would be. There is no chance of rescuing him." Sprikeson wiped the dirt from his sweating brow.

"I would not dream of asking you to open up the passage." Merlin smiled. "I merely ask you to stop filling it till we return."

"Return from where?" demanded Dorf. "You have only just arrived. Where are you going?"

"To middle earth – the land of the gudgers," replied Merlin. "Now, pray listen while I tell you how I propose to get there."

"All the years I've known you, I didn't know you had a familiar." Yzor scratched his head.

"As I said to you the other day," said Merlin. "It is not wise to let other people know you can transform. Using transformation can be a means of escape. But if it is known that you can turn into a dog or a cat, your pursuers will be watching for you. Plus it is a useful way of collecting information – no one would suspect it was actually me hanging from the ceiling, listening to what they are saying."

The sorcerer turned to Lennox. "You are very brave, Lennox. I was afraid you would refuse to accompany me."

"I am willing to go in Lennox's place," Flambeau put in. "Sprike is my friend. Lennox doesn't know him and has no reason to put his life in jeopardy."

"Alas." Merlin tried not to sound unkind as he spoke to Flambeau. "Glubber's price is to see a unicorn. A unicorn with no horn may not satisfy his curiosity."

"Sprike is my father," Sprikeson stated. "I should also accompany Merlin."

"I understand your wish to help rescue your father, Sprikeson, but I am not sure what service you could provide. If anything happens to me then Yzor might be able to work the magic that could help Lennox and perhaps even Sprike to get back. A fourth person might make our task more difficult. What is that saying, 'Too many cooks spoil the broth'?"

"And there's another saying," Sprikeson responded quickly. "'Many hands make light work.'"

"That's true enough," echoed Jonathan. "I'd like to go, too."

"No, Jon," said Merlin. "You have a young wife. Besides, a magician must remain here. If Yzor and I were not to return, who would turn Lennox or Sprike back into themselves? I have written down the words of the spell. Try to memorise it. If I fail to return and you can't get the spell to work then take whoever returns to the Brambles and ask them to try. If you still have no success take them to Wormald, he will be able to put them right."

307

"I have no doubt you can transform yourself." Yzor was looking more than a little anxious. "It's a skill some wizards happen to have, but have you ever transformed anyone else before?"

"Well, I have to admit, it was a long time ago but it did eventually work."

"Eventually?" Yzor shook his head. "What am I letting myself in for this time?"

"Try it on me." Sprikeson spoke up. "I am not afraid."

Merlin raised his eyebrows. "Well, if you don't mind?" He was somewhat taken aback by the goblin's offer.

"I don't mind at all," said Sprikeson. "And if I let you experiment on me, will you let me go with you?"

Merlin tightened his lips in annoyance but Sprikeson interrupted before he could speak. "I helped dig the tunnel you are about to enter, along with other passageways which run off it. I may well be of service to you if you get lost. The tunnels have changed much in appearance since I last stepped foot in them, but I still know them better than you. If you get lost, or find one route completely blocked, I would be the only one able to assist."

"Well said, Sprikeson!" said Merlin. "You have persuaded me. You are a very brave fellow to put yourself in this position."

"What about me?" Flambeau asked. He had not understood the words spoken between wizard and goblin but he could guess. "Sprike was *my* friend. He is the sole reason I stayed behind instead of going to the Forbidden Forest with my mother and the rest of the herd. I wanted to stay in order to help in any rescue attempt."

It was Lennox who spoke. "That is true. Let Flambeau come with us, Merlin, but on one condition." Lennox did not wait for the wizard to give his consent. "If you come with us, Flambeau, no matter whether or not the rescue is successful, promise me you will go to the Forbidden Forest and one day take up your rightful place as leader of the herd. You may have lost your horn but you will have children. One of your offspring may well be born with a golden horn."

"It was always my intention to find my way to your forest one day," replied the young black stallion. "I promise I will go there if I return. I hope we will both return and you will teach me to follow in your footsteps."

"So, it seems as if Lennox has made a decision for me," Merlin told the rest of the party. "Flambeau will join us too. The rescue trio is now a rescue quintet."

Taking his wand, he looked at Sprikeson. "Are you sure about this?"

"As sure as I ever will be."

Without giving Sprikeson a chance to rethink, Merlin drew his wand, muttered some words, and struck the goblin none too gently on the head.

Dorf looked on in awestruck silence as his colleague disappeared. "Where is he?"

"There he is." Jonathan pointed to a small dark spider on the ground.

Even Zan and Muffle, who had listened in silence to the plan to rescue Sprike and the subsequent arguments, leaned forward to see the insect. The spider was turning in circles trying to get its bearings.

Ned got up from the bed of straw he shared with Muffle, and walked over to take a closer look.

"Careful, old timer!" Lennox called out. "Don't tread on him. I don't think even Merlin could turn a squashed spider back into a goblin."

Ned stood stock still, afraid to move, before pacing backwards.

"Right, Jon, have you got the words? Try to memorise them rather than read. Always look directly at your victim, or in this case volunteer, and speak the words with as much meaning as you can put into them. Remember you must replace the word 'wizard' with 'goblin' – not that I think Sprikeson would actually return as a wizard."

"Stay still, Sprikeson," Yzor ordered. "How can the boy make the spell work if you keep moving. If you want to be the subject of a successful spell try not to move!"

The spider stood motionless.

Jon read the words to himself again. When he finished he pointed his wand at the unmoving spider. Staring into its eyes he said,

"A spider's life is not for thee,

From this spell I set ye free,

A goblin again ye must be!"

Jonathan flicked his wand at the spider but Sprikeson remained as an eight-legged arachnid. The warlock looked at the people watching him. Every face, including his own, was full of dismay.

"Silly me, I forgot to give you the powder." Merlin searched through his pockets, and drew out the blue posy bag which the royal ladies had made for him. "Wrong one. It reminds me, though, I should have asked the Brambles to make a nosegay for you, too, Yzor." He searched again in the depths of his long pockets. "Here it is. I knew it was in there somewhere."

He pulled out a dirty brown bag and gave it to Jonathan.

"As you say the last word, of the last line, throw a pinch of this into the spider's face. Take a pinch before you start and hold it between your thumb and finger on your left hand and hold your wand in your right. I seem to remember you must get your timing right so flick the powder and the wand at the same time."

"How long ago is it that you last performed this spell, Merlin?" asked Yzor, his face betraying his anxiety.

"A while ago," admitted Merlin.

"More than fifty years?"

"Probably."

"More than a hundred?"

"No. Not that long."

"This stuff looks like it's more than a hundred years old." Jonathan felt the fine powder within the bag. "What is it, Merlin?"

"Ground spider webs. What else would you use to perform an arachnid related spell?"

Jonathan considered the question. "Silk, perhaps?"

"What a good idea," Merlin declared. "I never thought of that. We must try it sometime."

"But not today!" Yzor was getting agitated. "Try again, Jon. Just as Merlin told you."

Jonathan tried a second time. He stared at the spider first to concentrate his mind. Then he raised his wand in his right hand, holding a pinch of the powder firmly in his left.

"A spider's life is not for thee,
From this spell I set ye free,
A goblin again ye must be."

This time he flicked his wand and threw the pinch of cobweb dust at exactly the same time. The spider started to spin, gradually turning back into Sprikeson, who sneezed and coughed as he emerged as himself again.

"Ugh, that cobweb powder is disgusting. Did he have to blow it in my face? Couldn't he have done it from behind?"

"No, it's very important that you breathe it in and blow it out." Merlin gave the warlock a wide smile. "Well done, Jon. You are becoming a highly accomplished magician."

"Yes, well done, my boy!" Yzor beamed with pride.

Jonathan, who was naturally quite a shy warlock, started to turn crimson.

Dorf the Dwarf scratched his head with one hand and pulled his beard with the other. Then he decided to pinch himself. "I am awake," he said to himself. "And I haven't been drinking."

Dorf and Sprikeson commanded the workers to stop what they were doing and called them together. They chose two large rocks, a short distance apart, on which to stand. Dorf spoke first; burly men and women came together to listen to him, surrounding the rock on which he stood.

Meanwhile, the wiry goblins surrounded the rock on which Sprikeson stood but all maintained a respectful silence to hear Dorf's words.

Both dwarves and goblins had faces lined with hard work. Hair, faces, hands and clothes were dirty with the quarry dust which filled the air. Dorf spoke in a loud voice which echoed across the quarry. First of all he introduced the three magicians who bowed politely before taking seats on nearby boulders. Dwarves and goblins looked at the wizards. Some came forward to touch them and look into their faces as if to make sure they were real. *Perhaps*, thought Merlin, *they think we are plainfolk dressed up*. Lennox and Flambeau stood close by.

"Don't worry," Lennox whispered to Merlin. "They are just curious." Nevertheless, the unicorn still resented being touched by people he did not know. As hands brushed him he moved uneasily from hoof to hoof, until the younger black unicorn nuzzled him to give him reassurance.

The leader of the dwarves told his people that the wizards had a plan which 'might', as he put it, rescue Sprike. Dorf didn't describe the plan, and made it quite clear that he had no faith that the project would be successful. However, he added, "If these kind people and unicorns are willing to put their lives at risk then who am I to try to stop them."

There were a flood of questions but the army of workers remained well behaved. Most wanted Dorf to describe the plan but he said he would leave that to the old sorcerer who stood before them.

One dwarf asked, "If we stop filling the tunnels which lead to middle earth are we not putting our lives at risk as well?"

"If we stop for any length of time and the rescue party does not return then, yes, that's right, we would be putting the whole of Zanadoo at risk, but we have to give them this chance," answered Dorf. "After all, it is not just Zanadoo at risk; the gudgers seem to be burrowing through in other places. Even if Sprike is not rescued we may find out things about these creatures which will put a stop to their capers, once and for all."

There were murmurs of agreement all round but expressions of anxiety reflected in every face.

Next it was Sprikeson who spoke. The wiry goblins looked up at their leader while the dwarf turned in his direction. "I hope that I will find my father again and bring him back. He is, or was, a fine man." Voices from his audience confirmed that they too missed the goblin king.

"I have feared since he was kidnapped that he is dead. However, Merlin here, this old magician, has spoken to a gudger. The gudger has told him that my father, your king, is still alive."

The idea of anyone speaking to a gudger seemed extraordinary to the audience who raised voices with a myriad of questions.

"How did he talk to them?" asked one.

"How do you know this man, magician or not, is speaking the truth?" asked another.

"Even if the magician can speak to gudgers, who would believe such odious creatures? This gudger is trying to dupe the old magician! Why can't he see that?"

"How can you rescue Sprike without opening up the tunnel and putting all our lives at risk?"

"Those reptiles are setting a trap to let themselves in! They would take over our home in no time!"

Sprikeson bid them to be quiet a moment. "Merlin is Zan's nephew-in-law," he continued. This fact seemed to calm the audience which had become quite agitated. "He is not planning to open the tunnel, merely to access middle earth by creeping along the crevices." Heads shook and voices of mistrust were loud.

"Please be patient," pleaded Sprikeson. "Let Merlin show you how he intends to find his, or rather our, way to the land of the gudgers."

Merlin stepped forwards. The dwarves and goblins made way for him. He looked even taller than usual as he walked through the audience. He stood next to the boulder on which Sprikeson was standing so that they were eye to eye.

"Merlin is going to transform me into a spider," said Sprikeson. "Please do not be concerned."

The little man turned to the sorcerer, who stood in front of him with wand poised. "Let's get on with it then, Merlin," he said.

The sorcerer wasted no time in striking the goblin across the head. The watchers echoed cries of horror as they watched the goblin leader shrink before their eyes until they could see him no more.

Goblins started to move, in a single crowd, towards the boulder on which Sprikeson had stood. Hands sought to find his whereabouts. A small black spider on a grey rock with dark crevices is not easily seen.

"Stop! Stop!" shouted Merlin. "You are going to squash him."

"Get back, you fools!" yelled Dorf. "Give him space."

Muffle hee-hawed in a warning tone.

The goblin workforce realised the danger and stood back.

Merlin gave a sigh of relief.

Dorf fell off the rock on which he stood. He got up, without bothering to dust away the dirt, and paced to the boulder on which Sprikeson had stood. "Where is he?" the dwarf leader cried. "I can't see him."

"Probably hiding in a crevice," answered Merlin. "He'll come out when he knows it is safe."

Rose-Grace glided through the crowd like a ghost, silent and without any need to push anyone aside she found her way around the mass of onlookers. She carried with her a small shallow dish made of rose stone. She was so tall she peered over the rock, casting a pink shadow across its grey face. In one graceful movement she scooped up the spider and placed it on her dish. Then she glided to one side.

"Thank you Rose-Grace." Merlin bowed his head in acknowledgement of the strange woman's assistance.

"Right, let us continue. Yzor, you're next." The sorcerer turned to where he thought his fellow wizard sat, but he and his son had moved further towards the tunnel entrance. They appeared deep in conversation. Merlin's brow furrowed; *what are those two up to?*

"Do Lennox next, will you?" Yzor turned momentarily before returning to his conversation with Jonathan.

Merlin looked at the pair with some irritation but, as Lennox stepped forward, he got on with the job. "Stand well back everyone, *please!*"

The crowd stepped further back.

Lennox gradually shrank into a large white spider, with a strange point on its forehead. The crowd murmured in wonderment. Jade-Grace slid across the floor. In one elegant movement she scooped the spider up and gently placed him into the green bowl she carried. She took her place beside her rose sister.

"Well, he'll be easily spotted when he comes back. This place is full of spiders and as you say it would be easy to tread on one. Have you thought of that?" asked Dorf.

"These lovely ladies obviously have," Merlin replied. "If the dishes are left at the point where the blockage starts, we will each be able to crawl down into these colourful dishes."

The graces sang some sort of response in their musical voices.

Merlin looked over at Yzor, who was still in discussion with Jonathan. They were pointing at the tunnel entrance and their hands and head movements told him they were debating something. In the meantime, without any bidding, Flambeau stepped forward.

One strike of the wand and some magic words and the ebony unicorn became a large black arachnid. This time it was Topaz-Grace who came forward to lift him into her small yellow plate.

"Yzor, are you ready?" the sorcerer shouted. There was an impatient tone to his voice.

"Yes." The wizard hurried to the rock on which Sprikeson had stood. "But before you turn me into an insect, may I tell everyone that my son has to leave for a day or two. Don't worry, he will be back. If any of us return and Merlin doesn't, just keep us in these wonderful dishes until Jonathan gets back."

"Where is he going?" asked Merlin and Dorf almost in unison.

"Home to the forest." Yzor spoke to the crowd. "Some of you may be aware of how Tannus and I sealed the entrance to Zanadoo in the North. My son and I are wondering if we can do the same here, but we have our doubts."

"Ah," said Dorf, "I have seen the seal myself but I didn't know you were the architect. A vine which burns, bites and strangles if touched. We all have to keep well away from it."

"I'm sorry about that," said Yzor. "But as you know, the only way to stop an invasion by the northerners was to seal the Karminesque entrance."

"That is true." Dorf bowed his head in acknowledgement. "You and the young wizard Tannus have served us well."

Tannus again. Merlin bit his lip. *Can that warlock do no wrong in anyone else's eyes?*

"I make no promises whatsoever in this case," Yzor stated firmly. "All plants need light and fresh air and that is something the quarry lacks. But Jon will do his best. He is a skilled plant wizard. However, the Bramble family are the experts in protective bindweed. Jon will fly back to the forest and seek help from the witches who live there. Jonathan will be back with some samples and see if he can persuade one of the lady witches to help."

The proud father added, "Jon married one of the Bramble ladies recently, you know."

"Congratulations." Dorf nodded in recognition and there was a small round of applause. "We will do all we can to assist you, Jon."

Jonathan turned red again.

"Now, I am ready." Yzor took a deep breath. He was not looking forward to the experience at all but did his best not to show his true feelings.

Merlin struck fast. He didn't want to give the reluctant Yzor time to change his mind.

"Good luck, dad," Jonathan called hoping his father would hear him as he shrank away.

This time it was the Grace of Lapis Lazuli who swiftly scooped the brown spider on to her blue dish.

"Now who will I get?" asked Merlin, looking round before transforming himself. He was pleased to see Amethyst-Grace glide towards him. "Ah, purple, my favourite colour. Thank you, dear lady."

The sorcerer had transformed himself so many times into his familiar that he did not need his wand, which he had carefully placed in his pocket to take with him. He didn't shrink either, he was merely replaced by a grey spider. The grace gently removed him from the rock on which he stood and placed him in the safety of her amethyst dish.

The graces made their way to the blocked tunnel where Jonathan still stood. The young man looked down at each of the creatures standing on their individual plates.

"Take care, dad. Please come back safe and sound," he whispered to the brown spider.

Fiery and Feerce pushed their way through the crowd of dwarf and goblin workers; Ned followed. The unicorns whinnied and pawed the ground. Ned hee-hawed and he too brushed the ground with his hooves. The crowd of workers raised their voices with cries of "good luck", "come back safely", "The graces be with you."

The small black spider, which was Sprikeson, led the way. He crawled up the debris which blocked the tunnel to a crevice at the side of the passageway, with his four companions following behind him in a line. As the five arachnids disappeared from sight, every face in the watching crowd showed signs of trepidation.

Jonathan made his way up to the platform where he had left his broom and where Merlin and Yzor had left theirs for him to look after. He had been followed by Dorf, Ned and the unicorn foals. Zan and Muffle were still slumbering and softly snoring.

"Will you look after these, please?" the warlock asked Dorf.

"Do you think I could try one out?" asked the dwarf leader.

"No, sorry, they won't work for you; besides, Merlin and dad would be very cross if they came back and found their brooms damaged." Dorf looked miffed. "Right, I'm off now. Please look after dad and anyone else who gets back before I return. If Merlin is with them then he'll turn them back to their real selves again, but if not please take care of them." Jonathan knew he was repeating himself but he was nervous about the whole project.

Dorf gave him the assurances he needed and he set off on his broomstick. The workforce below stood and watched, waving their goodbyes. As Jonathan weaved his way along the passage he was conscious of hoof beats behind him. He looked around to see Feerce and Fiery following. Knowing that the unicorns could not travel fast on such hard flooring, he slowed down so they could keep pace. Then he picked up speed again as he saw daylight.

The warlock took the gnomes, guarding the equines outside, completely unawares. They stumbled to the ground as he whizzed past. "Sorry," Jonathan shouted as he looked back over his shoulder. Comet, Lucky and Bunty looked up. He waved as he passed them by. *They are probably wondering why I am leaving so soon. I wish I could speak the equine language.* Looking back over his shoulder he saw Fiery and Feerce joining the horses. *I hope they come home with us. Those magnificent creatures shouldn't be living in what is little more than a huge cave. I hope Comet and Lucky will persuade them that life could be so much better for them in the forest. That little dun pony would like the forest life, too. She is so cute; I've never seen a horse wink before.*

Jonathan's heart skipped a beat when he saw the Forbidden Forest in front of him. *I'll be home with Heather tonight. I'm missing her already and I've only been away for a day.*

Chapter 15 – Middle Earth

The spider rescue party wove its way along the filthy crevices. All, except for Sprikeson, who was used to dust and dirt, coughed and spluttered for the first few hours. Gradually the four, who were not used to living in a mining environment, became better able to cope with their surroundings. Nevertheless, they longed to breathe fresh air again. During their journey they met many other types of insect. They were surprised to find that they could understand what other spiders said, and other spiders could understand them, too. However, different species of insects spoke diverse dialects which only Merlin was able to comprehend.

"I've never seen a white spider before," one large arachnid commented. "Nor have I seen one with a spike on his head."

"Oh, he's a foreigner." Merlin gave one of his explanations which was not untrue but still provided misinformation "He comes from a place where humans capture unusual creatures like him. We let him join us in this new land where he hopes he will find wives and father other beings like himself."

The large spider tut tutted as it looked the white spider over with interest. "I am glad you managed to escape. Where did you come from?"

"A place called Briton," Lennox replied truthfully.

"What was it like there?"

"Much the same as Twydell but there were more humans."

"There must have been a lot then, there are too many here. You have to watch where you crawl or they simply tread on you; they just don't care where they put their flat feet. Others scream and point at the sight of you – usually the females. Next thing you know you've got a male chasing you for frightening his woman, when the only crime you've committed is to go about your usual business!"

"Shameful," agreed Merlin.

"Mind you, bad as humans are, those gudger reptiles are much worse."

"Are they?" asked Yzor. "I've never seen one."

"If you do, keep your distance," the spider warned. "They have long tongues which reach out and grab every insect which catches their eye. I've lost at least fifty sons and daughters to those vile creatures. I've lost a few wives too."

"I am sorry to hear that," said Sprikeson, not wanting to miss out on the conversation.

"Have none of you seen gudgers before?"

"I have," replied Sprikeson.

"Me, too," added Merlin.

"I saw them once," Flambeau put in.

"Then why are you not warning your other friends about them? Your white companion will easily be spotted. They won't even appear to be looking at you when wham! That long pink thing they keep in their mouths will strike and you won't have a chance."

"You seem to have survived," commented Merlin. "I suppose the older you get the wiser you become. Youngsters think they know it all; they don't pay heed to what advice their elders give them; then when they get themselves into trouble we have to pick up the pieces."

"True, my friend," said the spider. "So very true. I have watched many of my family die. Painful as it has been to see them devoured by reptiles, my other offspring learn by the mistakes of the ones we lose. I always tell my children to get back into narrow cracks as far as they can when they see gudgers. But there are always some who are curious and want to watch the ugly beasts. They get too close to the edge, thinking their small bodies are hidden by shadow; next thing they know they are being swiped by a pink tongue. Those long tongues can slither into the narrowest crevices if the gudgers think there are titbits hiding within."

"We will make sure we stay within the deepest cracks in the walls," Yzor, the brown spider, assured their new friend.

"I suppose you have heard about the limitless supplies of insects in middle earth," the large spider queried. "I can't think of any other reason you would be travelling in the direction you are going. Personally, I think the benefits of keeping away from gudgers outweigh the reward of sweet food. There are still plenty of flies and other insects in Twydell so that is where I am headed. Well, it's been nice chatting to you but I'd better be on my way. Goodbye."

"Please, tarry a few moments longer," Merlin implored the spider. "Pray tell us, how far are we away from the gudgers? We don't want to go walking into them."

"Walking into them? You won't do that! They are making a terrible amount of noise clearing away the rocks that the little men keep throwing down this hole. Put your ear against the wall, and you will probably be able to hear them from where you stand. They get closer every day to the place where those horrible little humans and the nearly transparent man live."

"Really?" Sprikeson's tone was somewhat indignant. He didn't like the Zanadoonians being described as horrible.

"Oh, yes," replied the spider. "Gudgers and humans deserve each other. I hope they wipe each other out and leave the world to decent creatures like us."

Flambeau placed one of his eight arms round Sprikeson to pacify him. The small spider kept his mouth shut.

"Quite so," said Merlin, playing the diplomat. "Well, goodbye my friend. I hope you find what you want in Twydell."

"Goodbye, again," said the spider. "By the way, you may find a few of my old webs on the way to middle earth. If there is any fresh food in them, feel free to help yourselves. I won't be returning."

"Thank you," Merlin called after the arachnid. His companions politely uttered words of gratitude. However, none had any desire to empty the spider's larder.

All five pressed their ears against the wall to see if they could hear the approaching gudgers. Sure enough faint sounds in the distance were apparent and they could even feel a slight tremor beneath their feet.

"We have only been travelling for two days and we can already hear them." Sprikeson showed the alarm he felt as he shifted from one set of feet to another. "They are even closer than I thought. This is dreadful. My people have stopped work while we travel to middle earth and back. The time our journey will take is a waste of valuable time which could be used filling the tunnel. My father would never want us to risk other people's lives to save his. We should return to Zanadoo now and get everyone back to work!"

"Only by educating ourselves about the gudgers' way of life will we find a mechanism to stop their progress," said Merlin philosophically. "We may not be able to free your father, but we can learn more about gudgers and the world they live in."

Sprikeson was not pacified and put up a variety of arguments as to why the companions should turn around and go back to Zanadoo.

Eventually Merlin grew weary of this arguing. "Sprikeson, you cannot continue to have your people working every day of their lives filling one hole continuously!"

"We don't work *every* day," said Sprikeson. "We have rest periods."

"How many people work, for how many hours, each day?"

"We take it in turn to work three shifts a day. About thirty, or forty people, labour at any one time."

"And the goblins, who are skilled craftsmen, have had to join with the dwarves who are the miners to fill the hole. So there is not much crafting going on these days."

"It is the only way," Sprikeson replied. "We all need to work together to keep those murderous beasts out!"

"But despite craftsmen and miners working together, all day and all night, the gudgers are getting closer," Merlin reasoned. "We must find another way of stopping them."

In desperation, Sprikeson turned to Yzor. "Your idea of sealing the tunnel with spiteful bindweed, do you think it will work?"

327

Yzor tried to shake his head. A spider shaking its head looked rather queer; it simply wobbled from ear to leg. "In all honesty I don't think so. Plants need sunshine and fresh air; there is little of either in Zanadoo but let's see what Jon can achieve."

"You should be back there helping him!" Sprikeson was growing more agitated and was now levelling his frustration at Yzor.

As the goblin and wizards were arguing in spider language, Lennox and Flambeau could understand all that was being said and joined the debate.

"We have come this far, let us not turn back when we are so close." Lennox tried to reason with the goblin.

Everyone except Sprikeson agreed that the quest should continue. The small arachnid stamped all eight of his feet in frustration and tumbled over, naturally rolling into a ball just like a real spider as he did so.

"Glubber said he would meet me at the entrance to the tunnel." Merlin remained calm. "If the gudgers think I can hear them working they will worry that I will turn and go back. They will stop work when they think I am approaching with a unicorn."

Do you think it is a trap, then?" asked Yzor, aghast.

"Of course I do."

"Now he tells me!" Yzor shook his head in dismay; at least, he tried to shake his head, which simply wobbled again. "How did I let you get me into this?"

"Very easily," replied Merlin smartly. "We all knew we had to find out more about these creatures in order to protect the Forbidden Forest as much as Zanadoo."

"Which I can do with bindweed," retorted the herbologist.

"Which is one option," Merlin answered rather sharply.

Flambeau cut in before the two wizards got into another argument. "I thought the reason for this expedition was to rescue Sprike and to protect Zanadoo? Even if we don't rescue my friend, even if we find ways of protecting your Forbidden Forest and Zanadoo, what about everywhere else? Are you going to put your magical vines around the Great Forest or the Twydell plains?"

The four older spiders looked at the sleek black spider. The youngest member of their party continued to speak. "I have relatives in the Great Forest. I left that home when I was just a few weeks old, but I still have feelings for the unicorns who still live there; I even have feelings for my father who would have had me killed. Do you think you can protect everywhere with your magical bindweed? Have you forgotten your friends in the place you call Avalon? If the gudgers get into Zanadoo again they won't take long to invade other countries."

The other four remained silent for a while thinking about Flambeau's words.

"Well said, Flambeau." Lennox broke the silence. "The boy is right. I believe we should continue."

"I agree," Merlin stated. "Despite his youth, Flambeau speaks words of wisdom. The gudgers may be setting a trap for us but they are expecting a wizard and a unicorn. They are *certainly not* expecting five spiders. As long as we keep out of the reach of their rather enormous feet, and their long tongues, we will be safe."

Sprikeson's only response was to crawl ahead. Everyone else followed him.

❀ ✦ ❀ ✦ ❀ ✦ ❀ ✦ ❀ ✦ ❀ ✦ ❀

For two further days they journeyed on. They were not tempted by the unclaimed insects caught in spiders' webs along their route. However, they were always relieved when they found water dripping down the walls.

"I've got some food," Merlin told them as their bellies rumbled. "The trouble is I would have to transform to get it out of my pockets, and there is not enough room here to do so."

They kept going. The noise of gudgers working grew louder as they drew closer, although it stopped for long periods at a time.

"They are not working round-the-clock shifts." Sprikeson was relieved. "They seem to have long rest breaks and probably don't work at night."

Eventually the sound of mining stopped altogether.

"It must be getting close to full moon," Merlin stated. "They must have stopped work because they think we are approaching."

"We *are* approaching," Yzor stated in a flat tone. "You said they stunk but you didn't say the smell would be this bad. I feel sick."

Despite the stench, they crawled on until the blocked tunnel opened up into an open passage. Although it was dark in the passage, their spiders' eyes allowed them to see.

"They have got rid of a lot of the rocks and debris we used to block the tunnel," commented Sprikeson. "I wonder how long this passageway is? I can't see any daylight."

"It may be night time but I think it best if we climb to the ceiling," Merlin advised. "If the gudgers are

330

watching out for us they will be anticipating a wizard and a unicorn on foot. They would never guess their visitors were approaching upside down on the ceiling."

The companions knew when they were nearing the end of the passage because a warm breeze could be felt. The smell was still putrid but the air was easier to breathe because there were fewer dust particles.

A strange deep red glow could be seen in the distance, but it wasn't till they reached the end that they realised it was the sky.

Insects, of all types, emerged from every crack, inside and outside the mountain, heading in the same direction.

"Where are you going?" Merlin asked the insects.

"To feed," they replied.

"What about the gudgers?" Merlin called after them as they raced past.

"You must be new here! They go to the hot rocks to sleep at night. We finish up the leftovers from the meals they eat during the day. There is plenty for everyone. Just make sure you are gone before morning."

"Or simply build your web in the cracks and crevices and wait for these little critters to make their way back," said another voice as a spider, even larger than Merlin, crept along beside them. "I'm going to eat my fill of the sweet stuff then set my traps to catch some fresh meat on the way home. Why don't you join me?"

"We'll certainly join you for the sweet stuff," answered Merlin.

Outside the red sky was deepening to maroon. The creeping darkness was lit by fires which leapt from the tops of tall funnel shaped mountains. The dull maroon sky was streaked with the same colours as the dancing flames.

"Where are the gudgers?" asked Merlin.

"Over there, they sleep on the rocks surrounding the fire hills. They don't like the cool of the night," the big spider responded just before he started nibbling at a sticky yellow substance which surrounded some white pips. A thick yellow peel had been discarded nearby.

Merlin looked at the fire hills, which must have been at least half a mile away. He thought of the sculpted volcanoes in Queen Shirley-Poppy's pleasure garden. He looked at the yellow peel and thought of lemon water. The discarded peel was strewn everywhere and was now swarming with insects of both foot and wing varieties. *Those can't be lemons. Lemons are quite bitter.*

"Cool?" Yzor whispered when he and Merlin were out of earshot of the big spider. "Did he say cool? I'm hot, dusty and sweaty. The first thing I'm going to do when I get home is to bathe in the pool outside of your cave."

"I'm looking forward to doing the same thing myself," admitted Merlin. "I am also most uncomfortable." Suddenly Merlin emerged into his normal self. "There are no gudgers around. Anyone else wishing to transform, stand here."

The four spiders dutifully stood in the spot where Merlin pointed his wand.

"Huddle together. I'm going to try to do a four in one spell. Don't forget to breathe in the cobweb dust and blow it out again."

A few seconds later a goblin, a wizard and two unicorns materialised.

"I must admit," Yzor said, wasting no time in examining the plant life around him. "This is a very interesting place."

"I should have asked our new friend if there is any water nearby, before I transformed," Merlin commented.

"No need," responded Yzor. "Plants like these require a lot of moisture. It has to be nearby." He picked up a large green fruit and with his pocket dagger cut a slice. The flesh inside was ruby red with brown seeds. "I thought as much. It's a melon. Back in Briton, when I was a young man studying to be a plant specialist, I took a trip across the sea to places with sunnier climes. I've seen melons before but none so big or growing in such large quantities."

Yzor took a large bite of the slice of melon. Liquid ran down the sides of his mouth. He put the melon on the ground and cut slices for Merlin and Sprikeson. "Try some, it's very succulent and will quench your thirst."

Lennox and Flambeau had already started munching the sweet grass on which they now stood. Leaving their comrades to dine on melon, the unicorns wandered slightly further afield. However, they were careful to remain between the large leafed plants and a cliff which sloped down to the sea. Although the hot rocks, which surround the fire hills, were too far away for the gudgers to see them, they made sure they remained out of view from any approaching predators.

"What a fabulous land this is!" Despite his earlier despondency, Yzor sounded excited. "I've never seen flowers like this before. Look at the size of them. They are larger than anything I have ever seen."

Merlin took the cheese he had been carrying out of his pocket. He managed to find a bunch of carrots he had snuck away which he threw to the unicorns. However, the unicorns continued to take advantage of the moist grazing.

Sprikeson and Merlin tucked into a meal of melon and cheese.

Yzor continued to inspect the plants. Even in the dullness of the night sky, it could be seen that flowers of all colours grew in abundance; some on stems and others on the vines which grew on the mountainside. In between slices of melon, the wizard filled his pockets with seeds.

"Water over here," Lennox called. "It's a bit on the warm side but it's okay."

As the night progressed, the companions took it in turns to stand guard whilst the others slept. Sleep in the clean fresh air came easily. Gradually an orange sun rose above the horizon. The sky started to brighten until it turned a vivid red with smudges of orange and yellow.

"This must be daylight." Merlin stared at the red sky. "What a very curious place this is. It is alien to anything I have ever known before."

Daylight gave them an opportunity to take in their surroundings. The cave in which the tunnel had been excavated looked out on to luscious green grassland until it reached a beach made up of brown sand speckled with pink. Beyond the beach was a purple sea. The cave was set in a cliff; no different to the granite mountains in Twydell, it stretched as far as the eye could see on one side; on the same side stood a pile of rocks and stones which must have been cleared from the tunnel. On the other side of the cave, the mountains bordered the grassy area where the melons grew until it sloped down into the sea. The companions had spent the night on the grassy side between the tall plants and the sloping cliff where the unicorns had grazed.

In the daylight, Yzor was disappointed to see that some of the large plants which he was admiring had been trampled down by large feet. "Those gudgers have no respect for the environment in which they live," he grumbled. "I presume they've trodden all over those flowers to get to the fruit."

"You are probably right," Merlin agreed. "I think it is time to return to our arachnid forms. One or more of the beasts will no doubt be approaching soon." And so saying, he used his wand to strike each of his comrades in turn. He watched them spin, and shrink into spiders, before tucking his wand back inside his cloak, and transforming into his own familiar.

"I suggest we climb up there, find a nice spot, and wait," he stated, looking up at the granite cliff in front of them.

Although inaccessible to humans, the steep cliff did not present a problem to the eight-legged insects. The five spiders found a ledge about eight feet off the ground. It was a good vantage point from which they could see the distant fire hills in front of them. They also had a good view of the entrance to the cave.

As the sun rose higher, the gudger workforce could be seen approaching. They walked on all fours rather than on two feet as Glubber had done when he met Merlin. Unlike Glubber, none wore clothing but the wizard noticed that they had his same swinging head motion. Their long heads swayed from side to side as their shoulders moved to and fro with each pace.

The gudgers marched into the tunnel. From time to time they walked out on two feet, carrying stones, which would have been too heavy for human arms. Larger boulders were pushed along by foot or, in some cases, feet as the gudgers worked in pairs. All the rocks were piled haphazardly on the far side of the entrance. The smaller stones must have been left on the passage floor with other debris.

"They have no tools," Sprikeson remarked. Whilst Merlin, being an old man, kept dozing off, and Yzor examined anything and everything which grew from the soil, the goblin kept his spider's eyes on the gudgers' method of working.

"They have nails like talons; probably as hard as a metal tool," Merlin said in a matter-of-fact fashion. "I looked very carefully at Glubber's nails when I met him."

"But it will make their progress slower," commented Sprikeson. "Nails can't be as efficient as all the different tools used in mining, and they must hurt themselves occasionally. Our tools have varying types of points, which we use depending on the sort of surface we are cutting."

"Their current lack of knowledge won't slow them for long. They will be learning to use tools in the Kernan mines," Merlin advised. "I'm surprised they are not already using them. I'm even more surprised they haven't bought any of those poor pit ponies to haul those stones."

As realisation dawned, Sprikeson stared at Merlin the spider. "You have to stop the Kernans using them. Don't you see? There is a great deal more to mining than digging holes in the ground. Once they learn how to use tools they will be able to work at a much faster pace."

"Yes, they will, and one of the reasons we are here is to prevent that happening. Look over there," he said. "There are a lot of crumbling rocks in those cliffs on the far side of the cave. It must be from the impact of the way they throw stones and rocks in a heap. They are causing the cliff to crack. Even some of the stones above the entrance appear to be loose."

"And there are a couple of large loose boulders on the cliff above that heap," added Lennox who, with Flambeau, had been to take a closer look.

"We could probably organise a rock fall before we go," Merlin stated casually. "That might give us an extra hour or two if we have to leave in a hurry."

Yzor had found a small cave further up the cliff face. He asked Merlin to accompany him so that he could be transformed back to his real self. Merlin had to turn back into himself before he could transform Yzor. Once back to his normal self, the garden expert filled his own pockets with seeds and roots until they were full; then he found enough plant life to fill Merlin's pockets, too.

The companions spent another restful night feasting on melon and other fruits. They finished off the cheese Merlin had brought.

The next morning the watchers, all in their arachnid state, waited for the gudger workforce to arrive. This time it was early afternoon before they could be seen in the distance. They surmised this was because the day and time of the meeting arranged with Glubber was approaching.

Gradually, as the gudgers came into view, a much bigger gudger which had not been there the previous day could be seen leading the others. On this occasion the creatures did not go into the cave. Instead, the big gudger rose up on to his hind legs and bellowed orders. He pointed to four gudgers and then to the grassy area, behind the large plants. The four made their way to the place indicated, crouching down so that they would be out of sight from anyone coming out of the cave.

The watching spiders, who had settled just above the four gudgers, felt anxious. The creatures were in the same spot where Lennox and Flambeau had grazed the night before, and the ground was marked with hoof prints. Thankfully, the gudgers seemed oblivious to the tracks which the unicorns had left.

"They would not have seen hoof prints before unless they have worked in the Kernan mines. The marks mean nothing to them," Merlin realised, and gave a sigh of relief.

The big gudger ordered another with a large neck to stand at the tunnel entrance. Others were sent to either hide behind the pile of rocks on the far side of the cave; or to climb on top of the heap and conceal themselves behind large boulders.

"They are setting a trap for us." Merlin told the others what was already obvious to them. "You can hardly see the gudgers on top of that heap of rocks, their skin is almost the same colour. There are only four beneath us because there is nowhere we could run in this direction. We would be blocked by this slope. The only way we could get up this cliff is to fly."

"Which we could do if we had our broomsticks with us," Yzor put in.

"Hmm… I don't think they would have fitted into our pockets. Next time we will try transforming with our carry cases on our back and see if the brooms get moulded in to our spider forms." Merlin gave the thought some consideration.

"Next time?" muttered Yzor. "If there is ever a next time, count me out."

"I thought you were enjoying yourself collecting all those plants." Lennox tried to be upbeat.

"I must admit the plant life here is fascinating," Yzor conceded.

"I have found my way out of many human traps," Lennox stated firmly. "I shall find my way out of this one laid by gudgers."

The big gudger bellowed a command which brought the other gudgers out of their hiding places. They marched off, behind their leader, in the direction from whence they came.

"So that was the trial run," commented Sprikeson. "They have established their positions and gone back to their hot rocks."

"The question is will they be back tonight or tomorrow?" Merlin was lost in thought. "The rendezvous is supposed to be the night of our full moon but I've quite lost track of days. Last night's middle earth moon looked as if it was fairly full. I wonder if it mirrors ours."

"Or if our moon mirrors theirs," Yzor commented as he gave a weed closer inspection.

The watchers spent a fairly restful night but Merlin insisted that he should give Yzor lessons in transformation. "Have you had much experience with transformation?" he asked.

"I watched Tannus turn a dog into a mouse once and on another occasion he turned a girl into one." Yzor was excited at the prospect of learning a very complicated spell which few magicians were sufficiently skilled to perform. "Ever since seeing what Tannus could do I've always wanted to try transformation. Jon soon learnt that spell you taught him."

"And this is your chance, but it is me who is teaching you, not Tannus." Inwardly Merlin chastised himself for becoming irritated at every mention of his successor's name.

Yzor practised the spell to perfection. His companions turned from goblin or unicorn to spider and back again several times.

"How's your stunning spell?" asked Merlin.

"Good. I practised with Wormald when he was giving training sessions before the Battle of Merlport."

"Mine are excellent, so that's one spell we don't need to practise."

"Thank goodness for that," muttered Flambeau. "I feel as if I've been the victim of enough practice spells for one night!"

Lennox and Sprikeson agreed.

Despite the time taken up practising spells, the unicorns still had plenty of time to graze. The rest of the party were again able to fill up on melons and berries to the point they could eat no more: they looked forward to going home to a plain meal of bread and butter. In the light of the new day they returned to their arachnid forms. However, Yzor carefully removed the hoof prints from the ground and brought the trampled grass back to life before Merlin transformed him to a spider once more.

As the hours passed the spiders explored the cliff, identifying loose rocks and looking at the view. From above the cave they had a clear view of the landscape. It was obvious why the gudger leader had not placed any of his men in front of the cave. The entrance looked out on grassland, beyond which was the beach made up of brown sand speckled with pink. On the far side of the beach the purple sea stretched to the red horizon.

"There is nowhere for them to hide out there." Lennox summed up the situation. "They can only conceal themselves on two sides. I don't think they would attempt climbing the cliff, the face is too sheer and the stones appear to be loose."

"As Merlin said, the stones in the cliff have probably been loosened by the way they throw those rocks on the heap which leans against it," Sprikeson mused. "That growing pile of rocks and the damage it is doing to the cliff face is extremely dangerous. Dwarves would never work in such a haphazard way."

"Which is to our advantage," stated Merlin. "One loose rock up here falling on that heap below could inflict quite a bit of havoc on our gudger friends."

"So, what is your plan?" asked Lennox. "Are you still going to meet Glubber?"

"We will wait and see what happens when the time comes," said Merlin. "I just wish I had not lost track of days. I don't know if our rendezvous is today or tomorrow."

Merlin's question was answered later on that same day. They saw the big gudger marching towards the cave, followed by about a dozen others. Two carried a metal structure which glinted in the orange sunlight.

"What's that they are carrying?" asked Sprikeson. "I've never seen anything like it before."

"I have," Merlin stated, feeling sick. "It's similar to the cages the Kernans kept fairies and elves in."

The big gudger pointed to a spot directly in front of the cave. The two gudgers dropped the cage on the spot; it clattered as it landed on the ground. The big gudger stood back and reviewed the cage's placement; then he pointed to another spot a few feet further back. He shouted an order and the cage was lifted again by the two who had borne it. They lifted the cage deliberately high before dropping it on the new place, indicated by the leader. The two gudgers, which had carried the cage, slithered back on all fours to allow their leader a better view.

As they moved away, the contents of the cage were visible to the watching spiders.

It was Sprike!

Despite his diminutive size, he was still too big for the cage and his naked body was cramped inside. He was very thin and, as he grasped the bars of the cage and shook them, the watchers could see his skinny arms.

The gudgers made a strange guttural sound. They all now stood on their hind legs and pointed at the prisoner trapped inside. Sprike pushed his bony arm out between the rungs; he clenched his fist and shook it at the gudgers. The helpless gesture made the guttural sounds, made by the gudgers, become louder.

"They are laughing at him!" Sprikeson tried to stamp his eight feet but instead he tumbled off the ledge. In true spider fashion, he rolled in a ball until he landed on a piece of rock which jutted out.

Flambeau lowered himself on a strand of silk. Merlin had spent some of the waiting hours teaching his comrades the art of creating strands of silk and how to weave cobwebs. Now Flambeau was finding out how useful his new skill was.

"Come on Sprikeson." Flambeau the spider spoke kindly to his friend. "Let's climb back up on my silk ladder. We need to keep together."

Sprikeson did as he was bid and found that he could work his way up the strand with ease.

A gudger with a large neck was called forward by the leader. He appeared to be carrying some pink and black pieces of material over his shoulder, which he dropped on the ground. First, he picked up the black item, which he proceeded to put on.

Merlin recognised the black waistcoat. "It's Glubber. I didn't recognise him. What's he done to his neck? He didn't have a big neck like that when I met him."

"He must have caught mumps from you," Yzor commented smugly.

"How marvellous. I hope he suffers as much as I did. In fact, I hope he suffers more."

The comrades continued to watch the spectacle in front of them. As Glubber picked up the pink piece of material, they could see it was a frock. The big necked gudger opened the cage door and pulled Sprike out. Grabbing the goblin's hair, Glubber lifted him up and held him there. To the merriment of the watching gudgers, Sprike wriggled and kicked. Unfortunately, Glubber held him at arm's length and none of the goblin's kicks or punches made any impact. Glubber dropped the poor little man on to the ground before forcing the pink frock down over his slight body. The dress was much too big and Sprike stumbled over as he tried to stand up. The gudgers' laughter continued as they watched the show.

One of the gudgers stepped forward and gave their leader a sparkling object. The big gudger held it up. It was the goblin king's crown. With one arm the big gudger picked Sprike up by his hair before dropping him on the ground again. Next, he forced the crown so far down over Sprike's head that it covered his eyes. Then the big creature grabbed his prisoner and roughly pushed him back in the cage.

The cruel laughter subsided when the gudger leader pointed to the positions in which his fellow creatures were to conceal themselves. The gudgers dutifully made their way out of sight to anyone exiting the cave.

Sprikeson looked on helplessly but he kept his wits about him. "If the gudgers don't have tools, how did they make that cage?"

"Only one place they could have got it," commented Merlin. "Glubber or one of his cronies must have bought it in Kerner. That's where they must have bought the dress, too."

"Can you work magic in your spider form?" Sprikeson asked.

"No, not really. I've tried a couple of times but my spells weren't very successful."

"My father might as well be dead as to spend the rest of his life as the gudgers' play thing! Is there nothing we can do?"

"You can do as I tell you," said Merlin, remaining calm. He turned to Yzor. "You said your stunning spell was good."

"I believe so." Yzor tried to smile, but spiders have no means of smiling so his head wobbled instead.

"Well, this is my plan..."

They waited until the hour between day and night when the light dimmed and little could be seen. Merlin scuttled down to the cave. Glubber waited at the entrance for the wizard and unicorn to arrive as arranged. Merlin slipped back into the darkness of the passage before materialising into himself.

He squinted to see what was going on within the tall plants, where four gudgers hid. He concentrated his gaze on a ledge above the spot where the would-be assailants hid. At last he saw Yzor slide along the ledge on his belly. Yzor's brown cloak made him almost imperceptible in the dusk; to add to the disguise, the wizard had also wound leafy vines around his head.

Merlin crept up behind Glubber, saying a few words under his breath as he pointed his wand at the gudger. Dressed in dusty grey travelling clothes and standing behind Glubber, he was out of the sight of the other gudgers. Glubber froze stock still as he felt the force of the stunning spell.

"You might not be able to move but I know you can hear every word I say," the wizard told the motionless creature. "I have kept my word. I am here and I have brought a unicorn with me. However, far from helping me rescue my friend's friend, you have laid a trap for us."

From the corner of his eye Merlin could see four quick movements from Yzor's wand and knew that the four gudgers hidden in the tall plants were now as powerless as Glubber.

From behind Glubber, Merlin pointed his wand at a loose stone on the cliff. The stone fell down on to the heap of rocks on which some of the other gudgers had concealed themselves. Rocks and gudgers tumbled together from the top of the heap on to others below. The creatures' painful screeching seared the silence of the night.

Two spiders spun down from the ceiling on silk strands; one was sleek and black, the other white with a spike on its forehead. The wizard spoke the necessary words, and threw a pinch of cobweb dust at the pair, and two unicorns stood before him.

"Stay out of sight," the wizard commanded. "But ready yourselves for our escape. How I hate making you beasts of burden."

"We do what is necessary to rescue Sprike," Flambeau stated.

Under bellowing orders from their leader, some of the uninjured gudgers started to settle back on the heap of rocks.

Still hiding behind Glubber, Merlin raised his wand again. This time he took aim at a larger boulder, further up the cliff. "I'm so glad this one didn't fall with the others," he told Glubber, who remained stock-still. "Let's see how your friends react this time."

The boulder rolled down the cliff. It made a thunderous noise. Screams from the gudgers below could be heard before it reached its target.

Whilst the gudgers were in complete disarray, Sprikeson and Yzor ran to the cage.

"We are here to rescue you, father," Sprikeson told him. "Hurry, we must get away before those creatures realise what we are doing."

Sprike tried to get out of the cage but tripped on the dress, and found his cramped limbs difficult to move. Yzor picked up the goblin. Although Sprike had lost a lot of weight, he was still an additional burden to carry, and the short distance from cage to cave took fractionally longer than it should have done. During the delaying seconds, one of the gudgers saw what was happening, and shouted a warning to the others.

Only a few of the gudgers had not been hurt by the falling rocks and others remained frozen by the stunning spell. But the big gudger leader had not been injured; he leapt from behind the fallen rocks, shouting orders in his deep throaty voice. Five subordinates loped behind him on all fours.

Yzor stumbled to the cave where he mounted himself and the goblin king, complete in pink frock and crown, on Flambeau. Flambeau made his way along the passage as fast as he could but the floor was littered with stones, which slowed his pace.

Merlin stepped out from behind Glubber. This time he swapped his wand for his staff, which he kept in his magical long pockets. The end of the staff was encrusted with a crystal. The crystal glowed red. The sorcerer thrust the staff towards the assailants. As he did so his loud voice uttered a curse which echoed across the bay. A flash like forked lightning shot from the staff. All six attackers cried out in shock as the force of the beam hit them.

The wizard turned. Sprikeson was already sat on Lennox's back. Merlin mounted behind him and the unicorn set off as fast as he was able on the hard floor.

Merlin could hear the sound of footsteps behind him. *One, maybe two still in pursuit. They are very brave, the fools.* He yelled for Lennox to stop and turn. Lennox did not question the wizard's command. Merlin raised his staff again, the crystal glowed green; he pointed it down the tunnel towards the entrance. A wind blew up in front of them which took with it the loose debris lying on the floor. Yells of pain could be heard further along the passageway as flying rubble struck the assailants – then all went quiet.

Yzor waited at the point at which they could travel no further as themselves. He had already transformed Sprike and Flambeau into spiders and lifted them into a high crevice.

"Three in one," stated Merlin. Yzor, Sprikeson and Lennox stood together and were soon turned into spiders. Merlin carefully lifted them up into the crevice before transforming himself.

Despite the goblin king's poor state of health he forced himself on over the next two days. They found water dripping down the sides of the tunnel, on which they filled their hungry bellies. As the six spiders progressed, they were relieved that no sounds were heard coming from the gudger end of the tunnel. The gudgers did not seem to be making any attempt to follow them. At last they reached the end of their journey.

Lennox was the first to slide on his silk strand of spider's web on to the jade dish. All five dishes were lined up along the wall. Small people had been watching for the comrades' arrival for days. A cry went up and applause as they saw Lennox sliding down a cobweb thread and crawl to the jade coloured dish. A sleek black spider fell to the ground shortly after, and made its way to the topaz bowl.

Jonathan, who had been busying himself with his plants, wasted no time in bringing the two unicorns back to themselves. The equines pushed their way through the crowd to the pool where water fell. They walked into its depth to wash away the dust and drink before returning to the buckets, which had been filled with oats, ready for their arrival.

Jonathan's anxious gaze never left the crevice as he sought his father's arrival. However, two small spiders who clung to each other, as they slid down a silky strand, came next. Jonathan flicked his wand and threw cobweb dust at the pair. There was uproar as Sprikeson landed on the floor holding his father. The goblin king was emaciated and still wearing the pink frock and crown. Goblin hands raced to lift their king and give him food and water. There were cries of joy at seeing him still alive and cries of anger at the state he was in.

Little attention was given to Yzor, as he made his way out of the crevice. Only Jonathan and Heather, who had been helping her husband with his vines, saw him drop to the floor. The warlock flicked his wand and threw the cobweb dust.

"Hello, dad, am I glad to see you?" Jonathan gave his father a hug.

Heather flung her arms around her father-in-law's neck.

Merlin's arrival was also unnoticed until he materialised as himself. "Is there any bread and cheese?" he asked loudly. "A jug of ale would be much appreciated, too."

349

The graces appeared from nowhere with food and ale.

Yzor ate a piece of cheese between two slices of bread as he inspected the spiteful vines which Jonathan and Heather had tried unsuccessfully to grow across the tunnel.

A tall wooden structure had been erected nearby.

"What's that?" asked Yzor.

"It's scaffolding," explained Jonathan. "Dorf is intending to tunnel upwards to open the top of the mountain. I feel sure the vines could grow if they have natural sunlight. But he was afraid to start work before you got back in case the rubble fell on you."

"Very interesting." Yzor gazed at the structure. "But I have a better idea."

Merlin had made his way to the stone platform above the quarry where Zan rested on his couch; Muffle sat on his bed of straw beside his master.

"You knew we would arrive back safely?" the wizard asked, between mouthfuls of food.

"I saw you in my crystal ball but couldn't make out whether you had Sprike with you or not. I was fooled by the pink frock and thought you had found a sick child somewhere on your journey."

Lennox and Flambeau, having eaten their fill, made their way up to the platform where the old wizard and the ancient soothsayer supped ale.

"I must make haste to get home," said Lennox. "Sheba is expecting our foal. We need to make arrangements to go."

"Yes, indeed," replied Merlin. "Let us get everyone together."

Merlin told Zan of their plans to leave as soon as possible. He called to Yzor, Jonathan and Heather, who were still in the quarry below, to join them.

Whilst they were waiting Lennox spoke to Merlin, "Flambeau has been suffering with headaches since you started transforming him into a spider and back again. He has been afraid to say anything since it was he who insisted in joining the rescue party; he wants me to tell you that if he has made himself ill, he places no blame on you."

"Let me take a look at him." Merlin stroked Flambeau's neck and lifted the fringe which fell across his forehead. He stood to one side to allow Lennox and Zan to witness his examination of the black unicorn.

"I think it is only natural to feel some temporary discomfort but I think the pain will gradually ease," said Merlin matter-of-factly.

"I am sure a mother's kiss will help," stated Lennox. "You have missed your mother's company and the attention she should have given you as a child. No doubt she will make up for it when we get to the Forbidden Forest."

Zan nodded wisely. "I have seen in my crystal ball that Blaize will ease her son's pain."

"When you leave, I think Bunty might like to join you." Zan managed a smile. "She has become very fond of Feerce. While you have been away she and the two unicorn colts have spent almost all their time with Comet, and that little pit pony who pulled the cart for you. They have told her how delightful it is to live in the Forbidden Forest. You could take another pony with you, couldn't you?"

"Of course," Merlin replied, although he was not sure how many more equines the forest could support. However, he considered Bunty to be an exception.

Yzor, his son and daughter-in-law joined them on the platform.

"Right, are you ready to go?" asked Merlin, already picking up his broom in its carry case.

"We are not going home yet," replied Yzor. "I am returning to middle earth. Jonathan and Heather are coming with me."

"What? What are you talking about?" Merlin was aghast.

"The spiteful vines won't grow here because of the lack of light. They might grow one day when Dorf opens up the ceiling to let the sun in. However," Yzor paused to give his words added momentum, "I have no doubt whatsoever that they *will* grow at the other end of the tunnel. We will plant vines at the entrance to the cave in middle earth. If the gudgers attempt to break the vines, at best they would get a nasty sting; at the worst they would be strangled."

"Then we had better make arrangements for Dorf to take the unicorns back to the forest, whilst we set off for middle earth immediately," said Merlin, returning his broom to its carrying case.

"You are not going back to the forest!" Yzor stated firmly. "Your wife is expecting your twins any day now."

"Yes." Heather spoke in earnest. "My family and all the children have been chanting prayers for their safe delivery. Great Grandmother says they should have been born already. Mother says somehow Helen is holding on till you get home."

"But it is impossible for you to go back to middle earth without me," said Merlin. "How would you transform?"

"Easily." Jonathan smiled proudly. "You taught me how to turn your transformed spiders back into themselves."

"And you taught *me* how to turn willing volunteers into spiders *and* how to bring them back to their original beings again," stated Yzor.

"Yes, but none of you can transform *on your own*," Merlin stated. "You need a wizard who has a spider as his familiar, and the only wizard who has such a familiar is me!"

"Not any longer," stated Jonathan. "Do you remember when you were ill and I was caring for you? You told me that to find my familiar form all I had to do was to wish hard for whatever form I wanted to be, and suddenly it would happen."

Merlin nodded.

"Well, when dad was gone I got myself in a real state worrying about him and wanted to follow. I wished hard to be a spider so I could go and find him – when suddenly it happened. It was a good job Heather was here and I hadn't put your written instructions and cobweb powder in my pocket. I'm not sure I could have brought myself back on my own."

"One second he was Jonathan and the next he was a spider," Heather added. "I was frantic. I picked up the instructions. They didn't work the first time but it was second time lucky. Suddenly there he was again." The young witch's smile lit up her plain face.

"Heather made me promise to wait a few days longer before going off to find you. We spent the time practising the transformation spell. Now I can transform easily – watch this." Jonathan disappeared. A brown spider appeared on the spot where he had stood.

A few seconds later, Jonathan materialised as himself again.

"Well done, Jon. I am so proud of you," said Yzor, and was joined by Zan in giving a little round of applause.

Muffle hee-hawed and wiggled his ears. Lennox and Flambeau stamped their hooves.

"Well, I still think I should go with you," stated Merlin. "There is safety in numbers."

"You will not go with them!" snapped Zan in a more ferocious voice than anyone had heard him use previously. "Your place is with my niece. It is time for you to bring an end to your adventures, and for you to become a full time husband and parent."

Merlin was taken aback.

"Zan is right." Yzor spoke gently. "Your place is at home. You are a mighty sorcerer and few, except perhaps your children, will ever have your skills. Go home, Merlin. My family and I are the plant specialists – it is the one area in which our talents exceed yours." He turned to look at his son and daughter-in-law. "On this occasion we do not need your help."

Merlin found it difficult to bite his tongue. "Very well, I shall leave you to it," he conceded. However, his reluctance showed in his face.

Chapter 16 – Time To Go Home

The dwarves provided an escort of two carts full of men with bows and arrows, ready to fend off any human huntsmen or large predators.

Merlin scouted above on his broom. Bunty pulled the cart. It was a task she seemed to enjoy and it gave Lucky the chance to enjoy the freedom of the plains. The goblins had placed a bag of precious stones and ornaments in the cart, as a present for the forest people. Yzor's plants were also in the cart. He had given Merlin instructions for their wellbeing which he was to relay to the Brambles. "My plants are more valuable than any colourful stones or fripperies," he had told the sorcerer.

When they reached the forest boundary they said their goodbyes to the dwarves and the escort departed. Bunty was more than a little excited to see her new home. She was awed by the first sight of the woodland.

Blaize and Luna had waited patiently just inside the forest for days. They were delighted to see their offspring again. Feerce was nearly fully grown; Flambeau was now as big as his father and towered above his mother.

"Where is Sheba?" asked Lennox, concerned that she was not with the other mothers.

"She is at the pool near the cave," replied Luna. "The children have laid straw for her so she can be comfortable. The other mares are looking after her."

357

"Hurry, Lennox," Blaize stated. "It will not be long before your new foal arrives."

"Come along, Fiery," Lennox told the youngest of the three young unicorns who had made the journey with him. "Your new brother or sister will be here shortly. Follow me."

Fiery galloped behind Lennox, doing his best to keep pace with the white stallion.

Blaize and Luna greeted their sons with nuzzles and licks. Blaize started to lick her son's face but he pulled away.

"What's the matter?" she asked.

"I don't want to worry you, mother, but I have had headaches since being transformed into a spider and back again so many times."

"A spider?" Blaize was aghast. "What are you talking about?"

Flambeau tried to explain to his mother about their expedition to middle earth. Blaize didn't seem to be able to take it in.

"My forehead keeps itching where my horn used to be. I am worried that the scar might be turning septic. Will you take a look for me, please? Lennox says the witches who live here have some healing potions but thought that your kiss would be enough to cure me."

Blaize pushed Flambeau's fringe out of the way with her nose. She looked at the spot from which his horn had been torn. "You don't need my kisses although I am happy to give them. The only thing unusual about your forehead is that your horn is growing again."

"We could all see it when you came back from your trip to gudger land," said Feerce, who had been listening. "Lennox told us not to say anything. He wanted your mother to be the one to tell you."

"That's wonderful news!" Flambeau whinnied and stood on his hind legs to celebrate.

"Does it look all right, mother?"

"It looks splendid, my dear. It is golden, just like your father's."

Lennox arrived at the waterfall to find Sheba lying on her bed of straw beneath an overhang. The other mares were watching over her.

"How is she?" he asked.

"She is doing very well," replied one of the three carers.

"Lennox, my dear husband, you are home!" Sheba was delighted to see him. "Where is Fiery? Did you bring him back with you?"

"I promised I would. Listen, can you hear his hoof beats? He is not far behind me."

The brown colt came into view. It was a long time since he had last seen his mother and the other mares. He came to a halt and shyly walked forward.

Sheba tried to stand up to greet him.

"Lay still, mother. You might hurt yourself if you try to get up," said Fiery, leaning over and licking his mother's forehead.

"Welcome to your new home, Fiery," said one of the attending mares. The others echoed her greeting. Fiery's shyness drifted away. This was his family.

"I am very happy to be here. I can't tell you how wonderful it is to be with my family again, in a place where trees grow and birds sing." So saying, the young unicorn raced around the small grassy area, and then standing on his hind legs, he whinnied with joy.

The next morning Sheba gave birth to a pure white filly.

"What shall we call her?" Sheba asked her husband.

"Whatever you like, as long as it is not Snowy or Magnificent One," replied Lennox.

"Hmm…" Sheba seemed disappointed at her stallion's comments. "But she is as white as snow. What about Snowdrop? Snowdrops are white and they are one of the first signs of life after winter. Our newborn is the first child in this woodland since I don't know when. Since that young witch girl was born, I suppose. What is she, seventeen now?"

"About that," replied Lennox.

He looked down at the small creature. "True, she is as white as snow. And she is the first likeness of my family to be born here. Yes," he said, "Snowdrop is a good name."

One of the other mares had kept Fiery occupied, chasing rainbows in the waterfall, whilst his mother gave birth. Now he stepped forward to see his new sister. "Snowdrop is beautiful," he told his mother. "I am so proud of her. I love her as much as you and my new home."

Merlin waited anxiously outside of the room in the Brambles' house where his wife lay. She had been in labour for several hours. The Bramble witches were at her side.

His voice and powerful magic joined that of the witches and children who chanted prayers for the safe delivery of his twins.

Ethel, Yzor's wife, busied around bringing dock leaves soaked in cold water to cool Helen-Joy's heated brow.

"How much longer must this go on?" Merlin asked her. His brow was furrowed and his eyes reflected the worry he felt.

"As long as it takes," Ethel answered smartly. "Why don't you go in and see her? Hold her hand and try to comfort her."

Merlin did as Ethel suggested but each time he entered the room the attending witches made him feel as if he were in the way. Helen-Joy, however, always welcomed his company.

"Don't worry." She tried to smile at him. "Not long now."

"Go and join the children," Great Grandmother suggested. "They always sing louder and wish harder when you are present."

Merlin wandered off to the garden where the children sat around a fire. The weather was getting cooler as autumn progressed and winter started to set in. As he joined in their chant their young voices did indeed grow louder.

At last the cries of a newborn baby were heard. Merlin hurried back in the house only to be shooed away by the witches.

"We are still busy in here!" Maura told him. "There's not enough room for too many people."

The wizard stood outside the door feeling helpless. In spite of all his magical skills there seemed to be nothing he could do. Time seemed to drag. At last he heard the cries of a second baby. He tried to enter the room but was pushed out yet again.

Eventually, the witches left the room. "In you go, Merlin." Nora and Maura spoke in unison. Bertha just gave him one of her near-toothless smiles.

His wife lay in the bed, propped up by pillows. A small bundle lay in each of her arms.

"Meet your son and daughter." She smiled. "What shall we call them? You have been away so often we have not had time to discuss names."

"What would you like to call them?" Merlin felt humbled.

"Well, I would like to call our daughter Myrtle."

"What a lovely name for a fine witch."

"What about Mazillion for our son?"

"Perfect." Tears rolled down the wizard's face as he looked at his baby boy. "An ideal name for a warlock, whose skills will be a zillion times more powerful than any other could wish for."

"I am so glad you are back, Merlin," Helen-Joy sighed.

"I am more delighted to be home than you can possibly imagine." Merlin beamed with pride.

The three magical beings, disguised as spiders, made their way to middle earth. Their journey had been much easier than they expected. There was not a gudger in sight.

Heather and Jonathan were as intrigued by the plant life in middle earth as Yzor had been. They emptied their pockets of spiteful vines and filled them with as many different species of plants as they could find.

Heather was particularly interested in the flowers and carefully aged them so she could collect their seeds.

Yzor cut a sweet yellow melon and let it lie on the ground. Soon all sorts of insects, including spiders, were feeding on the edible part of the fruit. "Let's find out what is going on. Turn me into a spider again, will you, please, son?"

Jonathan obliged and transformed himself at the same time. Heather chose to stay as she was.

"Where are the gudgers?" Yzor asked a spider who was drinking the melon juice. "Were they all killed by that rock fall a while ago?"

"You're joking!" said the spider as he continued to feast. "There are thousands of the beasts."

"So where are they then?" asked Yzor. "I haven't seen any working here for a while."

"I think they are ill," was the reply. "They seem to have developed large necks and although they have always liked the heat, they now seem to be bathing in the sea to keep cool."

Father and son wasted no time returning to themselves. They've got mumps," Jonathan told Heather.

"Merlin will be as delighted as I am." Yzor grinned. "Now let's take another look at these spiteful vines. I want to go home."

In the rich soil, and with a bit of helpful magic, the vines made steady progress. The three plant specialists were soon on their way back.

When they arrived in Zanadoo, Yzor told the waiting dwarves and goblins that there was no doubt the spiteful plants would keep the gudgers out. "There is no way they will get through those vines," he told them. "We have woven them tight and if they try to

363

break them down they will sting anyone who touches them. The more they try to cut them down the quicker they will grow. If a gudger got through the first layer he would be trapped and end up either strangled or starved."

"It is all such a relief. You have all done so much for us," Sprike told the magical beings who stood before him. "When I was held captive by those horrible creatures I never thought I would see my home again. I cannot thank you enough. There is a saying, 'there is no place like home'. How very true that saying is."

Yzor, his son and daughter-in-law were each given a bag of trinkets to take home with them.

Yzor opened his bag and found, among many other items of jewellery, a lapis lazuli pendant. The polished stone was set in a gold surround and hung on a golden chain. "Ethel will love this," he said. "Perhaps it will help make up for all the time I've been away."

The three said their goodbyes and set off on their broomsticks.

It didn't take long to reach the forest. Heather opened the bindweed which sealed the forest and was surprised to see her mother-in-law sitting outside the shack that had been built for Merlin when he was ill.

"What are you doing there, Ethel dear?" Yzor was equally surprised to see his wife sitting in front of a fire, frying mushrooms.

"I may not be a soothsayer or a magician," she said, "But even plainfolk can sometimes have a sixth sense. I just had a feeling you would be home today. The Brambles made fresh bread this morning and I picked some mushrooms on my way here. I thought it would be nice to have some time on our own. I know you like mushroom sandwiches and I've brought a flagon of wine."

"It would be very nice to have some time together." The wizard was taken aback. "I have a present for you." He took the pendant out of the bag and gave it to his wife.

"It is beautiful," Ethel remarked as she held it up to her neck. "Oh, Yzor. I have missed you so much. I am glad you are home."

"Can I have a mushroom sandwich, too, mum?" Jonathan asked.

"I'll make you one when we get to the cottage," Heather put in before her mother-in-law could answer. She gave Ethel a shy little smile as her cheeks turned pink.

Ethel gave her son and daughter a hug and kiss before the pair set off.

Jonathan and Heather arrived at the Brambles' cottage to more hugs and kisses. Jonathan felt overwhelmed by the affection Heather's family showed.

He spent some time telling the children about his adventures while Heather admired the new babies.

Merlin was delighted to hear that the tunnel had been successfully sealed and that the gudgers had come down with mumps. He poured Jonathan a mug of wine to celebrate.

"So, now you are married, are you sure you wish to stay in the forest and not take your new wife to Avalon? You would not be so confined there."

"We both want to stay here." Jonathan did not hesitate to respond. "I can't think of a better place to call my home."

The royal ladies of Kerner were delighted to hear the lighthouse bell ringing. They each found a window from which to lean to get their first sight of Prince Steven's ship.

They tried to be patient as they waited at the door for the prince to arrive.

He greeted his wife first, then his mother and finally his aunt. Jeanette clung to his arm whilst his mother and aunt continued to talk at the same time, asking where he had been and who he had seen.

The chatter stopped when the king's secretary made a polite cough, to draw attention to his presence.

"The king awaits you in the meeting hall, my prince. The lords of Kerner are here to give their reports today. Your father wishes you to provide a summary of your voyage."

"Yes, of course," Steven replied. He gave the ladies a wink and a smile. "We'll catch up later."

King Jeffrey sat at the end of a long table. He bid Steven take a seat. The lords each made their reports, took questions and afterwards instructions from the king.

Lord Jecquin was one of the last to speak. "Work at the silver mine, which you visited, has slowed down. The gudgers have not been seen for over a week."

The king considered the lord's words. "Do you think this has anything to do with Merlin's visit to middle earth?"

"It seems too much of a coincidence not to be," Jecquin replied.

"My lords." Jeffrey decided to give more information to his noblemen who had previously been aware of Merlin's visit, but not about his trip to middle earth. "Merlin the magician arranged a meeting with one of our gudgers. It transpired that the creatures had burrowed through near the Forbidden Forest and kidnapped one of his friend's friends. He did not tell us who this friend's friend was but it would appear to be someone of importance to the magicians. In normal circumstances I would say only a fool would attempt a visit to middle earth, let alone rescue someone who had been captured by those beasts. However, Merlin is not normal."

"Have you heard anything from the magician since his last visit?" enquired Jecquin.

"Nothing, except your reports about his serious illnesses and miraculous recovery," responded the king.

Just then a servant walked into the room carrying a box and a rolled up parchment.

"Sire," said the servant, lowering his head timidly in fear of being reproached for his interruption. "This message has just been brought to the palace by an old man and a boy in a cart. They say it is from Lord Merlin."

"Read it," the king commanded his secretary.

The secretary broke the seal and a long parchment unravelled which was so long that it tumbled on to the floor. He started to read the contents out loud for all to hear:

Dear King Jeffrey
I hope you and all your family are well.

First of all I must thank the royal ladies for their wonderful gifts. My wife and I were overwhelmed by their kindness. I am delighted to tell you that we are now the proud parents of a boy and girl. Two healthy young magicians.

Helen has had great fun with the old curtains making them into patchwork—

"Stop," ordered Jeffrey in a loud irritated voice. "Is there nothing of substance in that long missive? We do not wish to be informed of Merlin's mundane home life!"

The secretary glanced through the roll of parchment. "Ah, here we are." He picked out a section towards the end of the letter and started reading again.

Many thanks to you and Lord Jecquin for arranging my meeting with Glubber. As instructed I met him at the middle earth entrance to the tunnel. It is with much regret that I have to inform you that Glubber laid a trap. It may be that neither Glubber nor his colleagues return to work at your silver mine. Indeed, I do not know if he is alive or dead. There was a land slide which left several of our would-be assailants lying helpless. The last I saw of him he had been hit on the head by a falling rock. The landslide was followed by a streak of forked lightning which disabled the other attackers. However, I am sure you will be pleased to know that my companions and I escaped unharmed taking my friend's friend with us. The entrance to the tunnel has now been sealed.

There is a small gift for you in the box. I think it will be a very suitable item for the good Queen Shirley-Poppy's pleasure garden.

Kind Regards,
Merlin

"So that explains what happened to our gudger workforce," King Jeffrey stated in an even tone. "That was a piece of luck for Merlin," one of the lords commented. "A landslide, followed by lightning, which wiped out the creatures who tried to lay a trap for him. That must have been a chance in a million."

"No chance at all," Jeffrey replied in a bored tone. "Merlin is warning us in his usual over-friendly manner what tricks he can perform."

The king looked towards another lord who sat at the end of the long table. He was a young man, short with black hair and a face dotted with the pimples of youth. "Lord Queron," said King Jeffrey. "I am sorry to learn that your father is indisposed and thank you for attending in his stead. Your land borders the Forbidden Forest and I am aware that your father maintains a watchful eye in case the magicians enter Kerner through that border. I now require additional watchers to patrol the boundary. Do you understand me?"

"I understand, sire," the young lord responded. His eyes widened. He had not expected the king to even notice him, let alone speak to him.

"Any unusual activity is to be reported to me without delay. These people are not to be trusted."

"Yes, sire," responded Queron dutifully. Then he added, somewhat nervously, "Wouldn't it just be easier to make friends with them though? They seem to get on well with the Twydellers – and they did clear our land of that poisonous weed."

Jeffrey's eye twitched slightly. "We are Kernans," he said. "An ancient race bound together by blood and

369

traditions. We do not trust foreigners. It was a foreigner who sold us the seeds of the poisonous weed disguised as fertiliser. And it was a foreigner who just eliminated our entire gudger workforce. You have a lot to learn, Lord Queron."

The young man's face turned red and he lowered his head.

All the other lords at the table remained silent.

"If the gudgers were to return," Lord Jecquin said, "should I re-employ them, sire?"

"Of course." The king did not hesitate. "The gudgers are good workers. However, we have been warned. Keep skilled archers around the mines and if trouble arises order them to fire without hesitation. A few skilled spearmen would help resolve any situation."

Jecquin nodded

The king spoke to all the noblemen around the table. "My lords, I am sure all of you can spare some skilled archers and spearmen to guard our mines should the gudgers return."

No one refused the request.

The king continued. "My Lord Chief Justice, I want more workers to be sent to the mines. Lord Jecquin's managers must be short handed at present."

"As you wish, sire." An elderly lord with white hair nodded graciously.

However, Lord Queron still had questions. "If the gudgers return, and trouble arose at the mines, wouldn't the prisoners and the men who supervise them get hurt?"

"Convicts are no loss to anyone and can soon be replaced. The mine supervisors know the risks involved in their work when they accept employment. You are young and too kind hearted by far, Lord Queron. As I said, you have much to learn."

The meeting continued until Steven, the last to speak, gave his report. When he finished he gave a sigh. It had been a long day. He and his father took refreshments with the noblemen of Kerner before bidding them a safe journey home.

"Now," said Jeffrey. "Let's see what this present is that Merlin has sent." He opened the small box to find a miniature plant inside.

"Splendid." The king almost smiled. "I have seen these melon fruits on my trips abroad and tried to grow them here but never with any success. Merlin is right, the plant will be an ideal addition to your mother's pleasure garden."

"It is rather nice," responded the prince, who was not afraid to smile. "I will help mother plant it. I am glad to be home. Tomorrow I hope to enjoy a game of Strike the Ball with Jeanette."

Glubber stood in front of King Globbalot, the large gudger who had set the trap for Merlin and Lennox.

The swelling in his neck had subsided but Glubber had a big bump on his head and his face and body were covered in red spots.

"So, you promise me a wizard and a unicorn, and what do I get instead?" Globbalot pointed to his own neck, which was so swollen it wobbled when he spoke. His bloodshot eyes reflected the pain he felt. "A big neck is what I get! At the same time I lose my little pet with the pretty crown. I liked watching the little man in his cage. He was most amusing, especially when I made him angry. Now, thanks to you, he has been stolen!"

"I am so sorry, glub glub," Glubber answered.

"Sorry won't do!" snapped Globbalot.

"When I feel better I will go back to the human land and find you another one," Glubber grovelled at his king's feet.

"You will not!" Globbalot's anger was rising. "Look at what you brought back from the human world the last time you visited. We are all suffering with these swollen necks and now I see you are covered in spots. Do the rest of us have the red spot misery still to come?"

"I don't know," muttered Glubber. "I am so sorry, my king."

"You will go home and stay there!"

"Yes, my king, I will go home as you command."

It was over a week before Merlin and his wife returned to their home. The Brambles had insisted they stay long enough for mother and babies to build up their strength. Bunty pulled the cart in which Helen-Joy sat holding her son and daughter. She still looked very pale and tired. Merlin hovered above on his broomstick. He was worried about his wife.

Maura and Nora had gone on ahead of them. They had spent some time cooing over Snowdrop before setting to work in the cave where Helen-Joy had dwelt for many years.

They had lit the stove and boiled the kettle ready to make mint tea when the family arrived. One of Nora's home-made cakes had been placed on the table.

They covered the bed with a new patchwork quilt, which Helen-Joy had stitched with the help of the children, whilst she was confined to her bed. The two cots which Dexter had made were placed near the fire, where the occupants would be kept warm. White crochet shawls were spread across the wooden cradles.

Helen-Joy and her husband went to see the new foal before taking their own babies inside. Mazillion was dressed in hand-knitted blue clothing. His sister was dressed in an identical outfit, except hers was pink. Both were wrapped in blankets knitted by the Bramble family.

Lennox and Sheba stood either side of their offspring. The little white foal wobbled slightly but made its way around the small clearing without aid from either of her watchful parents.

"Snowdrop is exquisite," the wizard and his wife agreed.

"Thank you. Your babies are delightful, too. But your wife looks poorly."

"The Brambles and I will take care of her," acknowledged Merlin, as Maura came to help his wife inside.

Merlin gently handed his son to Maura before turning back to Lennox. "You and I have helped create a new generation in the Forbidden Forest."

"I am glad you persuaded me to come this new land," said Lennox. "My blood line would have been extinct if I had remained in Briton. I have had many adventures on my travels and now a beautiful daughter. Unicorn foals are rare, yet we now have a fine little filly to add to this new herd. I can't believe this is the final chapter in my story."

"Final chapter?" laughed Merlin. "I think not!"

Epilogue

A sleek mahogany ship with fifteen white sails made its way across the Northern Sea. The crossing was not smooth. The Avalonian passengers were on their way back from Barrden, the capital city of Barrmin which ruled the whole of the North. They had attended the wedding of Princess Delphine of Barrmin to Count William of Vanddalasia.

Prince Edward stood, a lonely figure at the aft of the ship, leaning over the railings. He watched Barrden slip away in the distance.

Esmerelda, Queen of the Witches, stood some way behind with Tannus. She had brought Edward from Briton, when he was just a young boy, to be reunited with his father.

Everyone in Avalon knew that Edward regarded Esmerelda as his big bossy sister. She frequently scolded him and he took her reprimands in good humour. They had never been known to fall out.

This evening was different. Green sparks flew as the Witch Queen let her anger erupt.

"Look at him sulking," she told Tannus. She gripped the railings to keep herself steady as the ship rose and fell with the waves.

Tannus put his arm around the woman he loved. "Let him be, Esmie. I'm sure his father has a few things to say to him when he gets home."

"I'd love to be a fly on the wall when that happens!" Esmerelda's eyes still glinted emerald.

"If that's what you want I'm sure it can be arranged," Tannus responded with a smile.

❀ ✦ ❀ ✦ ❀ ✦ ❀ ✦ ❀ ✦ ❀ ✦ ❀

To find out more about Prince Edward's visit to Barrden and his subsequent adventures, read *Edward's Story,* Book 6 in *The Tales of Avalon* series.

Characters

List of main characters, in alphabetical order:

Allarond: King of the Elves

Arthur: King of Avalon (formerly King of Briton); husband of Gilda the Witch; father of Edward and Rosalie

Bramble Family: Bertha (Great-grandmother Bramble), mother of Nora (Grandmother Bramble) and Maura; Nora (Grandmother Bramble), mother of Dilly, Dally and Sally; Dilly Bramble, wife of Jerry; Dally Bramble, wife of Garod; Sally Bramble, wife of Isaiah and mother of Heather

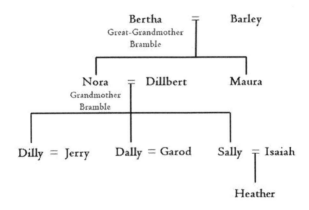

Comet: Merlin's white stallion

Edward-Arthur: illegitimate son of King Arthur (usually referred to simply as Edward)

Elvira: Queen of the Witches; all her witches migrated to Avalon

Esmerelda: Queen of the Witches (after Elvira); daughter of Elvira

Ethel: a plainfolk married to Yzor a wizard and mother of Jonathan

Helen-Joy (referred to by friends as Helen): a soothsayer

Hyacinth: sister of Queen Shirley-Poppy

Iwan: a young warlock rescued from the Kernan mines

Jeanette: Princess of Twydell and Kerner; married to Prince Steven of Kerner. Daughter of King Frederrick and Queen Elise

Jeffrey: King of Kerner; married to Queen Shirley - Poppy

Jonathan: a young warlock who specialises in plants (herbologist); son of the wizard Yzor and Ethel a plainfolk

Lennox: last of the British unicorns

Merlin: powerful wizard who organised the migration to Avalon; adviser to King Arthur

Shirley-Poppy (referred to by family as Poppy): wife/consort of Jeffrey, King of Kerner (given the title of queen at the time of marriage)

Steven: Prince of Kerner; son of King Jeffrey and Queen Shirley-Poppy

Tamarie: Unicorn mare. Wife of Lennox; mother of Bryant

Tannitus: powerful wizard; father of Tannus

Tannus: powerful young warlock recently elected leader of the Avalonian clan of wizards; son of Tannitus
Wormald the Wise: wise old wizard

Yzor: a wizard who specialises in plants (herbologist); father of Jonathan

About the Author

Daisy Bourne was born in England in 1917. Nothing much is known about her real parents except that their lives were changed dramatically by the First World War. At the age of six, Daisy was unofficially adopted by a farmer and his wife. They changed her name and took her to Canada.

There are several similarities between the real Daisy Bourne and her namesake in the *Tales of Avalon* series.

 To a small child, Canada, with its heavy snowfalls, huge forests and grizzly bears must indeed have seemed like some kind of new world. Although Daisy loved Canada and the farm on which she lived, she was not happy and ran away. She returned to England at the age of 16. In later life, she took up farming again. She also enjoyed her garden and preserving much of its produce. This is where the similarities between the real Daisy and the character in the *Tales of Avalon* end.

I am proud to use my mother's birth name as a pseudonym when writing the *Tales of Avalon*. My ambition is to one day write the story of the real Daisy Bourne. In the meantime, I will continue to complete this series.

A note from the Author

I love hearing from my readers. If you would like to contact me, please use the link on my website: TalesOfAvalon.co.uk or message me on Daisy Bourne's Facebook page. You can also register to receive my newsletter with details of myths and spells.

If you enjoyed reading this book, why not recommend the *Tales of Avalon* series to your friends. But please suggest that they start on Book 1, right at the beginning of the tale, so that they do not miss out on any of the adventures.

More from the Tales of Avalon series

The ***New Land*** is the first book in the *Tales of Avalon* series. It was published in 2016.

What happened to Arthur, King of the Britons, after he was allegedly killed on the battlefield? Legend has it that Merlin, the mighty sorcerer, put the king's body in a boat and set sail for a mysterious place called Avalon. However, many Britons refused to accept that Arthur was really dead and believed instead that Merlin had taken the king to a place of safety. There have been many theories as to the whereabouts of Avalon, but none have proven to be accurate.

The New Land tells the story of how Arthur, magical beings and other Britons who feared for their lives sought refuge in a far-off land. They hoped their new home would be a place where magical beings and humans could live together in peace and harmony. Did the travellers find the new life they so desired? Well, they certainly found a land full of surprise and adventure.

The Avalonians soon find that they have to form new and unusual alliances in order to protect themselves against an unexpected enemy.

If you like stories about witches, wizards, fairies, elves, giants and unicorns, you will enjoy this book.

The Land of Twydell and the Dragon Egg is the second book in the *Tales of Avalon* series. It was published in 2016.

What happened during Merlin's trip to Twydell? Who, or what, did he meet? *The Land of Twydell and the Dragon Egg* describes the wizard's extraordinary adventures in Twydell and the people and creatures he meets there. As he flies across the countryside on his broomstick, he is puzzled to see a long line of people leaving the capital of Dalton and heading towards the outlying villages. Entire families are fleeing the capital. They look ragged and downcast and appear to be taking their possessions with them. As he approaches Dalton, Merlin is shocked to see billowing smoke and that large parts of the city have been destroyed by fire.

The wizard learns that the devastation has been caused by a pair of dragons which have lived near the city for many years without any problem. King Frederrick is bewildered as to why the dragons should suddenly seek to attack the Twydellers, for no apparent reason.

The Exchange of Rings is the third book in the *Tales of Avalon* series. It was published in 2016.

The Exchange of Rings follows on from *The New Land*, the first book in the series. It describes the preparations for the wedding of Princess Jeanette of Twydell to Prince Steven of Kerner. Rosalie is excited at the prospect of meeting Derrick, Prince of Twydell, who many hope will be her future husband. The weddings are an opportunity for each country to build new alliances.

Everything seems to be running smoothly, but news is brought that wizards who have been missing from Twydell's Forbidden Forest for many years are being held in a Kerner prison. It is also revealed that fairies and elves have been similarly treated with cruelty by Kernans. The magical people of Avalon are furious and some want to take revenge on Kerner.

King Arthur of Avalon, Merlin the wizard and their new found ally, King Frederrick of Twydell, try to resolve the situation. They are concerned that revenge will be the beginning of war.

The allies hope that a solution can be found when the King of Kerner is forced to ask the magical people of the Forbidden Forest for help.

A Story Never to be Told is the fourth book in the Tales of Avalon Series. It was published in 2018.

What happened to Azgoose, the clever old witch, who delayed the Trajaens at the Battle of Merlport? Although the Avalonians sent out search parties, she was not found. In this book we meet the Rabbart lll, the powerful King of Barrmin, and his family. King Rabbart rules all the former kingdoms and tribes in the northern lands. King Rabbart befriends Arthur and the magical people of Avalon. He offers one of his beautiful daughters in marriage to Edward. Is Rabbart III's friendship with Avalon sincere? Will Edward remain loyal to Daisy, or will he marry a Princess of Barrmin to strengthen the alliance between the two countries?

Edward's Story, the sixth book in the *Tales of Avalon* series, is planned for publication in 2019.

Is Princess Rosalie safe from King Rabbart's scheming? Will he murder the young princess before her marriage to Prince Derrick? You will have to read *Edward's Story* to find out.